AWASH WITH DESIRE

Victor Maurier's brilliant blue eyes were afire as he took in the tantalizing sight of Talleha by the edge of the creek. She was so stunning that his whole body came alive with wanting her as he'd never ached for any woman.

When Talleha entered the waters of the creek and lay back, allowing the stream to flow over her, he wished it was he covering her with his body. He watched the pleased smile on her face as the cooling waters caressed her flesh, and he yearned to see that same look on her face when he touched and caressed her.

Just at the moment the bathing beauty realized she was being watched, Maurier's hands grabbed her around the waist. She turned, startled, to see those blue-fire eyes of his devouring her.

Now she knew why such titillating sensations had fired within her. She'd *wanted* him to come to her—to love her as he had so briefly that day by the lake. Now he was here and his hands were holding her. Her flesh felt the searing heat of his touch. . . .

TEXAS CAPTIVE
WANDA OWEN

ZEBRA BOOKS
KENSINGTON PUBLISHING CORP.

ZEBRA BOOKS

are published by

Kensington Publishing Corp.
475 Park Avenue South
New York, NY 10016

First printing: January 1988

Printed in the United States of America

My special thanks to all the nice people I've heard from this year expressing how much they've liked my books and are eagerly awaiting my next one. That's my inspiration!

Part I

The Many Faces of Love

Chapter 1

Each night Eliot Penwick took a ride on his fine thoroughbred through the dense, piney woods surrounding his home: he found it to be a soothing, calming interlude before he retired. Nothing except foul weather ever hindered Eliot from taking these evening jaunts. But on this night his serene interlude was interrupted when he spied a young maiden lying on the forest trail.

When he dismounted from his stallion and picked up the young girl in his arms, he saw that her thick, glossy hair was as black as the night surrounding him. Never had he seen a night as black as this.

Penwick was not considered to be a compassionate man and he certainly did not have a gentle nature, but the tiny, helpless female he cradled in his arms pulled at his heartstrings. He'd gazed upon many a fair face as an English nobleman before coming to the Texas countryside.

She was obviously in a stupor; she could not speak to him, but her thick-lashed eyes fluttered, and she opened them to look up at him, wide-eyed and trusting. Eliot felt instantly protective, wanting to comfort her. Never had he gazed on a more beautiful face, and as he held her in his arms he swore she seemed so fragile she might break. He held her tenderly.

He didn't give a damn how much his wife, Marjorie, would rant and rave; he could not leave the girl here. He would take her back to Penwick Manor. Now, this side of Eliot was not known by his friends, who considered him coldhearted and unfeeling. He would have agreed with them that he was reserved and stern, but he knew what the depth of his emotions could be if he desired to give of himself. This little ragamuffin aroused his sympathy.

As he managed to mount his stallion with the girl in his arms, he pondered the strange feelings churning within him for the little creature he held.

Her black hair fanned out across his arms and he glanced down to see her giving him a sweet, weak smile. His heart melted with warmth.

When he arrived back home, it was his trusted housekeeper, Flossie, who took charge of Penwick's new guest. He instructed Flossie to see to her bath and to quarter her in one of the many guest rooms in the spacious mansion. He knew how capable Flossie was and he himself felt rather helpless now.

The thirty-five-year-old Eliot had to think carefully about how he was going to approach Marjorie in the morning about their guest. There were enough problems where Marjorie was concerned without this. He'd not anticipated just what he'd face when he'd married the attractive Texas widow some months ago.

If Marjorie's old friends and neighbor ranchers considered his English ways strange, he bloody well considered the whole lot of them boring and crude. But Marjorie's vast wealth was enough to whet his interest and to make a few sacrifices well worth the price. At least, that was what he'd thought in the beginning. Now he was having some grave misgivings.

The last few months, she was constantly ailing, and the difference in their ages was having a distinct impact on Eliot. At first, Marjorie had been a most attractive woman of a certain age who certainly didn't look or act much older than he, but after a few weeks of marriage, the masks were removed. Eliot had had several rude awakenings.

This evening, Eliot Penwick knew he'd found in the forest what he'd searched for all his life, and he didn't intend to lose it. So he spent a very restless night.

The next morning, when he went to check in on his new guest, the encounter proved perplexing. His first question to her was to ask her who she was.

In a soft voice, with her big black eyes staring up at him, she declared herself to be Talleha.

Raising a skeptical brow, Penwick quizzed, "Your name is what?" He'd never heard the name before.

"My name is Talleha. Tall . . . le . . . ha. That is how you say it." She smiled sweetly and her black eyes sparkled brightly. "It is different—yes?"

"Yes, it is different." He returned her smile, thinking to himself privately, she was so rare, so different from any female he'd ever known. She *should* have an unusual name. It was only fitting.

She sat on the massive bed, looking very tiny surrounded by the mountain of pillows lining the headboard. Her eyes danced busily over her strange surroundings, then back at him, as if she were waiting for him to speak. She showed no fear of him, and this endeared her to Eliot Penwick immediately. He realized his power to intimidate people, especially the ladies.

But not this minx, he mused. He'd never seen such black sparkling eyes, so alive with curiosity.

In that dignified way of his, he took a seat on the velvet chair. Crossing his long legs, he said to her,

11

"Now, young lady—I know your beautiful name, but I need to hear more about you." He gave her a broad smile, and there was even a hint of warmth in those piercing blue eyes of his.

"I—I don't think I can talk about it right now, or else I will cry, sir." Her lovely face changed quite suddenly; it was etched with sadness.

A surge of tenderness washed over Eliot as he reached over to grasp her small hand. His deep voice consoled her, "Well, we don't want you to cry and spoil that pretty face. So, we'll talk later, and now I'll send Flossie up to tend to you." He rose from the chair beside the bed and Talleha's eyes stared up at his towering figure. Such a huge man! How very kind he had been to her, both last night and now.

Eliot was glad to have the services of his devoted Flossie once again. She was the only servant in the house that was completely loyal to him. The rest of the staff were doggedly devoted to his wife, Marjorie. Their eyes always reflected their resentment for the Englishman who'd married Marjorie Greenfield, a wealthy widow.

Two years ago when he'd married, he'd instantly recognized how harsh disliked he was by her friends and neighbors, and he knew his acceptance in this Texas countryside was not going to be easy. But Penwick didn't care about that, for he was now in control of thousands of acres and all their cattle. What had been known as the Greenfield Ranch was now Penwick Manor.

But old, loyal friends of Marjorie and her dead husband, Frank, refused to consider the property Penwick's. It was Greenfield land and cattle. They wondered how the poor forty-two-year-old Marjorie could have allowed herself to be played for such a fool. Frank had been a fine, respected man.

Eliot Penwick had failed to win any of the neighboring ranchers or friends to his side or to change their opinions of him. But he didn't concern himself with that.

Like a beautiful flower which goes uncared for, Marjorie had withered in spirit. For months now she had been constantly ill. Friends who saw her were shocked to discover the changes in her and felt it was Penwick's doing. Some feared she'd lost her will to live.

Marjorie had not been informed of the strange little guest Eliot had brought home last night; nor had she been told this morning when she and Eliot had eaten breakfast. Eliot considered it none of her business. However, he knew sooner or later one of the tattletale servants would inform his wife. So far, he thought Flossie and the cook were the only ones who knew of Talleha's presence in the north guest room upstairs.

Now he prepared to leave. "Rest, my dear, and I'll look in on you a little later."

She gave him a nod of her head and a sweet, lovely smile.

At the door, he paused for a brief moment to declare, "Talleha, you may address me as Lord Penwick." His tone of voice was most impressive.

"A lord, sir?"

"That's right. I have a home and holdings back in my native country. England is my home, not Texas."

Talleha sensed his distaste of his surroundings as he spoke and wondered why such a wealthy man as he sought to stay here. But she remained silent.

Eliot left. Only to himself did he question why he'd so delighted in boasting of his title and wealth back in England. But for his marrying Marjorie, those holdings would have been gone by now. Marrying her was his saving grace. All Eliot cared about was the vast wealth he'd acquired to make his coffers richer.

13

He cared not about the blacklands, as the neighboring ranchers called this rich, fertile farmland. The dense, fragrant forests which sheltered magnificent streams of water and lakes flourishing with fish and wildlife meant nothing except insofar as they provided sport for him. He did not hunt to provide food for his larder, but only for the sheer thrill of the hunt.

But the mysterious bayous along the borders of the land did intrigue Eliot, for he knew of their treacherous quicksand, which could suck a man to his death. The force of that strength and power was something Penwick could respect.

Perhaps it was why he enjoyed his nightly rides through the pines in the evening and the solitude they provided away from Marjorie and their ranch.

No one knew better than Eliot that he didn't belong here. England was his home; his roots were there. England called him to come back and God knows, he could not wait to return. To endure Marjorie and this abominable place was more than he could bear at times. The only thing that made it all worthwhile was the reward he'd receive once he was the sole owner of this vast, sprawling ranch. It would be enough to last him a lifetime.

When he left the house and headed toward the stables, he allowed himself a few moments of whimsy. His towering figure walked with a slow, unhurried gait, his head held high in an arrogant manner. His fine-tailored attire fit his firm-muscled body to perfection. There was no doubt that Eliot Penwick presented the image of a fine gentleman. There was an elegant dignity about him, and this was the side he always showed to Marjorie's friends.

But a different man quickly appeared when they were alone. He could be cruel and vulgar. He enjoyed playing his childish little games of torture, which were surely destroying poor Marjorie. This was exactly what Eliot desired.

By the time he had mounted his stallion and reined the spirited thoroughbred toward the woods, he was lost in his fantasy about the magnificent young creature he'd rescued the night before. He'd take her back to England with him someday very soon, he hoped. She was something to behold, and he'd mold her into his love goddess.

He'd never been so stimulated by any woman before. The tantalizing little Talleha was innocent and untouched, he just knew it. Eliot was the first to admit his amazement, for he'd never before allowed himself to have such feelings about any woman.

Flossie knew him well after having been with him for many years in England. She noticed the strange attitude he showed the new guest. She also felt some misgivings about the furor little Talleha was going to create.

Like her Lord Penwick, she yearned to be back in the English townhouse where she'd begun her employment. Coming to this house had been against her better judgment and only out of loyalty to him had she agreed. But it still wasn't pleasant, and Marjorie Greenfield Penwick was not even as cordial and friendly to her as she was with her own Mexican servants.

But fifteen years of loyalty in working for Eliot Penwick made her try to endure it here in this strange place called Texas.

By the end of the first day, Flossie had spent a considerable amount of time with the young girl up in the bedroom, and she had much to tell Lord Penwick. Her kind, motherly manner had urged Talleha to talk as the day wore on. Flossie found herself feeling very sorry for the little miss. But she could not figure out what Lord Penwick intended for her once she was well.

She knew he would come to her as soon as he returned to the mansion. He depended on her greatly, and this was a source of pride to Flossie. They shared a common bond in a strange place. Oh, to be back in England! Lord Penwick had sworn to her that he would return someday and she would accompany him, and Flossie lived for that day.

The American he'd chosen for his bride was a complex woman, Flossie considered, nothing like the ones she'd served in London before she was hired into Penwick's household. The American ways and customs were still impossible for Flossie to get used to.

Things had been so orderly and simple when she'd been in charge of the Lord Penwick's townhouse in London, where he resided with his young nephew, Ralph. If only he'd never come to this godforsaken country with its crude, rugged ways.

Now Flossie felt a heavier burden on her shoulders: a young woman had entered the lord's life. Oh, she was bound to be trouble! The matronly servant could figure it no other way. When the mistress found out, there would no doubt be a terrible scene, and Lord Penwick would get into one of his black moods. She'd seen many such moods during the last two years.

But what was the answer to her lord's present situation? In the past there had been several occasions when Eliot had sought her sage advice. She didn't have an answer for Talleha's case. The poor little thing had been abandoned there in the woods by the men who'd already killed her mother, and obviously they'd expected her to be destroyed by the bears known to roam the forest.

The very fact that Eliot Penwick had rescued her and brought her here made him a hero to Flossie. Ah, yes, she swelled with praise for her employer, the arrogant Penwick!

Flossie's sentiments were hardly shared by Marjorie as she slowly strolled through her garden, now flourishing with redbuds and dogwood in full bloom. Not even her glorious varicolored azaleas interested her this evening.

She gazed up into the Texas sky she'd always loved, now so full of twinkling stars, and cried out pathetically to the man for whom her heart ached: "Oh, Frank . . . Frank . . . how could I have been such a fool! Why did you leave me when you did? I . . . I was not smart enough to run my life . . . to manage this place without you."

Marjorie had no one to turn to in her dilemma. She knew she could not cope with the power of Eliot Penwick. He was such a forceful, determined man, and he drained her dry.

There was no hint of the voluptuous, happy-go-lucky woman she'd been two years ago when she'd met Eliot. She'd come to terms with being a widow and she didn't exactly enjoy life without Frank by her side, but she'd learned to endure. Their many friends constantly rallied around her. If only Eliot Penwick had not entered her life! How much better off she'd be! But he had, and she'd been smitten in a way she'd not been since she was seventeen. That love affair at seventeen had been as dismal and disappointing as this one. But Frank had come along and made her forget the first unhappy experience. This time, though, she could not be rescued.

Each day she felt herself being smothered a little bit more, and she knew instinctively that her days were numbered. Soon she would be free of all this. Soon she'd find some peace. Perhaps she'd reached the point where she really didn't care, for in death she could be with Frank. Anything—even dying—would be better than living with Eliot!

When she slowly left her gardens that evening, Marjorie felt a serenity she'd not known for many months. Her devoted lady's maid, Lucita, noticed the change in her. She was pleased that her mistress was improving.

Lucita detested the vulgar Englishman who'd tainted this household from the moment he'd arrived. He did not belong here!

But there was another reason Lucita hated Eliot Penwick. She had dwelled in whimsical anticipation after his arrival that her sensual looks and shapely body would attract his attention. The sultry Mexican servant usually found gentlemen visiting the ranch staring at her with eager eyes whenever she came into view.

While it was true that Penwick had been in residence but a month when he sought her out for a romp in her bed, it had been only a brief interlude for Eliot, and now he turned a cool, aloof shoulder to her.

A devious urge overcame Lucita to see the young lady the kitchen help had been gossiping about. Lucita picked a time when she knew Flossie would not be in her room and slipped up the long, winding stairway to the second floor.

Quietly, she moved down the hallway toward the room she'd seen Flossie enter that morning. Cautiously, she turned the heavy brass doorknob and opened the door. She moved through the narrow opening and her dark eyes flashed brightly. Whether she wanted to or not, she could not help admiring the stunning beauty lying there—her hair looked even blacker fanned out against the snowy white pillows.

Talleha jerked up to sit erect in the bed, and her black eyes stared straight into Lucita's as she addressed her, "Hello—Who—who are you?"

It was an eager, friendly face Lucita observed, but she could not feel friendly toward that gorgeous creature, now curled up in bed in a fine, lacy rose-colored gown Flossie had dressed her in. She sashayed cockily over to the bed to get a better look at the girl and almost haughtily replied, "I am Lucita, lady's maid to the mistress of this house—Marjorie Greenfield Penwick."

"Oh, I see. The lady must be Lord Penwick's wife?" Talleha quizzed.

Lucita exploded into a gusto of laughter. "Lord Penwick, is it?"

Quite innocently and somewhat perplexed, Talleha nodded her pretty head. "That is what he told me."

A smirk came to Lucita's face. "You are, indeed, an innocent one, I think." She had best bridle her tongue, or the girl might tell Penwick. So she didn't add that no one around the ranch called him "lord." Whether Eliot Penwick liked it or not, he'd finally accepted that the ranch hands addressed him as "mister" or "señor."

The sweet-natured Talleha did not suspect the wicked, naughty thoughts running through the servant girl's mind. Instead, she was thinking that they were about the same age and had very similar features, both dark-haired and dark-eyed.

Lucita bade her goodbye and Talleha waved to her as she swayed through the doorway and declared how glad she was they'd met.

Under her breath, Lucita muttered that the little niña would soon be regretting those words. This one named Talleha would be anything but glad that they'd met. The naive little señorita was surely under the impression that they would be friends.

The very thought made Lucita laugh as she continued to saunter leisurely down the hallway. How would Señora Marjorie take this? Would this be the blow to drive her over the edge of madness she'd been so close to the last year?

The feisty Mexican servant girl bounced down the front stairway as the plump English housekeeper moved slowly up the back stairs to check in on her young charge, Talleha. No sooner had Flossie opened the door and greeted the young girl than she was told about Talleha's visitor. The pretty little black-eyed miss was delighted and pleased by the visit of Lucita.

But the abrupt change in Flossie's demeanor was noticed by Talleha and she did not hesitate to ask, "You do not like Lucita, Flossie?"

The girl's candid inquiry caught the matronly Flossie by surprise, and for a moment she hesitated. "No, no, sweets—it is not that. I'm—I'm just surprised that she came in here, for she's usually so busy with her duties to the mistress."

Flossie was pleased that the vulnerable young girl accepted her exclamation, and the housekeeper breathed a sigh of relief. She must inform Lord Penwick of this fact.

Before Flossie left the room, she realized something else. The impish young girl leaped out of the bed to declare, "I am feeling marvelous tonight, Flossie. See what I mean?" She whirled around in the full flowing sheer rose-colored gown and her face glowed with radiance.

Flossie could not deny that her strength had been miraculously restored. But neither could she help thinking about the immediate problem this might cause.

"It's a picture of health you are, child," Flossie said, giving her a warm, friendly smile.

"Yes, so now I can go back to my home."

"Home, child? But I thought you told me some men killed your mother and abandoned you there in

20

the woods?"

"It is true, but we had friends—my mother and me. I want to go back, Flossie."

"Well, dearie—that you will have to take up with Lord Penwick." She smiled at Talleha, who had a frown on her face.

That frowning face turned into a stormy one, and Flossie was about to witness the first outburst from the young Talleha.

Determined and sure of herself, Talleha sat up in the bed. Her rosebud lips were tight as she spoke slowly, but as firmly and unwavering as Lord Penwick himself. "There is nothing to talk about, Flossie. I shall not stay here and I *am* going back to where I came from. I do not belong here. I am most grateful to all your—the Lord Penwick has done for me, but I shall not stay here. I can't!"

Flossie had no reply to make, and this young lady, as young as she was, had a mind and will of her own. She would prove a formidable challenge to Lord Penwick —to anyone, Flossie immediately decided.

She was what the Texans called a little firebrand!

Chapter 2

There was a chill to the night even though this part of Texas was usually blessed with mild temperatures. The damp, penetrating, chilly nights of England were missed by Eliot Penwick. He'd found it rather pleasant this evening when he'd returned from his ride to discover that his always thoughtful Flossie had lit the oak logs in the massive stone fireplace of the study.

The crackling sounds on the hearth, the dancing reddish-orange flames, and the special scent permeating the room seemed utterly delightful to him as he entered. He could not wait to shed his light wool coat, help himself to a glass of his favorite brandy, and get cozy in his overstuffed leather chair by the fireplace.

He could sit there and dream his dreams of the future, which he figured could be rich and fulfilling now that he had the means to take care of his lavish way of life.

He could enjoy the fruits of this rich Texas land, but he bloody well wouldn't have to live here. He would not have to put up with the people who hated him. Let them burn in hell—he couldn't care less.

Removing his coat, he went to the liquor chest to pour a generous serving of dark amber brandy into one

22

of Marjorie's cut-crystal glasses, and he strode over to the armchair to sit down. The sparkling fires of the burning logs instantly turned his thoughts to the breathtakingly beautiful Talleha. He could imagine what another year or two would do for her and all that blossoming loveliness. So very rare she was! Like an exquisite gem!

Eliot had never felt this way about a woman before, and it was exciting beyond anything he'd ever experienced. He'd had the sophisticated ladies of the English court and he'd had his fair share of the maids from the pubs and taverns on Fleet Street in London. After he'd arrived in this country, he'd enjoyed the lovely women along the Eastern coast of this country, and down in New Orleans, he'd tasted the sweet nectar the sultry Creole ladies so generously offered. Never would he forget one golden-skinned octoroon he'd spent the night with in Natchez before he'd traveled on to Texas.

Once he'd arrived here, he'd been fascinated by the sultry charms of the dark-eyed señoritas. They were hot-blooded and passionate, and for a while he was as utterly fascinated as he'd been with the feisty little Lucita right here under this roof. He had no doubt he could bed her any time he wished, but he had no desire to have her again.

In fact, she'd presented a problem—he'd found her a pest. There was no challenge, for Lucita was too eager to jump into bed with him, and that had dampened his ardor.

His wife, Marjorie, had become dull and boring a week after he'd met her. She was like all her Texas neighbors and friends, who could talk about nothing but this wonderful land. He cared nothing about the Hasani Indians and their culture or the old mission nearby, built in 1716. For Texans like Frank Greenfield and Marjorie, the Mission of San Francisco de los Tejas had a significant meaning and sentiment, but to him it meant nothing.

He was never so bored as he was when Marjorie's friends had gathered at the house for dinner in the evening. He'd had to endure hour after hour of the grand, glorious history of this country. What a bunch of bloody braggarts they all seemed to Eliot! God, he'd never known such a crude lot!

But for now he forgot all this; he leaned his head back against the chair and closed his eyes, having taken the last sip of the brandy to let his thoughts focus on Talleha.

His patrician face was creased in a smile as he lay there daydreaming. But for the soft rapping on the door, he would have liked to linger longer. Yet he was sure it was Flossie coming to report to him as he'd instructed her.

"Enter," he called out, sitting up straight in the leather chair.

Flossie came in, expressing her apologies for disturbing him, for his eyes looked heavy with sleep to her. Sometimes, she found herself feeling motherly toward the thirty-five-year-old Penwick. Perhaps if he'd married earlier in life, when she'd first started as his housekeeper in England, and he'd had a wife early on, her attitude toward him would have been different. But he'd been a young bachelor sought after by many London ladies.

"Cozy in here this evening, sir," she warmly smiled at him. "But I have a few things to tell you that I was able to find out about our young lady upstairs, and I was sure you'd want to hear about them."

"Come, Flossie—sit down and tell me. More than that—let me pour you just a nip of brandy. Make you sleep good after your busy day, eh?" He grinned, for it wasn't the first time he and his matronly housekeeper had joined one another in a nightcap. Flossie was one of those rare individuals who'd managed to stay in Eliot's favor for a very long time.

She took a chair across the hearth from Eliot and folded her hands on her apron-covered lap, waiting for him to hand her the glass.

"Well, sir—the poor little thing was flung there in the woods to fall prey to some wild creature by these horrible brutes who murdered her mother. Can't learn of a father—that is, if there's one around. Seems she and her mother lived in a house near a big thicket, but she gave me no name of any village or town."

Eliot listened intently, and when she finally finished enlightening him with all she'd found out about Talleha, he declared, "You did fine, Flossie. You never fail me—never have. I set great store by you."

"Thank you, sir." She took a sip of the warming brandy. Now she must tell him more, and she didn't quite know what to expect. "Sir, that little lady is determined to go back where she came from."

"To what, pray tell? The mother is dead and she is just a child."

Flossie thought to herself that he had not observed her very carefully if he thought her to be just a child. She told him, "There are friends, she says, sir. The young lady is a very strong-willed person for one so young. I thought it would be well that you realize this. I was taken by surprise, for she seemed so very shy the night before. I must also tell you she has quickly recovered her strength after the ordeal she's been through. By goodness, she was so full of spice tonight she hardly seemed like the same girl you'd brought out of the woods. No paleness on that pretty face tonight, and no lifelessness about her, either. She was full of spirit and energy."

25

"Wonderful! Yes, that is wonderful, Flossie! Couldn't be happier to hear anything." What he didn't tell Flossie was that he rather *expected* that to be her nature, and if she thought for a minute she was leaving him, his little Talleha was crazy. He was not about to let such a precious jewel slip through his fingers. *His* will was strong and determined, too!

Already he plotted the days ahead, and his mind was whirling with plans that included Talleha. But he could not let his loyal Flossie suspect what he was scheming to do. He must be very shrewd and calculating these next weeks, so that each little piece of his devious puzzle would fit with perfection, for otherwise it would not work.

Never was Eliot Penwick so determined. He shrugged aside any problems the young Talleha might create, for he was sure he'd be able to manipulate her, regardless of Flossie's warnings.

Eliot welcomed the sight of Flossie getting up out of the chair to take her leave, for he wished to be alone again in the quiet study; he had a lot of thinking to do.

For all his daydreaming, Eliot realized that there was the annoying obstacle of Marjorie Greenfield Penwick standing in the way of everything he wanted. It was clear to Eliot that he had to eliminate the obstacle. But this was going to be tedious!

The Penwick household and its very strict routine went against Talleha's nature and what she was used to. This was not how she and her mother had lived in their simple, meager little cottage. Outrage and resentment boiled within her each time Flossie chided her about running around with her slippers off. Lovely, dainty slippers they were, but Talleha found them restraining, and she wore them only a short time before taking them off and flinging them to the floor.

So divine it then seemed to let her feet caress the thick, plush carpet of the bedroom! Flossie stood shaking her head in utter dismay as to how to control this urge Talleha had of going around in her bare feet.

Talleha was not accustomed to the many perfumed baths in the strange bronze tub which Flossie was always preparing for her. Talleha considered herself completely clean, by her standards. A strange custom this family observed, this constant bathing, she thought to herself.

There seemed to be no time around this place for just a leisurely stroll in the verdant, dense woods she could see just beyond her bedroom window, across the way from the fine gardens of the property. Oh, she swore she could smell the pines! She knew the woods flourished with ferns and wildflowers.

She could hardly complain about all the fine food they'd served her during the last two weeks, but she wondered why they didn't enjoy the bounty of the fine bass swimming out in the stream not far away or the wild fowl nesting in the woods. She recalled how her mother had made dumplings and squirrel and how delicious the wild onions were. These poor people seemed to miss so many good things provided for them by the land.

Talleha found it almost impossible to mask her feelings when she'd tasted the miserable bowl of strange stuff Flossie had served her for breakfast. She could not swallow it, so the housekeeper had not insisted that she eat it; and Talleha had eagerly accepted biscuits and jam instead.

The clothing Flossie insisted she wear was just as unfamiliar to Talleha. The gowns had been fine, with their generous, flowing material, but the garb Flossie was now laying on the bed was like nothing Talleha had ever worn before. Oh, it was all very beautiful to look at, Talleha had to admit, with delicate lace and frills, but she was not used to the waistlines of her simple little frocks being so tight. She could not believe the undergarments she was expected to wear!

Reaching a height of frustration one afternoon, she'd rebelled against Flossie and declared, "I find this place not to my liking, Flossie. These clothes—I could wear what Lucita wears, but this—this mountain of clothing is overwhelming me. I'm tired from just being dressed. Perhaps I shall just stay in bed all day in my comfortable gown." She sat with her legs crossed as though she had no intention of getting out of bed.

"Now, miss," Flossie tried to soothe her as she urged herself not to be impatient with the girl. "You are not a servant in this house, like Lucita. You are a guest of Lord Eliot's. It would not be fitting for you to dress like Lucita."

"Well, I am not going to be a guest much longer, Flossie. I can tell you that for certain! I will be getting away from here if your Lord Penwick doesn't return me to my home. I told him this last night."

Flossie scurried around, attending to her chores of straightening Talleha's room and hoping she would be able to persuade her to get into the clothing still lying at the foot of the bed. Such a stubborn little imp she could be at times!

Yet the housekeeper found her so adorable that she could not dislike her, even when she was proving to be a handful. Those eyes could sparkle brightly, and she had spirit. Flossie had concluded that Talleha had been allowed to roam with unrestrained freedom in the woods where she lived alone with her mother.

When she spoke of her dead mother, the young girl's voice was warm and loving. Her face was glowing with admiration when she told Flossie, "She was as beautiful as her name. She was called Dawn by her friends. Isn't that pretty, Flossie?"

"Yes, child—it is beautiful. And I bet she was pretty—just like you."

Talleha's black hair cascaded down around her face as she sat there on the bed with her legs crossed. She fidgeted with her hands clasped around her legs. "Such animals those men were that killed her! They called her a savage—a half-breed squaw! Oh, I'll hate them until the day I die, and I pray I can kill both of them someday!"

Flossie could not resist rushing over to the girl sitting there with her head bowed. Flossie's plump arms went around her small shoulders. "Don't ever fear that they'll get what they deserve, dearie. The good Lord will take care of them. Rest assured of that!"

A mist of tears framed her eyes and she looked directly into Flossie's understanding face to declare her firm intentions, "But I wish to be the one to give them what they deserve. I want that pleasure. I must right the wrong done to my mother, for there is no one else to do it, Flossie."

Flossie just hugged her closer to her bosom, admiring her courage—so much for one so young.

Chapter 3

The Casa del Lago Ranch joined the land of the Greenfield ranch. Its fertile blackland was fed by a magnificent crystal-clear lake and springs. There were always fine black bass, crappie, or catfish to be caught in the cool streams that flowed there.

For decades the land had been owned by the Cortez family, and Emilo Cortez expected that it would always be that way. Yet each year more intruders invaded his Texas countryside to lay claim to the bounty of the land. The most recent newcomer to the region met with the dignified Cortez's distaste and would never hold his respect as Frank Greenfield had throughout all the years of their friendship.

He still could not understand the impulsive marriage of Señora Marjorie Greenfield to the despicable Englishman, so arrogant and obnoxious. Emilo found it hard to be neighborly and friendly, even for Marjorie's sake and out of respect for Frank's memory.

He knew he was not alone in his feelings, because his rancher friends to the north and west had voiced the same opinion.

There had been some speculation among Emilo's friends, he knew, that he and Marjorie would have made a fine couple. But it had never entered his mind to try to court Marjorie, not even after Frank had been dead almost a year. Actually, there had been no woman to attract his attention since his wife's death. His ranch kept him busy and filled his days. At night he was ready to rest and relax in the comfortable surroundings of his sprawling ranch house. While it was certainly true that much of the spacious house stood empty—he wished some of those rooms had been occupied by sons and daughters—Fate sadly had not complied with his wishes.

But Emilo loved this adobe-and-stone house, with its red tile roof, and his housekeeper kept it immaculate. His expanding waistline was a testament to the fact that she was a magnificent cook as well. Why, he could not imagine living anywhere else.

One thing marred his contentment these days: an overwhelming desire that this land remain Cortez land. Since he had no sons, he must choose one of his nephews. But which one? Neither had evinced a strong ability to take over the tremendous job involving the vast acres of blackland and timber.

But the young man who'd arrived a week ago and was still his guest had shown traits of character Emilo wished his nephews, Raphael and Mario, possessed.

But this stranger, Victor Maurier, had made it a pleasant week for Emilo. Had he not had business to discuss with his foreman this morning, he'd have gone along with Victor to fish in the lake. He'd joked with his guest as he departed for the lake, "Catch a nice big bass for our dinner tonight, young man."

Maurier had grinned as he descended the front steps to leave, "I'll catch one or maybe a couple before I return, Señor Cortez."

Emilo watched his tall figure move across the grounds toward the gate. Emilo was tall and robust himself, but young Maurier easily matched his six feet two inches of height. His biceps were as strong as steel, and his firm, muscled legs took long strides as he walked.

His skin was so tanned by the weather that Emilo could have taken him for a Latin like himself, but he knew he wasn't. His hair was as black as Emilo's hair had been at one time. His eyes were as blue as the bluebonnets growing in the pasture lands. There was a directness about the young man's gaze—his eyes were so blue against his dark face.

Emilo was very grateful to his old friend down in Brownsville for sending young Victor his way. It was sad to learn, though, that his old friend Captain Crawford was ill and fading fast. As tempted as he was to travel to Brownsville to pay his respects, Emilo knew he could not be gone that long from the ranch right now.

Victor Maurier's tale about how he and Captain Crawford had met years ago was most interesting to Emilo. Never would he have imagined the salty old captain he'd met down in Brownsville so many years ago turning out to be so tenderhearted and generous. That tough, rugged exterior of his never gave off any hint of such compassion. Obviously, this was not the man Victor Maurier had described to Emilo when he was a tousled-haired youth of nine and the old American captain had rescued him roaming on a wharf in the late night hour, all alone with nowhere to go and nobody to turn to.

Ah, yes, it was a most intriguing story Maurier had told him, and Emilo's esteem for Captain Glenn Crawford had instantly grown.

Maurier had been a lad of nine when his old friend, Crawford, had invited him to come aboard his boat, docked in the harbor of an English coastal hamlet a

32

short distance from Dover. Crawford had offered him a night's lodging aboard his schooner. Maurier had accepted his offer, for he was a frightened young lad who'd just run away from a horrible scene his young eyes had witnessed back at a cottage in the woods where he'd lived with his mother.

Two of the most fierce looking men he'd ever seen had broken into their quiet cottage and attacked his mother. She'd screamed for him to flee. He'd obeyed her as he always did and raced into the forest.

There, on a dark, moonless night, young Victor had hidden in the thick underbrush, trembling as he'd never trembled before, until he saw the two burly men leave the cottage. When he'd gathered his courage to enter the cottage, he knew instinctively that he was likely to find his mother gravely hurt.

The nine-year-old Victor had found his beautiful mother dying; but she'd had enough life left to urge him, "Go, my darling! Just run so they can't get you too!" Her soft, French-accented voice spoke to him with such urgency that Victor knew he must do as she asked.

He knew he could do nothing to help her. It was not that he didn't care about his mother, for he loved her beyond description and she knew that. She died with a smile of contentment on her face, watching her dutiful son obey her last command. It was exactly what Colette Maurier wanted as she saw him rush out the door. She prayed that God would guide him.

A passionate woman, Colette could not resist in that last moment of her life calling out to her young son her secret wish that he'd seek revenge for the wrongs done to them.

Young Victor rushed through the dark forest with tears streaming down his face, but never did he look back. His mother would have been very proud of him.

Already, young Victor had vowed to avenge her death.

But when he'd accepted Captain Crawford's offer that night on the wharf in England, he had not expected to wake up the next morning out in the ocean, leaving the shores of England and sailing to America.

As a youth of nine, he could hardly change the turn of events, and he had to submit to the will of Captain Crawford. Oh, their stubborn, hardheaded wills clashed frequently during the following weeks of the crossing of the vast Atlantic.

But by the time they docked in their first port, Victor had learned many things about life; especially, he'd learned to admire Glenn Crawford.

Having never had a father, Victor found himself admiring and trying to imitate the captain. In fact, he yearned to be a sea captain just like Crawford, for he loved the sea and the ship he'd called his home.

The rugged American sea captain had no inkling of the impact he'd made on the youth. But he'd kept the lad so very busy, and spent so much time with him, explaining the proper running of his fine schooner, that he'd made the quest of vengeance fade for Victor.

Victor Maurier admitted this to himself years later. Those first days with Captain Crawford went by so fast! His fascination with the strange American sea captain had turned the days swiftly into weeks and the weeks into months. Young Victor did not even think about time. For the first time in his life the sharp, clever lad who learned quickly had the figure of a powerful, strong man to pattern his life upon.

Lately Victor had reflected upon those ten years under the protective wing of Crawford. Perhaps he did think about his mother on certain occasions. But his world was dominated by men—men who were rugged and strong. There were no weaklings among Crawford's crew.

34

Victor had learned about life—about tavern brawls and women—at an early age. By the time he was eighteen, he'd enjoyed the pleasures of many ladies; his rugged, handsome face and muscled, virile body had made his conquests easy.

The high point of his life was when he knew he'd earned the respect and great trust of Captain Crawford. On his twentieth birthday, Crawford acquired a second schooner, for Victor, and it was a sleek, magnificent beauty.

The only sad thing about being the captain of his own ship was having to part company with his beloved captain, who was sailing for the coast of Texas to the port of Brownsville. It was an emotional day for Victor, and the rest of the summer of 1880 was a time of change for him. He was on his own without the sage wisdom of Crawford to guide and direct him. Decisions were his to make, and there was no captain to go to for advice.

His schooner, *Destiny,* sailed to the West Indies and the Caribbean Sea that first summer, and his cargoes were rich and prosperous. Victor felt a great pride knowing how highly Crawford would think of him.

It was when fate led him back to the shores of England and he docked in the small fishing village just outside Dover that a horrible, ugly trauma which had happened more than a decade before came back to haunt him. The twenty-year-old Maurier revisited the little cottage secluded in the woods where he'd lived the first years of his life with his lovely French mother.

No boy could have wanted a more loving, giving mother than Colette Maurier, and Victor never missed the absent father he did not have living under his roof. All he remembered about the man was what Colette had told him: his father was a stately gentleman who'd paid occasional visits to the cottage. His visits were usually nocturnal, Victor realized as he'd grown older.

Circumstances had not allowed him to take his father's name, and at the time of his mother's unfortunate death, Victor did not even know his own real name.

It seemed to Victor that the summer of 1880 was to be a season when his whole life took on a new meaning—almost a new beginning. It had shaped the last six years of his life and driven him with an insatiable desire to forever cleanse his soul for the need to avenge his beloved mother's death.

Yes, it was strange that the path had led him to this ranch in the eastern part of the state of Texas. But it had started back in England, in the woods near the cottage where he'd been born and raised.

He'd roamed through the deserted cottage with all its familiar corners and little alcoves. Layers of dust and massive cobwebs draped the ceilings and corners. Neglect was obvious in every room and the smell of mold and musty decay sickened Victor, for he remembered how sweet-smelling and fresh everything had seemed while his mother was alive.

He'd rushed out the door, wishing not to linger there. It was his past! She was no longer there and he had no need to remain there either, for the cherished memories were locked forever in his heart.

He ambled aimlessly into the woods before going to get the horse he'd hired from the livery in the small village. He was not prepared for the sudden appearance of a wizened-face little man who reminded Maurier of a leprechaun. His small body was bent over; he was a hunchback.

"You were her son, weren't you? That beautiful Mademoiselle Maurier's son is who you got to be. Knew you'd come back someday."

"I am," Victor told him, watching as he walked with

36

a cane in one hand and a knapsack in the other. "And who are you?"

"They call me 'Paddy,' but my name is Patrick McHugh. I have been the caretaker for this property—the owners hired me. It should be your land and not theirs, you know? He meant it to be for you and your mother."

Victor arched his dark brow, puzzled by the old man's remarks. "I'm—I'm afraid you've lost me, Paddy."

"Young, you were. Hardly more than a tadpole. But I've something to pass on to you, for I can see you never knew that you were the son of Lord Penwick. You were a child conceived in great love, even though Edward Penwick could not marry your mother. Neither could he stand to leave her in France when he had to return to England."

"Not that I'm doubting you for a minute, old man, but how come you are privy to so many intimate details about my mother and this Lord Penwick?"

"Well, it might be hard to believe it by the looks of me now, but I was Lord Edward's manservant until he died and that wife of his kicked me out of the house and assigned me duties around the grounds of the estate."

If he was to believe what this little gray-haired gnome was telling him, then he was the bastard son of Lord Edward Penwick, the very tall, dignified man he'd seen in their cottage and with his mother. Never could he recall any mention of a name. Usually they addressed one another in terms of endearment.

"Only his untimely death kept Lord Edward from getting this land and cottage put in your mother's name. I know that was what he intended to do. He was a good man, that I know full well. He was also unhappy that he could not be with your mother as he would have desired, but he was married to someone else."

Victor had absorbed all this with a consuming interest. He repeated all the facts to assure himself that he had heard them right. "You're telling me that my mother and this Lord Penwick fell in love in France, and when he had to return to England he could not stand to part from her, so he brought her here and set her up in this cottage on lands he owned. Obviously, she later gave birth to me and they remained loyal lovers during all that time. Then, suddenly, Lord Penwick died and my mother was left without her protector. So now I must ask you, Paddy, is this why she became the prey of the brutes I witnessed murder her that terrible night?"

"Ah true, my bucko—a lady as beautiful as your mother always needs a protector, but it was hate that murdered her. Lord Edward's wife hated both her and you, his bastard son. She was a vicious woman and still is. She wanted your mother driven from the countryside—she wanted her destroyed. Greedy she is, too. With all the vast fortune Lord Edward left her, she could not stand to allow your dear mother to have this little plot of ground and cottage. And just as greedy and evil is Lord Edward's younger brother, Eliot. They were in league with each other to drive your mother and you away."

"So they were the ones who did that horrible thing to my mother that night?" Victor trembled with the anger devouring his soul. His palms were clammy as he rubbed them together while the old man talked.

"Ah, those two would not have sullied themselves; but there was a bloke willing to do it for them while they stood back in the woods to watch. You, my fine young man, were sought in these thick woods by the three until the dawn's first light, when they gave up their search. I applauded you that night when you escaped them. I watched, knowing I was helpless to do

38

anything. I was no match for the three of them."

Maurier quizzed the elderly man for a few more details before bidding him farewell and insisting he take a leather pouch of gold coins. "My mother would want me to reward you, Paddy. Add some comfort to your life, eh?" He grinned and patted the old man's humped back. "She will be revenged, Paddy, and you can know that you have helped me."

They said their goodbyes, Paddy went back into the dense forest and Maurier returned to the hitching post for his horse.

Perhaps Paddy would never know about Big Tom meeting his untimely death in a dark alley in the city of Dover. But three weeks after his meeting with young Maurier in the woods, he was to remember the fierce look on Maurier's face when he'd said Colette's death would be avenged. Was it just a coincidence that Lord Edward Penwick's wife, Elaine, was taken suddenly ill and died two days later? Paddy's superstitious nature was convinced that Maurier had managed to seek revenge.

Paddy was right! Maurier sailed out of Dover on his slick-lined schooner, and there was no question about his destination. He was a man possessed, and his goal was to find Lord Eliot Penwick. He'd paid a handsome price for the information he'd gathered in the last three weeks.

His first port of call was Brownsville, a city at the southern tip of Texas. Before he went on with this quest of his, he must seek out his old friend, Captain Crawford.

But when he docked in the Texas harbor a month later and located his friend, he was hardly prepared for the dilapidated state of Crawford's health. He told his beloved friend what he'd found out about his mother's death and that he was going to avenge the wrong.

In a faltering voice, Crawford declared, "I wouldn't think much of you as a man if you didn't, Victor. Go, and godspeed! And after that, I want you coming back here to see me." His rheumy eyes still had a hint of a twinkle in them.

"You can count on that, captain!" Maurier gave a forced grin, for it pained him to know his dear friend was surely dying.

"There is an old, loyal friend of mine, Victor, who will be able to help you: go to the Casa del Lago and tell him I sent you. His name is Señor Emilo Cortez. Just tell him Crawford told you to seek him out. He knows the country and everyone around that part of east Texas. Beautiful country, Vic—that blackland and those pine forests. Go, my boy, and do what you must do."

He went purposefully from Crawford's bedside that night in Brownsville to travel to east Texas and seek out Señor Cortez.

He'd never questioned the wise advice of Captain Crawford and he didn't now. Somehow he knew the trail would lead him where he wanted to go.

When he arrived at the Casa del Lago, he wondered that first evening if he was wasting his time. But the very next day he realized how wrong he had been, for he found out that Emilo Cortez's neighbor was Lord Eliot Penwick.

He could not believe his good fortune.

Chapter 4

Sitting there on the riverbank by himself, Victor found it very easy to drift into a peaceful languor. He had been pleased that Señor Cortez had not sought to accompany him, for it gave him some time to think and plan what his next move should be.

But once he'd reached this particular spot and sat down on the grounds to lean back on the trunk of the big oak, he found it hard to do any devious plotting against anyone, even Eliot Penwick. Damn, this was beautiful country, and Maurier had to admit that he could easily stay here much longer than he'd planned.

He removed the wide-brimmed, flat-crowned black hat and flung it aside, then removed the kerchief from his neck. The urge to catch a big bass suddenly didn't matter that much; he propped his pole against a supporting boulder so the line could go into the water below the bank.

A short time later there was a tug on the line, but Victor's eyes were closed so he knew nothing about it— nor about the pair of wide, sparkling black eyes appraising him. The girl's dainty feet had made no sound as she'd stepped along the riverbank. She'd tethered her horse a short distance away.

The whole countryside seemed so quiet and peaceful that Talleha felt like she was the only one stirring on this hot afternoon. Like Victor Maurier, she felt the need to be alone to plot how she was going to get away and return to where she belonged. There were things going on in that big house she didn't understand or like.

No one could have been sweeter or kinder to her than Flossie. And Lord Eliot had been a generous and thoughtful man. But Talleha had come to realize that behind Lucita's smile there was a hint of distaste for her, though Talleha could not figure out why.

There was certainly no doubt about how Lord Eliot's wife felt about her. It was written all over her pinched, pale face every time they met, yet Talleha felt sorry for the woman. She was miserable in spite of her obvious wealth.

Lord Eliot promised to send her home each time she approached him about the matter, but Talleha grew impatient and irritated as the days wore on.

All the fancy clothes and the fine little mare he'd purchased especially for her did not break her determination to return to where she lived with her mother. Lately, something had gnawed at her as she lay awake at night: perhaps he was never going to let her leave! This frightened her.

Last night, she'd decided to start her own plan of departure from the Casa del Lago. She'd reasoned that she was no helpless, fragile child—her mother had taught her well. She knew about the herbs and berries there in the woods, and what could be eaten. There was water in the river to drink and bath in; even if it took her days to reach her destination, she'd have what she needed.

The spirited young lady felt no fear of traveling alone through the woods or at night. She'd roamed the forest around her mother's cottage and the little creatures of the woods had been no threat.

As she'd ambled down toward the edge of the river in her brand new black twill riding skirt, she wished it was just a pair of faded old blue pants like the ones she usually wore. The low underbrush caught at the material and she had to yank it free. The sheer ruffled-neck blouse was not as comfortable as her old loose-fitting cotton tunic.

She'd mumbled to herself, "Guess rich people don't seek the simple comforts Mommie and I did. All this fluff. It's—it's miserable!"

She unbuttoned the first three buttons on the sheer blouse and the feeling was wonderfully pleasant. She flopped back the ruffles.

It was then that her dark eyes spotted the young man sitting under the big oak tree, and he was the most handsome man she'd ever seen. His eyes were closed, but his wavy black hair was tousled, giving him the appearance of a young lad. But his broad shoulders and long body destroyed that image. In his faded blue pants bulged firm, muscled legs. Talleha knew he was very much a man.

She stood there quietly for an unhurried moment or two, letting her eyes dance over him. Why was her heart pounding so fast, she wondered? She wanted to rush away, but it seemed her feet were made of lead. She remained in the same spot wondering who he was.

Her black eyes lit up and she broke into a gale of laughter as she noticed the sharp movement of his fishing pole. He had lost a big fish by sleeping. It would have been too late, even if she'd have rushed to grab the pole herself.

As her laughing black eyes focused on the fishing pole, Maurier's eyes opened to view the breathtaking sight she made standing there less than a hundred feet away.

43

The sheer blouse opened at the neck gave her a most provocative look; the mounds of her breasts were tantalizing to his senses. Hair black as a raven's wing framed a lovely face with a most kissable pair of lips.

Maurier let his eyes leave her lovely, laughing face long enough to follow the source of her amused delight, and he broke into a slow, easy grin. She was giggling about the fish below the water taking his bait, but escaping his hook. The way the line was being tugged, Victor had obviously lost a fine, big bass.

But that didn't faze him, because he'd been rewarded with the sight of a beautiful girl he was far more interested in catching.

As Talleha edged her way closer, she had no idea that Victor lay tensed and ready to leap up off the ground. The sight of her aroused every muscle in his body. The lazy sway of her walk gave her a sensuous air that she was not aware of but that any man would find delightfully stimulating. And Victor Maurier, all man, was stimulated indeed!

Her back was now turned to him and Victor rose up so quietly that she did not hear him. When he stood up directly behind her, he saw she barely reached his shoulders. His hands reached out to encircle her waist and he said to her with a hint of teasing in his voice, "I might have lost the fish, but I caught you, my lovely lady."

Talleha whirled in the circle of his arms, which held her captive. His eyes sparked with blue fire and there was a devious grin on his handsome face. He held her pressed so close to him she felt wicked, liking the warmth of his firm, virile body.

Handsome as he was and as excited as she was to be in his embrace, she sensed he was a man far too sure of himself. But the innocent Talleha had never encountered such a man as Victor Maurier and she dared to taunt him as she did the young men she'd known back near the village where she and her mother lived.

Boldly, she inquired of him, "Now that you've caught me, what do you intend to do with me?"

A broader grin creased Maurier's face and he replied, "This!" Without any further delay, he bent down to capture her half-opened lips with his. Honeysweet, they were, and Maurier wanted the kiss to last forever.

Talleha swore she could not breathe as his sensuous lips seared hers. But her lips were not the only part of her aflame. She felt consumed by the nearness of his heat as it seemed to trail all over her trembling body. She'd never suspected a kiss to ignite such a wild, wicked emotion in her. It had never been this way before.

When Victor finally released her lips and she stood there, wide-eyed and wondering, he knew he was the first man to really kiss those rosebud lips. He, too, stared down at her silently without speaking for a minute, for he was amazed that one so beautiful had not known a man's kiss before.

The fathomless expression revealed no clue to her feelings as his eyes pierced hers. Did his kiss thrill her as her sweet lips had pleasured him? Did the feel of his firm, muscled form pressed against hers excite her as much as she had tantalized him? God, he wanted to know and yearned to see a warm, loving smile crease her face!

But the little minx just stared up at him, saying nothing. He was at a loss for words, for he was filled with emotion. Not for one minute did he regret the kiss, or holding her close to him, but there was a sparking effect in her dark eyes that reminded him of a frightened little creature. He didn't want that! He had not intended to scare this beautiful girl, only to make love to her.

Talleha felt the release of his hands around her waist and she suddenly realized just how firmly he had held her. Maurier finally broke the silence by confessing, "I won't say I'm sorry for kissing you, for that would be lying; but I didn't mean to scare you, miss." He backed away from her and ran his long, slender fingers through an unruly wisp of hair falling down over one side of his forehead.

Talleha placed her hands firmly at her hips and tilted her head haughtily to one side to declare, "Scare me? Oh, I hate to shatter your illusion, but I was not scared." Without any hesitation, she whirled around to walk away.

Maurier stood for a moment watching her feisty paces taking her away from him. Just what was she trying to tell him?

"Well, pardon me, ma'am, for my concern. Just let it be known that I am a gentleman. Glad I didn't insult you, then." His voice was laced with mockery.

By now Talleha's swift footsteps had taken her about a hundred feet from where Victor stood. Bad judgment on Talleha's part urged her to give way to the impulse to call back to him, "I didn't say I wasn't insulted. I said I wasn't scared. The truth is, I don't think you are a *gentleman!*"

She turned her back on him and started on her way, her long, black curls bouncing.

Her impudent air and smirking little face riled Maurier so, he broke into long strides to catch up with her. Just who in the devil did she think she was to turn that pert little nose up at him? When Talleha turned to see him dashing toward her, she started to run like a gazelle to get to her horse, which wasn't too far away.

As fast as she ran, she could not compete with the long, strong legs of Victor Maurier. He quickly closed the distance separating them and Talleha felt the force of him attacking her. His powerful arms crushed her to him as he muttered angrily, "Well, damned if I'll be a gentleman this time, you little vixen. But I'll assure you, by the time I release you, you'll know the difference."

He captured her lips roughly with his mouth and there was no hint of tenderness as there had been the first time. Talleha fought against him, wiggling and arching to try to free herself, but Victor only held her tighter.

"I'll kill you—so help me!" she hissed angrily. Her arms were now trembling with weakness and she knew what strength and power she had left was the weapon of her legs. She sought to position herself so she might thrust a blow to his groin. But Victor was too clever to allow that to happen and together they fell to the ground.

He lay heavily atop her, and the rapid beat of each of their hearts could have been just one. His hungry mouth sought hers again, and so fierce were his lips with his tongue seeking entry that she was forced to surrender to such overwhelming power.

But Victor chanced to gaze into the black pools of her eyes and he saw a mist gathered there. All his fury quieted, even though he still lay across her petite body. His lips were still greedy for one more kiss and he took that for himself.

Raising up, he propped himself on an elbow as he calmly murmured in her ear, "Now *that,* my darling, was no *gentleman.* But I've yet to take a woman against her will, and I'll not force you. One day you'll come into my arms willingly, and then you'll be loved as you've never been loved before."

Talleha muttered under her breath that the day would never come, but she was now too smart to be

47

bold with this man. She dared not be so foolhardy again. So she said nothing as she watched him raise up away from her to stand there, towering.

She took his hand as he offered to lift her up from the ground. Neither did she give a protest when he suggested, "I'll help you on your horse. That's your mount, isn't it?" She merely gave him a nod of her tousled head.

Her silence bothered him almost as much as her spitfire tongue, but this time it was not anger consuming him. It was confusion stabbing at him as he assisted her up to straddle the mare. So occupied with his own thoughts was Victor that he forgot the question he'd meant to ask her before she rode away.

Talleha immediately spurred the little mare into a fast gallop and she didn't look back or answer him as he yelled at her, "You didn't tell me your name! Hey, what is your name?"

By then the dense, piney woods had devoured her fleeing image and he could not see her. She was gone like the lovely petals of a beautiful blossom swept away by a breeze.

The vision of her loveliness would remain with him, Victor knew. He'd find her if he had to search the whole Texas countryside. She had to live nearby at one of the ranches close to the Casa del Lago. Señor Cortez would surely know such a strikingly beautiful young lady.

When he finally turned to go back to where his fishing pole lay, he grinned as he kicked at the ground with the toe of his Spanish boot. How would he describe that dainty damsel to the señor? How sadly lacking it would be to say only that she was a black-haired, black-eyed young lady who stood five feet and a few inches high.

That would not do justice to the vivacious little vixen

he'd met and hoped to find once again. But it would hardly be fitting to tell Señor Cortez about the perfection of such a female figure for one so petite, nor that her lips were made for a man's kisses. For a brief moment his nose had nuzzled the side of her cheek and his senses were intoxicated by the sweet fragrance of her: it reminded him of wild honeysuckle.

No woman had ever made such a startling impact on Victor Maurier and he didn't even know the name of the girl with the wicked sparkle in her eyes.

Chapter 5

When Talleha came bouncing through the bedroom door, Flossie noticed immediately the rosy flush of her cheeks and the brilliant sparkle in her dark eyes. The plump housekeeper had been searching throughout the spacious house for at least an hour to find her impetuous charge.

"Where in saints' name have you been, child? I'm exhausted from going all over the house and up and down these stairs. You've made it very hard on poor Flossie." She wiped her forehead with the bottom of her starched white apron. Happy at the sight of her, Flossie took a seat on the edge of the bed.

"I'm sorry about that, Flossie, but I just went for a ride. I was bored." Talleha flipped her long hair up off of her neck and shrugged her shoulders frivolously.

With her hands on her hips and a frown arching her brow, Flossie insisted on knowing, "By yourself, missy?"

"Of course! I didn't want to have anyone with me, if you must know the truth, Flossie," she confessed with her usual candor.

"Oh, Lord Penwick isn't going to like you disobeying his orders, Talleha. You know he told you not to ride off the ranch alone."

"I was still on the ranch. I rode through the woods and down to the lake." She didn't mention the handsome devil of a man she encountered, though.

"Oh, mercy! That far?" As she stared at the lovely little creature, Flossie thought to herself what a sight she would have provided for those hot-blooded Mexican ranch hands employed at the Casa del Lago by Emilo Cortez. She also knew Lord Eliot Penwick was not at all fond of the señor.

Talleha obviously had not met up with any of them or surely she would have told her. The young lady was quite a chatterbox when they were together.

"Flossie, dear—I'm used to going where I please because my mother allowed it. She was a free spirit; she understood my yearning to wander." She smiled so sweetly at the housekeeper that it was impossible for Flossie to remain displeased. The adorable little imp was unruly and certainly willful, but Flossie concluded that no one was going to change that.

Eliot Penwick was not even that forceful, Flossie mused.

When she left Talleha, she decided to make no mention of the incident to Penwick. If he found out, it would have to be through the stableboy or someone else. Flossie didn't want it to be through her, because after all, no harm had come about by the girl's disobeying him. She was upstairs safe and sound.

But the jealous Lucita took devious pleasure in mentioning that Talleha had gone for a jaunt in the woods. She made a casual remark as she busily dressed Marjorie's hair while Eliot paid a visit to his wife's boudoir before dinner.

"She is a very good horsewoman, this Señorita Talleha. I admired the way she galloped into the clearing near the woods." Lucita addressed her

51

mistress. But Eliot perked up and barked out to the Mexican servant girl, "You must be mistaken, Lucita!"

"It was her I saw, because I watched her ride right up to the stable. Romano can confirm it, for he helped her dismount, Señor Penwick," Lucita remarked meekly.

In a snapping, resentful voice, Marjorie demanded to know, "So what does it concern you whether the girl does or doesn't go for a ride, Eliot? It isn't exactly uncivilized country here." Her voice and her manner cracked with indignation.

She still felt the deep passion for Texas that Frank Greenfield had when he was alive. But Marjorie learned quickly that her new husband looked down his aristocratic nose at most of the things she held dear to her heart. The crude, sarcastic remarks he'd made after meeting some of her friends at the first annual barbecue on Marjorie's ranch after their marriage was enough to make her despise him.

After that, each new slur of Eliot's heightened her distaste. The romance that had blossomed so freely and clouded her good judgment was replaced with repulsion. A stinging resentment erupted within her as he began to act as if *he* owned her ranch. His arrogance was so overbearing that Marjorie felt a weakness to cope, and this frayed her nerves more as the time went by.

As he so often did, Eliot turned his back on Marjorie, choosing not to answer her question regarding his concerns about Talleha' riding alone. With Lucita's and Marjorie's eyes glaring at his back, he stalked out of the room.

Right now, he was angry at all the females in this house, including the pretty Talleha. She had defied his direct orders, and that he could not tolerate. As he marched down the hall he changed his mind about going to Talleha's room to lecture her until he confirmed what he'd just heard from Lucita with Romano.

There was the possibility that Lucita was telling one of her devious lies, and he wouldn't put it past her. She was a conniving little witch, he'd found out after he'd come to live here. He'd often wondered what Marjorie would think of her "devoted Lucita" if she'd known how easy it had been to take her to his bed. Even now, all he'd have to do was snap his fingers, and she'd come running.

So there was all the more reason why she'd invent a falsehood about Talleha in the hopes that he'd be displeased, Eliot thought to himself. He went down the stairway to go to the stable instead of seeking out Talleha.

A deep purple twilight pervaded the countryside as Eliot walked across the grounds toward the barn and stable. He hastened his pace, hoping to catch Romano before he left for his own cottage about a halfmile away. A couple of ranch hands were moving through the corral to go to the nearby bunkhouse.

Eliot sneered, thinking that they'd have probably given Frank Greenfield a friendly wave of the hand or a wide-brimmed hat if it had been him going toward the barn. The bloody bastards!

Why should he care, though? He didn't intend to spend the rest of his life in this godforsaken place. In fact, the sooner he could leave, the better he'd like it.

He caught sight of the short young Mexican darting out of the back doorway and yelled out at him to wait. Romano halted and turned around to see the tall, lean Penwick behind him.

"Maldito sea!" Romano cussed, wondering what he wanted, for he knew his supper was waiting for him and he was tired and hungry. "Si, señor?"

Eliot swaggered up to him to ask if he'd saddled

53

Talleha's mare that afternoon. "She is not supposed to go alone again. Those are my orders for the future, do you understand?"

"Si, I do now," Romano muttered, trying not to sound insolent, but he disliked the señora's husband very much.

"Be sure you do. That is all, Romano." He turned sharply to go back to the house. Romano thought to himself that the young lady was not going to be too pleased by this new rule laid down by Penwick.

His conclusion was exactly right. Talleha was more than displeased that evening at dinner—she was infuriated. Before Eliot's demanding voice spoke of her afternoon jaunt alone and the fact that she'd obviously ignored his orders, she had looked gay and beautiful with the candlelight shimmering against her skin. She wore a pale-yellow gown trimmed in white lace on the puffed sleeves and scooped neckline. Flossie had pinned a yellow forsythia blossom behind her ear. Eliot admired her loveliness as he sat at the head of the table. He'd noticed the graceful motions of her hand and her long, slender fingers, thinking that they did not need rings or bracelets to draw attention.

Marjorie's exquisite gold bracelets and her expensive diamond and ruby rings did not impress him. But then he was never excited or impressed by her beauty. It was the fortune she possessed that attracted him, for few ladies could provide the same.

When he addressed Talleha he tried to soften his voice, especially with Marjorie sitting there, but even if he had whispered the words, Talleha would not have taken kindly to them—to be told she was essentially a prisoner in this house.

She sat up straight in the finely carved walnut chair and her nostrils flared; her black eyes sparked with fire.

"I was never unfortunate enough to be confined, Lord Penwick." Her soft voice was as cold as a winter wind blowing in from the north.

"You are not confined, my dear; hardly that." He gave a nervous chuckle.

"I consider it so. I had best be getting back to my village as soon as possible, so I won't put any more burden on you here." Her thick black lashes fluttered nervously as her eyes stared down into her lap.

Marjorie wore a sly grin, for she detected instantly that Eliot was not expecting such a reply. It was one of those rare occasions Marjorie sought to assume her role as the mistress of her own house as she hastened to remark, "Well, I see no reason why that can't be arranged, if this is your desire, my dear."

Marjorie's eyes were directed away from Eliot and focused on Talleha. She didn't have to be looking at him to know there was a frown on his finely chiseled face.

His voice was laced with indignation as he addressed his wife. "Such arrangements will be made by me, Marjorie, so you'll leave that in my charge. I've things calling for my attention the next few days. Talleha will have to wait for a while."

The rest of the dinner hour was quiet and restrained. Talleha did not finish Flossie's delicious dessert, which she would have normally devoured with relish, but instead asked to be excused. Eliot gave her a nod of his head but said not a word to her as he watched her move away from the table. It was obvious to him from the way she marched away, her yellow gown swishing back and forth, that she was vexed. How haughtily she carried that beautiful head! She was a vision to behold, he thought to himself.

He didn't know whether she was more appealing

with the sweet, inviting smile on her face or when she was fired heatedly with a temper, as she was this evening.

Marjorie was thoroughly enjoying herself, for a change. Poor Eliot was so miserable, and she knew why. She could not resist goading him, "No meek little lamb, that one. Stubborn as a mule, too, I'd wager."

The eyes that turned on her at that moment were fierce, and the way he looked at her told her what she'd suspected for many months now; he cared for her not at all. Oh, what an absolute, utter fool she'd been ever to marry Eliot Penwick!

His tall physique was rigid and tense as he pushed back from the table. "Good evening, Marjorie. I'm going for my ride." He walked out of the room, leaving his wife sitting there staring at the wall. Flossie entered to see her there alone and figured the couple had just gone through another of their many fusses.

Quietly, she went around the table to remove Talleha's half-finished dessert and wondered what had happened to her hearty appetite this evening. Politely, she inquired of Marjorie if she wanted anything else. Poor Flossie received a curt reply as Marjorie slammed the napkin down on the table and turned to leave the room.

All Flossie could say was that this was a miserable house to live or work in. How she yearned to be back in London and walk those cobblestone streets!

Sometimes she felt like taking the savings she'd acquired from the wages Lord Penwick had paid her and going back alone. Regardless of what he said about their returning together soon, Flossie wondered just how long it would take. She could hardly wait.

She began gathering up the remaining plates because she wanted to look in on Talleha before she retired. She left the burden of all the cleaning up in her kitchen to her helper.

Without taking the time to remove her apron, she rushed to check on Talleha. When she entered the room she found Talleha standing at the window; the pensive look on that charming face melted Flossie's heart. "You look a million miles away, child," Flossie remarked, moving over to where she stood.

"No, not all that far away, Flossie. But I *am* going! I don't care what your *Lord Penwick* says!" Her tone of voice was assured and determined and there was a haughtiness when she mentioned Penwick's name.

"Dearie, I can't help what Lord Penwick does. You are obviously out of favor with him." Flossie now knew why her tasty pie was left on Talleha's plate and why Lord Eliot had made his hasty exit. It also explained poor Marjorie's foul temper, and Flossie felt sympathy for her. She was a very unhappy woman.

Talleha never ceased to amaze her. Flossie saw her as still almost a child with all that blossoming beauty of hers. But there were times when the black-haired girl spoke with the wisdom of an experienced, worldly woman. Flossie knew she wasn't that at all.

Talleha had turned from the window and her black eyes were now soft and warm. "Oh, I don't hold you responsible for Lord Penwick's actions, Flossie, but you seem to worship him so! I doubt if he deserves it. Call it the Indian blood that flows in my veins, but I know this house is not a happy one—not like my mother's and my home. Love was there. Faith and trust were there. Perhaps we were poor by Lord Penwick's standards, but in other ways we were far richer than those who live here."

Flossie said not a word but only stared at the girl. She could not argue with her, for she spoke the truth. As they stood there in silence, Talleha knew Flossie agreed with her. She walked over to pat the English housekeeper on the shoulder affectionately. "That is why I must get away from here, Flossie. This place would smother me. He has even denied me the privilege of riding alone. I cannot accept that!"

Flossie understood. Talleha was like a beautiful butterfly who would die if her colorful wings were clipped.

Flossie could not bring herself to speak the words she felt then. But after a moment of thought, she admitted: "Talleha, I care very much for you and I hope you know this. I'm—I'm only a simple lady—a housekeeper—but I'll help you in any way that I can."

A searching look was on Talleha's face as she declared, "I may just ask your help, Flossie. I just may."

As Flossie left, she realized she was in a state of confusion. The young lady certainly had a winning way about her, she would have to say that. The housekeeper was under her spell; she felt herself drawn to the girl more than she was to Lord Penwick after all these years of service.

Was Talleha some kind of wicked little witch capable of casting spells? Flossie tried to shrug those thoughts aside, telling herself she was just weary; but the next day she was still feeling the same way.

Talleha was a mysterious little creature.

Chapter 6

There was a marked change in his young guest, Señor Cortez observed during the dinner hour. The young Maurier was most thoughtful and preoccupied about something. When he'd returned to the house that afternoon without so much as one fine bass from the lake, Emilo decided this young man was not much of a fisherman. Anyone could catch one fish in that crystal-clear stream!

Maurier had told him he'd had only a few nibbles. Emilo raised a skeptical brow at that remark, but he shrugged it aside. This young gent probably found his relaxation elsewhere, but Emilo found fishing a most peaceful way to enjoy himself.

Cortez had invited Victor to join him out on the covered veranda, where he'd have Margarita serve them a cooling glass of lemonade. There they sat and talked for over an hour as Emilo's servant refilled their tall glasses.

Victor asked casually about the nearby ranchers in hopes of learning which one had a daughter with a mane of midnight-black hair. Emilo spoke at length about all the neighbors whose lands bordered his property, but he gave no response to encourage Victor that the charming little creature lived nearby.

But Maurier's eyes remembered certain details about that fine-tailored riding skirt she wore and the luxurious sheer blouse so perfectly molded to her sensuous body. Those clothes were expensive, so she was no wandering little vagabond.

There was only one answer, Victor decided as he left Señor Cortez there on the veranda to enjoy his cheroot. The girl was visiting one of the rancher families living in the vicinity and Cortez was probably not aware of it.

A few hours later, when he joined his host for dinner, he could not get Talleha off his mind. He became aware of how preoccupied he was when his congenial host had to repeat questions to him. Victor offered his apologies to Señor Cortez.

Emilo gave him a lighthearted chuckle, "Ah, young man, I was young once, and I'd venture to guess that some pretty young lady awaits you. Maybe you are pining to be with her, si?"

Victor broke into a guilty grin. The elderly gentleman was very observant. He was reminded of Captain Crawford. Oh, the two of them looked nothing alike, but their ways and their thinking were so much the same.

"I'd not try to deceive you, sir, for it *was* a young lady I was thinking about," Victor readily admitted.

"Ah, I thought so—I imagine a most beautiful one, too," Emilo replied.

"A gorgeous young woman, sir. Her hair is as black as a raven's wing, and so are her eyes."

"Hmmm, she sounds lovely."

"I must confess to you I don't even know her name, so I'm at a disadvantage, wouldn't you say, sir?" Victor shrugged his broad shoulders.

"Well, I imagine you'll find out who this mysterious young señorita is shortly."

How absolutely right Emilo Cortez was, because it happened quite unexpectedly the next afternoon, as he and Maurier rode across the pasture where Cortez cattle grazed leisurely on the knee-high grass.

Emilo rode his handsome, dappled-gray stallion and Maurier was astride a magnificent black horse Cortez had just acquired. Maurier realized the señor was quite a fine horseman, a striking figure of a man his age. Dressed all in black with a flat-crowned black hat on his gray head, Señor Cortez projected the picture of dignified elegance.

As Maurier's eyes caught sight of a buggy coming down the dirt road and a cloud of billowing dust rose upward, he reined up on the black horse. Cortez halted his mount, too.

As the buggy passed them, Emilo remarked with the hint of a smirk in his voice, "Ah, my neighbor, Eliot Penwick."

Maurier could not care less about the man, for he was mesmerized by the beautiful vision sitting next to him. She was a glorious sight with an ecru straw bonnet tied under that pert chin with green velvet ribbons. She turned her head to glance in the direction of him and Cortez, but hastily her gaze was directed back to the road.

Did she recognize him, Victor wondered? If so, was it distaste that caused her to swiftly turn away?

In a hesitating voice, he inquired of Cortez, "Is that Penwick's wife with him?" He did not know whether he wanted to hear the answer Cortez would give him.

"Oh, no—that is not his wife. That is not Marjorie, Frank Greenfield's widow. Frank was my very good friend and this—this Penwick could never be that, I'm sure."

"I see," Victor drawled with no doubt about Emilo's feelings for the man.

61

"I still can't understand Marjorie's marrying this—this Englishman, who is younger than her, and especially after being married to such a fine, upstanding man as Frank Greenfield."

"So then, who might this lady be, Señor Cortez?" Maurier quizzed with overwhelming relief that she wasn't Penwick's wife.

"It can only be the young lady Penwick is reported to have found in the woods, lost and deserted some time ago. I've heard talk from my friends at the other ranches. They say he took her in and has been caring for her. My friend Bill Driscoll says she has some kind of funny name—sounded like an Indian name to him."

"Indian? But she doesn't look Indian to me, sir."

"Oh, certainly not full-blooded, from what I just saw. Not even a half-breed, from all I've known in this part of Texas. A white man or woman had a part in her breeding, I'm sure." Emilo glanced in Victor's direction: the admiring warmth in the young man's eyes told Emilo how fired Maurier was at the sight of her. The shrewd Emilo recalled the mention of black hair and eyes during their conversation the night before. Could this be the one Maurier was thinking about?

It made the elderly Mexican smile with amusement. A young lady like her could not help finding a man like Maurier very appealing, with his handsome features and magnificent physique. He noticed as they traveled down the road that the young woman turned her head back to look in their direction.

Señor Cortez did not think his young friend was aware of this. Now the elderly Mexican would be the first to admit that he was a romantic, even though he was now in the winter of his life. Young or old, he always had been a romantic, and he did not apologize for it, for he knew that he and his beautiful Carmalita had had a glorious marriage. He took a great masculine pride that he helped make it so, because he was a very sentimental fellow. How often his wife praised him for that; he swelled with pleasure.

Señor Cortez pitied the man who was not willing to be tender, for it had yielded him such a bounty of rapture that the warmth remained with him still. He desired no other woman to sleep by his side if it could not be his Carmalita. No woman could match her in his eyes.

He knew the consuming warmth he'd seen in Maurier's eyes just now. So perhaps Maurier was romantic too. Perhaps there was only one woman to hold him for eternity. His pleasant musings brought forth a serene and contented smile.

Victor Maurier had no inkling of the thoughts of his elderly companion. He was too absorbed with his own thoughts; he wished not to involve this beautiful girl in his plans for the man in the buggy beside her. This changed everything, he realized.

Victor remarked to Señor Cortez, "His wife must be a very understanding woman to permit such a beautiful young girl to stay under her roof. You say she is older than this Penwick?"

"That is right. Knowing Marjorie as long as I have, I rather doubt that she is taking it too well. All her old friends share the same opinion that this cocky so-called English lord is an overbearing rascal."

Victor gave him an understanding nod, having already concluded that it was the Greenfield fortune Penwick wanted, just as he'd greedily wanted all his older brother's wealth. He'd not hesitated to kill his mother to be rid of her, Victor knew, so he'd certainly not hesitate to do the same to Marjorie Greenfield Penwick.

The sly Emilo baited his young friend. "I sense you are glad the pretty black-haired lady is not his

63

wife, Victor?"

With a solemn look still on his face, Maurier admitted honestly, "I'm glad, señor."

"Well, shall we continue on our way, then?" Señor Cortez suggested. Victor reined his horse to follow behind the dappled gray, but his head was giddy. It struck him just now that he ought to get this business with Eliot Penwick over and done with so he could get on with his life.

Strange as it might seem, Eliot Penwick had similar thoughts as he reined the bay pulling his fancy buggy into town. He'd insisted that Talleha accompany him for a very specific reason. Like Maurier, Penwick was ready to get on with a new life—one which did not include Marjorie. Last night he'd made his mind up to act upon it without any further delay. The longer he waited, the more difficult it would be to gain control of the wild little vixen sitting beside him. He was now obsessed with a desire to have her.

When they arrived in town and he'd halted the buggy in front of Brown's Mercantile Store, he offered his hand to Talleha and urged, "Come inside and we might just find you some little pretty you'd like, yes?"

But Talleha shrugged her shoulders, declaring, "I wish nothing, sir. At least no 'little pretty,' as you call it." She'd been preoccupied with her own thoughts since her eyes had unexpectedly caught the sight of the handsome devil she'd met down by the lake. Today he was just as winning as she'd remembered. She knew now she had not been just imagining his devastating good looks.

As they'd gone on down the dirt road, she'd felt her heart pounding erratically, and she was glad Penwick didn't attempt to carry on any conversation. She didn't know whether she could have talked.

"Come on," Eliot coaxed her. "I cannot leave you in

64

the buggy alone." His firm hand insisted she get down and come with him.

The owner of the store greeted Eliot, but his eyes were on Talleha. Noticing this, he urged Talleha to go over to look at the colorful bolts of ribbon while he gave his order to Mr. Brown.

Enos Brown was a wiry little man who had lived in this region long before Texas was a state. He'd sold to the Greenfields since they'd first come to Harrison County. Like everyone else in these parts, he'd greatly respected and admired Frank Greenfield, and he still had high esteem for his widow, Marjorie. But the foreign dandy she'd married he could not abide.

Looking over Eliot's list, he quizzed, "Got some pesty critters you want to kill, eh?"

"That's right. Poor dear Marjorie was heartsick to find moths were ruining her fine woolens, and I intend to get rid of them for her."

"I see," Enos drawled. He moved to get some arsenic powder, along with the other items on the list.

When Enos's back was turned, Eliot's face creased with a smirk, silently calling him a nosy bastard. All these Texans were that way, it seemed to him. He turned to look for Talleha and spotted her at the long rack holding the bolts of velvet and satin ribbon.

Enos gathered up the articles. He'd also appraised the fair young companion with Penwick as he'd moved along the counters. She was certainly a tiny little thing, Enos thought to himself. He'd heard the story about the girl; a kindhearted soul, he felt sorry for her.

When he happened to glance her way again, he noticed the arrogant Penwick had moved to stand behind her. Enos was reminded of cat ready to lunge at a little mouse to devour it. He also noted something else with very curious interest as he watched the pretty girl turn away from the ribbons to glare up at him. She didn't seem too fond of Eliot Penwick, and Enos surmised she had to be one smart girl.

Enos inquired, "Well, how's Miss Marjorie doin' these days? Haven't seen her in ages."

Eliot highly resented Enos's referring to his wife as "Miss Marjorie." It bloody well galled him that everyone refused to admit that she was now a Penwick—his wife, not Frank Greenfield's.

"My wife is just fine. As I told you, she'll be more content when I rid the house of moths."

Enos was no fool, and he caught the snapping in Penwick's tone of voice. He ignored it and turned to Talleha to inquire if he might get something for her. "You need any of them pretty ribbons I saw you lookin' at, miss?"

She gave him a nice smile and politely thanked him. "No, but those are pretty colors."

"Aren't they, now?" Enos agreed as his eyes continued to enjoy the sight of her. She was lovely to look at and it had been a long, long time since Enos Brown had seen such a beauty.

Eliot Penwick bristled to think she could be so friendly and warm to a common merchant when she had nothing to give him but a frown or a pout. He had plans to change all that, though. There were ways to break a female, just like there were ways to break a filly.

If it took that to have the woman he desired in Talleha, then he'd do it!

Chapter 7

It was long past midnight, but Maurier still had not removed his pants or boots. Bare-chested and puffing on a cheroot, he'd ambled out the double doors of his bedroom onto the small roofed patio just outside. Leaning against the porch railing, he looked out into the surrounding darkness. The sweet fragrance of night-blooming nicotiana wafted on the gentle breeze.

Killing Eliot Penwick seemed hardly enough to Victor, for it appeared that the evil of the man harmed anyone he encountered. Not that Marjorie Greenfield meant anything to him . . . but Eliot was obviously playing her as cruel as he had his mother.

Yes, there had to be more than just the swift punishment of death for Penwick, something more fitting for the scoundrel. Tossing the remains of the cheroot to the ground, he strolled back into his room to remove his boots and pants.

Tomorrow, he was going to take a ride over by the Greenfield ranch; with what he had in mind, he did not want the companionship of the señor.

The same darkness that surrounded Victor engulfed

Talleha a few miles away from the Casa del Lago. Restless and wide-eyed, she looked out into the night, promising herself that tomorrow would give her the solution to getting away from this place. Eliot Penwick was impossible to reason with and she was beginning to think he was a liar as well.

She did not care for the touch of his hand reaching over to take hers as they traveled back to the ranch from town. She certainly didn't like the way those same hands clasped her tiny waist to help her down from the buggy nor the way he'd intentionally pulled her against him as her feet had hit the ground. She saw the salacious grin on his fine-featured face when he sensed she was flustered by his nearness.

Again during dinner she sat witnessing the harsh, cruel way he acted toward his poor wife. She felt so sorry for the woman. Once again, Talleha had not finished her dessert so she could excuse herself. But Penwick had stopped her before she could get out of her chair. "Talleha, I was planning to invite you to stroll in the gardens after we dine. Such a wonderful evening. Marjorie doesn't care to go walking this late."

Talleha looked from him to his wife and wondered what in the world he was attempting to do. She felt embarrassed and ill-at-ease standing there in Marjorie's presence while this man carried on like this.

Giving a tug at her full-gathered skirt, Talleha politely but firmly refused him. "I'll—I'll have to disappoint you, sir. I don't care to go for a stroll tonight." She made a hasty exit before he could stop her and she did not see the fury on his flushed face.

Talleha raced through the hallway and up the steps as quickly as she could. She didn't slow her pace until she was halfway down the hall and ready to go into her bedroom. Suddenly a shadowy figure appeared in the darkened hallway and Talleha gasped and froze on the spot. But when she realized it was only Lucita her trembling ceased.

"Oh, Lord, Lucita—you frightened me for a minute," Talleha confessed breathlessly.

"Frightened, señorita? In this grand house who would frighten you?" There was a smirk there in the sultry little servant girl's voice, but Talleha had too much on her mind at this moment to notice it.

"That—that doesn't matter—really. I was just in a hurry to get to my room to take off this miserable gown and be comfortable. I am—was not used to such fancy clothing."

"Ah, yes, I recall you telling me this," Lucita remarked. The Mexican girl found it hard to dislike Talleha, for she was very outgoing and friendly. While she was consumed with envy that Talleha had managed to captivate Eliot Penwick when she couldn't, she admired her down-to-earth honesty and her unpretentious ways. If she had let herself, she could have been friendly with the girl. Right now, she was on a mission for her Señora Marjorie, though, and she'd best be about getting it accomplished, for the señora would be back in her boudoir requiring her services any minute.

"Talleha, the señora wishes to talk to you tomorrow. She will meet you in the back of the east garden courtyard at eleven. Be sure you are not observed—by the señor. The señora insists that you say nothing to anyone about this meeting if you wish her assistance in getting away from here."

Wide-eyed with curiosity, Talleha prodded, "Are you saying that the señora is offering to help me?"

A devious smile lit up Lucita's face and she almost whispered her next words: "I am saying, niña—I am saying that the señor has no intention of letting you leave here; the señora knows this. The señora is your only hope, so you must be discreet and careful. You understand now?"

Talleha nodded and replied, "Yes—yes, I think I do. Tell her I will meet her there at eleven, and tell her I appreciate her offer, Lucita."

"I shall." Lucita turned to leave and swayed down the hallway in that sensuous way of hers.

There was much to think about this night, Talleha told herself as she entered her room, and she prayed Flossie would not make an appearance, for she needed to be alone. If what Lucita said was true, her fears had been well founded. After today, she was sure she'd been right all along about Lord Penwick.

Oh, how she wished to be sitting next to her beautiful mother, enjoying one of their quiet, serene moments back at home. She missed the wonderful evenings when they just sat quietly by the bank of the river, listening to the night birds calling, smelling the wildflowers, and cooling themselves on a hot summer night as a rustling breeze fanned them. They did not need to talk to enjoy one another's company.

Talleha knew no one so wise or smart as her mother had been, and how she wished for some of that wisdom right now! Her curious nature would make her fret tonight and until she learned what Marjorie Penwick was prepared to do to help her leave. From the way Lucita talked, she was willing to oppose her husband on the matter, and Talleha was more than ever convinced that theirs was a strange marriage.

If her mother had had a husband, Talleha wondered, would the two of them have been so unfeeling toward one another? She found it hard to believe of such a warm and loving woman, someone always giving her a kiss and a hug.

When she finally urged herself to get to bed, she was miserably restless, lying on one side or the other. She tossed and turned, becoming weary, but sleep still escaped her. When she disgustedly sat up on the side of the bed, the hands of the clock on the nightstand told her it was only midnight. She would have sworn it was much later.

She rose up to walk across the room and gaze out the window. To her amazement she saw two men walking on the grounds and she strained to see who it was. One was Eliot Penwick, but the shorter man she did not recognize. It seemed awfully late to receive a guest, she thought to herself.

She listened to see if she could hear their conversation as they paused there by the huge oak tree. All she could hear was their muffled voices. But she recognized Eliot's voice, and she could detect a gruff tone in it.

When they moved on out of sight and through the double door to the library below, Talleha returned to her bed.

Below her room, the men's discussion was still going on and would continue for another hour. The unexpected arrival of his nephew, Ralph, coming to the ranch had put him in the foulest of moods. The last person he'd dreamed of finding on his doorstep when he returned from his nightly ride was Ralph. But there he was with his valise as if he were planning a visit.

Ralph was not what he needed to contend with right now. He had enough on his mind without that irresponsible idiot underfoot.

Marjorie would be more waspish than she already was when she learned of Ralph's presence in the house. Eliot had decided that tomorrow he'd set his devious plan in motion, and he was patting himself on the back for having Talleha accompany him. Now, if she became headstrong and stubborn with him, he had a weapon to use on her. She was with him when he purchased the arsenic, and so it appeared that she was

71

in league with him in ridding himself of Marjorie. That would make the little firebrand stop and think. He could hold that threat over her pretty head as long as he wished, he convinced himself.

But now there was Ralph, and that could prove to be a handful. The wild story he'd told him about what had taken place back in England and why he had fled to come here to Eliot was completely unbelievable.

Ralph's voice had cracked and trembled with the fear consuming him when he told Eliot about Big Tom being found with his throat slashed in a dark London alley.

"One could expect such an end for someone of his character, Ralph. Why do you suppose I paid him the price to do the job I didn't wish to soil my hands with? Would you have wanted to do it if I'd asked you? Any number of characters could have taken care of old Tom."

But Ralph was firmly convinced that it was only one man as he pointed out to Eliot, "And what about Elaine and her sudden death, Uncle Eliot? She was as healthy as a horse one day and the next day she was gone—dead. That's when I decided to get out of England. I tell you, I know it was that Colette Maurier's son who came back to punish us all for what we did to his mother."

"Ralph, you talk like a frenzied old woman! Her son was too young to know much of anything that went on that night, and he'd certainly have no earthly way of finding out." Eliot did not credit Ralph for too much intelligence and he wondered just why he'd jumped on this ridiculous idea in the first place. So Elaine had been taken with a fatal malady. It was possible.

"I know he was only a lad then, Uncle Eliot, but he'd be a man now—a man in his mid-twenties. Besides, old Paddy said he saw him—even talked with him."

Eliot burst into laughter. "So it was that crazy old loon that struck this note of fear in you! The old fool probably did it on purpose and is laughing himself silly that you hightailed it away, scared out of your wits. God, Ralph—you are a bloody milksop!"

Eliot flinched, for his uncle's cruel, harsh words wounded him, but he did not waver one bit in his theory. "Well, Uncle Eliot—don't say I didn't warn you if this Maurier shows up unexpectedly. From what old Paddy told me, it is you he hates the most. It's you he will punish to avenge his mother's death."

"Drink your brandy, Ralph, and go to bed. It's been a long day, and a longer night for me. I've a very busy day to put in tomorrow," Eliot suggested.

Ralph finished his nightcap and sat the glass down to stand up from his chair. Already Eliot's thoughts were churning and Ralph's presence was being ignored.

With his valise in hand, Ralph ambled toward the door; Eliot had told him he did not wish to summon one of the servants this late. Besides, he didn't want Marjorie to know about Ralph's arrival until he told her himself.

"Now, which room am I to take, Uncle Eliot?" Ralph stammered.

"The very first room on the right as you get to the upstairs hallway. Now, remember—I said the right, not the left," Eliot cautioned, knowing how easily Ralph got confused. His nephew wasn't the brightest young man, but then, neither was Ralph's mother, Eliot's older sister.

He would never have taken Ralph into his home as Edward had done. But Eliot always considered Edward's generosity one of his faults, just like his romantic heart.

To give that cheap French woman Penwick land could not be tolerated, Eliot decided. Neither did a bastard son deserve it!

Edward might have been the elder son, but he was not the smartest one, Eliot consoled himself. Fate had denied him, for their father had died before their mother, who had always considered Edward her favorite. Edward was a sweet, gentle soul like her.

It was his father Eliot had respected and admired. That was very understandable since he was a selfish, cruel man who cared about no one but himself.

Chapter 8

Talleha followed Lucita's instruction to try to leave the house without being observed when she kept her rendevouz with the señora in the garden. She followed the wall to get to the far corner, which was sheltered by tall oleander bushes blooming profusely. She saw the señora sitting there, awaiting her arrival on one of the white wrought-iron benches.

She always looked so sad and weary, Talleha thought as she appraised Marjorie Penwick. It showed in her eyes, and yet Talleha considered her a very attractive woman. There were hints of warmth about the señora at unguarded times when Lord Penwick wasn't around.

"Señora," Talleha greeted the lady and gave her a friendly smile. Marjorie gazed up to see her and returned her greeting, motioning her to have a seat.

Fidgeting with the white lace cuffs of her frock, Marjorie wasted no time explaining the reason for their meeting. "You have to understand, Talleha, that if anyone finds out about this, there will be nothing else I can do for you. But if you truly wish to get back to your village, I will help you. I have my reasons—but they are none of your concern."

"Yes, ma'am, I do wish to. But I don't want you to think that I've not appreciated your generous hospitality and Lord Penwick's kindness all this time." For a short minute Talleha saw warmth in Marjorie's eyes.

Had she been able to read her thoughts, she would have known what Marjorie was thinking: there was no kindness in Eliot. It was only his lusting after the lovely little creature that made him seem kind. Marjorie realized that Talleha was too naive and innocent to know this.

"Where is this village of yours, Talleha? Has Eliot even asked you, for I've not heard him mention it," Marjorie inquired.

"You know, I don't think he *has* ever asked me," Talleha declared with a slightly puzzled look on her face. "It's called Cedar Springs, near the Lake of the Pines. A beautiful place, señora."

"I see. I have heard of it. My husband—my late husband, Frank, had a friend who lived there for a while." Marjorie's soul was churning with her own private musings. Of course Eliot had not inquired; he had no intention of taking her back.

But the girl had a longer journey to make on her own than Marjorie had counted on. She had imagined a jaunt of only a few miles. A young, innocent girl traveling over a trail of some twenty miles or more could be in terrible danger, and Marjorie wasn't heartless in this matter, even though her heart was cool most of the time.

A change of plans was quickly developed. On horseback the girl could travel more swiftly; it would require the services of her devoted servant, Lucita, to obtain one of the many horses in the stables. But it could be done late at night, Marjorie was certain.

"I will provide you with some funds and one of my horses, Talleha, for I've seen that you are an excellent rider. Lucita will come for you when the time is right; I will have to be the judge of that for the plan to work, you understand?"

"Of course I do, and I'll be ready when Lucita comes, señora. I—I thank you very much." Her gratitude showed in her gleaming eyes. "And I'm happy to know you don't dislike me as I'd imagined. I apologize for such thoughts."

"Go, now," Marjorie urged, for the humble honesty of the girl had affected her. She was actually fighting tears. "I shall wait until you are almost to the house."

Talleha turned to leave. Marjorie sat watching her go and detested Eliot Penwick more than ever. Perhaps she also detested herself a little, too, for ever believing his silver-tongued lies.

She'd paid for that mistake over and over again. Her pride had been shattered; Marjorie was no fool, and she knew what her dear old friends thought about her. It was probably the biggest hurt of all.

Recently, she'd thought about paying a visit to her devoted friend, Emilo Cortez, and confessing the nightmare of her life. She was not strong or forceful enough to order Eliot to leave her ranch, for he would only give her one of those smirking laughs of his. But Emilo and a couple of his strong, muscled hombres could oust him from the house—and from the countryside as well!

She'd always dismissed the idea, for it was asking too much of any friend to get involved so deeply. A truly gallant gentleman like Emilo would not have refused her, either; and of all the nearby rancher's wives, it would have been Emilo's wife to whom she could have admitted her foolhardy mistake in marrying Eliot.

There was another solution to solve the dilemma she found herself drowning in, but it was one that really frightened her. Never before had Marjorie harbored thoughts of killing another human being. But Eliot had brought such hellish torment into her life that the thought had crossed her mind lately, and a terrible wave of guilt always washed over her afterward, for she was not a wicked woman.

As she'd sat watching Talleha scamper away, she tried to convince herself that her motives were not completely selfish. Eliot might have rescued her once, but Marjorie knew she must get away from her if she was to be saved from her conniving, lusting husband.

Just at that moment another pair of eyes ogled Talleha as she bounced along the flagstone path toward the roofed veranda. Ralph had never seen such a lovely creature in all his life. Who in the world was that, he wondered? Was she the daughter of his uncle's new wife?

He'd not met Eliot's wife yet, and curiosity consumed him. His uncle did not seem to be the typical happy bridegroom. His manner was strange last night, and this morning as they shared breakfast together, it had not improved much. But Flossie's warm welcome was pleasant, at least.

Ralph would have expected Eliot and his new wife to have dined together in the morning, but when Eliot inquired about Marjorie, Flossie told him she'd already had her breakfast and left. Ralph noticed that a frown creased his uncle's solemn face. Eliot might not have considered his nephew too sharp or clever, but Ralph sensed that something was not exactly right here at the ranch.

Eliot decided to blame Ralph's arrival for the miserable way his day went. It did not start out with its usual routine: the breakfast hour. He'd bid Ralph good-bye to be about his own affairs, telling him to roam the ranch as he wished.

Marjorie was not keeping to her regular schedule. In fact, when he appeared in her boudoir to be greeted by Lucita, he curtly inquired about his wife's whereabouts, only to be told that she'd gone to take a walk in her gardens alone. This was strange behavior for Marjorie, who usually insisted that Lucita accompany her.

Eliot had left the house and searched the gardens, but he could not find his wife. Was he merely imagining it, or was Marjorie becoming more strong-willed lately?

By the time he encountered Flossie in the entryway back at the house, his mood was foul. He stopped the housekeeper, asking her, "How is our little Talleha this morning, Flossie?"

"Ah, sir—she was like a ray of sunshine. That one— she is nature's child. She loves the outdoors. Can't stand to be within the walls of a house if she can be outside."

"She isn't in her room?" Eliot shot back at his housekeeper.

He seemed annoyed that she wasn't sequestered upstairs, and Flossie considered that he was being far too strict. Lord Penwick must surely understand that she was no child!

"She's just enjoying herself by taking a walk in the gardens, sir. She—she loves the flowers and the birds. I think she's always been allowed to roam freely." Flossie sought to plead for some understanding for Talleha from Lord Penwick.

A snarl curled his lips as he spit out his next words, "A half-breed mother! Raised up as a little savage, I imagine! I can't tolerate that here, Flossie. You can understand that."

The housekeeper did not agree with the lord. Eliot

Penwick was aware of this when Flossie quickly replied, "Oh, sir—I think Talleha's mother was a most gentle, loving woman, from what the girl has told me. She adored her."

Flossie's attitude did not help Eliot's mood and he was now so vexed that he gave her a grunt before he marched away.

Flossie knew he was displeased with her, but she did not know why. Later, when she was through with her chores and had some time on her hands, she realized how she'd defended Talleha and her mother.

Talleha's spirits were high after her encounter with Marjorie, and she took no notice of the young lanky Englishman standing across the grounds and staring at her as she rushed up onto the veranda. She decided to go up the back stairs instead of those at the front of the hallway entrance. The decision was the reason she did not encounter Eliot and the reason he missed her being in her room. Neither did he find her taking a stroll in the gardens as she told Flossie she was going to do.

Eliot Penwick would have been appalled if he'd known what the willful Talleha was about while he made his hasty search of the garden courtyard. She was in her bedroom now, gathering up a camisole and pantaloons to tie up in a small bundle. Perhaps Lord Penwick had given orders at the stable for her to not be allowed a horse to ride out alone, but he couldn't stop her from slipping out of the house and off the grounds on foot. Once she reached the nearby woods, it was only a short distance to a delightful little creek. She intended to enjoy the cool, clear waters of the stream without any approval of Lord Penwick. She could not see how anyone would have to know.

It had all gone so smoothly that she felt smug by the time she arrived at the creek. She removed her clothing to hang it on the branch of a sapling. There in the quiet serenity of the woods as she stood barefooted in only her white camisole and pantaloons, she was reminded of the stream close to her home.

Perhaps it was the memory engulfing her that made her linger, her hands lifting her thick long tresses off her neck as she arched her body, gazing skyward. She felt so alive!

Victor Maurier's brilliant blue eyes were afire as he took in the seductive, tantalizing sight of her there by the edge of the creek. She was so stunning his whole body came alive with wanting her as he'd never ached for any woman.

He'd not expected such a rare gift of pleasure when he'd left the Casa del Lago to snoop around the Penwick property. When she entered the waters of the creek and lay back, allowing the waters to flow over her, he wished it was him covering her with his body. He watched the pleased smile on her face as the cooling waters caressed her flesh, and he yearned to see that same look on her face should he touch and caress her.

Suddenly he was like a man possessed, with no will of his own. He was driven by wild desire, out of control. Like an animal stalking its prey, he moved stealthily in, around the bushes, getting closer and closer to her. The nearer he got, the more beautiful she looked. The rivulets of water on her bare shoulders sparkled as the rays of the sun reflected against them, and her flesh reminded him of gold satin.

Her jet-black hair looked even longer now that it was wet and she flung it from side to side, playfully enjoying herself. A capricious little vixen, she was!

Now he was close enough to see the beauty of her eyes, and when she closed them to lean her head back in the water, he saw how long and thick the lashes were.

What better way to initiate his first stroke of revenge on Penwick than to take away something he desired,

Maurier convincingly told himself. Victor was not ready to admit to himself that Penwick really didn't matter to him; he was entranced by the girl himself. He did not realize the power she held. He was completely bewitched.

By now, she was so close that he could have reached out and pulled her into his eager arms. He yearned to hold her; his tensed, muscled body moved and his strong arms stretched out to enclose her.

At that moment, Talleha felt the force of his powerful presence. She did not know it was the nearness of Victor Maurier, but she felt a strange stimulation.

It was like a primitive instinct churning within her, so wild and savage her head whirled with an excited giddiness. In the moment that Maurier's hands grabbed her around the waist, she turned to see those blue-fire eyes of his devouring her. She knew why those titilating sensations had gone off within her.

She'd wanted him to come to her, to love her as he had so briefly that day by the lake. Now he was here and his hands were holding her. Her flesh felt the searing heat of his touch.

Chapter 9

Victor Maurier's hand impatiently yanked the strap of Talleha's camisole away from her damp shoulder, and before she realized what he was doing, the other one was torn away. She started to gasp but her half-parted lips were captured by his sensuous, demanding ones. She gave in to the sweet surrender of pleasure she recalled about his first kiss.

Maurier took her honeyed lips in a long, lingering kiss and his hands busily struggled to remove the clinging camisole so her firm, rounded breasts would be free. When he had finally managed to do that, his lips trailed down to the hollow of her throat. His lips finally took the hardened, rosy tip of her breast, and he sensed her deep intake of breath and felt the rapid beating of her heart throbbing against his broad chest.

His tongue stirred a wild, exciting feeling Talleha had never imagined, and she arched her body to absorb more. Victor cradled her back with one hand but his other hand cupped the satiny flesh, lifting it closer for his caressing. It pleasured him to know he was arousing her so, but he had no intention of remaining on this bed of pebbles.

Reluctantly, he forced himself to lift her into his

arms so they might lie on the grass a few feet away. As he carried her, their eyes locked together; neither uttered a word. She was entranced by the way his eyes danced slowly over her face, by his crooked grin. She found herself responding with the hint of a smile.

"You're the most beautiful creature these eyes have ever seen," he huskily murmured as he gently laid her on the ground. He moved to bend his head so their lips could meet once again. Now his hands searched the waistline of her pantaloons and he tediously worked them downward.

Talleha felt the touch of his fingers against her flesh and she knew she was soon to be lying there naked for his eyes to see. But something rendered her powerless to stop him from having his way with her. Instinct told her she would never be the same after this rare summer afternoon.

She felt the firm muscles of his thighs touching hers now and he played with the wisps of her hair as he whispered her name softly, "Oh, Talleha! Talleha!" His hands urged her to roll with him on her side and she felt his leg encircle hers.

He willed himself to be patient so he could absorb all the loveliness he saw there on that face, but all the time he kept her pressed tightly to the front of him as they lay on their sides. Talleha felt the tremendous strength of his physique.

"Tell me, little black eyes—tell me you like my kissing you—my loving you. I want to hear you say, 'Victor, I want you to love me.' I know you do, Talleha."

She could not deny it. She wanted him to continue making love to her desperately. His amorous hands moving over her body urged her to softly moan, "Yes, Victor—I do."

Many things about this beautiful, sultry looking girl

told the experienced Maurier that she'd never known the touch of a man before. Penwick had not tasted the sweet nectar of this glorious body—Victor was convinced of it—so he measured the time before he made that vital thrust of his maleness to enter her. He did not want her to freeze with disillusionment.

When she did give out a stunned moan as he entered her, he quickly sought to soothe and calm her with his gentle touch. Instantly he felt her responding to it, a new excitement igniting within her again. He was overwhelmingly pleased that she so willingly clung to him, swaying to and fro. He whispered softly, "I tried to make it easy for you, my darling. But that won't ever have to happen again. Now I can give you nothing but pleasure." He buried himself deeper in the moist velvet softness of her to let her flaming flesh devour him.

He loved to hear her sigh with delight as her passion mounted, calling out his name urgently. As strong-willed as he was, he could not restrain the mounting explosion ready to erupt. His powerful body gave forth a mighty tremble and Talleha dug her fingernails into the bare flesh of his back to give out a sweet moan of anguish. Maurier was a man feeling the height of ecstasy, for he had satisfied and fulfilled the beautiful young lady just as he'd yearned to do.

Maurier had never known such rapture in all his life though he could lay claim to having bedded many women. Most of them had given Victor a few moments of pleasure simply gratifying an immediate need. A couple of times he'd thought he might be in love, but he had always quickly dismissed the idea.

This black-haired lovely had fascinated him from the first. Something he could not define intrigued him in a strange way. He was drawn to her like a magnet. He knew now he was the worst of liars if he tried to justify what he'd just done as merely revenge against Penwick.

85

It had nothing to do with Penwick. He had deflowerd this little vixen because he desired desperately to make love to her.

Holding her now in his arms, watching the lazy fluttering of her long black lashes, he gave her a grin as her breathing slowly calmed. He could not resist being a bit devious as he teased her, "I told you, my little Talleha, that you would come into my arms and want me to love you—remember?"

A slow smile came to her face as she purred playfully, "I remember what I told you that first day we met—that you were no gentleman, Victor Maurier! I think you are conceited as well."

He gave her a deep, husky laugh and pulled her over to lie atop him. "It is true, my darling, that I'm no gentleman—but I'm not conceited. It doesn't flatter me to know I conquered you, Talleha, but it does please me to know we shared a rare, special moment. You mean much more to me than this one afternoon. I've had many afternoons. Do you know what I'm trying to tell you?"

"I—I guess I do. I've never had such an afternoon as this," she confessed honestly. Of course, Maurier knew that already, but he loved her unabashed honesty, her unpretentious nature. It was refreshing.

His handsome face mellowed with adoration as he confessed, "Can I tell you how glad I am that you hadn't made love to any other man before? Now, that can make me feel very conceited, Talleha. I'm proud to be the first one, and I intend to be the only one. Do you understand what I'm telling you?"

"I think so. A long time ago my mother told me that she'd loved only once," she remarked with a glowing warmth coming to her eyes.

"Then I would say that your mother was lucky to have found it even once in her lifetime, because some people never do. I think your mother and my mother may have had a lot in common."

As they lay there like nature's children, unashamed and naked, encircled in one another's arms, they spoke about their mothers both sharing the same fate. It was somewhat startling that both had been murdered.

Talleha told him about Lord Eliot Penwick's rescuing her there in the dense woods and bringing her to his home. "I have to be very grateful that he came riding along when he did." She omitted telling him that she was not so grateful to him that she'd permit herself to remain a prisoner in the huge, sprawling house, to be denied her freedom.

Maurier could well imagine how Penwick was counting on this innocent young girl being so beholden to him that she'd succumb to his demands. It puzzled Maurier that he'd not yet tried to trifle with her after all these days and nights of her living under his roof. Perhaps he didn't want to gamble on his wife finding out and kicking him off the ranch. He had no doubt that Emilo was right about him marrying Marjorie Greenfield for her wealth. Knowing about his unsavory past, Maurier wouldn't put anything past him.

God, he hated the thought of the lovely black-haired girl now in his arms going back there. He wished he could just ride out of here with her and head down Brownsville way to Captain Crawford's home. But that was just a fantasy for now.

Soon, he knew, they must go their separate ways, but his heart would ache until he could be with her again. Talleha harbored similar thoughts and she knew that she'd been gone a long time. There were grave doubts that she'd manage not to be missed almost immediately. Her original plans had been merely to come to the creek for a refreshing dip and then get dressed again in the clean, dry camisole and pantaloons she'd brought along.

Now she recalled how Victor had yanked the camisole off; it was left in the waters. Chances were, the garment had floated downstream a long way by now. The thought of it made her give out a giggle.

"Now what is that all about? Do I suddenly amuse you?" Victor asked, leaning on one elbow to look down on her with a broad grin.

"You dropped my camisole in the water and the current has probably carried it a long way from here."

He bent down to kiss the tip of her pert little nose. "I'll buy you the fanciest camisole you've ever seen, my Talleha, for I have to confess to you that I didn't just drop it—I flung it, for I was in a frenzy to rid you of it."

"Well, I thought to bring another one when I left the house. Speaking of the house, I must go, Victor. I've been gone far too long. I—I had to walk, for Lord Penwick has forbidden me to ride out alone anymore."

The bastard, Maurier muttered under his breath! "Well, you won't have to walk back—I'll take you to the edge of the clearing so you'll have only a short walk from there." He wasn't ready to make an appearance at the ranch just yet, but he couldn't explain this to Talleha.

She reluctantly raised up from the ground and in doing so, became shy about her nakedness and covered her breasts. Victor smiled, seeing the pleading in those black eyes. He obliged by turning his eyes away, then gallantly marching over to gather up her garments for her.

"Thank you," she murmured quietly, then started scrambling into her undergarments, as he went to fetch his own clothes.

When they were both dressed, Maurier swung her up into his arms and walked toward his horse. They could have been two children giving in to a lighthearted gale of laughter when he stubbed his boot on a rock and almost lost his balance.

He hoisted her onto the horse and straddled it behind her, reining the animal into motion. All too soon they were at the edge of the woods with the clearing ahead of them.

As he helped her down to the ground, he held her close and took one final kiss before they parted. There was a more serious look on his face now, Talleha noticed. When he spoke there was a ring of sincerity, "I'm staying at the Casa del Lago, Talleha. That's not far from here, should you ever need me. More to the point, I'll take you home in a few more days when I've finished my business."

"I'll remember that," she said, hesitating a moment longer before breaking away from his embrace. "I—I must go!" She hastily dashed into the clearing and Victor watched the feisty swinging of her skirt and was fired again with a flaming desire to have her back at his side.

Giving out a deep sigh, he finally reined the horse around to start back toward the Casa del Lago. More than ever he was eager to get this business with Eliot Penwick done with.

Talleha made it so!

Chapter 10

As much as he hated to admit it, Eliot had to acknowledge failure in his search for Talleha. He wasn't in the best of moods when Ralph approached him with an eager and excited look on his face to inquire about the beautiful girl he'd seen while he'd been roaming the grounds.

"Who is she, uncle? Is she your new wife's daughter?" Ralph looked like he could actually explode, he was so fascinated.

"God forbid, no—she's not Marjorie's daughter," Eliot snapped. But trying to sound casual, he prodded, "Where did you see her, Ralph? Here in the gardens, perhaps?"

"Well, yes. She'd been in the back garden but she was going into the house."

So Flossie had been right, Eliot concluded. He'd no doubt missed her by a few minutes. He dismissed Talleha from his thoughts and spent the next hour with his nephew, assiduously outlining what he might expect from this household and the people under his roof.

"They've not got the grace and charm of us more reserved Englishmen, Ralph. This includes my wife as well. Our dear Flossie could tell you that. It has not been easy for her here in this house. It seems to be their nature to be outspoken, with a lack of refinement."

Ralph was perplexed, then, as to why his uncle had married this Texas widow. His reputation back in England had been that of the elusive bachelor who squired many young women around the city. But he never allowed himself a long affair with any one of them. He could not have courted this woman too long, since they'd been married almost a year, if memory served. He recalled the letter his aunt had received from Eliot.

In fact, his Uncle Edward's wife, Elaine, swore at the time that Eliot had deserted her to face any repercussions from their act against Colette Maurier, and she was quite disgruntled about his behavior. Until a few weeks ago, all had gone well, and he and his aunt had decided nothing was ever going to come up after such a long period of time.

During those first months, there had been no inquiries at the Penwick estate and their life followed its usual routine. His aunt had laughed many times to Ralph that Eliot had hightailed it out of the country when he hadn't had to.

There was no one to be concerned about the Frenchwoman, Colette Maurier, or her vanishing son, Victor, since Lord Edward was dead. Lord Edward's wife wasted no time in removing Edward's devoted servant, Paddy, from the premises and changing his duties to the stable, where there were small quarters up above.

Recalling all these things in a few short moments urged Ralph to ask his uncle, "There must have been something attractive about this woman, Uncle Eliot, for you to have married her."

"Oh, there was something attractive, Ralph. These

91

rugged Texans don't do things in a small way. They call themselves ranchers, not farmers. The ranches out here in this godforsaken country spread over a thousand acres and as many cattle roam there. There are also as many wild horses to be caught and tamed."

"Really?" Ralph was agog listening to this amazing tale.

"And these woods could supply timber and lumber for years to come. A man could get wealthy on that alone, Ralphie boy." There was a smug, arrogant look on Eliot's face.

Ralph gave out a chuckle. "Sounds like you got yourself a great future laid out, Uncle Eliot."

"A great and glorious one, Ralph. It's very important you realize this, now that you've arrived here."

"Oh, yes sir! I understand," Ralph replied, but his thoughts during the conversation always went back to the beautiful black-tressed young woman. His uncle had still not explained her. Consumed with curiosity, he inquired once again, "Uncle Eliot, you never told me who the beautiful young lady was I asked you about earlier."

Eliot told him about the circumstances of Talleha's being at the ranch and how he'd come upon her in the woods. Ralph listened with intense interest as his uncle related the strange tale.

When Eliot had finished, Ralph remarked casually, "Then why would she venture back in the woods today, Uncle Eliot?"

"What in bloody hell are you talking about, Ralph?"

"I saw her go that way this afternoon," he replied.

"I fail to understand you, Ralph. Before, you told me you saw her going into the house from the garden. Now you're telling me you saw her go into the woods. Which is it?"

"I *did* see her go into the house, but a short time later

I saw her come back out and go toward the woods."

Eliot said nothing for awhile. He sat silently and thoughtfully. "Thank you, Ralph, for telling me this."

He was able to disguise his anger, which he'd failed to do around Flossie earlier. But he was already wondering how he was going to deal with this headstrong, willful little bitch who seemed determined not to obey him. She really was a little savage, taking it upon herself to do as she bloody well pleased. Eliot Penwick knew she would prove to be a handful. The reward titillated his senses, though, and he'd never be bored with her as he'd been this last miserable year.

With her, his days would provide a variety of challenges and his nights would be spent in sensuous delight.

"I've some work to do in my office now, Ralph. Perhaps you can find something to occupy you if the mid-afternoon heat is too much. There's a fine selection of books in the library. You might enjoy browsing in there," Eliot suggested, knowing what an avid reader Ralph was. He decided he should try to be more civil to his nephew. While it was not likely, it could be that Ralph would come in handy in his scheme later on.

Ralph nodded and started to head for the library. Eliot reminded his nephew that dinner was always promptly served at seven, "a tradition Marjorie insists on keeping."

Once again Ralph detected a hint of distaste in Eliot about his new wife. Uncle Eliot had certainly become a complex man, in a way confusing to Ralph.

He found himself enjoying the solitude of the library, and there was a vast selection of books lining the dark wood shelves. There was a magnificent collection of leatherbound volumes, which must have cost a handsome price, he knew.

The time passed quickly for Ralph and he suddenly realized he must get to his room to freshen up for dinner.

When he got to his room, he immediately laid out his clothing. It had always displeased him that he could not have inherited some of the good looks of either his Uncle Edward or his Uncle Eliot. Both had striking features and such trim physiques! But Ralph knew he was gawky and awkward when he walked. He was small in the shoulders and too large in the waist and hips.

His eyes were too big and his mouth was too small. There was an unruly strip of his brown hair which would never lie down as it should, regardless of his endless brushing. No one was more aware of his unattractive looks than Ralph, but there was little he could do about it. However, he did take special care to dress himself neatly, for he hoped to make a favorable impression on his uncle's wife.

When he'd done all he could possibly do to make himself presentable, he turned to leave to join his uncle in the parlor, as Eliot had suggested.

Just as Ralph reached the base of the stairway and started to turn to go to the parlor, he heard a familiar voice call out to him, and he turned back to see Flossie in her snow-white apron.

"My goodness—how nice you look, Mister Ralph," she declared cheerfully. Flossie had a tender spot in her heart for the young man since the time he'd stayed at Lord Penwick's townhouse back in London. There was a shyness about him and Flossie decided that he didn't have much self-confidence. The poor young gent had been cheated on his looks, to judge by the other Penwick men she'd known.

Ralph gave her shoulder a friendly pat and thanked her for the compliment. A broad grin lit up his face as he remarked, "Something smells awfully good, Flossie. My appetite is already whetted."

"Well, you just wait until you taste it. As I recall, you've a very healthy appetite," she playfully teased.

"I plead guilty to that charge, Flossie. Well, I guess I'd better go along. Don't want to keep Uncle Eliot waiting."

"Yes, be off with you! I think I saw him go to the parlor a few minutes ago." She returned to her duties, checking to see that the meal was properly prepared and that the setting of the long dining room table was perfect. Already she'd placed a colorful floral arrangement in the center of the table and put the candles in place.

When the lanky young man entered her parlor, Marjorie immediately decided she was going to give Eliot a surprise and not react as expected. She would be cordial to the young man who was nothing like what she had anticipated. A younger version of Eliot was what she'd expected, but this young man did not appear to be cocky or arrogant. Bashful and ill-at-ease was how he acted as he awkwardly approached them where they sat sipping sherry.

Stiffly Eliot rose up to introduce his nephew and Marjorie extended her hand to greet Ralph. "Nice to have you in our home, Ralph. Please sit down. Eliot, why don't you get a glass of sherry for your nephew?" Marjorie gave Ralph a warm, friendly smile as she motioned him to take the rose brocade chair closest to her.

Ralph did as she requested. He was instantly impressed by her friendliness. He thought her right pretty in her deep blue gown with its wide, white lace collar and cuffs. She did seem pale, without any glow in her cheeks. She wore her dark hair pulled back severely into two huge coils at the back of her head, displaying a pair of exquisite pearl teardrop earrings which matched a bracelet and ring she was wearing.

There was a reason Marjorie had taken such special care with her appearance tonight. She did look more attractive than she had in a long time. Only she knew why her spirits were lifted after her talk with Talleha this morning.

Eliot tensed with resentment to have to comply with her request to pour Ralph a glass of sherry. How dare she attempt to order him around? All the time he went through the motions of pouring the sherry and handing Ralph the cut-crystal glass, he pondered her syrupy-sweet mood tonight. Where was the waspy witch he was used to? He'd expected her to be rude and snappish and she wasn't. God, he'd never understand women!

But he didn't have time to dwell on these thoughts long, because out of the corner of his eye he caught sight of a blue-green vision of loveliness entering the parlor. The dark hair cascading down the gown was a sight to see!

The gleaming sparkle in her eyes and her glowing golden skin, so tantalizingly displayed by the low, scooped neckline of the gown, made him swell with desire.

The sight of her as she approached them made Ralph gasp and his hand tremble so that he almost dropped the glass of sherry. Marjorie watched the young man and found it amusing. Oh, Eliot would not like his nephew's attitude at all!

It might just prove to be an interesting evening, Marjorie thought to herself. She gave Talleha a friendly greeting. After this morning, Marjorie was less bitter toward the young girl, for it was Eliot who deserved her wrath.

Marjorie's simple efforts at being the gracious hostess this evening had had a devastating effect on her husband. Actually, she was punishing him far more severely than she realized. He was utterly befuddled by the Marjorie who sat at the dinner table this evening. Furthermore, he had to sit there, watching his stupid nephew ogling the young lady he adored. Across from Ralph sat Talleha with all her radiant beauty. It bewitched him and tempted him to the point that he'd do anything to possess her.

As he sat there gazing at the loveliness of her in candlelight, one thought overpowered him: he must rid himself of Marjorie so he could go forward with his magnificent plans for him and Talleha. He could imagine how much he'd be envied with her on his arm as he escorted her around London amid that elite circle of his old friends. What exaltation he would feel! Ah yes, Eliot's vivid imagination was running wild tonight!

Flossie's delightful, thick bisque made no impression on him tonight, though he would normally have raved about it. Neither did her delectable duck à l' orange, served with tender carrots and peas, draw any mention of praise from him. Flossie was feeling somewhat hurt as she moved around the table. It happened to be Ralph who complimented her on how good the duck was as she moved behind his chair.

She muttered softly, "Thank you, Mister Ralph. Glad you are enjoying it."

She noticed the distinct change in Mrs. Penwick tonight. She'd never known her to be such a chatterbox and amazingly, Flossie found herself liking her mistress for the first time since working in this house.

Talleha, too, was an interesting study this evening. There was a very special glow to her lovely face and a wistful, faraway look in those beautiful black eyes. Flossie knew one thing for certain—she should wear that glorious blue-green more often, for it enhanced her sultry dark beauty.

Talleha daydreamed of the afternoon she'd spent with the handsome Maurier. She had only to think of his sensuous lips touching her and his strong hands caressing her body. Just remembering his forceful body making her surrender to him was enough to bring a serene smile to her lips.

The others sitting around the table gazing her way had no inkling of her secret thoughts. If Eliot Penwick had known what was going through her head or what had happened this afternoon, he would have been devastated.

He would not be the first man to love her, for no longer was Talleha a virgin.

Chapter 11

Flossie's sweet dessert, made with whipped cream and lightly beaten eggs, was enjoyed by everyone except Eliot Penwick, who was more occupied with his own secret thoughts about Talleha's tantalizing rosebud lips.

He was completely bewitched by her charms. Nothing registered with him—not the muffled tones of Marjorie's voice ringing in his ear nor Ralph's irritating chuckles. It was only Talleha's soft voice that made him sit up and take notice.

As the evening wore on, Eliot found himself absolutely befuddled by the strange turn of character in Marjorie. She was completely destroying the image he'd painted to Ralph. The truth was, he could have sworn that his nephew was intrigued with his dear wife. But then, what else should he have expected from the simple-minded, easily swayed young man?

Just when Eliot had decided that the evening could offer no more surprises, he was stunned again by his audacious wife.

Flossie was removing their dessert plates when Marjorie broke the silence surrounding the table by saying to Ralph, "You and Talleha should take a nice walk in the gardens, Ralph. It's a divine evening and there's no reason why two young people have to be stuck with us old married folk."

Eagerly, Ralph leaped at Marjorie's suggestion and turned to Talleha to ask her, "Would you do me the honor, Miss Talleha?"

Damn her, Eliot muttered under his breath! The bitch was taxing him beyond the limits of his endurance. Fury welled up in him as he saw that she was deliberately pushing Ralph at his beautiful Talleha, and resentment consumed him when she labeled him an old married person. He didn't feel married and he was not old.

It took all his inner strength to control the burning rage within him, and he tried to moderate his voice when he spoke to Ralph. "Don't linger too long, Ralph. I've some things I must discuss with you tonight before I retire."

Unsuspecting of his uncle's overwhelming displeasure about him being alone with Talleha, Ralph gave him a hasty reply, "Yes, sir. I'll—we'll not be long." His complete attention went back to Talleha. "Shall we, Talleha?"

She rose from her chair. Marjorie could hardly suppress a laugh as she observed the disgruntled Eliot. Ah, revenge was sweet!

At least, this was what she was thinking as the young couple left the dining room, but finding herself all alone with Eliot, her moment of amusement quickly changed to an alarm which made her shudder. She saw something in her husband's eyes that was violent and dangerous.

She moved back in her chair to rise and leave the table. It taxed her sorely to try to act cool and unaffected by his malicious manner. She did not make the effort to speak, nor did she excuse herself. Instead, she marched out of the room into the hallway and was more than grateful to see Lucita coming toward her with a fresh pile of linens cradled in her arms.

"Ah, señora—we shall go up together and I will put this linen up and help you, too," Lucita suggested.

Marjorie was more than happy with that. The comforting presence of her maid would ease the disturbing thoughts whirling in her head right now. She was convinced Eliot could kill her.

"You enjoy your dinner, señora?" Lucita asked as they walked down the thick-carpeted hallway together.

"It was a very nice dinner, Lucita. Very nice."

"Well, you look very pretty this evening—better than I've seen you in a long time. It pleases me so." The Mexican servant girl gave her a warm smile. Lucita could never forget the señora's generous ways during all the time she'd been her maid, even though she had allowed herself to forget about the señora's feeling that one night she'd shared Eliot Penwick's bed. While her hot-blooded nature had surrendered to his will that one time, she found him despicable all the same.

As crazy as that might seem, her loyalty lay with Marjorie Greenfield Penwick. She'd have been much happier if the lady had remained a widow. But if she'd had to marry, why had she not picked someone like the gallant Señor Cortez? Now, there was a true gentleman —as respected as Frank Greenfield had been.

Lucita's endless chatter as she went about taking down the coils of Marjorie's hair and helping her slip into her nightgown and wrapper was welcome. As the soothing strokes of the brush calmed her, Marjorie pushed all disturbing thoughts aside. Lucita left the room unaware of the great service she'd performed for her señora.

*   *   *

Eliot did not take the usual evening jaunt on his fine thoroughbred. Instead he paced the floor of his study, his anger mounting steadily. This was what poor Ralph would have to confront as he left Talleha and ambled down the hallway to enter the study. He had enjoyed the brief and wonderful interlude with the beautiful black-haired girl. He found her to be sweet and nice, and he'd enjoyed their light-hearted, casual conversation.

Ralph had found the story about her mother being part Indian most interesting. The strange beliefs of her mother's heritage completely intrigued him. Talleha had spoken about the signs of the moon, and the good and bad omens of the owl and the eagle. Her mother, Dawn, was part Choctaw. Talleha had described the various tribes of the territory; all this was a revelation to Ralph.

Oh, he'd heard about American Indians in his native England. Now he was fascinated and excited about actually being here. Talleha had performed a miracle merely by being so nice to him: Ralph actually felt confident and self-assured.

When Eliot's stern voice gave him permission to enter, Ralph went in with a particular look of cockiness about him. It had a devastating effect on Penwick.

There was a snarl as Eliot muttered, "Well, did you enjoy your stroll, Nephew?"

"I did, sir. Talleha is a very nice young lady," Ralph said in a faltering voice, for he sensed his uncle was well into his cups. There was a vivid flush on Eliot's face, but Ralph did not realize what this raging fury was. For the first time in his life, Ralph saw an ugliness on Eliot Penwick's striking features. Ralph was possessed by a fleeting thought: could this be the true Eliot Penwick, and the other image he'd always admired and envied be

102

just the mask his uncle wore?

Ralph observed Eliot sway as he moved toward him with a glass of liquor in his hand. There was a strange glaze in his eyes which seemed to pierce Ralph. Eliot's voice hissed like a snake as he told his nephew, "You are never to be with Talleha alone again as you were tonight. This is my order, Ralph. As long as you are under this roof you will do as I say. Do you understand?"

"I—I guess I do, sir," Ralph said, utterly perplexed that his uncle was so upset by such an innocent act—a stroll in the gardens after dinner with his uncle's houseguest. He questioned at this moment his uncle's sanity, for he acted like a man on the edge of madness.

"You'd better do more than guess, young man. You'd better know without any doubt whatsoever that I mean what I'm saying."

"I do, Uncle Eliot. I understand exactly," Ralph quickly replied. Right now, he would have said anything to appease him.

But that did *not* seem to appease Eliot, Ralph quickly realized; his uncle continued to address him with anger in his voice. "We'll see if you understand by how well you obey me in the days ahead."

"May I go now, Uncle Eliot? I'm rather tired," Ralph mumbled in a faltering voice, for he could not anticipate what his uncle's foul, surly mood might bring out next.

"Be off with you, Ralph. I find you about as dull as my wife, Marjorie. Perhaps that is why you two seemed to have such an interesting time chattering away tonight," Eliot smirked.

Poor Ralph was utterly confused by now. "I—I found your wife to be very nice, and yes, Uncle Eliot—I

103

enjoyed talking to her." Why was he being so insulting?

Eliot Penwick threw his head back and roared with laughter, and Ralph was so befuddled that he said not another word, but turned to make a hasty exit before his uncle delayed him any further.

As he made his way up the steps to go to his room, he wore a concerned look. What had happened to the Eliot Penwick he knew back in England? This man seemed like a stranger to him. Why, he was saying insulting things about his own wife, and she'd been absolutely kind and charming all through dinner. What more could his uncle expect?

For a long time after Ralph slipped between the fresh, white sheets on his bed, he wondered about his uncle and the strangeness of his behavior.

It was a laborious effort for Eliot to raise his throbbing head off the pillow the next morning, and he realized he'd consumed far more liquor than he should have. There was a horrible taste in his mouth, and he sought to get a glass of water to relieve the dryness.

But he had to get downstairs before Marjorie arrived to be served her breakfast. How else was he going to accomplish the feat of getting that little powder into her coffee to mingle with the sugar she so lavishly stirred into the cup?

That was enough incentive for him to get out of bed and get dressed immediately. When he was satisfied with his grooming, he tucked the tiny packet of powder in his waistcoat pocket and left his room. Luckily, when he walked into the dining room only Flossie was there, standing by the sideboard.

"Good morning, sir. You're the first one to come down this bright, cheery morning, and it is certainly a fine day we're to have, I think."

Flossie's words were exactly what Penwick was hoping to hear. Marjorie was yet to arrive. "A glorious day I'd say, too, just looking out the window, Flossie." Eliot gave forth that charming side of him and insisted that Flossie need not serve his coffee—that he could do that as he waited for his wife to appear. "I'll let you know when she arrives so that we can eat together this morning before I leave the house."

His pleasant manner was a welcome change to Flossie from the way he'd been yesterday. He could be so very nice when those awful moods weren't upon him. She gave him a smile and a nod of her head, turning to go back to her kitchen.

Eliot was encouraged that things were going according to his plans for a change. He was more than pleased when he smelled the carnation fragrance Marjorie always wore, and he turned to see her there in the archway in her dressing gown with Lucita not by her side.

Gallantly, he rose up from his chair to announce that he'd serve her coffee and refill his cup. "Flossie will be in shortly. She had to check the biscuits."

Marjorie observed that he seemed to be in a civil mood, and the offer to serve her coffee certainly indicated that the fury of last night had burned itself out.

She took her seat, remarking, "Yes, I'd like a cup of coffee, thank you."

"Well, you shall have it, my dear," he said, pouring the coffee and fumbling for the packet in his waistcoat pocket. His breath seemed to stop until he'd managed to pour the contents into the steaming cup as she sat with her back turned toward him. He was feeling smug when he left the sideboard to walk back to the table and place the cup in front of her.

He watched her put the two heaping spoons of sugar

105

into the cup and stir it. Eliot sat feeling pleased.

Marjorie did not immediately take a sip of her coffee because she was busy considering his solicitous air and his pleasant facial expression. Those striking good looks had surely been her downfall, because the face he wore last night would have made her immediately turn away from him.

"Ah, delicious," Eliot sighed. "Flossie brews a fine pot of coffee." He hoped to entice her to start sipping hers.

Flossie's keen ears had heard Penwick speaking to his wife, and knowing how the mistress wanted her breakfast served the minute she got to the table, the housekeeper did not wait for Eliot to call her. Instead, she rushed through the door with Marjorie's and Eliot's plates and a warm, cheerful greeting to Marjorie.

Marjorie was jolted out of her thoughtful state, and in doing so, she'd turned to respond to the cheery greeting of the housekeeper. The turning of her body caused her hand to brush the cup just enough to cause the fine china to tumble from the saucer onto the floor. The thin china shattered on the expensive Aubusson carpet.

"What a bloody mess!" Eliot yelled angrily, caring not one whit about the fine china cup or the carpet. He was venting his irritation that she'd not drunk the powder he'd been so careful to sneak into the coffee. His frustration was so overwhelming that he leaped up out of his chair and left the room. Flossie and Marjorie sat there aghast, their eyes darting to each other.

For the first time since she'd come to the ranch, Flossie disapprovingly declared, "There—I'll get this all cleaned up. There's no call for Lord Penwick to get that upset! Isn't the end of the world. Give me just a moment, ma'am, and I'll have you a fresh cup."

106

"Take your time, Flossie." Marjorie appreciated the housekeeper siding with her and faulting Eliot. The fine Sèvres china was her cherished heirloom, not Eliot's. What was all the fuss about?

His own devoted Flossie was very disturbed by his erratic behavior. A broken cup should not provoke such rage in a man!

She felt sorry for Marjorie Greenfield Penwick, and sadly disappointed in Lord Penwick. It destroyed a little of the respect and admiration she'd always felt for him.

Chapter 12

Ralph was wary as to what he could expect this morning when he encountered his uncle. In fact, he had delayed going downstairs as long as he could and still hope to have his breakfast. His hearty appetite urged him to brave whatever tempest he might face.

At the base of the stairway he saw Eliot riding his thoroughbred down the long drive away from the ranch. He was grateful and felt as if a heavy weight had been lifted from his shoulders.

When he saw Marjorie sitting all alone at the long dining room table, a dejected look on her face, he speculated that his uncle's tongue was perhaps as cruel and venomus toward her this morning as it had been with him last night.

"Good morning, señora," he greeted her, with that boyish, friendly expression on his face. A strange feeling consumed Ralph as he looked at her forced, weak smile. He felt there was a common bond between them as she invited him to have a seat, calling out to Flossie to bring some more coffee for her and tea for Ralph.

"I trust you slept well, Ralph. Your—your uncle has already left," she told him.

"I know. I saw him riding out as I came downstairs. He'd told me he had business to attend to today and besides, I don't expect him to change his schedule just because I showed up," Ralph said.

There was a humble, meek air about this nephew of Eliot's. "It doesn't matter that you had no formal invitation to visit us, Ralph. I'm—I'm rather glad you came. I didn't know Eliot even had a nephew, for he's never talked much about his family." Her mood suddenly changed from serious to lighthearted as she sought to enlighten Ralph. "Besides, this was my home long before Eliot called it home. He may be my husband, but this is my ranch and my land."

As they shared each other's company for the better part of an hour, Ralph found her as pleasant as she'd been the night before. More than that, he found her to be very interesting to talk to. And it was just as rewarding for Marjorie to have someone like this young man to give her his attention.

Just about the time Marjorie was preparing to go upstairs to get dressed, Talleha bounced into the room looking bright-eyed and radiant. She was apologizing for sleeping so late.

"I ate so much of Flossie's good food last night that I slept like a baby. The truth is I only want some coffee. I certainly don't need one of her hearty breakfasts this morning." She let out a soft laugh.

Ralph gave her a broad smile, thinking to himself that she looked as beautiful in the morning light as she had by the twinkling candlelight.

Had Eliot Penwick entered the dining room just then, he would have been frenzied to see the camaraderie shared by Talleha, Ralph, and his wife, Marjorie.

Marjorie delayed her departure for a while to linger with the two young people. Before she finally rose to leave, she directed her words to Talleha, "I might have some news for you later, my dear, about what we discussed yesterday."

"All right, señora," Talleha replied.

Marjorie moved to leave, telling the two, "Enjoy this lovely day." Ralph assured her that he certainly planned to, and Talleha gave her a nod of her head, her two long thick braids of hair hanging down over her shoulders. It was the first time Marjorie had noticed the girl wearing her hair in braids. But on such a warm day as this, it was very practical, Marjorie thought.

But as she slowly mounted the stairway, she stopped on the steps to ponder a fleeting thought. At first her thoughts were indistinct, but it was something—something that went back to her life with Frank. What was it?

Marjorie sat at her dressing table while Lucita styled her hair. When Lucita had the final wisp smoothed into place, Marjorie dismissed the Mexican girl politely. She knew what she was going to do, and what better time to do it than now, while Eliot was away from the house. He always resented that she reserved one special room in the house to store Frank's special belongings. Whenever she went into that room, which she kept locked, he shot horrible accusations at her.

She went to the secret place where she kept the key, and when she'd tucked it inside the pocket of her frock, she hastily left the room. She knew instinctively that what was plaguing her would be revealed there in that cluttered storage room.

Just passing through the doorway and closing the door behind her was a bittersweet experience for Marjorie. To view a lifetime of Frank's special articles was to recall her own life, too. There were his hats, his fine tooled-leather saddle, and his vast collection of rifles and guns.

She smiled, noticing his vast assortment of wood-carved animals and the knives of all sizes and shapes. The man kept everything, she recalled fondly. Oh, how she teased him about this!

Marjorie could not look over these things without remembering how loved he had been by all their friends, and how they were always giving him something they knew he'd appreciate. He always treasured their gifts.

She thought to herself that Eliot Penwick could rant and rave all he wished, but as long as she lived, this room would remain just as it was right now. Just looking at a particular article, she amazed herself that she could recall the individual who'd presented it to Frank.

Slowly, she moved along the sides of the walls of the room and time was forgotten. She became engrossed in her memories.

Seeing all these things that had belonged to Frank, she began to recall friends who no longer lived in Harrison County. Some had died and others had moved away. Marjorie found herself wondering about some of them.

There had been one old pal of Frank's she'd not exactly approved of. She considered him a drifter who'd accepted Frank's hospitality greedily, for her husband had been a most generous and kindhearted man to his less fortunate friends. One such friend was Richard Talbert, and Marjorie had been glad to see him move on.

Now, she saw a huge pile of cloth-draped paintings and recalled how Richard had promised to send for them later, though he never had. He'd been an artist of sorts, and he'd drifted into Harrison County after a sojourn up around the Lake of the Pines region. Like a bolt of lightning, Marjorie recalled her conversation with Talleha. That was the region she'd come from.

Marjorie knew now what she was seeking in this dust-covered storeroom. It was a painting done by Talbert while he'd stayed many months in a village called Cedar Springs. The painting was of a woman, part-Indian.

Marjorie quickly began to pull away the dusty covers. If she was right she knew why she'd been consumed by strange feelings this morning as she looked upon the lovely, tawny-skinned Talleha.

After she had fumbled through at least a dozen paintings, she found the one she sought. Holding it up she saw a distinct resemblance of the features of Talleha to those of the woman in Talbert's painting. Yet there were differences. The lady in the painting had a deeper-hued skin, but she wore the two long braids in her hair as Talleha had fashioned hers this morning. Marjorie knew that that was what had ignited her memory this morning.

Could it be mere circumstance that Talleha came from the same region and that this old painting of a woman resembled her? Maybe her imagination was just running away with her. Nevertheless, she had satisfied her curiosity.

Replacing the cover on the painting, she tried to trace back in time how long ago it had been since Talbert had bidden them farewell and left the ranch. Frank had never heard from him before his death, nor had she had any word from him since. Both she and Frank had suspected that he'd died, since he'd never returned for his cherished possessions.

In a short time she left the room and tried to leave the memories back there, too, behind the locked door. It wasn't so easy, she found as she placed the key back in her secret hiding place. At least she'd managed to accomplish all of it without Eliot's intruding on her, and for that she was pleased.

It was a strange day for Marjorie, one she enjoyed very much, for she was going back in the past, recalling the good times with her dear Frank and their friends. She even enjoyed thinking about the hard times of their early married life, for they were far more exciting than her life now with Eliot.

Thinking about her past and about Frank, she knew she must not wait too long to help Talleha depart from the ranch. If there was the slightest chance—the most remote possibility—that Talleha could be Talbert's daughter by the lovely Indian woman she'd heard about when he'd stayed with them, she'd never forgive herself for not helping that poor girl.

Marjorie had no doubt about what lustful thoughts ran through Eliot's mind. He had not been in her bed for months now, and she had done nothing to encourage it, for all the romance of their marriage had died. There was no amorous fire consuming her, for he had put it out.

As the afternoon wore on, she decided that tonight would be as good as any to see about Talleha returning to her village. She would go over her plans with Lucita when she came to help her prepare to dress for the evening meal.

Marjorie was far from the empty-headed woman her arrogant English husband thought her to be. She'd known about his one-night escapade with the little Mexican servant. But she knew that it had began and ended all in one night. Actually, she'd laughed about the incident; if Eliot's pride had swelled about the fact that he'd taken her maid to his bed, many more men had probably been granted the same privilege.

Lucita was a hot-blooded señorita, and Marjorie knew all about her little rendezvous with the foreman of the neighboring rancher, Emilo Cortez. That had been going on for months now. She knew also about

113

the stable boy, Romano. Eliot was just one of many!

Marjorie had not sought to trouble herself, though, with any effort to enlighten him about the truth. Let him live in that fool's paradise of his! Let him think she was the stupid one, for time was going to prove him wrong, Marjorie reminded herself.

The only thing that galled her was that he dared to think he was so cleverly playing her for the idiot. Well, soon she would have the great joy of laughing in that handsome face of his. Soon, she promised herself, he would be the one humbled as he'd tried to humble and debase her.

The afternoon had given her a strength she'd not known she possessed, and when Lucita came to her room, she found a lady of confidence and self-assurance. Lucita sensed this right away: "You have had a good day, señora?" she asked.

"I've had a divine day, Lucita."

"Ah, I am glad, señora."

Marjorie knew she meant it, and that was what endeared Lucita to her. She'd never faulted Lucita for Eliot's indelicate behavior.

She knew who was at fault—Eliot Penwick!

Chapter 13

Victor Maurier had hoped to be rewarded by the glorious sight of Talleha when he heard the prancing beat of the horse's hooves approaching him there along the path in the woods. His thoughts had been almost solely of her for the last twenty-four hours.

Instead, he saw that the rider on the horse was a fancy dude, for so early in the day he wore dark-brown tailored riding attire. Victor didn't have to be told that he was facing Eliot Penwick, nor did he have to be told why the Texas ranchers found him a strange character. None of the ranchers wore this kind of clothing unless they were going to some grand social affair. Their daily attire was duck or twill pants, with a plain cotton shirt and maybe a kerchief tied around their necks, handy to wipe the sweat from their brows as they rode.

Their sturdy leather boots were selected for service and endurance, unlike the fancy black leather Hessian-style boots Eliot wore.

As Eliot pulled up on the reins of his thoroughbred to glare at this intruder and Victor sat astride Emilo's stallion, giving Eliot a bold, defiant look, it was clear each had an instant hatred of the other.

Eliot was at a disadvantage, for he had no inkling

who this broad-shouldered, rugged-looking man was. But the indomitable image Maurier projected was noted by Penwick as he inquired, "May I ask what you seek on my property?"

Under his breath, Maurier called the man a bastard. The devil it was his property! With a crooked grin on his face and a flippant tone to his voice, he quipped, "Your land? I thought I was riding over the Casa del Lago spread."

So this was a new hand working for Cortez, Eliot mused. "You just started to work for Emilo Cortez?" Eliot asked in his own arrogant way.

"No, I'm a guest of Señor Cortez," Maurier replied in a blunt, insolent air.

"Well, so you'll know in the future, the border of the Cortez land ends about a quarter of a mile due south, Mr. . . ." Eliot hesitated for a moment. Then he asked his name.

"Oh, I'll try not to trespass again." Privately, Victor cussed him again, wanting him to look into his eyes and see that eight-year-old who'd fled from a cottage in the woods back in England some sixteen years ago. "I'm Victor Martin. Who are you?"

"I'm Lord Eliot Penwick, Mr. Martin." There was a snobbish haughtiness about his demeanor and Victor could hardly restrain himself from accusing him of being a murderer. Not only was this man vile and evil, Maurier suspected he was a little mad. If old Paddy had spoken the truth, then this man would be his uncle. Victor did not want to accept that fact, but Paddy had told him he was the son of Lord Edward Penwick; this scoundrel was Edward's brother. God, that sickened Victor!

"What's an English lord doing here in Texas?" Maurier prodded deviously, raising a skeptical brow.

Instant resentment flared in Eliot at this man's

116

brashness. How *dare* he be so insulting? Sitting up straighter and more rigid in his saddle, Penwick curtly dismissed Victor. "What I'm doing here is my business, wouldn't you say, Martin? I suggest we both be on our way."

"Didn't plan on wasting any more time, Lord Penwick," Victor drawled, the hint of a smirk in his deep voice. Tipping his flat-crowned hat in a departing gesture, Victor whipped the reins around to urge the stallion into a swift departure and Penwick watched the man gallop away.

"I don't like that man!" he mumbled to himself. "He's dangerous. The look in his eyes is mean and menacing."

It never entered Eliot's mind that this might be the man his nephew, Ralph, had warned him about—the one who might be coming here to Texas to seek his revenge.

Victor Maurier was consumed with one thought as he rode away from Eliot Penwick. Never did a man deserve killing as much as the one he'd just encountered. He would take great delight in it. The only consideration he had to think about was the tantalizing Talleha. He had to get her away from that house.

On his ride back across the pastureland, he watched the magnificent herd of grazing longhorns belonging to Cortez and he wondered if he should take Emilo into his confidence. He was a friend of Crawford's and Maurier never doubted that he could trust him.

That night he came very close to confessing to Emilo what his mission was as they dined in the sprawling old hacienda. But something stopped him. Even so, he did not fool the very perceptive Emilo, who knew that something was hanging heavy on his young friend's shoulders.

Emilo had requested that his best Madeira be served

with their dinner. From the very first moment Victor Maurier had entered his home, Emilo knew this was no ordinary man. This was a rare breed, and he captured Emilo's interest. He knew Glenn Crawford well enough to know that if he put his stamp of approval on this fellow, then he was all right.

Cortez was also shrewd, and he knew instinctively that this young man was not lingering at his ranch as a courtesy call out of respect for their mutual friend, Crawford. The captain was a man of the sea and so was Maurier, from what he'd been told about his fine, trim-lined schooner, *Destiny*.

But this man was a man on a mission, a very important mission! Maurier was a man who would let nothing stand in his way.

Emilo was curious by nature, and he'd not been so intrigued in a long time. Victor impressed him immediately: he was everything Emilo would have desired in a son, had he been blessed with one. How could he let young Maurier know that he would help him in any way he could?

The right moment never seemed to come, and Victor bade Emilo an early good-night. Emilo knew he was a man driven by some overwhelming passion, but what it was, Emilo could not determine.

An hour later, in his bedroom, Emilo chanced to look out his window, and the full moon in the dark Texas sky shone down on his gardens and grounds. He noticed his magnificent stallion trotting down the long, winding drive from his stables. And on the fine beast was Victor Maurier. Emilo's curiosity was whetted as to where and what this late night rendezvous was all about.

Victor Maurier could not have answered the

question himself. He felt driven to go out toward the Greenfield ranch. It was sheer madness, he told himself. It was a need to be closer to his lovely Talleha, for he knew he was a man bewitched. There was no point in trying to deny it.

Something called to him, and damned if he could turn his back on it. All through the dinner hour, she seemed to be calling to him to come to her. There was no way he could have slept. He had to go.

Maurier was not a superstitious man, but this was as close to a premonition as anything he'd ever experienced in his life. He could not shrug his broad shoulders and casually dismiss it.

As he rode away from Casa del Lago, he noticed that the light of the moon up above was suddenly blotted out by dark clouds moving in. The countryside was shrouded in an overwhelming darkness.

A short distance away, in her bedroom, Marjorie Penwick observed how swiftly the moonlit night had changed. It spurred her to make a hasty, impulsive decision. What better time would there ever be than now to help Talleha get out of here and back to the place she belonged?

She knew Eliot had returned to the house from his nightly ride and was already sequestered in either his study or his bedroom. While Lucita was here turning down her bed, she could send her to Talleha. Marjorie knew that she must make a decision fast if it was to be tonight that she helped the girl. With Lucita's assistance, Talleha could saddle the mare she'd been riding lately and be on her way before anyone would notice what was going on.

Her nightly duties for her mistress done, Lucita was about to leave the room, but Marjorie called out to her to stay. "I think, Lucita—I think this is the night we should help our little friend leave here. I want you to give her this," she said, handing Lucita a velvet pouch with gold coins inside. She motioned her maid to have a seat as she laid out her plot.

Attentively, Lucita listened to the señora, and when she had finished telling her what she had in mind, Lucita agreed. "It will work, señora. Romano has been gone from the stable for hours, and Talleha and I can easily get the tame little mare saddled and ready to ride. That Talleha is an expert rider. She's told me she has ridden a horse without a saddle. She is part Indian, you know."

"I know. So what are we waiting for? Be off with you, niña! I will be most grateful to you for helping me."

"Ah, señora! It is my pleasure, for I never forget how good you are to me," Lucita exclaimed. A pang of guilt stabbed at Lucita: she'd been indiscreet and disloyal with that Englishman husband of the señora's. When the masterful Frank Greenfield ruled this empire, Lucita knew she would never have thrown herself at him the way she had with Eliot Penwick.

"Go, Lucita—go, and God go with you!" Marjorie urged her.

Obediently, the little maid rushed from the room. She hesitated only long enough to give the señora an assuring smile before going out the door. Marjorie sat there watching her, and she knew as only a woman can know that Lucita felt a degree of remorse about her sinful little escapade with Eliot.

However, when Lucita rushed to Talleha's room to carry out the señora's plans, she was not there. Lucita's excitable nature moved her to pace the floor in Talleha's room. Oh, wherever could she be, Lucita wondered.

There was no more welcome sight than that of

120

Talleha dashing through the door with her hair tousled, the flowers hanging limply out of place. Her lovely face was flushed, and she was taking deep breaths, as if she'd been racing down the hall. The truth was that she had to get to the security of her room and away from Eliot Penwick.

It had been her misfortune to encounter him as he'd returned from his nightly ride. Eliot was in a most desperate, strange mood tonight. He'd dared to be more bold this evening than ever before. Talleha had found herself cornered by him, and his hands had clutched her waist, moving boldly to fondle her breast. She was mortified!

Talleha had reacted instinctively, as was her nature. She voiced her disapproval, "Lord Penwick!" Her face reflected shock.

"Now, come on, Talleha—you're no child, and we both know that. I've been most patient with you, and I've certainly been generous. Is it so hard to grant me a few favors? Am I so repulsive to you? Most ladies find me very appealing." In his boyish plea, he was almost whining.

She tried to control the trembling in her voice as she replied, "You've been most generous, Lord Penwick, but that does not give you the kind of liberties you obviously expect. I—I shall never grant you them. You might as well know that right now."

Eliot Penwick could not accept that sort of rejection, and his fury was so intense that he slapped her. She was stunned by this act of brute force. Her thick eyelashes fluttered and her eyes grew misty, but she was damned if she was going to cry. She was stubbornly determined that she'd show this bastard no sign of weakness.

She amazed herself when she spoke in a cool, calm voice. Her dark eyes locked with his as she backed away from him. There was a strength and force in her

121

petite body that she was not aware of as she told him, "You ever do that again, and I swear I'll kill you!" The hate in her eyes blazed brightly.

She turned and Eliot watched the swishing of her silk skirt and the swinging gait of her walk as she marched away from him. She meant it and he knew it. This lady was not one to take lightly. He'd acted rashly.

Needless to say, Talleha was receptive to Lucita's news. She was ready to leave. With Lucita's help, she quickly changed from the silk frock she had on and donned a simple cotton tunic with her black riding skirt.

She took the shawl Lucita handed to her. There was an eager look on her face as she announced, "I'm ready, Lucita! I'm more than ready to get back to the Lake of the Pines."

"Then let us be on our way, señorita," Lucita replied.

The two girls draped in their shawls slipped cautiously down the steps and out the door. As cloudy as the skies were, and under the cover of night, it would have been almost impossible for anyone to have spotted then moving through the courtyard garden.

Everything went without a hitch, and in no time at all, the mare was saddled and Talleha mounted it. Lucita led the pair out through the stable door. Once outside, Talleha said a brief farewell, but Lucita urged her, "Please, tarry no longer. God be with you, Talleha!"

Funny as it seemed, Lucita felt concern for the girl as she watched her spur the mare into action. She was going all alone into the vast countryside.

It seemed not to faze Talleha in the least.

Chapter 14

The only thing occupying Talleha's thoughts was that she was finally free to return to her home after all these weeks of being denied her right by Eliot Penwick. She knew why he'd sought to detain her. Now she knew why the señora agreed to help her leave, for she must have suspected her husband's evil intentions.

The stiff night breeze touched her face and the fast pace of the mare caused her hair to blow back wild and free. She felt her spirits soar, for she was filled with happiness to be leaving the Penwick household far behind her.

Now all she could think about was the cozy little cottage she'd shared with her mother, surrounded by her belongings, including certain cherished little keepsakes which might not mean anything to anyone but her. There was certainly no high value on anything within the walls of their cottage, but all of it was dear to Talleha. Until this moment, it had not dawned on her that her home might have been emptied of all the furnishings. What had their friends thought? What had they done when her mother was found dead and she was missing? What were friends like Hunter and his good wife, Salina, to think? A horrible thought struck her, making a startling impact: it was possible, since she was missing, that *she* could have been the one who'd done that terrible thing to her mother.

She could not accept that, though. Salina and Hunter knew how much she loved her mother. Never would they think that!

These reflections made her spur the mare to move faster and she guided the horse quite skillfully through the thick growth of pines. She flinched, though, as she heard the nearby shriek of an owl. Her mother'd always said an owl shrieking was a bad sign, and Talleha never questioned her wisdom about such things.

Quite suddenly, she was subjected to a startling sight: straight ahead of her loomed an imperious, phantomlike figure on a huge horse, blocking the trail. She pulled up sharply on her reins. The mare must have been frightened and panicked. Talleha was not prepared nor had she expected the usually calm mare to rear up so.

For the first time since she was about seven years old, Talleha found herself tumbling off the back of a horse. There was no way she could prevent it.

Her firm derrière hit with a mighty slam, giving her a harsh jarring. She responded with a shriek of cuss words. When she'd hit the ground, the force of the fall had caused her to fall backwards and her thick hair had caught on something. She was rendered utterly helpless. Whatever it was that held her hair, she could not find it with her hand. She wiggled there on the ground, struggling to free herself.

She was actually so occupied by the miserable dilemma she found herself caught up in that she forgot about the fierce, imposing figure ahead of her who'd caused all this in the first place.

She didn't even hear the deep, husky laughter as the man's eyes watched her writhing on the ground. Just watching her, Maurier was convinced that she was a hotheaded little firebrand. A devious streak in him gave way, so he let her suffer for a brief moment or two before he sought to come to her rescue.

He found he could not let her linger too long in her miserable state, and so he leaped down from the huge stallion. He had her gloosy, black hair free of the fallen branch in a moment. Just as quickly his arms claimed her as he whispered her name lovingly. She barely had time to recognize who her rescuer was before she felt his searing lips branding hers.

Flames of passion consumed her. The liquid heat he stirred traveled the full length of her body. She felt herself arch up to him so that his arms could enclose her.

Maurier would normally have allowed himself to become completely bewitched by the magic of the moment, but his keen ears heard the sounds of what he suspected were riders fast approaching in the distance.

"Come, Talleha—we've got to get out of here," he whispered. In one swift motion of his strong arms, he gathered her up and swung her up onto his stallion. Grasping the reins of her little mare, he mounted his horse behind her and spurred the stallion into movement with the little mare following behind them.

She didn't ask where he was taking her, but she heard the beating hooves of the horses too, and she knew it could very well be Eliot Penwick and his men out searching for her. She did not want him to find her and take her back to his ranch.

Maurier was not ready to present Talleha to Emilo— not just yet! But he had only one other place he could deposit her until he could think this thing out. He'd not anticipated this turn of events, but there was the small little shack on the north end of the Casa del Lago Ranch that he'd happened upon when he'd been riding.

Tonight that would have to do, he told himself as he rode in that direction.

In an effort to try to prepare her for what they were facing at this secluded cabin, Maurier told Talleha, "It's not a very tidy place I'm taking you, Talleha, but at least you'll be safe there. I'm assuming you were leaving the Penwick ranch, shall we say, unceremoniously?"

"You might say that," she confessed.

"May I ask where you were heading at this late hour, little one?"

"Home. I was heading home."

"And where is home?"

"Cedar Springs, on the Lake of the Pines."

"Lake of the Pines—sounds nice," he murmured, letting his lips tease her ears. He found himself delighted by the way her sensuous body responded to his nearness.

"It—it is beautiful. I—I've wanted to be on my way for a long time, but Lord Penwick could not seem to arrange to get me back."

"Or perhaps, my pretty, he didn't want to get you back there. I would venture to guess that he might not have intended to take you back at all, ever."

Talleha turned around to face him with a quizzical look on her face. How could he have been so perceptive about Lord Penwick? When she saw his face, so handsome it took her breath away, his self-assurance was astounding.

She almost resented his all-knowing expression as his eyes took her in. He seemed to know exactly what she was thinking, and she seemed to have no defense against that.

"Why do you say that, Victor? Do you even know the man?"

"It must be true, or you would not be running away

this late at night. As to knowing the man himself, the answer is no. I only know about him, Talleha."

She noted a strange tone in his voice now. But before she could respond, he pulled at the reins to change the direction they'd been traveling. There was a narrow path with a huge bluff on one side and a row of trees growing along the lake just a short distance away.

"Do you remember what I told you about this place?"

"I have not forgotten," she replied in an offhanded manner, for she was intrigued by the jutting boulders of the high-rising cliff. There seemed to be no end to it. Maurier had to veer to the right to move around it. Another horse could not have gone around them, for it was too narrow.

"We're almost there. I'm certain Señor Cortez won't mind our using the cabin," Victor gave her a lazy smile. But he noticed her eyebrow arch as he spoke.

"*Our* using it—is that what you said?" she muttered in a hesitating voice.

"It is. I'm not going to deposit you alone in this cabin and go back to Cortez's house to sleep, with Penwick searching the countryside for you already."

She sat silently, saying nothing for a moment. She felt his warm lips close to the side of her face and she caught the hint of devilment in his voice as he asked, "Now I could see you safely back to Penwick's, if you want me to."

She gave him a hard shove with her elbow and hissed, "Oh, shut up! You're ornery, Victor Maurier!"

He threw his head back and roared with laughter.

Talleha heard him but her attention was focused on the little cabin just ahead. A flood of sweet memories washed over her, for it was enclosed by a white rail fence, just like her mother's cabin was. There was a gate and an arched trellis over it. Beautiful blue morning glories always covered her mother's trellis. But this little cabin stood with knee-high weeds in the yard.

She was so engrossed in it that she was unaware that Maurier had halted the stallion, leaped down to secure the reins on the railing. He was preparing to swing her down from the horse.

He made no effort to place her there on the ground but carried her in his arms as he walked through the high weeds. When he reached the small porch, he let her down to stand on the floor of the porch. "Let me go in first, Talleha . . . I don't know what we shall find inside."

But he soon found out as he moved inside the door and was greeted by drapes of cobwebs clinging to his face. "Holy Christ!" he grumbled, swiping at his face with both hands.

"Wh—what is it, Victor?" Talleha wanted to know.

"Bloody cobwebs everywhere!"

She giggled with amusement. "Light up one of those cheroots you smoke, and I think I have the problem whipped." Already she was fumbling in the small bundle she'd gathered up to bring with her when Lucita had informed her that tonight was the night she was to leave the ranch.

When she spotted the orange-red glow of his cheroot, she held out one of the candles she'd quickly packed away to take with her on her journey. She held it to the fire of his cheroot until a glowing flame ignited. He saw a smug smile on her face.

Together, they slowly walked into the cabin with Maurier carrying the long, slender taper to survey the condition of the humble dwelling.

The meager furnishings reminded Talleha of her own home. The dirt and grime were anathema to her because her home was spotlessly clean. But Talleha knew how to remedy them. What did amaze her were the supplies she found in the cupboards, as though someone had used this place in the last few weeks.

Though she excitedly pointed out all these marvelous things—coffee, flour, meal, and dried beans—Maurier did not share her excitement. He was bone-weary and there were many things on his mind. The most distracting problem was the beautiful Talleha.

He'd not expected to have to deal with her to have to accomplish his quest. When he'd left England, his plans had been simple: his destination would be Brownsville. To find Eliot Penwick somewhere in Texas was his next goal.

What he had not planned on was losing his heart to a girl like Talleha. He'd had his share of beautiful, experienced women in many ports all over the world, but none had challenged him or held his interest; none had made him change his plans. Talleha had done exactly that. It perplexed him that he should allow it.

He did not want to admit it, and Talleha was certainly not aware of it, but she did have a power over him. If she had known it, it would have pleased her, because she knew how strongly he effected her.

Victor was happy that she was not appalled by the cabin. He watched her roam around as if she were appraising each corner of the room. Not once did she have a frown on her lovely face, and it endeared her to him.

"Well, what do you think, my darling? Can you sleep here tonight?"

She turned and he'd never seen a more beautiful smile. "I could sleep here many nights. This reminds me of my home, on the Lake of the Pines. It's dirty, but it can be cleaned up. It's a nice cabin; I feel a happy spirit here." Her black eyes turned to lock into his bright blue eyes. There was a look there as old and primitive as the ages. Maurier understood when she told him,

"Remember, Victor—I am a half-breed—I am part Indian. I probably don't think the way you do."

He grinned deviously and his hands reached out to snake around her tiny waist as he huskily declared, "Oh, my darling little Talleha—I think you think exactly the way I do."

He was too fired with desire to continue; his lips captured hers in a kiss. It was a long, lingering kiss which made her surrender completely. At first, it was only her sweet, moist lips; but then the rest of her found it natural to give herself up to him.

Nothing could have pleased Maurier more than the surrender of the beautiful Talleha in his arms. Ah, she was so much more than he'd ever expected to find in any woman!

He found himself instantly soaring to the loftiest heights of sensual desire. He forgot about everything else except the passionate woman he held in his arms.

Chapter 15

It was not the setting he would have chosen for this glorious night of pleasure. But he realized suddenly that none of this mattered when his lips were exploring the velvety softness of her flesh and his hands were teaching her the new sensual pleasures a woman could share with a man.

He knew that his precious Talleha had never shared with any man what she'd experienced with him. He had never been so gratified.

She was his now, and nothing was ever going to change that. He loved the way she returned his passion with a hot-blooded passion of her own. It happened between them naturally and easily, as though they had been meant for one another.

He loved the tantalizing sway of her body, moving eagerly to come to him, yearning for him to fill her with his whole being.

He loved her sweet moans of pleasure as his powerful body devoured her with delight. She told him as only a woman can that she adored his touch, loved the feel of him in their all-consuming lovemaking.

He'd never known such rapture. But at the first light of dawn, when he opened his eyes to look around, the miserable surroundings were somewhat shocking to him. Talleha would probably be horrified when she saw the terrible place he'd brought her to; she might think him horrible to have brought her here.

He asked himself what he could do to improve the scene her eyes would see when they first opened. With this in mind, he slowly slipped his arm out from under her head and heaved a deep sigh of relief that she still slept soundly.

Hastily he dressed and opened all the windows and doors to allow the fresh morning air to permeate the musty cabin. He took the kerchief he'd been wearing and wiped away the layers of dust on the oak table and wooden chairs. He did the same thing to two wooden rockers. There was nothing he could do to improve the looks of the old featherbed they'd made such passionate love on last night, for he did not wish to rouse her from her sleep just yet.

But he did find an old jar in one of the cupboards and he rushed outside to gather up some of the bachelor buttons growing amid a vast sea of weeds just outside the tiny porch. It was only when he was awkwardly stuffing them in the old jar that he recalled how he used to do this very same thing for his mother when he was a small boy. The pleasant memory brought a smile to his face. He recalled the lovely expression of Colette Maurier as she kissed him to thank him for his beautiful bouquet.

What was it about this one woman that seemed to bring out such a wild and wonderful insanity in him? He'd never been this way before about any woman—never!

But there he stood in the middle of weeds picking out the stems of the bachelor buttons and hoping he could find enough of the flowers to make up a nice bouquet.

When he returned inside the cabin, he was glad to

find her still asleep. Maurier had to accept the truth staring him right in the face whether he liked it or not. He was going to have to leave her here long enough to bring some supplies back; there was no other way. The other choice left to him was to take her to Emilo's house, but this was not the best thing to do right now.

He could leave her one of his six-shooters for protection while he went to Emilo's to gather up a few necessities, he decided. The whole operation should not take him an hour.

Part II

The Force of Evil

Chapter 16

His mind was made up by the time Talleha's eyes fluttered open. She lay there with a lazy smile on her face, and the sheet was tucked under her bare arms. Her smooth, soft shoulders urged Maurier to move to the bed so his hands could touch and caress them; but he'd be lost if he did it; he knew he must not.

There were some plans he must make before this day passed and the beautiful distraction of Talleha could prove to be dangerous. Victor was too smart to allow that to happen. Romancing Talleha must wait.

For a few moments Talleha was disoriented; she wondered if she was merely dreaming this strange surrounding and Victor standing there looking down at her. His broad chest was bare and he wore only his pants. Her eyes absorbed the firm, sinewy arms as his hands clasped his waist. His devious, gleaming blue eyes seared her, but there was a boyish look about his rugged face with his black hair falling over his forehead on one side.

"Good morning, sweetheart," he said tenderly.

"Good morning, Victor." She felt the cool, fresh air rushing through the door, and that was an improvement from the dismal, musty odor she'd smelled last night. When they'd arrived, there had been little time to check the condition of the cabin, for they had given way to the impatient passion churning within them. She remembered the fierce urgency of his virile body as well as the excited frenzy he stirred in her.

Maurier noticed the sheepishly wicked grin on her face and knew what she was thinking. "It was as wonderful for you, too, wasn't it, Talleha?"

She gave him a slow nod. A broader grin creased his face and he took a stride to sit down on the bed beside her. "I thought so; it wasn't just my imagination. It was wonderful because I wanted it to be. I wanted it very much."

"I never knew love could be so wonderful—between a man and a woman, I mean."

"Now you know it can, sweetheart, and it will even get better between you and me, my beautiful Talleha." It took all his will power for him to refrain from taking her in his arms as he yearned to, and he felt himself swelling with an overwhelming desire. But he released her dainty hands and rose up from the bed.

He ached with anguish, but he was determined not to give way until he accomplished what must be done. "We've got to talk, Talleha. This morning I have to admit that there aren't enough supplies to make do here."

She sat up in the bed with the sheet draped around her. "What can we do, Victor?"

"I've got to leave you here alone while I go back to the Casa del Lago to get some supplies. I don't like that one bit. Could you use a gun if you had to, Talleha?"

She suddenly realized how little they knew about one another. This man she'd given herself to so completely, without shame or regret, knew nothing about her, nor did she know virtually anything about him.

"I can use a gun if I have to," she told him. Would he

be surprised to know about her life with her half-breed mother? Dawn's friend, Hunter, was a Choctaw Indian, a guide and a hunter; he and his half-breed wife, Salina, were their best friends and neighbors back at Cedar Springs. He had taught her to ride a horse without a saddle and allowed her to shoot his rifle and pistol before she was ten years old.

She'd had no fancy bronze tub to bathe in as she'd enjoyed back at the Penwicks' lavish home. Her tub had been the lake with its cool, clear waters. She'd had no bath oils to luxuriate in as she'd had back at the Penwicks', nor had she ever owned a bottle of toilet water like the one Flossie had given her. Her perfume had been the wild jasmine she picked to tuck behind her ear or into the neckline of her tunic. But in her simpler life, Talleha had had a marvelous variety from which to choose as she roamed the woods. One day it would be the wild verbena; some days, it would be the yellow or white honeysuckle. Her favorite was the yellow blossom of the wild night-blooming jasmine.

When her eyes noticed the sight of bluish-purple bachelor buttons in the old jar, she melted with tenderness at Victor's thoughtfulness. That rugged exterior concealed a sweet gentleness that touched her to the core. It was the essence of the things her beloved mother had taught her about life. Perhaps it was the simplicity of her life and how she and Dawn had lived that made her feel no shame or embarrassment about giving herself so willingly to Victor.

And he saw such an assured air there that he did not doubt she spoke the truth about her ability to shoot a gun. He was now thinking that he did not really know this beautiful creature he adored. He was more intrigued about the mysteries he'd discover about this enchanting little temptress as they got to know one another.

"That makes me feel much better, my darling. I won't stay longer than absolutely necessary, I assure you." He raised a skeptical frown and gave her a crooked grin as he quizzed her, "So you can shoot a gun, eh? I'll have to remember that—just in case you get mad at me."

She gave forth a lighthearted giggle. There was a flirtatious glint in her eyes as she cocked her head to the side, challenging him, "Perhaps, you should, Victor Maurier."

He laughed, declaring, "You are a wicked little vixen, my gorgeous Talleha, and I adore you!"

"Well, if I am wicked then it is your fault. You are the devil that made me sin."

"Saucy imp! You're asking for a sound paddling, but I'll let you off this time since I must be about my business," he chuckled, playfully tousling her hair.

"Oh, Victor!" she protested and wiggled to the far side of the bed.

Maurier turned away to take his shirt off the bedpost; once again he chided himself to quit lingering, even though he was tempted to.

Buttoning the front of his shirt, he addressed her in a more serious tone, "I want you to get dressed, my little beauty, and then I want you to keep yourself in this cabin and out of mischief for about an hour until I can ride back here with some food and supplies. I'm going to leave you one of my guns—just in case you need it."

By now she was standing on the plank floor of the cabin with the old sheet clutched around her. "Turn around, then, so I can do as you requested."

"What? Oh!" he could not resist smiling as he teased her, "Isn't all this modesty rather silly now?"

"Not to me, Victor. Don't turn around until I say so," she insisted stubbornly.

"Yes, ma'am! Better be dressed by the time I count to

140

ten. One—two—three—"

"Victor—don't treat me like a child!"

His brilliant blue eyes appraised her from head to toe. His words were warm with passion as he admitted, "Ah, I know you're not, my princess." He was through pulling on his boots; he proceeded to place his hat on his head and turned in her direction.

Without further delay, he rushed over to give her a quick peck on the nose and a cautioning reminder not to venture out of the cabin while he was gone.

He dashed out the door and waded through the weeds to get to his horse. The moment he was in the saddle, he spurred the huge stallion into a fast gallop.

Talleha shut the cabin door as he'd suggested, but she decided not to close the shutters, for the breeze was refreshing. Now she had time to examine the unkempt cabin. It was much smaller than the cottage where she'd lived with her mother. Wishing to have something to do while waiting for Victor to return, she put the old broom to work. Not only did she sweep the plank floor; she also brushed down the walls, which were festooned with dozens of cobwebs.

If only she had a pail of water, some soap, and a mop, she could have really cleaned it properly, she thought to herself.

A few minutes of idly pacing the floor urged her to explore the cabin in earnest. In an ancient chest she found a pile of old rags, and on one of the window sills in the small kitchen she found a bar of lye soap.

All her good intentions to abide by Victor's orders quickly went astray. She rationalized that the river was not all that far away. Why, she could have a bucket of water and be back inside the cabin before ten minutes had gone by, and Victor was certainly not going to return all that soon.

She hastily grabbed up the bucket, dashed out the

141

door, and plowed through the high weeds to take the path which would lead her to the riverbank.

She returned to the cabin with her bucket full of water as quickly as she could. With the rags, soap, and water, she got down on her knees and scrubbed the tiny kitchen floor first. From there she went through the same process in the bedroom before going to the front room of the cabin.

By the time she stood up to stretch herself and toss the filthy brownish-gray water out into the yard, she was tired, but pleased by the fruits of her labor. When she turned to go back inside, she did close the front door. The fresh smell of the inside of the cabin and the added charm of Victor's flowers gave a pleasant air to the cabin.

She sat there with a smile on her face, enjoying the results of her work and thinking what a nice surprise Victor would have when he returned with their supplies.

She had no way of knowing how much time had passed since he'd left, but with everything she'd accomplished, she knew it had to be more than an hour.

However, once her vigor was restored, another idea came to her. She again justified a quick jaunt to the river. She picked up the bucket and took the same path. When she got to the riverbank, she quickly disrobed and plunged into the cooling waters. It felt wonderful to cleanse herself of the dirt. She swished her long, thick hair back and forth until it was completely wet like the rest of her.

But she suddenly realized that her wet hair would give her away to Maurier. Immediately he would know! "Damn—I didn't think about that!" she muttered. She reared up hastily out of the water to shake her head vigorously and was annoyed with herself. Because of this, she started swimming for the

142

bank. If she was lucky, maybe her hair would dry in the bright sunshine, she reasoned.

Back on the bank a pair of fierce-looking eyes were focused in her direction. They watched the graceful movement of her satiny body as she swam toward the river's edge. The very sight of her made the intruder on her privacy take a deep breath, and he pulsed with wild, savage sensations.

In another minute she would be stepping out of the water, displaying all her naked charms for his lusty eyes to behold!

Chapter 17

When Victor Maurier stepped through the doorway of the cabin to smell the odor of lye soap and saw the fresh, clean look of the place it did not please him at all, for he knew instantly that Talleha had not listened to his orders that she remain inside while he was away. That headstrong little vixen had gone and done just as she pleased.

After the short moment it took to scan the front room, when Talleha did not come scurrying out of the tiny kitchen to greet him, his anger turned to fear.

"Talleha!" He raged through the house and back to the front door yelling her name. But he got no response. He let out a flood of cusswords as he dashed off the porch and through the thick weeds. If she cleaned the cabin, then she'd obviously gone to the river. Like a naughty child, she deserved to have that little rump of hers spanked, and he'd darn well do it when he found her.

It was easy to track her path toward the river, for weeds were mashed down along the way. The closer he got to the river, the more his rage mounted. As he suspected, when he emerged from the thick growth of underbrush and the trees thinned out, he saw her there in the water as naked as the day she was born, like a beautiful wood nymph. Damn her, he felt himself melt at the very sight of her!

He was so beguiled by her beauty that his usually keen senses did not hear the slight rustling of another observer across the way from where he stood.

It was only when the intruder was sharply touching a quirt to his horse's backside and the horse broke into a fast pace that Victor became distracted enough from the sight of the black-haired goddess to realize there was danger.

"God damn!" He knew there was no point now to attempt to get back to the cabin and get his horse, to give chase to whoever was ogling Talleha. But it did make it more imperative than ever that he get her away from this cabin, now that she'd been spotted. The intruder might not be one of Penwick's men, but Maurier could not be sure of that.

As he marched down to the edge of the river, he had to admit that Emilo had given him the right solution to his dilemma when he told Victor to come back to get the girl. Emilo's words were ringing in his ears right then. "You took a dangerous chance leaving her there alone, amigo," the elderly Mexican had told him. Obviously, he'd acted stupidly.

He was as angry at himself as he was at her. He roughly yanked her out of the water. "Damn it, Talleha—you don't listen at all, do you?" His blue eyes blazed furiously. She meekly allowed him to lead her to the riverbank. No one had to tell her that he was out of patience with her.

"Get your clothes on immediately!" His hand freed hers. She couldn't understand why he was so insistent that she get dressed, now that he was back with her. She found herself fumbling with the garments because she was confused by his nasty mood.

"You don't have to be so nasty, Victor. There's—there's nothing to worry about," she grumbled, yanking up her divided skirt and tucking in her blouse.

"There could be, if you really want to get away from Penwick. You were foolhardy, Talleha, to disobey me and come down to this river alone—more foolish than you know!"

"I'm here, aren't I? I'm safe—well, I'm safe unless it's you I have to fear," she flippantly retorted.

"You're safe only because I happened to return to the cabin and came searching for you when I did. You obviously were not aware that there was someone right over there enjoying the sight of your naked body very much. I can imagine what might have taken place if another ten minutes had found me still away." His face was serious and worried.

"There—there was—do you mean a man?" she stammered.

"I mean just that, my pet! Come, we're getting out of here right now." He took her hand in his again, and this time he dragged her along, for each stride made her have to take two or three steps just to keep up with his pace.

"You mean after I scrubbed that cabin we're leaving it?"

"I mean just that. Señor Cortez insists I get you to his house, for he feels you'll be safer there. I'm convinced that he is right."

Talleha said no more as they reached the cabin and Maurier wasted no time hoisting her onto the stallion. There was no need to go inside, Maurier decided. Once she was astraddle, he mounted behind her and spurred the horse into action.

Only after they had gone about a mile did Talleha ask where he was taking her.

"To the Casa del Lago, owned by my friend, Señor

Cortez. You'll find him very nice. He's graciously offered to help us."

"This is where you have been staying since you came to Harrison County, isn't it? What brought you here, Victor?"

"A debt owed me. A debt I'm to collect before I can leave," he told her solemnly.

"It must be a big one to make you come all the way to Texas," she said casually.

"A very big one, indeed."

In a faltering voice she murmured, "And when you collect this debt, you will leave to return to the place you came from?"

"Probably," he answered, and there was a sly grin on his face which she couldn't see; her back was to him.

What he didn't venture to add was that when he left she would be going with him.

He welcomed the sight of the rambling house a short distance ahead. It would give his beautiful Talleha more sheltered protection than the small cabin.

It was a lengthy discussion with Emilo that had delayed him so long. Maurier had always credited himself with being a clever, shrewd individual, and he gave his beloved Captain Crawford the praise for this. But that sly old fox, Cortez, had drawn out the whole story about Talleha and how he'd rescued her last night. He confessed that he'd taken the liberty of using the old cabin on the river running along the narrow bluffside road.

Without any hesitation, Emilo had begun to shake his white head and grumble, "No, no, no, my young friend. You bring the little señorita right here to my house, and we shall see that she is protected from the likes of Eliot Penwick. It would give me great pleasure—believe me!"

What Emilo did not say to Maurier was that he, too,

147

sought revenge—for his good friend, Frank Green-field. Where he could not help poor Marjorie, he could certainly help Maurier and the gorgeous Talleha.

Señor Cortez had good reason for his insistent manner with Maurier. One of Penwick's men had been by the Casa del Lago today while Maurier's where-abouts were still unknown by Señor Cortez. However, he convinced the man he knew nothing about the girl he asked about and had not seen her. Emilo figured that explained Maurier's absence and somehow, he knew his young friend was involved with the girl's disappearance from the Penwick ranch.

Those wise old eyes of Emilo's had observed Maurier the day they saw the girl and Penwick driving down the country road in the Penwicks' fancy buggy. A raw, hotblooded passion was reflected in Victor's eyes as he gazed at that black-haired señorita, Emilo recalled.

A strange anticipation flooded Emilo Cortez. He questioned if it was just what his beloved wife always described as the soul of a romantic. She knew him so well. He wanted to help these two young people who he felt were in love with one another. He also recalled that pretty head of the girl called Talleha turning back to look in Victor's direction the same day Maurier had so hungrily stared at her. He could admit with all honesty that that could be the reason he impatiently awaited the young couple's return.

But there was more to all this than just the beautiful girl that involved young Maurier. Emilo would have given anything to have a heart-to-heart talk with his friend, Glenn Crawford. He knew then the mystery could have been unraveled.

Yet there was another side to the whirlpool of

intrigue that whetted Emilo's interest. Many times he'd felt the urge to go to the Greenfield ranch to try to talk to Marjorie and offer his help and his friendship. There were times he'd been filled with guilt that he was failing Frank for not doing just that. But how does one do what he'd have liked to do? Madre de Dios, his hands were tied!

Emilo's study faced the southern border of his land, and large windows gave him a magnificent view to the south and west. It was here he'd been pacing back and forth now for almost an hour wondering what was detaining the two young people.

As he often did, he sought to have counsel with his wife by talking to the painting of her which hung over the stone fireplace. He told her of the glorious sunset he could see just outside the window. He told her how he wished she could be standing by his side enjoying it with him, and as he spoke he allowed tears to dampen his cheek without shame. He knew no reason why he should feel shame, for how does one put a time limit on mourning the loss of a wife? His mourning would be endless. Forever he would cry out for her.

Few people had ever seen this side of the dignified, self-assured Señor Cortez, whose emotions were always in control. But this was one of those times when he wasn't.

He stood at the window watching some of his hired hands going off in different directions. Some meandered toward the bunkhouse just beyond the barn and stable; others mounted their horses to ride home, where their wives and families awaited them.

Emilo had hired on a few extra hands already to prepare for the busy season of roundup. He figured he'd get the best men seeking work before the other ranchers started to hire. Those signing on with Emilo Cortez knew exactly what the rules and regulations were around the Casa del Lago, and if they didn't comply they were immediately dismissed. There had been very few who'd presented any problems, and Emilo's foreman had sent them packing.

At long last, Emilo's dark eyes saw the couple on the fine stallion he'd assigned to Maurier when he'd arrived at the ranch. If that wasn't a picture to behold, the señor mused, as he watched with admiration.

Maurier was a striking image, a virile young man in his prime, handsome of face and physique. The enchanting young lady riding in front of him with Maurier's arms encircling her waist as he held the reins was breathtakingly beautiful. Their two black heads seemed to blend together; her long glossy tresses were swept back from her face. Emilo watched with intense delight as he could see her expression—she was laughing gaily. Emilo grinned, wondering what the young rascal had told her that was so amusing.

Ah, they were a fine pair! Like his prized thoroughbred, which he'd picked with such special care and scrutiny, he considered them a rare young couple. It would be his great pleasure to help them, for he had no respect for the likes of Eliot Penwick. It was a shame that he had to tarnish such a fine lady as Marjorie Greenfield, but to spoil such a young child as this would be sacrilege.

It was time he left his study to greet them on his front veranda. He spritely walked out of the study and down the tiled hallway toward his front door. He called out to one of his servants to prepare to serve refreshments on the east veranda.

Emilo was exactly where he wanted to be when Maurier and Talleha came up the stone path leading to the veranda.

Emilo had been impressed by Talleha, and now she was secretly admiring this gray-haired gentleman standing on the veranda with such a warm, friendly smile. He had to be the Señor Cortez Victor had spoken about so fondly, and she was already convinced that he was a very nice man.

In that gallant way of his, Emilo stepped forward, extending his hand to say, "Welcome to my home, Señorita Talleha. I am Señor Emilo Cortez."

She took his hand and gave him a lovely smile. "I thank you, señor. It is a pleasure to meet you. Victor has said so many nice things about you, and I can now see why."

Emilo looked from her over to Maurier to light-heartedly jest, "Your Talleha is quickly stealing my heart, Victor. I've not seen such a beautiful, charming young lady in a long time."

Victor's blue eyes gleamed wickedly as he glanced down at the tiny black-haired miss to reply, "Nor have I, but I saw her first, señor. You see, Talleha—you have two admirers."

There was a flirting glint in her dark eyes as she saucily declared, "I accept both of you." She gave forth a delightful, infectious giggle. Maurier and Emilo broke forth with jolly laughter. A friendly camaraderie enveloped the trio as they entered the tiled hallway with arms linked together.

"Señor and señorita, won't you join me for some refreshments? This is a happy occasion for me."

Maurier and Talleha readily accepted his invitation.

Chapter 18

A disquieting aura had settled in at the Penwick household for the last two days and nights. Lucita moved almost cautiously any time she had to leave her mistress's boudoir. Praying every minute that she would not encounter Eliot Penwick, she would leave Marjorie's upstairs bedroom and cautiously rush through the hallway. She just knew her face would reflect her guilt if he sought to question her with those fierce, piercing eyes of his.

The señora's cool demeanor absolutely amazed her. She dared anyone to tell her that Señora Marjorie was not a strong-willed lady. That period of her life seemed to have gone away, and it had all happened so suddenly. Lucita would have sworn that her mistress would have insidiously faded away, slowly weakening until she would find her some morning there, dead in her bed. It was horrible to think about, but those had been the thoughts invading her mind many times these last few months. A miracle had surely happened lately, though.

No one was more aware of this miracle than Marjorie. It was the greatest feeling, and she was relishing the sight of her husband's uneasiness; he'd been squirming for two days.

She sensed that she had succeeded in wooing and winning young Ralph to her side, and she also sensed that this did not please Eliot at all. He'd not expected this. Every time she'd recalled his utterly devastated expression when he'd found out about Talleha disappearing, she'd wanted to laugh in his face and flaunt the fact that she'd been the one who'd helped Talleha flee the ranch.

She'd actually felt genuinely sorry for poor Ralph the last two days, for he'd received such harsh treatment from his uncle. She'd watched the young man literally wilt from his uncle's cruel abuse. More than ever she was convinced that she'd married a man without any feelings whatsoever for other human beings. He was completely absorbed with himself.

There was something else which had plagued her. She had decided she could use only one weapon to protect herself. This morning she'd instructed Lucita to bring her a breakfast tray, and in the morning she planned to give her the same orders. Oh, it sickened her to feel or think this way, but she did. Damned if she was going to think it was she who was going mad!

As Lucita had pondered the transition in her, Marjorie herself had also tried to determine when it all came about. It had to do with Talleha, she had to honestly confess: the young woman had been too genuinely nice for Marjorie to hate. She had to keep this helpless young girl from being molested by Eliot. He was the worst sort of scoundrel, with the morals of a rattlesnake.

She also knew her little Mexican maid was very nervous about her part of the scheme to help Talleha escape. All day Marjorie had worried about Talleha riding through the rugged Texas countryside. She prayed she'd encountered no danger along the way. She

153

truly hoped that by now she'd arrived at her village among people who were her friends.

Marjorie would have been utterly amazed to know that the beautiful Talleha was sitting at this very moment only a few miles away, at her old friend Emilo Cortez's dining table, captivating the attention of Señor Cortez and bewitching the handsome Victor Maurier.

Eliot Penwick would have exploded into a rage if he'd known the goddess he fantasized about was so close. Hours had been spent by him and his hired hands combing the countryside and each searching trip had yielded him no clue to her. It was as if the earth had swallowed her up, but he knew that somewhere out there the woman he yearned for was alive. He would not rest until he had her back.

Lucita was loosening Marjorie's long tresses, but she was so nervous that her fingers were awkward; they were yanking at Marjorie's hair. "Good Christ, Lucita, will you please calm yourself! I have no wish to be bald!"

"Oh, forgive me, señora—I can't help it," she sighed, forlorn. "Every time I leave this room, I'm scared to death I'll meet him and he'll question me about that night. I know it is guilt that makes me feel this way. I know what we did was right, but I fear him, señora."

Compassion flooded Marjorie and she patted the girl's hand as she remarked, "I know I asked a lot of you, Lucita. Perhaps a good night's rest will help you. You may stay with me tonight. Sleep in there on the little daybed; I know you will be fine." She referred to the bed in the adjoining sewing room just off her room, which had a door that could be left open.

She witnessed a calm settling over Lucita's attractive face. Marjorie pointed out to the Mexican girl that if Eliot dared to question the arrangement, she would

154

simply tell him she wasn't feeling well this evening.

"Oh, señora! Señora! I thank you! You have an understanding heart!" Lucita soft and gentle touch was suddenly restored. Her quiet, thoughtful air had been replaced by her usual chatterbox manner, and Marjorie welcomed it tonight.

When Marjorie's hair had been brushed and she'd changed into her lace-edged batiste nightgown, she sat there watching Lucita hang her gown in the armoire. She thought to herself that the pretty maid got little out of life except hard work. Her mood was a generous one tonight and she told her, "Lucita, help yerself to the yellow gown and wrapper in the drawer . . . you know the one I'm talking about. You may sleep in it tonight and have it to keep."

"Do you mean it, señora?" Her black eyes were wide with disbelief.

"I mean it, Lucita," Marjorie laughed lightheartedly.

Exhibiting her delight, Lucita clasped her hands together, exclaiming, "Ah, señora—señora, I appreciate this—I thank you from the bottom of my heart! I've never owned anything so beautiful!"

A pleased smile creased Marjorie's face. "Well, now you do, Lucita. I've another suggestion when you've had time to change your clothing. I think a glass of my sherry would do us both good tonight. Will you join me?"

"Ah, si—si, I will join you!"

"Good. Go get yourself comfortable, Lucita, and we will have our nightcap," Marjorie urged her maid, amused by the eagerness glowing on Lucita's face as she scurried around the room putting everything in order for the night.

Marjorie was in a strange, pensive mood this evening, and her little maid's presence in the adjoining room was consoling. It was one of the many times she'd questioned herself most severely about her fool-hardiness in marrying Eliot. No woman should be so foolish as to believe that loneliness would be swept away by marrying some man! If she thought she'd been lonely after Frank had died, it was nothing compared to the type of misery she'd endured the last several months.

The lonely period after Frank's death was tempered by sweet, cherished memories, but this new anguish had almost driven her to the brink of insanity. She did not dare tell anyone what had kept her from going over that edge; it had been a dream. It was so vivid that she'd awakened in a cold sweat, so shaken that she'd sat up in bed for hours just staring out into the night. She yearned to go to her beloved Frank, for surely he had come to her to speak the words of wisdom which were her saving grace.

In a deep voice he had cautioned her about Eliot Penwick. He'd told her, "Don't let him do this to you, sweet darling. You were foolish, but I don't hold that against you. I love you too much, my darling Margie, and I always will. What I could never forgive is if you let him destroy you and steal our land. He will, Margie—he surely will if you don't stop him!"

It was all so real to Marjorie that she vowed she'd never let that happen. "Oh, my darling Frank! You've surely saved me!" She sincerely meant it, because she suddenly felt strong, with no fear of Penwick anymore. She would outsmart him and she would win in the end, for she firmly believed that the spirit of Frank would be beside her, guiding her. If this was so, she had nothing to worry about, she consoled herself.

Amazingly, she had not been apprehensive about anything since that night. Her plots to help Talleha had gone off without a hitch, and Eliot's young nephew seemingly held her in higher esteem than he did his uncle. It was Eliot who was the frenzied one, not her!

Her private musings were put aside as Lucita came from behind the screen in her pale yellow nightgown and wrapper. Marjorie praised her loveliness and she felt a wave of sadness come over her to think that this charming girl would never in her life know anything but hard work.

She gave Lucita a warm smile and kindly requested that she now serve them some of her favorite sherry. "It will soothe your nerves too, Lucita, and I think that would be good for you tonight."

"You are right, señora." Lucita found her mistress's mood delightfully strange this evening, but it was a change Lucita welcomed.

When Lucita handed Marjorie her glass, the señora's next words were most assuring. "Lucita, remember one thing: you are my servant, not Eliot's. You were working in this household long before my husband came here. You answer to no one but me."

Lucita nodded, saying, "I shall remember, señora. I shall remember." She savored the taste of the fine sherry which had been the señora's favorite for as long as she could recall.

By the time they had finished the first glass, Lucita knew she should have no more. Besides, it had been an endless day for her; she wished the comfort of that little narrow daybed in the adjoining room. "May I do anything else for you before I retire, señora?" she asked with a weary look on her face.

"Not a thing. Just go have yourself a good night's rest, and I will do the same."

Each gave the other an understanding nod and Lucita turned to go out the door into the little sitting room. Marjorie dimmed the light by her nightstand.

Both of them enjoyed a peaceful night's sleep.

*   *   *

That peace was not to be felt by Eliot Penwick nor by his unhappy nephew, Ralph. Ralph wished now that he'd never left the shores of England. He bloody well had found no peace of mind since he'd arrived here at the ranch. Now he was convinced more than ever that his fears were justified, even though his uncle had shrugged them off. He was as fearful for his own well-being here as he had been in England. But there was another fear here at the ranch. He feared his Uncle Eliot!

He supposed he'd changed his thinking since the night he'd arrived. Looking back on the misadventure he'd been part of as a thirteen-year-old, he did not find the enchantment that Eliot or his Aunt Elaine had seemed to feel at the time. Perhaps it was his youth and their influence on him. Since he'd met the kindhearted Marjorie Greenfield and the adorable, pretty Talleha, Elaine Penwick seemed little more than an evil bastard. That poor, helpless French lady had not deserved the vile treatment by Elaine and Eliot against her and her young son.

No longer was Eliot Penwick his image of a hero. That admiration had quickly been destroyed during the days and nights under this roof. The longer he'd been here, the more his admiration had mounted for the señora.

Knowing what his uncle was capable of doing to get what he wanted, Ralph's concern had heightened lately for the señora's welfare, and this time Ralph had already made up his mind: he'd do his best to stop anything bad before it happened to the nice señora.

Was Colette' Maurier's son out there in those shadows somewhere, just biding his time, waiting to punish those who'd wronged him and his mother?

In all fairness, Ralph could not fault him as he once would have. Now, after all these thoughts, Ralph felt a quiet peace settle over him and he quickly fell asleep.

Eliot could not rid himself of a gnawing restlessness; it seemed he had been deserted by his few loyal friends like Flossie and Ralph. He'd found it utterly impossible to corner that foxy little Lucita, and he knew bloody well that that little Mexican bitch could tell him a lot, if only he could get her alone for a few minutes. He'd put such a fear in her that she'd dare not hold out on him.

There was a feeling in his gut about Señor Cortez over at the Casa del Lago; Eliot knew he'd been lying when he'd said that he'd not seen Talleha. "That Mexican bastard was lying through his teeth. Sure as hell he was," Eliot had mumbled to himself, slurring his words, for he was already drunk. Instead of his nightly ride through the woods, he'd locked himself in his study and immediately had one glass of whiskey after another, pacing up and down the room.

No one in the household had been spared his grumbling. Not even Flossie had been spared this evening. The damned nosy housekeeper had come across one of his little packets of white powder and dared to quiz him about it.

Because she caught him unprepared, while he was preoccupied, Eliot had to concoct a lie quickly. But those all-knowing eyes of Flossie's reflected that she didn't believe him for a second. She quietly walked away, but he noticed a pensive look on her round face.

Violently, Eliot flung his glass into the hearth, cussing, "Damn them all to bloody hell! I don't need any of them!"

Chapter 19

Like most young girls, Talleha had indulged in fantasy and daydreams. The handsome Victor Maurier was the perfect image of a Prince Charming, as if he'd stepped right out of one of the storybooks her mother was always reading to her.

The very gallant Emilo Cortez would have been her choice for the father she'd never known. What young lady would not have enjoyed living in such a fine home as this: a sprawling house surrounded by beautiful gardens, with walkways and stone walls and grilled iron gates.

This house was no more lavishly furnished than the Penwick estate, but it had an aura of happiness and serenity that she never found within the walls at Marjorie Greenfield Penwick's fine spacious house.

She'd felt like a princess sitting at the long walnut dining table tonight as the señor's servants served their meal, and she enjoyed the company of two such charming men. There was an air of gaiety, and all fears of any impending danger were swiftly swept aside.

She had never seen Victor dressed so magnificently: he wore rich brown pants and a white linen shirt. Around his neck he sported a brown silk kerchief.

Usually when she'd seen him, it had been in a pair of twill pants and a faded blue shirt, with a cotton kerchief at his throat. Something else she'd never noticed was the striking gold ring he wore on the little finger of his right hand. In all the times those strong hands had touched or caressed her, she'd never once seen it.

There was a very simple explanation for this: it was only this evening, as Maurier had prepared to dress for dinner, that he'd come across it rummaging through his valise. He'd packed very few articles when he'd left his ship back in Brownsville. But this little trinket meant too much to him to be left in his cabin. This was his mother's ring and a most precious, cherished possession. For some unknown reason, Victor had slipped the ring on his little finger this evening, and there it had remained after he'd dressed to go downstairs to join Emilo for a drink before dinner.

After the meal was over and the three of them went into the parlor, Emilo served them a glass of wine. She sensed that both men's moods had changed to something more serious. She decided to excuse herself graciously so they could be left alone.

She rose from her chair. "I must confess, such a delicious meal and your fine wines have made me sleepy, gentlemen. I'm sure you'll understand if I leave you two to yourselves. Señor, it was a wonderful evening!"

"Ah, niña—you made it so." Emilo rose from his chair. "This old house has not been graced by such beauty as yours since my own beloved wife died. But I can confess to you, my two young friends, that I feel her presence forever with me here. This house knew great love," he told Talleha, a mist coming to his eyes.

"I was sure of that, señor. The moment I walked through the door, a feeling I've not known since I last was in my own home was with me again." Her dark

161

eyes gleamed, and she hastily bid them both goodnight and left.

As the two men sank back down in their chairs, Señor Cortez sighed, "She's a beautiful little thing!" Maurier did not have a chance to make a reply because Emilo hastily changed the subject. He had a more pressing matter to discuss.

Wasting no time, now that Talleha was gone, Emilo turned his searching eyes toward Victor to say, "Young man, I don't think I have to tell you that you and Talleha may be my guests as long as you desire. Under no circumstances would the likes of Penwick be allowed to darken my door. But I must confess to you that I've had an insatiable curiosity about your real motives for coming here. Think of me as a nosy old man, amigo, but I think you are someone with a mission. The Casa del Lago was just a handy place to stop by."

The old fox was too devilishly clever to be lied to, Maurier knew, so he did not try. "I am here for a reason. Talleha just happened to get caught up in my plans. I—I hadn't planned on her, shall I say. But now I have to change a few things."

"Once again, I shall be the curious old man and venture to say what is on my mind. You obviously care very much for her?"

"I care. I care more than I should with what lies ahead of me. She was on her way back to her village when I happened to rescue her, and I will take her back there after I've done here what must be done."

"You seek to avenge, then?"

"I seek to avenge a horrible wrong done to me years ago—to me and my dear mother." Fire sparked in Victor's eyes. "I can't rest until the act is done."

The keen mind of Emilo was already putting the pieces of the puzzle together. "So Eliot Penwick's evil

162

touch goes back much farther than Texas, I gather? It goes back to your country—England."

Victor saw no reason to be mysterious with this kindly old gentleman who he knew would support him in any way he could. He trusted him completely, so he told Emilo everything about his reasons for being here and what he intended to do.

If he thought that Emilo would be shocked, he was in for a surprise. The fine, upstanding Cortez did not blink an eye. Instead, he remarked, "Vermin like Penwick don't deserve to live and destroy good people like Marjorie Greenfield and your own mother. Had the lovely creature upstairs not left when she did, he would surely have made her his next prey."

By the time the two of them took their last drink and concluded their conversation, there was a bond firmly binding them, and Victor was glad he had confided in Emilo. As he went forward with his personal plans, the pressure of worrying about Talleha's welfare was settled. She would be safe here with Emilo.

Should anything happen to him, Talleha would have Emilo to turn to, and he would take care of her.

That had become very important to Maurier in the last two days.

The Mexican hired hand who called himself Mondo was not trusted by anyone, and none of the other hired hands around the old Greenfield ranch cared for him. It didn't matter to Mondo that they all shied away from him. He was interested in only one thing, and that was the money he was earning here since Eliot had hired him a few weeks ago. He figured he and the smug, so-called English lord were similarly disliked on the former Greenfield spread.

For a certain amount of money, Mondo could give

Penwick information he wanted and in turn, Mondo could have the funds to buy what he wanted—tequila and a woman.

Mondo could not wait until morning came, for he was going to immediately seek out Señor Penwick; then he would strike his bargain with the Englishman. Already, Mondo was anticipating what he would be doing in the evening. There was a little cantina where he would enjoy his fill of tequila, and then he would pay whatever it would cost him to get the voluptuous Linda into bed.

It had been an obsession to have this beautiful puta from the first moment he'd seen her at the cantina in town. Oh, he knew she was a whore, but that didn't matter in the least to Mondo. A night of pleasure with that luscious body of hers was all that mattered to him.

His dreams were wonderful this night. The first rays of dawn through the narrow, curtainless window of the bunkhouse brought Mondo awake. He leaped out of his bunk while the other hired hands still lay there sound asleep. He had no use for those hombres any more than they had for him.

When he had dressed and pulled on his boots, he took the time to take a brush to his coarse thick hair, which reached all the way down to his shirt collar. He wore his sideburns long and thick as well. As he held the old broken mirror up to the light to survey himself, Mondo conceitedly thought himself handsome. He set his sombrero at just the right angle to give him the cocky look he desired.

Feeling very satisfied with himself and what he was about to do, he swaggered out of the bunkhouse. When he was outside, he pulled one of the little narrow black cigarrillos from his pocket and lit it.

Taking a deep puff, he went toward the direction of the stable, where he was certain he would spot the señor.

While he passed the time with Romano there in the stable, he shared Romano's strong black coffee, and it was only a natural thing that these two young, virile men should discuss women.

"Tell me, Romano—did you ever get that snobbish Lucita in your hayloft? The truth now!"

"She has no time for the likes of me. Lucita has her head in the clouds, don't you know? She pants only for the foreman over at the Casa del Lago. He is one tough hombre!"

"Ah, so the little chiquita likes a rough, tough hombre, eh?" Mondo smirked deviously.

"Si. I would advise you not to try to trifle with Lucita, for she is the señora's maid. The señora thinks most highly of her."

Mondo sipped on his coffee and sat thoughtfully for a moment. "Tell me, Romano—what did you think about the lady who just recently disappeared from the ranch? You must have been around her some. I'd seen her out riding a couple of times."

"Ah, Señorita Talleha—she was nice! Very nice! She loves the horses and loved to ride until Señor Penwick forbade her to go alone," Romano told him.

Mondo's black brow arched upward as he echoed Romano's remark, "Refused to allow her to ride out alone, eh? Now why would the señor do that?"

Two things encouraged the easygoing, meek stable-boy to confess to the rugged Mondo: his dislike of Eliot Penwick and his gratitude for Mondo's friendliness.

In a confidential tone, he almost whispered his suspicions to Mondo and he bent low as though he was afraid he might be overheard, "I think the Señor Penwick feels most deeply for Señorita Talleha, and so he did not wish her out of his sight. I've watched him when they have gone riding together and he cannot take his eyes off of her. You know what I mean?" Romano smiled slyly.

"Ah, si—I know, amigo." Mondo could not have been more pleased to hear this, for Penwick would be most eager to hear what he had to tell him. Great could be his reward.

While he was anticipating that reward, Mondo was pleased to see the towering figure of Eliot Penwick coming toward the stables. What a regal, arrogant figure of a man he presented in his fine-tailored attire, walking jauntily out of the gate of his walled garden and across the grounds. Mondo had mixed feelings about the man approaching him. He detested men like Eliot Penwick, but he also envied the luxuries they enjoyed.

Mondo went toward him, his arms hanging loose at his side, so that they brushed the sides of his six-shooters hanging low on his trim hips.

Eliot watched the rough-looking Mexican approaching with his sombrero cocked to the side of his head. More than once he'd questioned his wisdom in having this hombre around. He wondered if Mondo might just be a hired gunman. There was an air of recklessness and danger about him, Eliot thought. He didn't like the way the man sometimes boldly locked eyes with him. There was a certain air of contempt about him which Eliot felt could spell danger.

He was already questioning what the man had on his mind. In his sharp, crisp, accent, Eliot addressed Mondo, "'Morning, Mondo."

"Buenos dias, señor. May I have a moment of your time?"

Eliot stopped and tapped his quirt impatiently against his legs. "What is on your mind, Mondo?"

"Valuable information for you, señor, if I have it

figured right."

"Valuable? It depends, Mondo. I must ask you to be more specific."

"Information, señor—information about the beautiful señorita missing from your ranch. Am I not right?"

"That would depend also, Mondo, on how accurate the information is. Idle rumors have no value." Eliot was vexed at the attitude of this conniving Mexican.

"Ah, this is firsthand information. This I saw with my own two eyes, señor." He gave an arrogant swagger.

"And what was this?"

"What would the señor say if I told him I saw the lovely young lady and stood only a few feet from her. Would it be worth the price of a few little pleasures for Mondo, eh?"

"You actually saw Talleha?"

"I did! And I saw as well the man who is her companion."

Mondo's revelation made Eliot seethe violently, and he would have paid a very handsome price to find out the man's name. But he tried desperately to keep his emotions under control.

"And am I to assume that you can direct me to where it was you saw Talleha and this man?" Eliot asked stiffly. Already his hand was fumbling in his pocket to take out the money he figured would appease the simple Mexican.

When Mondo's eyes beheld the bounty laid across the palm of his hand, he smiled with great pleasure. "Ah, si, señor! I can take you to the secluded cabin by the lake where I saw them. It is a place back off the main trail. Only one horseman can ride along the trail of the high bluff, and few ever travel that way. But Mondo can guide you."

Eliot listened to the boasting Mondo and without

any hesitation, he challenged Mondo, "Well, what are we waiting for, Mondo? I'm ready to ride if you are."

"Si, I am too, señor!" Mondo declared, and the two of them hastily walked back toward the stable so Eliot could have Romano saddle up his thoroughbred.

As if to warn Mondo in advance, Eliot declared as they rode away from the stables together, "I shall expect to find my just reward, Mondo."

"You will, señor! You will!" Mondo was already preoccupied with what he was going to do tonight with all the money in his pocket.

Chapter 20

Eliot Penwick allowed Mondo to take the lead along the narrow dirt trail, which hugged the edges of high bluffs. The jagged boulders seemed to climb all the way up to the heavens with no peak in sight. All the time Penwick had been living here in Harrison County he'd not known about this little trail. The countryside was vast and the ranchers owned huge amounts of land; it was enough to boggle the mind. What urged him to woo and win Marjorie Greenfield were her huge holdings in property and cattle.

Until Mondo told him, Eliot did not know that he was now no longer on his wife's property but rather on the land of the Casa del Lago. Knowing this, he was thoroughly convinced that wherever Talleha was now and whoever she was with, Emilo Cortez had played a part in it. Never had Eliot been fooled about the arrogant Cortez's opinion. Cortez had always looked down his aristocratic nose at Eliot—who was he to do that to a Penwick? He—a Mexican!

He considered all Mexicans unworthy of his respect. It had always galled him that Marjorie and her friends held Cortez and a couple of other established Mexican ranchers in such high esteem. Eliot looked upon Emilo much in the same way as he did Mondo riding there ahead of him.

Mondo called back to him, "We are almost there, señor." The Mexican enjoyed the feel of the bulk of the coins in his britches. However, Mondo had already figured out that Penwick would expect him to return the money if they did not come upon the couple he'd seen, and Mondo would not do that. A job never meant that much to him, for he'd been a drifter too long. He always felt free to move on to something else.

What he had in his saddlebags were all his earthly possessions; but they were few, and so he traveled light. His one prized possession was his horse, Fierro, a possession he would fight for. He and Fierro had been everywhere and had shared many things together. No one rode Fierro but him. No one could, Mondo was sure.

The small cabin surrounded by tall weeds came into view, and Mondo pointed out to Penwick that he had watched the couple leave the lake and go into the cabin. Without any hesitation, Mondo rode up to the hitching post and leaped down off his horse. He immediately marched through the gate and plowed through the high weeds, expecting Penwick to follow him. But Eliot was squeamish about walking through the thick growth of weeds, for he had a tremendous fear of poisonous snakes, which inhabited this region heavily. Reluctantly, he sat on his thoroughbred, watching Mondo go nonchalantly to the steps of the cabin. The happy-go-lucky Mexican reached the small front porch before he suddenly realized that Eliot was not directly behind him.

"Señor? I though you were interested in finding the señorita and the man who was with her." A puzzled look crossed his face.

"Obviously, Mondo, they are not here. You surely

saw ghosts," Eliot snapped arrogantly.

Mondo's rugged face showed his displeasure. He turned his back on Penwick and marched into the cabin. But when he came back out, there was an air of smug assurance about him as he flung an article of flimsy material like a lasso around his head. He gave a roar of laughter, "See, Señor Penwick—I was telling you the truth, and here is the evidence. I found the señorita's stocking."

Jauntily, Mondo waded back through the weeds with Talleha's stocking. When Eliot took it in his hand, he could not doubt Mondo; that stocking had graced the shapely leg of the luscious Talleha. Who was the bastard she'd spent the last two days and nights with? There had to have been some well-planned scheme to all this, for she was not all this smart, Eliot reasoned.

The lovely creature who'd so captured his heart and driven him to the edge of madness in a few short weeks was not an experienced young lady. Oh, no, there was a man at the bottom of all this. There was a man whose yearnings for her were as overpowering and consuming as his own. He had to find out just who this man was if he was to get Talleha back.

There was a strange glint in Penwick's eyes; he stared thoughtfully and his silence was eerie. Mondo thought to himself that there was a certain madness in this Englishman he neither understood nor wished to confront.

In that happy-go-lucky way of his, Mondo pointed out to Eliot Penwick, "You see, Señor Penwick— Mondo did not lie to you."

Eliot gave him an offhanded shrug. "You did not lie, Mondo, but neither has your information given me what I want. There is no sign of the girl here, so what have I to show for my ride out here or the money I've given to you?"

"You have exactly what I promised for the money you paid me, Señor Penwick. I could not know whether the señorita would still be here. I only told you where I had seen her." Mondo's dark eyes measured the Englishman cautiously. His husky body was now tensed to spring into action like a mountain lion if he must. He was leery of this man, and his eyes danced busily to assure himself where Penwick's hands were and what they were about.

It was rumored that Penwick carried small pocket pistols instead of the six-shooters worn by most Texans. Mondo was not about to play it stupid with this tricky foreigner. Whether it was a Mexican, an Anglo, or an Ingles, like Penwick, Mondo knew this type of hombre and he knew how treacherous such a man could be. Mondo had no intention of being shot or stabbed in the back.

But Eliot surprised him when he broke into a slow, easy grin and gave Mondo a nod of his head saying, "Yes, you are right. I did admit that, Mondo. Oh, well, let us just say it didn't work out, eh? You go on back to the ranch. I've another direction to travel."

There was a quiet expression on Mondo's face, but his mind was working furiously. It did not appeal to him to rein his horse around to ride off in an opposite direction, leaving his back facing Eliot Penwick.

Warily, Mondo veered his horse around to leave the cabin as Eliot sat there making no effort to be on his way.

More than once Mondo gave a backward glance as he spurred his horse into motion. It was only when he was moving around the sharp bend of the narrow trail at the side of the bluff that he began to breathe easier. He was not afraid of the Englishman face to face; but he did not like presenting his back as a target.

Mondo did not ride in the direction of the ranch, nor

172

had he intended to. It was in the opposite direction that he reined the horse. Mondo had been struck by something while he was talking to Penwick. So it was in the direction of the Casa del Lago he rode. It was the owner he planned to seek out.

He knew Emilo Cortez was considered a man of great honor and influence in these parts. The cabin was most assuredly on Casa del Lago land, and Mondo figured that perhaps the señor would be grateful for the information he could pass on to him about the strange happenings going on there. Mondo rode along with a sly grin on his rugged face, thinking about his scheme to ingratiate himself with Emilo Cortez.

With the money he had in his pocket and any reward he might receive from Cortez, he would not have to worry about working for a week or two. Mondo was not one to worry about the future, anyway. A day at a time was enough to think about.

Brad Castillo noticed the billowing cloud of dust rising up from the approach to the ranch long before he saw a rider. Castillo, Emilo's foreman, wondered who it was coming at such a gallop, so he lingered there in the doorway of the barn.

He was a man with a robust body, six feet, four inches tall, so he had to bend down to go through a side door into the bridle shed.

Something about the rider looked familiar as he came closer, but it was the magnificent horse which jogged the foreman's memory as to who the rider was. It had to be the new hombre just recently hired over at the Greenfield ranch. (Like most of the people in the region, he'd never considered it Penwick land.)

What could he want, Castillo wondered? But then he saw Señor Cortez and his guest, Maurier, leaving the house to go toward the hitching post where the rider had halted.

Castillo continued to watch as Cortez conversed with the one called Mondo. Castillo was no more curious than Victor Maurier, who stood silently as Cortez greeted Mondo. Maurier's nostrils flared as though he smelled a foul, fetid odor. He observed the rugged Mondo, whose manner was crude and cocky. It was instant dislike on Maurier's part.

"Good day, Señor Cortez. I am Mondo—Señor Penwick's new man. I may have some information you'd like to have." Mondo spoke hesitatingly. The piercing, measuring blue eyes of the man standing beside the elder señor had rattled him. Maurier looked like a cat ready to spring at the slightest provocation, and though few men ever intimidated the tough Mexican, this man was a force Mondo did not wish to contend with.

The dignified Emilo quizzed, "Information? What kind of information?"

"Señor—would you allow me to speak to you—in private?" Mondo found himself stammering. Actually, he wished he'd buried this little idea and made straight for the cantina instead.

Emilo's eyes darted to Maurier and then back to Mondo. "Would you excuse me for a moment, Victor?"

Maurier gave him a nod and turned sharply to walk away. When the towering figure was at a safe distance, Mondo leaped down from his horse and flung off his sombrero, letting his fingers run through his thick black hair.

His dark face reflected a humble expression as he remarked, "I am just a simple man, señor. You understand that I betray my patron to tell you this. But all of the people praise Señor Cortez, and I am

174

Mexican, too; so I have been urged to seek you out."

By now Emilo was becoming impatient; he measured the man with a slight distaste, as Maurier had. "I appreciate your kind sentiments, Mondo. But I'd be curious to know just what information is of my concern."

"Well—I thought maybe it would be worth something to you to know what was going on behind your back here on your property," Mondo said, apprehensive about asking bluntly for his reward.

"So you are selling this information?"

Mondo bowed his head as though he was ashamed and apologized, "Well, after I tell you this, I must get out of here, as you can understand. I'd need a little just to keep me until I can hire on somewhere else."

"I see," Emilo said, masking his amusement. He pulled out a couple of gold coins he had loose in his pocket and inquired of Mondo if that would buy the information. The threat of that blue-eyed devil only a short distance away urged Mondo not to quibble, and he began to tell Emilo about Eliot taking the liberty of searching the cabin for Talleha.

"Since it is on your land, I thought you should know that Penwick was there doing as he pleased without your permission." His revelation did not seem to bring any shocked response from Señor Cortez.

Calmly, Emilo inquired, "He is doing no damage to my property, is he? Just looking around?"

"Si, Señor—just searching the place. It seemed there was evidence that the young lady had been there but had left. Señor Penwick is like a raging bull because there was a man with her. He did not like that—not at all!"

"What you've told me, Mondo, is most interesting, but really none of my concern. I appreciate you thinking it might be, and it was well worth the price.

Good luck, Mondo." Emilo dismissed him by slowly turning to go in the direction Maurier had taken earlier.

Mondo was more than ready to mount his horse and make a hasty departure. He reminded himself that his greed could have put him in a dangerous position. There could be no more señoritas to bed and none of his favorite tequila to drink and it was not worth chancing that.

Chapter 21

"Amigo, over here," Emilo called out to his young friend wandering over by the courtyard wall surrounding his house. Victor acknowledged Emilo by throwing up his hand to wave. Immediately Victor started to walk toward Emilo, for he could not deny he was curious about what the Mexican had had to say to Cortez. While he'd waited for Emilo to speak with the man, Victor had tried to discern why he'd taken an instant dislike to a man he'd never seen before. But perhaps he had seen him before. He wondered where, but the answer remained in shadow.

Señor Cortez waited for Victor with an amused look on his face. He gave out a lighthearted laugh. "It seems Mondo's 'information' was of no real importance. Penwick had obviously found the cabin where you and Talleha took refuge the first night. I gave him enough money to make him happy and he went on his way. There are so many Mondos roaming the countryside. He is the typical drifter. They migrate from ranch to ranch with no ambition but to keep from starving, and in the end they usually end up in a gun fight because they've drunk too much liquor in some cantina."

Maurier smiled, reminded of some of the reckless

177

crewhands aboard his schooner, *Destiny*. He could always expect to lose two or three of his men when they made port. They'd go into the city with their pay from many weeks at sea and he'd never see them again.

Maurier laughed huskily as he related all this to Emilo. "I guess it is the same everywhere, eh, señor?"

"It must be." Emilo responded. The more time they shared, the more he liked Victor Maurier.

The Mexican's news was not earthshaking, but it told Victor just how determined Eliot Penwick was in searching for Talleha and how much he would do to get her back. Victor had no time to lose; he must finish his business so he could take Talleha and leave.

Besides, there was another pressing matter, and that was the grave condition of Captain Crawford's health. He wanted to get back to Brownsville before it was too late.

These thoughts weighed heavily on Victor. All Emilo had to do was to look at the young man's handsome face to know he was deep in thought.

Señor Cortez made it easy for Victor to part company with him. "I've got a couple of matters to discuss with Castillo about my herd grazing over on the north section. Ah, amigo—I tell you, there is no day of rest when you have this much land and cattle. There are times when you ask yourself if it is all worth it."

"Please, señor—you don't have to explain to me. I've been here long enough to appreciate what you're talking about. This state of yours amazes me more and more as I learn about it and the people here."

"Ah, I find your statement interesting, my young friend. Perhaps someday you will decide to become a Texan yourself."

"Who can say, señor? Six months ago I would never have imagined myself here as I am now. Things can change so quickly."

"Ah, it is true, Victor. Now, I must attend to my life and I shall let you attend to yours. I hope I will have the pleasure of your company at lunchtime—and our lovely little Talleha."

"You shall, sir," Maurier assured him.

Cortez took his leave and Maurier turned to go back to the house. The mention of Talleha urged Maurier to see about her. However, it was a peaceful feeling to know that here at the Casa del Lago she would be safe.

On his way to the house, Maurier made a hasty decision. Tonight, he'd settle the overdue score with Penwick. There was no reason to delay it any longer.

His boot heels made a sharp, clicking sound as he moved across the tiled hallway. He heard the soft laughter of Talleha's voice as he moved toward the sala, as Emilo called it. Maurier halted, deciding to go into the parlor to see just who was amusing his lovely lady so much.

Two giant palms in massive pots of clay on either side of the archway blocked his view. But he strained to see who it was through the dense foliage.

There was no mistaking the luscious curves of Talleha as she sat in the rich gold brocade chair, and he watched as she poured coffee for herself and the mysterious individual opposite. She did it with style and grace. She looked absolutely glowing this morning. She'd pulled her hair back and secured it with combs, and curling wisps tickled her ears. Her simple little sprigged muslin frock of deep blue with its dainty yellow flowers molded the sensuous curves of her body alluringly.

What a devastating challenge she was to a man! Victor stood there now and a part of him saw her as a darling, innocent child. But all his eyes had to do was dance up and down the tantalizing curves of her body to know she was all woman—a woman of passion!

179

He was fired with an overwhelming desire to make love to her. He wanted to kiss those sweet honey lips and let his tongue tease and taunt them. He liked the way he felt her sudden response when he did this. His hand wanted suddenly to touch the tips of her breasts so he could feel the instant hardening of them and the surge of her soft, supple body. He loved the simple, natural child–woman Talleha was. There was nothing false about her. She had obviously never played the stupid games of the sophisticated ladies he'd known before. He never wanted her to change. God forbid it!

He loved the way they made love. He gave himself to her and she took him eagerly. That, Maurier considered, was how it should be, but he never expected to find this perfection in a woman until he met Talleha.

All these romantic musings were quickly washed away when a deep voice, thickly accented, broke the stillness. He knew there was a man sitting opposite Talleha in the room.

He strained to see who it was who had the woman he loved so fascinated and amused.

Maurier's broad shoulders were leaning so far into the room as he strained to see that he almost lost his balance. The huge palm could not stand the force of his strong body and swayed. Utterly embarrassed, he grabbed it to keep it from falling. All this commotion drew Talleha's attention.

She saw it was he. She gave out a pleasant laugh and greeted him, "Victor! Come join us." Her dainty hands motioned to him.

Maurier felt like a stupid oaf as he steadied the huge, seven-foot palm, and he instantly caught sight of a striking looking Mexican sitting there with amusement in his dark eyes.

"Victor, this is Estaban. Estaban Cortez—Señor Cortez's nephew. He just arrived. Señor Cortez does

180

not know yet," she told Maurier, who was now slowly walking toward them.

Maurier's eyes appraised the handsome man, who was about his own age. "Victor Maurier, señor. Nice to meet you."

"My pleasure, Señor Maurier."

Maurier denoted that particular polished charm about Estaban Cortez which marked him as a lady's man. He found himself instantly flooded with a consuming jealousy. His fists itched to sock that handsome, swarthy face, which wore a winning smile.

He was damned glad he'd come to Talleha's side when he had. Resentment flared in him that she'd been so lightheartedly gay and seemed so enchanted by Emilo's nephew. He realized more than ever just how vulnerable she was to Estaban—or any man, for that matter.

Excited and wide-eyed, Talleha exclaimed, "Oh, Victor—Estaban was just telling me about his trip to Europe. He's been everywhere—England, France, and Spain."

Maurier was hardly impressed; he'd been to all those places and many others as well. It occurred to him that he had not revealed much about his life to the beautiful Talleha. His time with her had been spent making love to her, not talking.

His bright blue eyes turned to Estaban. "Those countries have some nice ports. I've hit a few of them. I'm a seaman actually, señor, not a man of the land. Did you enjoy your crossing?"

"Ah, most exciting! Most exciting, indeed!" Estaban's pleasant, smiling face did not change expression at all, but his insides bristled with indignation at this man interfering in his pleasant interlude with the lovely lady.

He wondered who this Maurier was. A seaman, he'd

called himself. For the life of him, he could not fathom what would bring a seaman to the Casa del Lago and his wealthy Uncle Emilo.

Each man was very preoccupied measuring the other up, but the naive Talleha was not aware of this.

Estaban had not come to the Casa del Lago just for a pleasant visit, and he'd certainly not come to the ranch because he felt any great devotion to Emilo. He came because his mother had insisted on it. It was about time he start ingratiating himself with his uncle, his mother had pointed out. If he didn't, he stood to lose a fortune.

His trip to Europe had been costly, and his mother was very displeased with Estaban. He'd failed to win the hand of the lovely Marcella Valdez, daughter of some dear friends of hers. His mother had been certain that her charming son would be accepted by the Valdez family and sweep Marcella off her feet. That did not happen, so Estaban's visit in Spain with his mother's old friends was curtailed when he saw that the family was not enchanted by him. To pursue his courtship of Marcella any longer would have been futile. It was obvious that Señor and Señora Valdez had someone else in mind for their future son-in-law.

Emilo's sister, Ernestina, was furious when her son returned home bearing this insulting news, for the price of such a trip had been a devastating blow to her shrinking bank account. That was why she'd told Estaban in no uncertain terms what he must do unless he wanted to change his lavish way of living.

As he traveled to the Casa del Lago, Estaban considered various schemes he might try out on his uncle. He decided on a sad tale he might use to enrich his funds for a few hundred dollars before he left the ranch to return home.

Even as curiosity about Estaban gnawed at him, Maurier was burning about this gorgeous creature,

Talleha. She was as rare as her name. When he'd quizzed her about a last name, she'd looked blankly at him with no reply for a moment. "Just Talleha," she'd told him with a sweet smile on her face.

It had not been Victor's plan to sit there in the sala making idle chatter with a man who he felt was wasting his valuable time, but he was damned if he was going to leave Talleha there alone with Estaban. Yet he did not absorb anything the other two said.

Twice Talleha had jarred his attention by repeating a comment she'd made to him. "You are awfully preoccupied this morning, Victor," she taunted.

"You are right, Talleha. I am," he told her quite honestly. She noticed a tone of seriousness in his voice. He knew she was wondering what was wrong with him, for he saw the way her fine brow arched. His mercurial mood was swept aside by the appearance of Señor Cortez.

Victor welcomed the sight of the señor because he did not have to delay his own plans any longer. Once Emilo had joined the group, Maurier made his move by saying, "Talleha, shall we excuse ourselves so Señor Cortez and Estaban can visit?"

Talleha mumbled, "Oh—oh, yes." She rose up from her chair slowly to go to Victor's side.

"But it is not necessary," Emilo graciously remarked.

Estaban echoed his uncle's sentiments, but Victor quickly made a point of insisting that they would join them later. "Besides, I have some matters to discuss with Talleha. Shall we go, my dear?" He took on a most possessive air with her which Estaban was quick to note. He planned to make a point of asking his uncle about this unusual couple when they had a moment of privacy.

Estaban watched the two as they left the room. Maurier's hand held her dainty arm in a most

183

protective way. It was tantalizing to watch the graceful sway of her body as they walked through the archway of the sala. His black eyes happened to glance over at his uncle and he realized that that old fool was enjoying the sight of the young lady just as he was. Latin men seemed to appreciate the sight of a beautiful woman, regardless of their age.

There was something about the silence in the room that made Victor sense that both men were staring at them. Emilo's admiring glances did not disturb him, but Estaban's bothered him tremendously. It urged him more to get his business in Harrison County finished so that he could take Talleha and leave.

More than ever he decided that tonight he would take care of Eliot Penwick once and for all. That nightly ride he always took after the evening meal would be the perfect time.

The gentle-natured Talleha would have been shocked if she'd known the thoughts rushing through the mind of the man she loved.

But Victor Maurier would have been just as surprised had he been able to read Talleha's devious thoughts.

It had pleased her to see jealousy in those blue eyes of his.

Chapter 22

The green-flowered muslin of her full skirt swished back and forth as she tried to keep up with Maurier. Her sensuous lips curled with a smile. He really did care for her in the extent that he wanted no other man occupying her time or her thoughts, she knew. Happiness flooded her, for she wanted desperately to keep his love.

More than that, she wanted him to claim her as his own—his wife. But he had not offered her this yet. What did the future hold for them, Talleha had asked herself when she'd ridden away from the Penwick house and into the arms of Victor. In a few brief moments her plans had suddenly changed. She'd known where her destination was until then, but now she wondered if she truly wanted to return to her village, if it meant parting with him.

A strange confusion had nagged at her the last day. Maurier had said he'd take her home as soon as he finished his business here in Harrison County. But then where would he be going?

Victor slowed his pace now that they had reached the cool hallway and turned to glance down at her. He grinned as he noticed she was almost breathless from walking so fast. Her thick black lashes fluttered as she broke into a sigh, "Well, thank God! Where are we rushing to so fast?"

"I'm sorry! I forgot that your shapely legs aren't as long as mine."

"No, they're not! But you've still not answered my questions. Where are we going? I believe you told the señor you had something to discuss with me?" She thought to herself that his real objective was to get her away from the devilishly good-looking nephew of Emilo's. She could not deny that he had a magnetic charm, and he made no effort to hide the fact that he found her very appealing, too. Talleha could not deny that this was flattering.

He hardly knew how to answer her question other than to tell her the truth—that he merely wanted to be alone with her. When she got no immediate reply from him, she posed her question again.

"Just wanted a little time with you alone." He bent down to kiss the tip of her pert little nose. "I'm rather fond of you, in case you've not guessed it."

Her black eyes gleamed like polished onyx, and she put on the air of a flirting coquette, something Maurier had not observed before. Softly, she purred, "Are you truly fond of me, Victor?"

His eyes danced slowly over her upturned face and his thick dark brow arched as he tried to figure out what this little vixen was up to. But he could not accept that she was using womanly wiles on him—not Talleha! She was too unworldly for that kind of trick.

"You know I adore you, you little imp. I've rarely had you off my mind since that first day we met. Remember when my fish got away?" he laughed.

"I remember."

"So you don't have to ask me that again, do you?"

"No, but I've other questions to ask you." There was

something in the tone of her voice he'd not heard before. This was a different, new Talleha, and he wondered what had made her change.

The look on that lovely face told him nothing, for it was the same. He could not put his finger on the unknown thing he sensed about her, but he knew it was there.

"So, what is your other question, my lady? You have only to ask and I'll try to grant your wish," he said, giving her a broad grin.

She pouted, declaring, "I am serious, Victor. I'm not the child you seem to think I am. I—I merely intended to ask you what your plans were after you leave Texas—and me back in Cedar Springs."

For one brief moment Victor found himself in a quandary. He'd actually not considered the time after he would leave her back in her village. He found his words slightly painful to say: "I suppose I'll return to my schooner down in Brownsville and spend some time with Captain Crawford before I set sail."

The two of them wandered down the long hallway aimlessly and now entered the garden courtyard. Neither had planned their destination. It had just happened that way, as had so many things with them.

A delicate spray carried by a gentle breeze caressed their faces as they stood there. Neither had been aware that Victor's hand was no longer holding her arm, but his tanned hand now clasped her tiny one.

"You love your ship and the sea, don't you?"

"Yes, I do."

She had only to look up at his face to see the passion there. She would have much to compete with—the sea was an all-consuming mistress. After all, she was a girl from the backwoods who'd never been anywhere outside her small village until she was taken away from that village to end up at the ranch of Eliot Penwick.

Such a girl could hardly expect to hold the interest of a man of the world like Victor Maurier. She'd allowed herself to dwell in the whimsy and daydreams of a silly young girl.

Standing beside him now by the fountain, she stole a fleeting glance up at his tanned face. She realized suddenly how much more experienced and worldly he had to be. Here was a man she'd made passionate love to not once but twice, and at this moment she felt suddenly ill-at-ease.

She could not even fault him for lying to her. He'd told her he was fond of her, and he'd told her he wanted her in a fever of desire, but that was not a man telling a woman he wanted to marry her or spend the rest of his life with her. She'd only wished that was the way it was.

Maurier noticed a reserve about her. Their hands still touched, but he could not feel the sweet warmth of her nearness.

"Why, Talleha—why did you ask me about my plans?"

She tried to sound flippant, but Maurier knew she was putting on an act. This was not like Talleha. Her voice did not ring with her usual honesty as she quipped, "Just my awful curiosity, I guess."

He felt a slight impatience. He had no time for games. He turned her around to face him and his bright blue eyes prodded her to be honest with him as he demanded, "Come now, Talleha—we've always shot square with each other. From the first, we wasted no time with silly pretenses. I've admired this about you."

Under her breath, she thought to herself that perhaps he hadn't ever pretended, but she *had* entertained all kinds of romantic imaginings. She wanted to scream out at him and demand of him just how fond of her he really was—fond enough to marry her and make her his wife? He'd bedded her eagerly enough—would he marry her as willingly? But there was a tremendous pride in Talleha, for Dawn had taught her that. Dawn had also taught her a certain brand of independence which would never have allowed her to ask Maurier such a question.

So when she replied to him, she discreetly lied, "I did not know I was not playing honest with you, Victor. As you say, I've always been honest with you. I—I guess as eager as I am to return to my home, I shall miss you, Victor, when you depart." Just saying the words made her have to fight back the tears.

It was rare for the self-assured Maurier to be rendered speechless, but he was; her sentiments were his. As insane as it might seem, he'd never really acknowledged to himself that at some point he'd be departing from her. Whether she knew it or not, she could not have made a shrewder move: it set his mind to thinking about such a time.

The choices were obvious. He could leave her behind in the village of Cedar Springs to resume his life as a bachelor. His other choice was to take her with him to Brownsville once he'd taken care of Eliot Penwick. When the sails of his schooner, *Destiny,* unfurled, and the ship at last plowed through the waters of the Gulf, she would be there at the railing by his side.

In that brief span of time, he privately envisioned her aboard the schooner and the two of them sailing to the islands of paradise in the Caribbean. Oh, he'd seen many places as he'd made port in the various islands, but how different it would be with his beautiful Talleha by his side, sharing the days and nights with him! But how would a woman's presence aboard his ship fare with his crew?

Next, he weighed how hard it was going to be for him to take her to her home back in that little village and tell her goodbye. The thought of that stabbed at him like a

189

sharp pain.

Now was not the time to make such an important decision, he concluded. Other things weighed too heavily on his mind. There was a long-overdue obligation he owed his mother. Until that was done with, he could make no plans for himself and Talleha.

There was a strange mood about Maurier, Talleha felt as she stole little glances in his direction. The only truthful answer he could give her was that he didn't know just when he would depart to go his own way. There was a hint of pleading in his deep husky voice as he suggested to her, "Talleha, my darling, let us just enjoy each day as it comes our way. Can you accept that for now?"

"I really haven't too many choices, have I?"

There was something about her manner which disappointed him. He would have expected her to accept his terms more readily. It was as if she were suddenly disillusioned by him, as if someone else had taken his place in her heart. So it was only natural that his thoughts turned toward the good-looking Estaban.

Manly pride prompted him to say, "Talleha, you have all kinds of choices to make. You're young and beautiful. Any man would have to be a fool not to recognize that. I won't try to deny that you've been a fever in my blood for weeks now."

For a man like Victor Maurier to admit that would have been enough for most women, but it wasn't enough for Talleha. She interpreted his declaration as a release of any claim on her, and this perplexed and disturbed her. Most of all, she felt devastation and pain.

The arrogance inherited from a French father she'd never known made itself clear as she told Maurier, "You are right, Victor. I have a choice to make, and soon. My mother always told me a fever meant you were sick. So if I've been a fever in your blood all these weeks, I should relieve you of that so you can be well again. Is that not true?" She whirled around so quickly that he did not have time to react, nor did she wish him to, for her tears were flowing now like a raging river.

When he did regain his composure, he mumbled to himself, "Now what the bloody hell did I say to bring that on?"

He watched her rustling green frock sweeping across the thick grass of the courtyard. Her jet black curls bounced up and down over her shoulders. What he could not see was her tear-streaked face as she rushed away from him. It would have broken his heart had he thought for a minute that she was assuming he did not care for her. He did care. He cared very much.

He stood there feeling utterly helpless—something he'd never experienced before with any woman. What was it about this slip of a girl that could stir up so much emotion in him? He wished to hell he could figure it out.

Women were a perplexing lot, he thought to himself, and this little savage had to be the worst of any it had been his misfortune to meet. Of all the times in his life, why did it have to be now?

Neither the courtyard garden nor the cooling spray of mist from the fountain held any fascination for him now, so he turned to go back into the house. He had no inkling that he was being observed by a most curious pair of black eyes behind the heavy velvet drapery in the dining room.

Estaban had witnessed what he considered a lover's quarrel, and he was conceited enough to think that he may have caused it as he watched the feisty little Talleha march away in a huff. If he was any judge of women, and he was sure he was, the lovely Talleha had left Maurier in a fit of pique.

This pleased Estaban, for he planned to be a distracting force where the gorgeous Talleha was concerned. He'd never expected to find such a delectable woman under his uncle's roof. She was worth the long journey here to the Casa del Lago. In fact, his spirits were heightened by the sight of her.

Now that he'd had his brief, boring chat with Uncle Emilo, he was encouraged. His uncle seemed to be in the best of moods, and Estaban wondered if Talleha's presence might be the reason for that. He usually found his uncle to be overly solemn. Such was not the case this afternoon.

He had received a cordial and gracious reception from Emilo, and this was not always the case in the past. He was tremendously encouraged that this trip to the Casa del Lago would be rewarding. His mother would be pleased with him again, and any disappointment about his failure in Spain would be washed away.

Somehow, he credited the petite, black-haired Talleha with all of it. The young girl with her strange name might just prove to be his good luck charm.

Under his breath, he sighed, "Ah, Talleha—I bless you!"

Chapter 23

There was an air of gaiety flowing through the spacious Casa del Lago this evening. Emilo had not felt so lighthearted in a long time. Perhaps it was this that had prompted him so generously to offer Talleha one of his wife's many gowns stored away all this time, for her to wear and enjoy this evening.

When the Mexican servant delivered the gown to Talleha's room, she was utterly speechless. Never had she seen material so exquisite; she was almost afraid to touch it. The lovely blue-green shade immediately reminded Talleha of a robin's egg she'd once found as a child.

When she was finally dressed and descending the long stairway, she felt like a princess out of one of the fairytales Dawn had read to her as a child.

The deep cut of the squared neckline was most alluring on Talleha with her firm, rounded breasts. There had to be at least ten yards of material in the flowing skirt of the gown. The bodice was tight-fitted, and the double-ruffled sleeves were edged in ecru lace. She needed no jewelry or hair ornaments to make her look like a vision of loveliness.

193

Emilo had only to take one look at her radiant beauty to know that he'd made the right decision in letting the pretty young lady wear his beloved wife's gown. Somehow, he felt his wife would have approved of her wearing it.

He'd taken her tiny hand in his and insisted that she turn in a circle so he might survey the full impact of this enchanting image. He told her his thoughts. "Only you, Talleha, could have had my wife's approval; but I know she would have wanted you to enjoy the gown. Somehow, I feel you are as special as she was."

When Estaban entered the room, he did not know that it was his aunt's gown the lovely black-haired señorita had on. But he did know she was the most tantalizing creature his eyes had ever beheld. He lavishly complimented her, and he made no effort to hide the way she effected him. She would have had to be blind not to see the flaming desire in his dark eyes.

It was only then that consternation began to stir in Señor Cortez. A beautiful señorita like Talleha could prove to be a tantalizing temptress for two randy young men like Estaban and Victor.

At least he could breathe easy, he told himself, until Victor made an appearance. Then he would worry about what this evening would hold. For now, he did not concern himself about Estaban playing the role of the gay caballero, and he had to applaud the handsome rascal: he did have a winning way about him.

Talleha's lighthearted laughter rang out as Estaban told her a funny story while they sipped their wine. She seemed to be completely entranced by Emilo's nephew.

For one brief moment, Victor's towering figure in the doorway went unnoticed. He stood with his legs slightly apart, and the black pants he wore seemed strained by the firm muscles of his thighs. His black silk

194

shirt was opened at the neck; it was a gift he'd purchased on his last trip to the Orient. It was soft and light, and Victor found it comfortable for this warm, late summer evening.

Victor had never had much time to worry about fine attire, since most of his time was spent aboard his schooner and practical clothing was what he found more to his liking. But he'd suspected that dandy, Estaban, would be impeccable and most debonair tonight, and he did not want to look inferior in comparison.

For all the extra effort he had put forth, he stood there now feeling like he scored low against the dashing, expensively attired Estaban. The woman he loved was obviously hypnotized by the handsome nephew, and this left a foul taste in his mouth.

He entered the room with an arrogant swagger. He greeted Emilo with warmth, but when Talleha's eager eyes turned toward him, she found him cool and indifferent. He gave Estaban a brief, nonchalant nod.

Emilo found himself watching a drama unfold during the next hour around his elegant dining table, and the actors were Estaban, Victor, and Talleha. He was reminded of a play he'd gone to see at a theater in San Antonio on his last trip there. For a while he watched the trio with amusement, thinking how marvelous it would be to be young again.

Seeing Talleha and Victor together here in his home with their love glowing in their eyes had made him feel a certain loneliness. Tonight he had witnessed that lovely young lady taunting her young man by giving so much of her attention to another. When it continued through the dinner hour, Emilo found the incident disturbing, and he questioned what the little señorita was up to.

Victor's face was tense and his mouth was tight-lipped. He looked like a thunderhead ready to erupt.

Emilo decided that it was time he played a role in this little drama. His sharp, astute mind had thought up a way he might break up the absorbing conversation Estaban was having with Talleha. But the señor never got to carry out his intentions, for Victor made his own move.

Rising up from his chair to tower over the others sitting there, Victor directed his word to Emilo alone, "I must excuse myself from this—this festive gathering, señor. Please accept my apology." By this time his back was turned on Talleha and Estaban, and by the time she turned back to stare at Victor, all she viewed was the broad shoulders which seemed to ripple in the black silk shirt and the jaunty motion of his trim, firm hips molded in the black pants.

A sickening anguish welled up in her, and she wasn't at all pleased with herself. She'd been haughty and spiteful toward him because he had hurt her. Now that she'd hurt him, it give her no satisfaction or pleasure.

She arched her fine brow and bit her lip, enormously regretting her performance all evening. What she'd really yearned for was for him to have told her how pretty she looked in her robin's-egg-blue gown. What she really hungered for was the kiss of his sensuous lips.

How he must despise her now! The one time she'd allowed her eyes to look into his, she thought she sensed contempt. It had spurred her to be more receptive to Estaban's constant attention.

Emilo had only to look on Talleha's distraught face to know she was experiencing the pangs of love's confusion. She was paying the price for all her flaunting and teasing. He knew that his nephew had been used to serve her purpose to make Maurier

196

jealous—for what reason, the señor could not know.

Whatever the problem between Talleha and Victor, Emilo knew that time would take care of things, for he was certain they cared very much for each other. He could see it in their eyes. Emilo had a theory that the mouth could utter false words, but the eyes did not lie. More than once, he'd listened to a man lie only to have his eyes betray him. The eyes were the mirror of a man's soul.

Estaban kept up his glib chatter with Talleha, but Señor Cortez watched her pensive face. Her laughter was now tediously forced. Her thoughts had wandered off to follow Victor wherever he might be.

It amused Emilo that his rather conceited nephew was so enamored of himself that he did not even sense that the young girl was not in the least interested in his conversation.

When he invited her to join him in an early horseback ride over his uncle's land, Talleha mumbled, "Oh, yes—yes, Estaban, I'll join you."

Señor Cortez would have wagered she did not know what Estaban had requested of her from that faraway look in her eyes.

When the señor finally rose up from the table and the other two followed his move to leave the dining room, Talleha quickly took the opportunity to excuse herself. Emilo could hardly refrain from laughter, for Estaban looked utterly crestfallen.

"Come on, young man—it is not the end of the world. Besides, you and I can sip a little brandy and play a game of chess. You can show me you are as clever as my sister is always boasting you are," Emilo playfully jested.

Reluctantly, Estaban followed his uncle, a disgruntled look on his handsome face.

*   *   *

Long ago, the dining room over at the old Greenfield ranch had been deserted and darkened. Flossie had cleared away all the dishes and left one of the Mexican servant girls in the kitchen to attend to the washing of the dishes and pots so her kitchen would be ready to begin the morning meal when she got there.

Eliot sequestered himself in his study, shutting and locking the door behind him. This was now the fourth night he'd not gone for his usual nightly ride through the forest of pines.

Marjorie invited Ralph to join her on the cool veranda. "It should be very pleasant out there with the light breeze stirring. You might as well, because that's all you'll see of your Uncle Eliot tonight."

Ralph understood what she meant. He had nothing better to do and he certainly wasn't ready to retire.

They strolled down the hall to go to the east veranda, and along the way they encountered Lucita rushing toward them. Poor Lucita, she seemed always to be going in a trot lately, Marjorie thought.

She instructed her maid, "Fold down my bed, Lucita, and lay out my gown and robe. Oh, yes—please bring me a breakfast tray as usual in the morning."

"Si, señora—anything else?"

"Yes, you may go on to bed when you've done that, to get yourself some rest."

This house was awash with a sickness, it seemed to the young Englishman. Flossie seemed cranky and out of sorts. Lucita, feisty when he first saw her, now seemed tense. Eliot drank himself into a stupor every night. Of all of them, Señora Marjorie seemed more lively and gay than she had that first night at her dining table.

198

They went through the French double doors out onto the dark veranda to take a seat on white wicker chairs. A most wonderful scent of blooming flowers wafted across the veranda. Moonbeams dappled the leaves as the mass of clouds moved off to block out the light of the full moon.

He was glad he'd accepted an invitation to join her out there. Ralph found her an easy person to talk to. They talked about the land and the cattle. Of course, Ralph finally had to tell her how much he admired the handsome thoroughbred his uncle rode all the time. "I've never seen a more magnificent beast," he declared.

"Nor I, when I purchased it shortly after Eliot and I were married. It was my gift to him. That devil's probably kicking up his heels to be ridden. Why don't you take him for a ride, Ralph? Eliot doesn't even have to know."

An apprehensive frown crossed Ralph's face. "I can't deny I'd enjoy that very much, but Uncle Eliot would violently disapprove of it."

"Then we'll let Eliot deal with me." She gave out a soft laugh.

"But I would not want you getting in trouble over me either, Señora Marjorie. You've been too nice to me."

"Go on, young man—enjoy yourself! You're only young once," she urged him.

A broad, excited grin broke on Ralph's face, and he jumped up to give her a hasty farewell before rushing out to the barn.

Marjorie sat alone and a devious smile etched her face. To the darkness surrounding her she declared with tremendous gratification, using Eliot's favorite figure of speech, "I'm still the bloody boss around here, Eliot Penwick—like it or not! This is Greenfield land

and always it shall be. You'll not get your bloody English hands on it!"

Alone in the darkness, she made plans for the future. Suddenly, she realized she had much to live for. It was Eliot's influence that had made her feel otherwise.

She'd never allow him to do that again!

Chapter 24

Marjorie Greenfield Penwick's deep, peaceful sleep was disturbed by an anxious rapping on her bedroom door and Lucita's voice calling out to her. Marjorie, still dazed by sleep, urged her to enter.

By the time the Mexican girl entered the room, still clad in her nightgown and wrapper, Marjorie had propped herself up in her bed with a questioning frown on her face.

"There's a commotion out on the grounds, señora. You have not heard it?" Lucita asked.

"No, I was sleeping too deeply," Marjorie admitted, but she wasted no time lingering in her bed. She looked out the window, pulling the sheers back so she could see more clearly. Two Mexican hired hands stood there beside Eliot's fine thoroughbred, and Marjorie suddenly realized it was Ralph they were lowering to the carpeted grass below her window.

"Oh, my God!" Marjorie gasped, her hands flying up to her mouth. Without hesitation, she quickly took charge, instructing Lucita, "Go—find out what's happened. I'll be down as soon as I can get my robe on."

Like a gazelle, Lucita dashed out of the bedroom,

her gown swaying around her bare feet. Marjorie hastily grabbed the robe from the chair and started on through the door, tying the belt as she ran.

By the time she reached the front door, Lucita was rushing back up the steps. "Señor Ralph—he's—he's been shot! Julio says he's in very bad shape, señora."

Marjorie gave quick, precise instructions to the two Mexicans. One was to ride immediately to bring Doctor Christy to the ranch as fast as he could; the other was to run to the bunkhouse to bring another man to help him get Ralph to his bed. Lucita was given her orders to bring hot water and cloths right away to help Marjorie administer aid to the injured young man until the doctor arrived.

As yet, Eliot Penwick had not come upon the scene, nor did he seem to have been roused from his stupor. By the time he did wake up, Marjorie was already busily struggling to remove Ralph's blood-stained shirt. When the bleary-eyed Eliot staggered through the doorway of his nephew's bedroom, he saw his wife cleansing the bloody wound in his nephew's shoulder. His first thoughts were not about Ralph's welfare but rather, he had to admit secretly, that the woman he watched was neither weak nor helpless. Unflinching, her hands moved to tend the ugly wounds in the young man's flesh.

She was unaware that she was being strangely admired by her husband there in the doorway. When she did sense his nearness, the sight of him filled her with disgust. There was no shred of the striking handsomeness in Eliot she'd once found appealing. Her voice declared her contempt, "Well, Eliot—you just wake up?" Without waiting for him to answer her, she curtly told him a doctor had been sent for.

"What—what happened? Where—"

"He was out riding your horse tonight. I gave him

202

permission, since the poor beast has been in his stall so much lately."

"How dare you do that, Marjorie! Is the horse hurt?" he barked angrily.

Slowly, she turned away from her patient with her hands clasped firmly at her waistline. Glaring fiercely at Eliot, she exclaimed, "I dare anything I wish, Eliot, on this ranch, and you'd best remember that! If my guess is right, poor Ralph took a bullet meant for you. Whoever did this figured it was you on that horse. This horse of yours can't be mistaken, but obviously the rider was mistaken for you!"

Her snapping words made an impact that Eliot could not shrug off. She was absolutely right, but he was damned if he'd tell her so.

Lucita worked by the señora's side, making sure she kept herself busy so she'd not have to look Eliot's way. When the two women had done all they could for Ralph, Marjorie told Lucita, "Come along." She turned to look at Eliot as she said, "I'll now turn your nephew's care over to you, Eliot. The doctor will be sent up just as soon as he arrives."

The two ladies left and Eliot was still trying to absorb the goings-on around him in the house at this early hour. His body and his brain were still sluggish from all his late-night drinking. He sank into the chair by the side of the bed.

Sitting there all alone, he stared over at the quiet figure of his nephew, whose upper torso was bare except for the huge wad of padding Marjorie had placed there to stop the bleeding. He began to tremble. He realized that it could very well have been him lying there instead of Ralph and his blood staining the thick padding. But who was the guilty party who'd shot his nephew, thinking it was him?

Who wanted to kill him? Could his dumb nephew

have been right that Victor Maurier was here in Harrison County, ready to seek revenge for the murder of his mother?

In that darkened room, Eliot lay his head back against the chair. He recalled that night so very long ago in the woods of his brother's vast estate, where his mistress, Colette, lived in her neat little cottage, and where Edward kept his secret rendezvous with her as many nights as he could. It was the little cottage where Colette had given birth to their love child with no assistance from a midwife. Only Edward had been there to assist her.

As he sat there thinking of what seemed like something from another lifetime, he could readily accept the truth as to why Edward or any other man could have idolized such a woman as Colette Maurier. She demanded so little and gave so much.

Here in Texas, Eliot could also see why Edward went so eagerly into the arms of this French lady after living all those miserable years with such a demanding bitch as his wife, Elaine. It was only after he'd left England to come to America that Eliot realized the influence Elaine had had on him. He was also a most vulnerable young man, and now he could admit he was over-whelmingly receptive to her older, sophisticated charm. Lady Elaine Penwick was an alluring woman, and Eliot had envied Edward, wishing it was he who was sharing her bed instead of his older brother.

Perhaps it was the ghost of the ravishingly beautiful Colette Maurier haunting him, Eliot concluded. Perhaps that was the reason his well-laid scheme had not gone as he'd planned.

He gazed over at the still figure of his nephew. He felt no compassion that he lay there hurt, paying the price which probably should have been his own to pay. Ralph had been his doting little lapdog in the same way

204

that he, Eliot, had been lapdog to the selfish Elaine.

All this reflection on the past was interrupted by the arrival of Doctor Christy. Recalling these events had left Eliot suddenly apprehensive and tense.

From the looks of things, it was questionable whether poor Ralph would make it. His face had taken on an ashen hue. Eliot looked at him and wondered if he was even breathing as Doctor Christy came through the door.

That made Eliot go into another spasm of trembling, thinking it could have been him dying.

Lights burned all night at the Casa del Lago. It was early morning before Talleha dimmed her lamp. The same thing was true in Emilo's suite. He had much on his mind. There was only one exception in the spacious, sprawling hacienda, and that was Estaban, because he had helped himself to one of his uncle's fine bottles of claret before bed the night before.

Maurier's lamp was still burning, for he was a man flooded with confusion. Who besides him was out to do Eliot Penwick in? Damned if he could figure what happened in the woods last night! No one was more taken by surprise than he'd been.

Now that he was in the solitude of his bedroom, his keen mind was trying to analyze things. He took time out to fill his glass from the silver flask sitting on the nightstand by his bed. Hell, yes—he'd taken deadly aim with his rifle, and his finger was ready to pull the trigger. More than anything he intended and prayed that a bullet would forever destroy Eliot Penwick just as surely as Eliot had destroyed his beautiful mother, Colette.

But it was someone else's shot that had struck the figure of the man astraddle the fine thoroughbred.

Maurier had stood there dumbfounded as he watched the slumped body bounce up and down while the panicky stallion broke into a frenzied gallop in and out of the thick pines.

Victor's long, slender fingers ran through his tousled black hair in an effort to brush it off his forehead. Crazy as it might seem, he knew she would probably not have approved of what he'd sought to do. The truth was that he wasn't a killer. He loved life.

His mother had taught him to love the creatures of the woods. He'd been exposed to her kind, loving nature all his life until that horrible night that changed everything.

And that wily old sea captain had taught him to love the things of nature with his consuming passion for the sea and the creatures in those waters. Captain Crawford had taught him so much that even Colette could not have. The signs in the sky and the force of the wind always drew Crawford's respect. He heeded them and made his decisions based on what they told him. Maurier learned so much from that old man that his words would guide him the rest of his life.

In fact, Victor wished he could have sat with Crawford tonight to get his opinion on what had happened. As it was, he wasn't sure of anything. Was Penwick merely injured, or was he fatally shot?

He was damned tempted to say to hell with everything here in Harrison County and get back down to Brownsville. He feared there wasn't much he could do for his beloved old captain except have one more visit with him. The truth was that he was sick and tired of the land and he yearned for the open seas and his schooner, *Destiny*. That was the tonic to heal his soul. And tonight there was an overwhelming need for it. Just thinking about his schooner lightened his heart.

Suddenly, his mood was interrupted, for he'd

206

forgotten something he'd yet to attend to before he could go south to Brownsville. There was the promise he'd made to Talleha that he would take her back to her village.

A devious voice deep within him told him to forget his promise. Shanghai the wild little vixen as the dashing pirate had done in days of old, and take her to all the exotic places he intended to see before he settled down.

He could not imagine a more exciting, little creature to take along on his wandering. A grin lit up his face even as he thought about this whimsy, and a most wonderful, relaxing feeling settled over him, inducing sleep.

By the time his firm, muscled body lay back on the bed with the vision of his tantalizing Talleha vividly parading through his thoughts, he was sure he was bound to have the most wonderful dreams this night.

His dreams were marvelous, but the dawn brought stark reality.

Chapter 25

Sheriff Dick Curley was not only reluctant, but embarrassed to have to go to the Casa del Lago to question that fine old gentleman, Señor Emilo Cortez. Like most everyone in Harrison County, Curley considered Emilo one of the finest, most trustworthy men he'd ever known. To dare to question that he'd harbored such a man as Eliot Penwick had described to him was insulting, as far as Curley was concerned.

The truth was that Curley would have refused to carry out Penwick's request that he investigate a stranger over at the Casa del Lago had Miss Marjorie not been standing there by his side. He could only assume that she was in accord with her English husband's wishes.

He didn't care a hoot for the arrogant bastard Miss Marjorie had married. Eliot especially rubbed Curley the wrong way when he dared to question Curley's bravery to confront Cortez.

It took sheer restraint and a healthy respect for Miss Marjorie to keep Dick Curley from punching that sharp-featured face of Penwick's when he snobbishly remarked, "What is it here in Harrison County that calls for a mere Mexican like Emilo Cortez to be looked upon as some kind of God? It's a bloody laugh to me." Eliot had stood there in his fancy clothes with his legs parted slightly, his hands on his waist, giving forth in that insolent, presumptuous way of his.

Curley turned sharply on his boots to mumble angrily, "Wouldn't expect the likes of you to understand that, Penwick. Wouldn't expect that in a million years." It was only when he'd mounted his horse and was attempting to rein it around to leave the ranch with his two deputies that he called out, "Bye, Miss Marjorie. Take care of yourself, you hear?" There was no farewell for Eliot Penwick.

A half-hour later, Sheriff Curley arrived at the Casa del Lago and was greeted by the gentlemanly Emilo Cortez. Curley had always wondered what it was about this man—he had a gracious air about him, yet managed to be an imposing, intimidating figure at the same time.

Curley was actually apologetic when he made his query to Cortez. Without hesitation, Emilo had quickly replied to Curley's questioning, "Ah, you must mean my young friend from Brownsville. Yes, he was visiting me, but he left the Casa del Lago some four days ago."

"Four days ago?" Curley echoed.

"That's right, sheriff. Was there some reason you need to speak to him?" Emilo asked, giving away no hint of the concern churning within him about what Maurier might have done. He'd made a point of not mentioning a name since Curley had not asked specifically.

"No, Señor Cortez. Figured this was a wild goose chase Penwick was sending me on, anyway. Still feel an obligation toward Miss Marjorie, though, so I thought I'd ride over here since I was so close, you know?"

"Oh, certainly, sheriff. Was there some trouble over

at the Greenfield ranch?"

"Yeah—seems Penwick's nephew over here from England got himself shot last night over there in the woods. Oh, he's gonna' live," Curley said, shrugging his robust shoulders.

Emilo gave forth a skeptical frown and an expression of complete puzzlement before he spoke next. In that impressive voice of his, he pointedly asked of Curley, "Why, I wonder, would Penwick pick a guest of mine to accuse of such an act, Sheriff Curley? It makes me question the man's sanity, I must say."

"God only knows, Señor Cortez. Hey, I'm not wasting any more time on him, and I'm sorry as hell I bothered you," Curley said, moving to take his leave.

Emilo smiled and gave him an understanding nod of his white head. But what the very clever Emilo could not know was how very important his casual remark about Penwick's sanity would be to his old friend Marjorie Greenfield in the days to come. Marjorie could not know what the future held for her any more than Emilo could. Nevertheless, the future was to bind them together, and already the wheel of fortune was turning slowly and surely that way.

Secure behind a massive fern, Estaban stood completely fascinated and intrigued by what a convincing liar his Uncle Emilo could be. The old man was a mere mortal like everyone else, Estaban realized. All his life he'd listened to people praise his uncle as some kind of paragon.

Never on any of his visits to the Casa del Lago had there been so much activity, except when his aunt used to give her gala fiestas. The enchanting little black-eyed señorita had certainly livened up his day and night yesterday. Now, this morning, he'd witnessed his uncle

210

lying to the sheriff, which he would never have suspected.

He was most curious as to why his uncle would cover up for Victor Maurier. There still had been no explanation as to why he was here at the ranch in the first place. Maurier remained a mysterious character as far as Estaban was concerned.

When Emilo marched back into the house, Estaban did not give away his presence but remained back behind the tall iron fern stand. Would Emilo now seek out Victor Maurier to inform him of the sheriff's visit?

And where was the delectable Talleha this morning? He'd seen no sign of her when he'd helped himself to the breakfast fare of sausage, ham, and eggs the cook had set along the sideboard. When the housekeeper had served his coffee and offered him a helping of the piping hot biscuits, he inquired of Talleha.

Rosa had shaken her head, saying, "She has not come down, Señor Estaban."

"And Señor Maurier?"

"No, he has not come down, either. Only your uncle has had his breakfast. Do you wish another biscuit while they are good and hot?"

"No, Rosa—this is fine," he'd told her, for his plate was already filled with delicious smelling food, and Estaban ate heartily. It was then, as he went to seek out his uncle, that he chanced upon the scene on the front veranda, where his uncle talked with the sheriff.

Now Estaban stood in the same spot, listening to the various noises of the stirring household: servants chattered and their footsteps echoed with their movement across the tiled hallway. He'd watched Emilo turn the corner of the hall which he knew led to the door of the study. He glanced upward at the long winding stairway to see if Talleha was about to descend. Unfortunately, he didn't see her.

There was a very good reason why Talleha had not come down the stairs. She'd rushed down the back stairs about an hour ago, after one of the Mexican servant girls by the name of Juanita had brought her a message.

Sleepy-eyed, Talleha had listened as Juanita relayed her message in hastily spoken Spanish; Talleha had had to ask her to speak slower so she could understand the girl.

"Lucita—she waits in the barn for you. She says she must talk with you immediately, señorita."

"Lucita—you said Lucita?"

"Si, señorita!"

"All right, Juanita. Please, could I get you to help me get dressed, then?"

"Si, señorita. What you wish me to get for you?"

Talleha told her what garments to bring and crawled out of her comfortable bed reluctantly, for she'd had a restless night. A weariness remained with her this morning from lack of sleep. But by the time Juanita had helped her get dressed, she was feeling more alert, and she questioned how in the world Lucita would know she was here at the Casa del Lago. If she knew, would it not be logical to think Eliot Penwick knew, too?

She hastily followed Juanita down the back stairway and rushed along the arbor, which went from the back door all the way to an entrance gate on the south side of the barn.

The only time she paused was to free her black hair when it caught on a low hanging branch of wisteria entwined in the archway of the arbor.

Juanita could not restrain a giggle when she heard the beautiful lady behind her giving forth with a flow of cusswords as she angrily yanked her long, thick tresses free from the vines. Juanita was reminded of the very

212

elegant señora who was mistress of the Casa del Lago when she first came to work here. As refined and elegant as she was, when Señora Cortez was riled or vexed, she, too, could cuss as fervently as any of the hired hands.

Once they were inside the barn and Juanita had led Talleha to the stall where Lucita awaited them, she excused herself to get back to the house and her chores.

"Lucita? How—what are you doing here? How did you know I was here?" Talleha insisted on knowing.

Shrugging her shoulders, she told her the answer quite simply: "Castillo, Señor Cortez's foreman, has been my lover for over a year. I am his woman and so we talk—si?"

"Oh, si—yes, I see. But is it so urgent, Lucita—so serious?"

"It is. I think you will surely agree knowing how loco Eliot Penwick is. His nephew was shot last night while he was out on a ride on Señor Penwick's horse. Señora Marjorie gave him permission because Señor Penwick has not ridden the poor horse in many nights. He has been most strange since the night you ran away, Talleha."

"Oh, how terrible! I'm so sorry to hear that Ralph was hurt. How is he, Lucita?"

Once again she shrugged her shoulders and told Talleha, "He will live and be no worse for the experience, I would say. I could not believe that the señora gave him the right to ride the animal in the first place, knowing how Señor Penwick dotes on that horse. But this is not important now, and that is not why I came here. I came here to warn you, Talleha, or maybe advise you to get that handsome hombre of yours to take you and leave here as fast as you can. If you don't, I fear something will happen to you or to him. Penwick will kill him if he gets the chance!"

Whatever had stirred a wariness in Talleha about Lucita was gone now. There was no doubt that she spoke sincerely. Talleha believed that she was really concerned for her welfare and that of Victor Maurier.

Talleha moved over and placed her hands on Lucita's shoulders. Her black eyes warmed with affection when she said, "Remember the first night we met and I told you I thought we could be friends, Lucita? I was right. You and I are friends, and I thank you from the bottom of my heart. I will give very serious thought to what you've told me, and I will tell Victor, too." Concern etched Talleha's lovely face as she prodded Lucita, "You did not put yourself in danger or trouble by coming here to tell me this, did you, Lucita? I would never have wanted you to do that."

A slow, sly smile came to Lucita's face as she confessed, "No, Talleha—I came late last night to spend the night with my Castillo in our little hayloft. That is worth any risk I might take. He is mucho hombre!" Her dark eyes sparkled brightly and she gave Talleha a wink of her eyes.

Talleha laughed with her as she declared, "I still feel beholden to you for your concern. Is—is the señora all right?"

"Ah, Caramba! I can't believe this lady. She's like the old señora. I will swear to you a miracle took place and I am so glad. She is no longer afraid of that vibora!" she hissed, expressing her distaste for Eliot.

"'Vibora?' What is 'vibora,' Lucita?" Talleha was curious to know.

"That, Talleha—that is a snake! That is what I consider Señor Penwick is—a snake!"

Talleha broke into a smile and declared that she was in complete agreement.

The two departed to go their separate ways. Talleha

rushed into the house to find Victor just as soon as she could. Lucita left the barn to return to the Greenfield ranch and her señora.

The night spent with the hot-blooded Castillo was like a tonic she'd needed for days. Her tense nerves had calmed and Lucita's courage had been restored. Her bravado was so heightened that she didn't fear facing Eliot Penwick now.

She whipped her little mare into a faster gallop as they moved through the pasturelands of the Casa del Lago, heading toward the Greenfield ranch. She was suddenly seized with an overwhelming feeling that the señora might have a need of her.

Never would she want to fail her dear señora!

Chapter 26

Emilo recognized Talleha's soft voice even before he saw her on the small roofed patio huddled close to Victor Maurier. Now that he was near enough to see the glowing radiance of her face, he noticed she seemed concerned or angry. He wondered what the two young lovers were disagreeing about now.

He heard the impatience in her voice as she admonished Victor, "Hate does nothing but destroy a person, Victor. I share your loss. I saw my own mother killed. It is a nightmare I'll live with all my life, and yes, I hate the men who did it."

Emilo was spellbound: he admired such wisdom in one so young.

"Damn it, Talleha—you don't understand. The bastard needs killing, and I failed."

"Perhaps it was meant to be, Victor. Have you never failed before? Obviously, from what you've told me just now, someone else is out to get Eliot, mistaking poor Ralph just as you did last night. In Ralph's favor, the other person wasn't as good a marksman as you."

"I have to admit that I'm glad I didn't pull the trigger; my bullet would have hit the target and Ralph would be dead."

"You see, my dear Victor? What I say is true."

Victor looked at her for a moment without speaking. At that moment he thought about Eliot's determination to get her back. Right now that seemed more important than his unsatisfied revenge against the man. He would do any underhanded thing it took to get to Talleha. With all the security the Casa del Lago offered, one unguarded moment could allow his hired man to snatch her away before someone could stop them, Maurier realized. That he could not allow.

He reached for her hand and brought it to his lips to plant a tender kiss. "All right, my darling—I bow to your wishes to leave. There is also Señor Emilo to consider in all this: my problems should not touch him."

Emilo had a pleased smile on his face now, and he decided that he must slip back from the doorway so they'd never know he had been so close by.

As he stepped back he saw the two of them move closer together until their lips met in a kiss. His back was turned to them when Victor released her to whisper in her ear, "I adore you, Talleha! For whatever made our paths cross, I'm grateful, my darling."

His sweet words pleased her; but she selfishly wanted him to say and feel more. His sensuous kiss had already flamed a wild, pulsing desire within her. She sighed softly, "So you do believe in destiny, Victor?"

"Oh, of course I do—I even named my schooner *Destiny*. But right now—and I know not what destiny holds for us, my beautiful Talleha—right now I want to kiss those honey-sweet lips of yours."

She was tempted to hold herself back from him, to declare that he could have no more of the honey from her lips until he swore he loved her and wanted to marry her. But his strong arms already enclosed her and he was lifting her off the bench to place her on his lap. She was powerless to resist such persuasion.

His long fingers ran up and down her back with caressing strokes and she found herself encircling his neck with her hands. By now his mouth was igniting such ecstasy that she gave out a soft moan of pleasure. Her breasts were pressed against his broad chest and she could feel the heat of his body warming her. Mounting sensations consumed her whole body now. She cursed herself and Maurier, too, for making her become so desirous by his mere caress. What was this mysterious quality of his that cast such a spell over her? What would her mother have called it? The lore and legends of her grandparents had always fascinated Talleha: they were so simple and logical.

But simple logic had not ruled her reckless heart where Victor was concerned; instinct had, the instinct of being Dawn's daughter. Their way of life would not have been considered conventional.

Talleha could not abide by convention. It would smother her, and she swore she would surely die if she had to exist that way.

As much as her wild side wanted Maurier to make love to her at this very moment, she stiffened against him. Her small hands pressed against his chest to push his searing body away from hers. "Please, Victor," she pleaded with him. "We're—we're hardly alone," she gasped breathlessly.

"What does it matter? You drive me crazy, Talleha! I don't have good sense when you get me this way. I—I don't think. I only feel!"

She understood exactly; she was feeling the same way. But she reminded herself of the very dignified Señor Cortez and his nephew, Estaban, and of the many servants constantly milling around this huge hacienda.

"I feel the same, Victor. Believe me, I do—but we

can't go any further. Please, my darling," she begged.

She looked into his eyes, now heated with a blue fire of passion, and he said nothing. Like her, his breathing was heavy with the wild excitement churning within him. Dejectedly and slightly disgruntled, he moaned his anguish, "Christ, Talleha—you—you are enough to drive a man wild!" His groin ached with an insatiable longing.

She showed him no sympathy, for his pain was no greater than hers. Perhaps it was time to point out that a man in the heat of passion was deprived no more than a woman. Talleha wore an impish smile on her lovely face, and there was a frivolous air about her as she declared, "And you can drive a woman wild too, mon cher." As she spoke the words, she was startled by the term of endearment, for it was something from her past—hers and Dawn's. It was something Dawn had called the man she'd loved—Talleha's father. He'd taught her certain phrases of his native language; he was a Frenchman.

Needless to say, her words brought forth a startled look on Victor Maurier's face. His blue eyes sparkled brighter and his lips parted slightly in amazement as he declared, "I like that, ma cherie—I like that very much. I'm going to believe that you truly mean what you just said. I want to be your dearest, for you are surely mine. But how—how did you know . . ."

"I had a French father, so I'm told." She gave forth a gay little giggle.

A crooked grin etched his face as he teased her, "I should have known there was a Frenchman around there somehwere, for all the passion and fire in you was hardly English."

"Now, why would you say that?"

He spoke before he thought and he realized that he was caught when he heard himself say, "Because I've had many English girls."

Jealousy and indignation exploded within her. She looked at him for a brief second before her savage instinct took over. What happened next was so spontaneous that Talleha did not know what she'd done until she'd done it. Maurier was certainly unprepared for the harsh, sharp blow that assaulted his cheek as her small, dainty hand stung him.

"I do not care to hear about your conquests, Victor Maurier! What a conceited bastard you are!" She was already marching swiftly away from him. He was consumed with rage that such a slip of a girl had literally assaulted him that he lunged forward, taking long strides to catch up with her. When he managed to do just that, his hands grabbed her roughly.

"Oh! Damn you, Maurier!" she spat at him, feeling herself being forced backward. She struggled desperately against him, but it was useless.

"And damn you too, Talleha. You talk too much!" he declared, taking full charge of her.

He took her in his arms in such a way that her willful nature could not resist; and she bent to his will. Once his arms surrounded her, she wanted him to possess her.

Before she realized what was happening, he had hoisted her up in his arms and carried her into the house and up the winding stairway. She said not a word but looked directly into those intense blue eyes. She was like someone in a trance.

Softly, but firmly, he told her, "You are a wicked little vixen, Talleha!"

She said nothing but gave him a devious smile which was enough to confirm his remarks. Neither of them had been aware of the giggling, amused Mexican servants who'd observed them. The young girls envied Talleha being carried in the arms of the handsome hombre, and each one of them was wishing she was in Talleha's place.

The older Mexican ladies seeing these strange things happening under the señor's roof were startled. For a moment or two, they were distracted from their mopping and dusting and just stood and watched the pair, exchanging glances of puzzlement.

It was not until Victor had entered her bedroom and unceremoniously dropped her on the bed that she uttered a protest. "For God's sake, Victor—what do you think you're doing?"

He towered over her, his blue eyes gleaming with amusement. "Come now, Talleha—you are no longer that innocent!"

She jerked up from the bed and, as a proper young lady would react, she fumbled to lower her rumpled gown, which temptingly displayed her knees and thighs. Swinging her body around so that her feet were planted firmly on the floor, she stood up, indignantly declaring, "Well, we both know who is responsible for that, don't we?"

A deep, throaty laugh erupted as his face took on a look of boyish mischief. He admitted readily, "We certainly do, and if you think I'm going to apologize for that, then you are wrong, my darling little Talleha. Never shall I regret it!"

His conceit riled her and her spitfire temper exploded. Hoping to wound his fierce male pride, she haughtily declared, "Did you ever stop to think that maybe I *do* regret it? I guess that never entered your puffed-up head."

Her venom hit its mark and Maurier felt its full impact. Tight lips and clenched fists were his first response. His gaze seared her for one lingering second before he made his move to grab for her.

"You little—you little witch! You have no regrets,

221

and we both damned well know it!" His lips roughly captured hers and held them until she was breathless. When he released her, he boldly dared her to tell him otherwise after the way she'd just responded to his kiss.

"Tell me, Talleha—didn't you like—didn't you want me to kiss you?"

Stubbornly, she willed herself not to answer him. She remained silent, her eyes boldly glaring up at him.

"Oh, I see, my pet. You want more than just a kiss! I forgot what a hot-blooded little wildcat you are, Talleha," he sarcastically challenged her.

Her voice cried out, "No, Victor!" But her body betrayed her, for his fingers were already unbuttoning her blouse, flaming the flesh of her breast with just that slightest touch. She silently cursed herself for being so weak where this man was concerned. She arched her back, feeling emotions of both desire and disgust.

He heard her gasps and knew she was trying her best to deny him as well as herself. It made him all the more determined to show her he could tame her if he sought to. He let his hand cup the satiny warm mound of her breast, slowly caressing it. His other hand had slipped behind her back to bring her closer to him; his lips were now covering hers, taking the sweet honey of them.

His hands and his lips were in no hurry. As she began to undulate against him, he knew from her soft, kittenlike moans that she, too, was hungry for his love. He was delightfully pleased.

"Ah, Talleha, my darling—you see? It is foolish to lie to me. We can't deny what is between us." His voice was husky as he kissed her cheek.

She moaned helplessly as the height of passion now consumed her. Her arms encircled his neck to pull him closer. She wanted him to fill her with the overwhelming rapture she knew so well.

His strong, sinewy thighs encased her and his

magnificent body moved to bury itself between the velvet, silken flesh of her thighs. He felt the stimulating arch of her body telling him how eagerly she yearned to be consumed by him. Powerfully he gave himself to her, and eagerly, she took him, sighing ecstatically.

A wild sensual joy mounted in them both as their bodies moved and swayed to a perfect cadence. They were lovers lost in time and space, for nothing else existed at this moment. They ascended to the loftiest heights of sensual pleasure. A breathless gasp came forth from them as they both reached the zenith; then they clung together desperately as though they didn't dare let go.

It was in that one magic moment that Victor Maurier knew he'd never take her back to her village and leave her. Never! Where he went, she would go, he secretly vowed!

Talleha lay in his arms, thinking to herself that she'd surely die should he ever leave her. Somehow, she must convince him to take her with him when he left Texas.

She was now his forever, whether he offered her marriage or not!

Chapter 27

Estaban had seen enough in the morning hours around the Casa del Lago to whet his appetite to linger on his uncle's ranch longer than he'd planned. Madre de Dios, who would have ever suspected so many surreptitious goings-on under the roof of the very refined Señor Cortez? He could not wait to relate all this to his mother and watch her face reflect her shock. The chances were she would think he was lying.

He'd seen Maurier marching up the winding stairway with the very ravishing señorita in his arms, an animal passion blazing in his eyes—and it had happened not during the late night hours that were the usual time for such sensual interludes, but in the morning.

He'd not deny for a minute that he would eagerly have changed places with Victor Maurier! The very sight of the amorous couple was enough to set an aching in his groin.

The truth was that he had immediately surveyed the scurrying house servants employed by his uncle to find a bedmate to satisfy his own needs. So far, all he'd spied going up and down the tiled hallway were two chubby middle-aged women who did not appeal to him at all.

He was not that much in need of a woman, he told himself.

It seemed he might as well forget about the riding date Talleha had promised to share with him. He suspected Victor Maurier was going to keep her occupied for a while; if he didn't, he was a fool.

But he could think of no other tonic quite like a brisk ride through the countryside, so he decided to go alone. At least, that was his intention as he made for the back entrance of the house. But his dark eyes chanced to see the housekeeper's daughter, Miranda, rushing out of the kitchen, where she'd been talking to her mother. She was exactly the kind of gorgeous young woman Estaban yearned for—she would satisfy his hearty virile appetite. His scrutinizing eyes missed nothing.

He liked the sway of her hips as she walked and he appreciated the ample fullness of her young breasts in a becoming, peasant-style blouse. The drawstrings of the neckline seemed to give a freedom to their fullness, and it aroused him to see the deep cleavage displayed.

A feisty little filly, she was, as she skipped out the kitchen door! Ah, yes—he liked that sort of fire in a woman! Estaban cleverly waited until her mother had returned to her kitchen chores before he went past the doorway. He knew his long legs could catch up with her in no time.

As soon as he felt he was far enough away from the house so her madre would not hear him, he called out to her, "Chiquita! Wait a minute!"

The young Miranda turned sharply to see a very handsome man beckoning to her. If she was not mistaken, he was Señor Emilo's nephew, and she was overwhelmed that he addressed her at all. She tried to calm her excited trembling. The very sight of him took her breath away; he was as magnificent as a matador.

"You are speaking to me, señor?" she asked, securing

225

one of her sandals, which had slipped off the back of her foot.

"No one else, señorita," he said with a most charming smile.

She stood there, trying to anticipate what he wanted of her. It seemed forever until he closed the distance between them, and when he did, she found she had to stare up at him because he was so tall.

For a moment, Estaban looked down at that lovely, innocent face, and he knew instinctively that she was a virgin. This was enough to fire his desire. "What is the name of one so beautiful as you?" he asked.

"Miranda, señor," she told him, feeling very flattered by his attention.

"Ah, that is a beautiful name, and so are you, Miranda. May I introduce myself? I am Señor Emilo's nephew, Estaban. May I walk with you? Or do you perhaps have something to do?"

She was so taken aback that the nephew of Señor Emilo wished to share her company that her heart pounded wildly. It was a great honor, and she could not wait until she could tell her mother about all this.

"Why—why, of course, señor. I was not going anywhere in particular." She was feeling very ill-at-ease with his piercing black eyes upon her. Never had she been around such a man; he had completely hypnotized her with his devastating charm.

"I care not where we walk, Miranda. I'd just enjoy your company. The truth is that I'm lonely."

She stopped abruptly and stared at him, wide-eyed. "You, señor? Lonely? I cannot imagine such a man as you ever being lonely."

Estaban could be a very convincing actor when he sought to be, and it suited his intention to win over this blossoming virgin. His hot-blooded nature cried out for a woman.

226

He took her by the arm and then held her hand tenderly. "You see, Miranda—you see how wrong you were, for I do have many lonely moments."

"Ah, si, señor—I do!" she confessed with sincere honesty. Somehow, it made her feel more at ease to know that such a fine-looking man as Estaban could admit to having periods of loneliness. Obviously, his wealth and lavish living did not fill enough hours in his days and nights to keep him from being lonely.

"So you see, we share a common bond, don't we?" He gave her one of his winning smiles. "I like very simple things, chiquita. I can think of nothing more exciting right now than a walk with you."

Oh, he was at his very best, and he knew it. He saw the way the pretty black-eyed little señorita believed every word he said. Those very same words had been used by him many times before.

Estaban's wild anticipation was heightening by the minute, for he knew he was going to have her in his bed before sundown. Conceitedly, he knew what his kisses could do to women, and he knew the expertise his hands possessed, for they'd had a tremendous amount of practice.

By now they were passing by the corral surrounding the barnyard, and Estaban knew about the hayloft inside the barn. It was probably time to make his move, for he could hardly take a servant girl to his room in his uncle's house.

"Is there someplace we could go to sit and talk, Miranda? I'm enjoying this time with you." He paused for a moment as if he'd just spied the barn. "I have a great idea! I used to go up there when I was just a lad to sit and enjoy an hour or two. Let's go up in the hayloft, eh?" There was a boyish charm about him that completely washed away any apprehension Miranda might have had about his intentions. She gave him an eager nod as he held her hand and led her toward the barn door.

Exhilaration swelled within him, for he knew he was about to add one more lovely young woman to his long list of conquests.

He broke forth with a lighthearted laugh, so Miranda laughed too. Never had she expected to have such a glorious day. The handsome Estaban had been in her dreams for many a night as she'd lain in her cot in their humble little cottage. A girl whose mother was a housekeeper and whose father was a hired hand had little opportunity to improve her station in life. Such a girl usually ended up marrying a younger hired hand and living in a cottage similar to the one her parents had lived in all their lives.

Miranda thought this might be the one special moment her life would ever offer and she did not think about the risks because she had never felt so wonderful.

As she dwelt on her own private musings, so did Estaban. She would have been utterly shattered if she had read his mind. But their mutual reverie was abruptly invaded by a thundering voice that broke the secluded quiet of the barn.

"Estaban! Oh, Estaban!" the demanding, insistent voice echoed. The dark barn was suddenly illuminated as the two double doors were flung open and an imposing figure entered those portals.

A disgruntled moan broke in Estaban's throat, for he knew the familiar voice. Dejectedly, he realized his quest was hopeless. Even before he turned to look behind him, he knew he was going to see Emilo.

Discreetly, he whispered to the girl, "Hide in the stall, Miranda. I don't want this to get you into any trouble."

She gave him an understanding nod, thinking him most gallant, and quickly dashed into the nearest stall.

Estaban turned to go back toward his uncle. "Si, Uncle Emilo." But Emilo was not about to allow his nephew to advance toward him, for he wanted the young girl to hear what he was about to say.

He took a longer stride to meet Estaban. When they were face-to-face, Emilo made a point of walking back in the direction Estaban had come from.

His manner and the expression in those deep-set dark eyes left no doubt about his sincerity when he spoke. "Estaban, the people of Casa del Lago are more to me than hired hands. They are my friends! My dear devoted housekeeper, her husband, and their daughter, Miranda, are like my family. For you to try what you were about to try is an insult to me. Do you understand, Estaban?" Emilo wanted the naive Miranda to hear his words.

"Oh, I certainly do, Uncle Emilo. I—I meant no harm or insult to anyone." What else could he say? His Uncle Emilo had destroyed any chances he might have had with the girl now.

"I trust you take me seriously, Estaban. Perhaps, you are not aware of it, but I can be a very mean man if I'm riled. I want no seed of yours planted in any virgins around the Casa del Lago. I want no bastards of yours here on my ranch, even if you are my nephew." Emilo hoped the little Miranda had got an earful, enough to shock her, for that was what he'd intended.

Estaban followed his uncle out of the barn, realizing as he never had before that the elderly gentleman could be ruthless if the occasion called for it.

He was cheated of the sensuous pleasures he'd anticipated with the tempting little Miranda, but he left the barn feeling an overwhelming admiration for his uncle. It was nice to have such a man to look up to, and it was even nicer to know that the same blood flowed in his own veins.

Estaban did not realize it then, but the incident would have an impact on his life. The course he sought to pursue in the days to come was influenced and guided by this day at the Casa del Lago. But more importantly, he had been greatly impressed by his uncle's actions.

This would have delighted Emilo, had he known. But the only thing concerning him at that time was that he'd kept a fine young girl from being ravaged by his own kin.

The two did not speak as they moved back toward the house. Each was deep in his own private thoughts. No one was more shocked than Emilo when Estaban broke the silence by saying, "I'm glad you came when you did, Uncle Emilo. I really am."

Emilo stopped, turning to his nephew to scrutinize his expression. When he had done so, he remarked calmly, "You know something, Estaban, I believe you."

"Gracias, Uncle Emilo. Mucho gracias!" He sincerely meant it; it was suddenly important that his uncle trusted him and had faith that he was telling the truth.

The metamorphosis taking place within Estaban was nothing short of a miracle and would alter his thinking and his actions from this day forward.

It would gladden Emilo Cortez and give him hope that after all, a Cortez could carry on after his death to run the Casa del Lago.

Chapter 28

The undercurrent of tension Emilo had felt when he and his guests had dined the night before was not present tonight. This was a congenial group. He could not have been happier that tonight was so much more pleasant as he sat conversing with the three young people sharing his meal.

He was proud of Estaban and his changed attitude toward Talleha. Oh, he was gracious and charming, but charming in a far different way than he'd been only the night before. It was as though he was telling Victor that he respected the fact that Talleha was his lady and he was honoring that.

This, Emilo was certain, made Maurier's mood not as black and morose as it had been last night. He was relaxed and most engaging.

As always, the beautiful Talleha was a joy as a dinner companion, Emilo thought to himself, appraising her rare charm and loveliness.

The dinner of roast wild turkey with all the trimmings had been delightful, and Emilo reminded himself that he must tell his cook how marvelous it was. He'd allowed himself an extra glass or two of his special white wine. Before he knew it, his guests had left to go their separate ways. He found himself all alone in the quiet seclusion of his study.

A warmth of serenity washed over him and he gazed up at the portrait of his lovely señora. He told himself she would be pleased to know he'd had this nice evening. He took another glass of wine and gave forth a toast to her, "To us, querida! I think maybe I have found an heir for the Casa del Lago. Yes, querida—I—I think if God gives me the time, I can mold him to stand in my shoes."

Someone hearing Emilo talk like this might have thought the dignified Mexican was senile, but senility had nothing to do with it. It was of Estaban he was speaking, and it was an incentive the elderly gentleman needed at this time in his life. It was the essence of his dreams.

Emilo had not felt so alive and eager for the future in a long, long time. He had a goal to achieve, and he now thought he could make it work. A wonderful eagerness engulfed him, and it was a glorious feeling.

This was Emilo's mood when he heard a rapping on his library door. He was not surprised to see that it was Maurier, who asked to speak to him. Emilo had rather expected to see him this evening before he retired. All during dinner he'd sensed that the two young people had made themselves some definite plans.

"Victor, come in," he cordially bade him.

Maurier moved through the doorway to the room, which he considered was one of the nicest in the spacious house. Everything about it appealed to Maurier's taste. The heavy, comfortable furnishings were to his liking, and the richly paneled walls gave forth an intimate feeling the moment he entered the room.

He knew he would have liked the lovely Señora Cortez had she still been alive. She was a beautiful woman, as the portrait reflected, but it was more than mere beauty, Maurier had concluded. There was an earthiness about her that would have endeared her to both her servants and her husband's hired hands, he devined from the gleam in those dark, all-knowing eyes of hers.

Most of all, Maurier saw a woman of deep passion, and he always felt he could recognize that in a woman. The señora was such a lady, and he knew his mother was. It was also the first thing he'd seen that day long ago down by the riverbank when his eyes had first gazed up at the sultry loveliness of Talleha.

Finally, he turned to speak to Emilo. "Señor, I hardly know how to begin. I guess it is best that I just come out and say it. In Talleha's best interests, I think I should take her away from here. You know what my business was here in Harrison County, but since everything has happened as it has, I must put that aside for the time being."

Emilo gave him an understanding nod of his head. "I am happy to hear you saying this, amigo. I had intended to give you the same advice. Penwick will not rest until he gets her back. We both know he is a man obsessed, and that is the worst sort."

"He is a devil! I was hoping to do the world a favor last night. If I could have done what I left here to do, then both Talleha and Marjorie Greenfield would have been saved. Damn it, I bungled it, señor!"

"No, no, amigo—you did not! Someone else hates him as much as you do; they were seeking to do the same. His poor nephew paid a hell of a price."

Maurier had not intended to punish the nephew of Eliot Penwick, but he remembered what old Paddy had told him back at his home in the woods on the outskirts of Dover. He recalled Paddy's explicit descriptions of who'd been at the cottage the fateful night his mother was killed by the devious plottings of Lady Elaine Penwick and her brother-in-law, Eliot.

Victor had taken care of the ruffian hired to do the job, and he'd see to it that Lady Elaine did not get to enjoy the spoils of her greed. Paddy had told him about the young nephew accompanying Eliot that night in the woods. That young nephew was a youth named Ralph. Maurier could not feel too sorry that he'd had his share of pain and been shot.

When he finally replied to Emilo, the señor found his words a little disquieting. "He, too, deserved a degree of punishment, señor." It was all he said, with no further explanation.

All Emilo could reply was, "Well, I am not God, amigo, so I can't say."

"I know, señor. I am the only one who can know that. Me and Eliot Penwick! But right now, this does not matter. I wish to purchase a couple of your horses, if I may."

"I have the feeling that you are not through in Harrison County, so take Sultana. He seems to like you very much. As for a mount for Talleha, the little red roan, Amapola, is perfect. Let that be my gift to her, Victor. Do I have to tell you how very fond I've become of that young lady? If my dear wife and I could have been blessed with children, I would have loved to have such a daughter as our little Talleha."

Maurier smiled at the generous man; his heart was as kind and giving as Captain Crawford's. "Ah, señor— you—you leave me speechless. I've only met one man in my whole lifetime like you, and that is our mutual friend, Crawford."

"You pay me a great honor, amigo. A very great honor!" His wrinkled hand reached up to pat the shoulder of his younger friend. They exchanged a smile. Their friendship was a binding one, the sort one cherishes knowing it happens so seldom.

There was a moment of quiet; it was Maurier who finally broke the silence. "I plan for us to leave at the crack of dawn, señor, so I want to tell you goodbye now." He broke into a grin as he added, "I've yet to advise Talleha of this, but I'm sure you can understand why I think we should."

Emilo wore an amused expression on his face. "You'd best go tell her, eh, amigo? Now, who knows—I might just be up at the crack of dawn to bid you two farewell." With a gesture of his hand, he urged Maurier to take his leave.

"Good night, señor," Maurier told him, appreciating him all the more.

"Good night, Maurier, and tell our little Talleha a pleasant good-night for me."

Maurier gave him a nod of his head, then turned swiftly to leave Emilo to his solitude.

As Maurier rushed up the winding stairway, light raindrops were just beginning to pelt the window of Talleha's bedroom, and she listened to them and the soothing sound they made.

It was a sudden chill sweeping over her that made Talleha leap out of the bed to close the window. How brisk and breezy the winds felt rushing through the open window! Autumn was there in the night breeze, and the rains added to the chilling effect. She stood there for a second hugging herself as she gave forth a little tremble, thinking that a long-sleeved gown would feel good tonight.

A low rumble of distant thunder invaded the quiet of the night. She saw outside her window no stars shining in the sky, and the moon was shadowed with clouds moving rapidly. A sudden bolt of lightning broke from the sky. She could not help giving a sharp flinch, and she began to move back from the window.

But something made her freeze, then slowly move closer to the window to get a better look at something below. There was only one horse like the one she saw now, and it belonged to Eliot Penwick. It was too dark and the rider was too far away from her, but there was no mistaking that horse.

The gentle rapping at her door was a welcome sound, and she scampered quickly to answer it. The sight of Victor standing there was consoling.

"I like that kind of response from a lady," he teased her lightheartedly before he felt the trembling of her petite body in his arms.

"Talleha, honey? What's the matter?" he asked, concerned.

"I don't—I can't be sure, Victor," she stammered.

"Now, Talleha—you're trembling like a leaf, and I know you better than that. Tell me," he insisted, wanting to know what had frightened her so.

"Out the window down there—just beyond that row of rose bushes . . ."

Maurier hastily left her side to go to the window. "I don't see a thing, Talleha." He walked back to her slowly, commenting, "It's so damned dark out there, it's impossible to see anything."

"There was a big flash of lightning, Victor, and I would have sworn that it was Eliot Penwick down there on his horse. I couldn't make out his face, but I'd never mistake that animal."

Maurier slowly sank down on the bed beside her. "Penwick down there in that rain? You mean just sitting there on his horse?"

"And staring directly up at my window," she said, with such assurance that Maurier knew she had not imagined it.

Maurier was convinced that the man was an insane fool obsessed with getting Talleha back. But Maurier did not voice these thoughts to Talleha.

She noticed the solemn, thoughtful look on his face; perhaps that was why she gave him no argument when he ordered her, as a father would a child, to climb into bed and try to go to sleep. "I'm going to stay with you awhile." Giving her a wicked grin, he added, "Now, don't ask me to lie by your side, because then neither one of us would go to sleep. I've got some things to think about. Besides, I intend to look at that window a few more times."

He was pleasantly surprised that she did as he'd asked without any fuss. There was no way he'd have any peace until he was rid of Eliot Penwick. He was sure of it now. He had no recourse once he got Talleha away from here except to return and finish what he'd come for.

The pleasant company of Emilo Cortez had delayed his action when he'd arrived at the Casa del Lago and the intoxicating distraction of Talleha had certainly made his quest for revenge fade. In a way, he, too, had been obsessed by the black-eyed vixen whose sweet angel face looked so innocent.

It was devilishly hard to sit in the chair and not go to the bed beside her to snuggle up close. He quickly shrugged his lusty thoughts away. That had to wait for now. If she would just be as agreeable in the morning as she'd been tonight, there would be no problem. He had to convince her that it would be dangerous for her to return to her village while he was away. She must let him take her to Brownsville and remain there with Captain Crawford until he could return for her.

If she proved to be hardheaded and stubborn, then he would have to use force. If he had to, he'd make her his captive aboard his schooner, *Destiny,* moored in the harbor at Brownsville. The three most trusted men of his crew were there keeping an eye on his ship while he was away.

He figured that old Snapper, his galley cook, his first mate, Davy Carron, and that big bruiser, Bruno, could surely handle one little slip of a girl for a while during the brief time he had to be away.

He walked to the window one more time before allowing himself to relax in the comfortable overstuffed chair. Somehow, his robust body and his long legs could not get cozy enough for sleep.

Did he dare cast aside his resolve? There was one solution if he wanted to get some sleep. He moved toward the bed and cautiously lowered himself onto it. His head rested close to Talleha's feet, and his feet rested up against the headboard.

Maurier was so exhausted he gave into the weariness he felt just thinking about the day facing him. Already it was early morning.

At least he could relax; sleep was possible for him now because he was beside the woman he loved, and he knew nothing was going to happen to her as long as he was close by.

He'd never allow that as long as he was alive!

Chapter 29

The rains continued to fall as the dawn was breaking and the skies were dark and heavy with clouds, gray and ominous. Maurier got up from the bed. Was it a bad omen, he wondered? Was it a warning to get out of here as hastily as he could? Well, that was exactly what he intended to do.

He'd slept in his clothes, so he had only to pull on the black leather boots. Talleha slept so peacefully he hated to rouse her, but he had to.

He bent down so that his lips teased her ears as he gently whispered, "Wake up, sleepyhead. We've got a lot of miles to cover."

She gave a lazy stretch of her curvaceous body and her long lashes fluttered as she stared up at him for a moment before she falteringly purred, "What—what did you say, Vic? Time to get up?"

She looked so tempting to Maurier that he would have loved nothing more than to get into that cozy bed beside her. She was absolutely beautiful! He'd seen many a lady in the first light of day, but never one as enchanting as Talleha. Her jet-black hair was fanned out across the pillows, and the golden, silken flesh of her lovely arms and her dainty shoulders was bared to him.

The soft, sheer batiste of the gown clung to the soft mounds of her breasts. He allowed his eyes a moment to savor them.

"Come on, my darling. We're leaving as soon as you can get up. Now, listen to me, Talleha—I'm going back to my room to gather my things. You get dressed and gather up what you have to take. Are you hearing me, my darling? I'll come back here in—say, fifteen minutes."

"I'll be ready, Victor," she mumbled, still slightly dazed.

He rose up from the bed, giving her little rump a playful pat. "See that you are ready, little one."

She'd show that cocky rascal, she vowed as she leaped out of the bed, rushing around in a mad frenzy to gather together her belongings and pick out the garments she wanted to wear. Noticing the horrible morning outside her bedroom window, she laid out the lightweight black shawl.

With all this done, she started to struggle into the black riding skirt, but she was rushing so much she was fumbling. She chided herself to calm down a little. In doing so, she found she got dressed much quicker.

When Maurier came rushing through her door, she stood there with a smug look on her face. She was dressed in her riding skirt and a soft muslin blouse. Her black hair was neatly braided and her black shawl was flung over one arm. "Well, Victor, what held you up?"

His eyes took notice of the small bundle, neatly tied and placed on the bed, before they darted back to see her smiling at him. Eyes twinkling and lashes fluttering, she presented the image of an imp full of mischief.

He liked this quality about her. He'd have to remember in the future that he'd better not dare or challenge her. She'd be damned sure to give it her all to meet any challenge.

"I compliment you, Talleha. Most women could never have done it so swiftly. I take my hat off to you." He offered her his arm and suggested, "Shall we go, then?"

Her beautiful black eyes were bright and alive with curiosity as she quizzed him, "Are—are we heading for Cedar Springs, Victor?" She could hardly breathe as she awaited his answer for she knew she could either be elated by it—if she was going with him—or saddened, if he planned to leave her at her village to go on his way alone.

There was something about her demeanor that made Maurier decide to be evasive when he answered her. So he told her, "There is only one thing important to me right now, Talleha, and that is to get you away from Harrison County and Eliot Penwick."

"Well, that's enough for me, Victor," she said, taking a double step to keep up with his pace, and when he gazed down at her petite figure moving beside him, he gave her an admiring grin. Such a cute little minx she was as she tried to keep up with him!

The fact that they were leaving this place for somewhere that he knew she would be safe and secure made his mood light and gay. He could not resist teasing her, "Do you know what a wanton little wiggle you have when you walk, Talleha? It's enough to drive any man crazy!"

A provocative smile came to her lips as she purred, "Really? I—I drive you crazy? I shall remember that!"

Her black braids bobbed up and down as she bounced along beside him, and he could have sworn that she was giving forth a more exaggerated sway of her hips. He stopped suddenly just as he would have descended the stairway to take her in his arms and firmly plant a long, lingering kiss on her half-parted lips.

"You may have been a virgin, Talleha, until I came along and changed all that, but you were born a coquette. Did you know that?"

She gave him a quizzical look, seeking to know, "This name you call me—what is that, Victor?"

"You were born a flirt!" he told her with an amused grin on his handsome face.

She raised her fine-arched brow and looked at him for a second before answering. "If anyone would know that, it would be you."

He broke into laughter and clutched her around the waist to bring her closer. She could not resist breaking into a soft giggle, for she was unusually happy.

Something told her that wherever he was taking her, he was not going to be telling her farewell. That was enough to make her swell with joy.

They were a glorious sight to see, Emilo thought to himself as he watched them at the top of the stairway. They'd taken no notice of him as he stood there watching. He loved these two young people in a way he did not exactly understand. They'd given him something special he'd needed very badly.

It was marvelous to hear their laughter. Emilo knew now what had been absent so long in this hacienda: it was the laughter of two people in love. Since his dear wife had died, he'd had no one to share his laughter with.

Maurier and Talleha saw Emilo awaiting them with that wonderful smile on his face. Talleha was thinking how she was going to regret telling him goodbye in a few short minutes, wondering if she'd ever get to see him again. It pained her to think that she might not, for she'd come to love him. Maurier, though, knew he would be coming back to Harrison County.

"There is a tasty breakfast waiting for you two before you depart in this miserable weather. I would have wished you a better morning, but we can do nothing about the weather, can we?" Emilo accompanied his friends into the dining room and made his suggestion that perhaps it might be wise to wait for the storm to pass.

"No, sir—we'll just hope we ride out of it in a few miles. I'd not had a chance to tell you, sir, but Talleha swears that she saw Penwick on the grounds last night—standing in that driving rainstorm. I think he's crazy as a loon, and that kind of man is the most dangerous of all!"

Indignantly, Emilo exclaimed, "He was here? I had two of my very best men posted at the entrance gate and around the barn, and Herman was checking the garden area every so often. They reported to me that they saw nothing all night. What time was this, Talleha?"

"When I had gone to my room, leaving the two of you downstairs talking."

It was obvious this news disturbed Señor Cortez, and now he understood Maurier's eagerness to leave with Talleha as soon as possible. He would not try to discourage him. On the contrary, he rose up from his chair to announce, "I'll send word to Romano to saddle up your horses, si?"

"Yes, sir, that would be appreciated," Maurier told him, struggling with a mouthful of food he was devouring hastily. Talleha broke into a giggle observing his awkwardness.

"We're not in that big a rush, are we, Victor?" she taunted.

Finishing the last bite of a flaky biscuit he'd lavishly covered with butter and jam, he told her, "I'm in a

243

devilish hurry to be gone with you from this place."

When Emilo returned to announce that Romano would be bringing the horses to the side gate of the corral shortly, Maurier rose up from his chair to caution Talleha to get into her long black twill cape before she came outside. He took Emilo by the arm to have a final farewell in private.

"I wish to talk with Emilo a moment, Talleha, while you finish your coffee. Join us when you're through."

"Yes, Victor." Like an obedient child she took the last sip of her black coffee, savoring it. Setting down her cup, she got up from the table, took the cape from the top of her bundle, and draped it around her shoulders, then tied a bright bandana around her head before going out to the side veranda, where she knew she would find Señor Cortez and Victor.

By the time she got there, Victor had told Cortez his plans for Talleha. "I could not rest, Emilo, if I left her in Cedar Springs. I'm going to take her to Brownsville with me if I have to hogtie her. She'll be safe there with Captain Crawford."

"Wise decision, Maurier. I shall wait for your return, amigo." He clasped Victor's shoulders in a comradely embrace.

Talleha witnessed the scene and found it warmed her heart. She suddenly thought to herself of the reason she had so readily taken to Emilo. Never had he seemed like a stranger from the minute she'd walked through the door of his hacienda. She knew he'd felt the same way about her.

Both men sensed her standing in the doorway, her cape draping her shoulders, her face framed in the bright-colored kerchief. Emilo went to embrace her as he had Maurier. "A safe journey, my little Talleha. I ask only one thing of you, my dear," he grinned with that special warm smile of his brightening his face.

"Anything, Señor."

"Someday, I wish for you to return to the Casa del Lago. I will not rest in my grave unless you do."

"Oh, my dear, dear, Señor Cortez, I would not want that to happen. We shall meet again, I'm certain." There was a brilliant twinkle in her black eyes that assured him they spoke the truth. Her hand reached out to hold his for a moment before they finally moved to go down the steps of the veranda.

Amazingly, the rain tapered off to just a light sprinkle, and for that Victor and Talleha were grateful as they rushed to the gate where Romano held the reins of the two saddled horses.

All Emilo could think as he watched them making their mad dash across his carpeted grounds was how excited and wonderful to be so young and carefree. How he'd love to do it all again!

In his heart he told them to enjoy these days of rapture while they could. It all went by so devastatingly fast. It reminded Emilo of the seasons of the year. He and his lovely wife had shared the marvelous blossoming of the spring, for he had been her first love. They'd been two of the lucky ones to know the flaming passion he likened to the heat of summer. The most rewarding times of their life had been the golden glow of autumn they'd shared together just before her death. Then there came into his life the cold, dreary days of winter, when he was alone without her love to keep him warm.

Talleha and Victor had brought back the springtime.

Part III

The Flight to Freedom

Chapter 30

Emilo's thoughts were with the young couple as he went through the rest of the day. It was a long journey if Maurier did go to Brownsville as he'd planned. A man could travel no farther south than Brownsville and remain in the state of Texas.

Knowing how Victor was feeling when they spoke, Emilo was certain the destination was Brownsville. He hoped that they were lucky enough to have found clear skies, for the heavy rain had stalled over the Casa del Lago countryside most of the whole day.

It had been a very pleasant, cozy evening for Emilo, because he and Estaban had played games of checkers, puffed on their cheroots, and sipped their brandy until it was time to mount the stairway to retire.

As they moved to go into their individual bedrooms, Emilo expressed to Estaban just how much he'd enjoyed the evening.

"And so did I, Uncle Emilo. I—I thought if it was all right with you I'd stay on a day or two longer than I'd intended."

A slow, delighted smile broke on the señor's face as he confessed to his nephew, "Why, Estaban, nothing would please me more."

Estaban smiled and told him, "Then I shall. I gave

my mother no particular day when I'd return, so she will have no concern."

Emilo gave him a pat on the shoulder and bid him good night. As he strolled thoughtfully into his room he could hear the light raindrops still falling against the windows, but they weren't so fierce, at least. He hoped his friends had a dry place to sleep this night.

Maurier knew he'd pushed a long, hard day of riding on Talleha. He also knew she would have fallen off the little mare, Amapola, before she'd have pleaded for mercy. But now that they were at their campsite on the banks of the Trinity River, eating a simple, but filling meal, he reached over to kiss her cheek, declaring, "We'll let up tomorrow, Talleha—I promise you that. I've put enough distance between us and Penwick now. That's all I was concerned about. I just want you safe, Talleha." There was such a loving look in his eye and such sincerity in his deep voice, Talleha knew he was speaking from the heart. He had to care for her or else he wouldn't be so concerned, she thought to herself. Elation swelled within her.

Her lovely smile told him his words had pleased her, even though she made no effort to speak. There was no denying she was tired. Every bone and muscle in her body ached with weariness. Yet, she'd enjoyed their ride over a strange countryside which she'd never seen before.

They'd been nearly as lucky as Emilo had hoped for. It was true that they'd ridden through a downpour for almost an hour before getting a break. But they'd only been spared about an hour of clearing sky when another downpour was upon them. However, they crossed the Sabine River and were greeted by the sun breaking through the clouds.

By the time they'd reached the spot where Maurier decided they'd make their campsite for the night and the sun was setting in the western sky, Talleha's long braids were dry from the heat of the sun and the wind whipping them as Amapola had galloped swiftly over the countryside.

When they'd finished eating and Victor had unrolled the blankets, which would serve for their bed, he challenged her, "Too tired to go for a dip in the river?"

She had removed her boots and stockings and was sitting there in her bare feet. He had no way of knowing that she'd already decided that a refreshing dip in the waters of the river was tempting her after a long day of riding. She could feel the dust and grime from the billowing dirt stirred by her little Amapola's galloping hooves.

The countryside was now lit up by a lovely golden fall moon and clear skies. It was a wonderful evening with a very light, calm breeze.

Before Talleha gave Victor her answer, she stood up with her back turned away from him, all the while hastily unbuttoning her blouse. Only then did she decide to answer him, for she figured to have him at a great disadvantage.

"Well, I guess so," she drawled slowly. "And last one in is a rotten egg!" By now she'd flung her blouse through the air and hastily wiggled out of her divided black skirt.

Maurier watched her frenzied undressing and he busily started pulling off his boots. By now, he glanced over to see that the little imp already had all her clothes removed except her underthings. If he was to beat her into the river and call her bluff, he could not worry about his pants or shirt. He admired her spunk, so he let her scurry down to the bank of the river as he rose up off the ground. Confident that he could outdistance her, he made his move. When she was about to plunge into the river, a mighty splash erupted in the water. Maurier was already there, rearing up, roaring with laughter and taunting her, "Come on in, you little rotten egg!"

With her hands clasped at her waistline and standing in her undergarments, she lashed out at him angrily, "That's not fair, Victor! You cheat! You're still dressed!"

"You said nothing about clothes. You said the last one in the water—remember?" he deviously teased her.

Before she could reply, he swam to the center of the river. Giving out a grumble, she stepped into the shallow waters lapping at the bank of the river. She lay back into the water, letting her long tresses be washed of the dirt from the trail they'd traveled today.

As she played in the water, Maurier swam a short distance away, hoping the cooling waters would ease her temper. Out of the corner of her eye she could see where he was in the river, and she decided that she would wait for him to swim to her. When a few minutes passed without that happening, she turned to see no signs of him. Immediately, she suspected that he was up to some mischief. She remembered how Hunter's and Salina's son used to play tricks on her when they swam in the Lake of the Pines: he would grab her ankles to yank her down into the water and dunk her.

She smiled slyly as she dived down into the water. She'd show him a thing or two, she thought to herself. But she was to be disappointed, for there was no sign of Victor underwater. Damn him, she muttered under her breath! What was he trying to pull on her?

For a few more minutes she lingered, searching for some sign of him, but she saw nothing. Giving a shrug of her damp shoulders, she decided she was through with their little game. Besides, she felt clean and pleasantly refreshed, so she stood up, shaking her hair to rid it of the excess water, squeezing out the long mane with her hands.

She made quite a sight for Maurier to see as she marched up the bank with her wet undergarments clinging temptingly to her curvy, petite body.

When she'd been searching for him, he'd come on up on the bank and removed his wet pants and shirt. He stood now with his handsome, muscled body draped in a towel. He made a most sensuous figure with the moonlight shining down on his bare chest and rippling arms. He was naked except for the towel around his middle. His strong legs and thighs were bared. He could have been Adonis.

The sight of him had an instant impact: she came alive all over. It irritated her that she allowed him to have such power over her. It would serve him right if she acted like she didn't even see him standing there arrogantly flaunting himself. She smiled, thinking about how it would wound his pride. Maybe, just maybe that would teach him a lesson.

But all the time she was indulging in her private little musings, Victor was striding closer to her with only the towel draped around his waist. If she could have seen the look in his eyes, she would have known that he was not about to be denied anything he wanted!

His long, slender fingers were already itching to remove the wet, clinging undergarments molding her satiny flesh. When he finally came to stand beside her and she gazed up into those solemn eyes, she could not speak. His playful mood had changed.

He said nothing as he took the liberty of removing her camisole, his intense blue eyes devouring the beauty he saw there. When all her garments lay on the ground, he still said not a word as he lifted her up in his arms to walk toward the bedroll.

Lying back on the ground, he carried her with him so that the length of her petite body stretched to press against his. His hands cradled her head and he pulled her closer so their lips would meet. Only after a long searing kiss did he speak. "You love me, my Talleha. You love me as I have loved you," he urged her. She could feel his flaming flesh moving so that she was straddling him and his forceful maleness sought to touch and tease her sensuously.

All the senses of her body were stimulated to wild excitement as he lay beneath her. He broke away from her lips so that he might caress the jutting tip of one of her breasts with his tongue. Ah, he stirred such a sweet, sweet agony within her that she arched her back to accommodate his powerful, thrusting body.

When he did answer her silent plea for him to enter her, she gave out a moan of pleasure, crying out his name. He smothered her lovely face with his kisses, answering her sighs with those of his own. "Oh, God— God, Talleha!"

Their bodies were bound together, as were their hearts and souls. It was a timeless moment that each of them wanted to continue endlessly. In each second the ecstasy mounted to a new plateau of sensual pleasure as they clung to one another eagerly. Victor loved the feel of her velvet softness capturing him. He fired with a new height of passion as he felt the faster tempo of her flaming body pounding against his with a savage eagerness.

His huge, muscled body gave forth a giant shudder, for he was forced to surrender even though he did not wish to. The same was true for Talleha as she collapsed against his broad chest and sighed breathlessly.

For a moment they lay still. Maurier listened to her soft little purring sounds and he felt the heaving of her body as it slowly calmed. He lay there with a smile on his face, still feeling the magic glow of what had just passed between them.

Talleha was still reeling from the new, strange ecstasy that was theirs. In her innocence she was amazed by the many ways there were to love, and she suddenly realized just how much more experienced Victor was. She almost felt shy now and because of that, she moved to sink down by his side. He allowed her to change her position without any protest, but he had no inkling that it was because she was feeling embarrassed about her ignorance of love and life.

"Did you like that, my darling?" His deep voice broke the night's silence.

In a hesitating voice, she replied, "Yes—yes, but I—well, I—"

Interrupting her, Victor insisted on knowing, "Why are you stammering so? God, you could have fooled me. I thought you were enjoying it as much as I was." His voice cracked with sharpness, for he was now feeling a painful disappointment.

"But I did, you hot-tempered fool! I was merely trying to tell you I didn't know—I don't know as much about making love as you obviously do, Victor," she snapped.

He roared with laughter and pulled her stiffened body next to him, knowing he'd riled her. "You silly little goose, I adore you! Well, we've just got to give you a lot of lessons, and I will certainly take delight in being your teacher. I've no doubt you're going to be a fast learner, my darling Talleha. No doubt at all!" And he knew he'd be an eager teacher as well.

She snuggled closer to him and with a provocative look in her black eyes, she retorted, "I've always heard that practice makes perfect."

"So true, my pet! So very true!"

Boldly, she challenged him, "Then should we not begin my lessons?"

He hastened to answer her challenge.

Chapter 31

True to his word, Maurier did not push Talleha so hard the next day. As they rode over the Texas countryside, they could have been going on a pleasure jaunt, for their mood was one of lighthearted gaiety. He told himself it would be smart to stop earlier to make their campsite, for it would give them a longer, more leisurely evening by the campfire.

He loved listening to her soft voice relating tales about her childhood and her remarkable mother. How simply and honestly Dawn had taught her about life. He realized that Talleha had never felt any shame that her mother had had no husband nor that she'd had no father, as the other children in the village had.

As it would happen, he was the one talking about his childhood on the third night of their journey. She listened with just as much interest as he talked to her. Both were struck by the strange coincidence of their similar pasts.

Talleha was intrigued by the lady he described when he spoke with such soft warmth about his French mother. What a bittersweet love each of their mothers had shared with their lovers. These men were never to be their husbands, even though each woman had given her lover a child.

It was on the third night away from the Casa del Lago, after they'd talked about Maurier's youth, that Talleha was dealt a stunning blow that she'd given no thought to before. She could not shake the thought aside when the time came for them to go to bed.

Maurier sensed her reserved mood with him, but they'd shared such a rapturous time the last few days that he told himself his darling Talleha was just weary from their journey. Whatever was ailing her, he decided to let her have some time to herself this night. He attempted to make the feeble excuse when she prepared to lie down in the bedroll that he was going to take a little stroll and smoke one of his cheroots.

Trying to sound very casual, he told her, "I won't be so far away that I can't observe you, so you can relax and get on to sleep. You look tired tonight, Talleha."

She gave him no fuss as she proceeded to obey him, for she had many things weighing heavily on her mind. But as she curled up on the bedroll, she did not go to sleep. In fact, she was still wide awake when he finally came to lie down beside her. He did not touch her, and she was glad. He assumed she was asleep.

Over and over again a voice kept ringing in her ear, telling her that she could have his baby, and she wanted to scream out for the voice to be still. She wasn't as brave as her mother, Dawn. She didn't want to have a baby and raise it without the man she loved, as her mother had done. How different she would have felt if he were her husband and she were his wife.

More and more she realized what a small, protected world she'd known with Dawn. Why, she hadn't even realized that anything existed outside of the river and lake country she'd grown up in. Now, she'd seen with her own eyes the wonderful rolling hills and thick piney woods. She and Victor had ridden into the valley of the

257

blacklands and past the flowing rivers of the Trinity and the Sabine.

Just today, they had come to the bottomlands, more level, where she could see for miles in the distance. Soon, Victor had told her, they'd come to the coast and she would see ships. She'd never forget the wonderful excitement in his eyes as he told her about the ships, describing them in great detail.

He loved the sea and his schooner, the *Destiny*. He spoke with a passion so devoted that she actually envied that ship of his. Would he sit and talk with such feeling about her, she asked herself? It was doubtful; and it was best she not try to delude herself.

Knowing her love for the animals of the woods, he told her about the creatures of the sea and the strange breeds of birds that hibernated along the coastline. She'd never seen a seagull, nor had she seen the majestic palm trees he spoke about. She had to confess that she was eager to see this place he was taking her to, because if it was as he'd described it, she could enjoy hours of strolling down sandy beaches, picking up the varied kinds of seashells, feeding the strange little birds he'd told her about. It all sounded so different to her than what she'd come to know in her woods at the Lake of the Pines.

It struck her as funny that Maurier had come to this country from England and yet knew more about the state of Texas than she did, even though she had been born and raised here.

If things had not happened to alter her whole life, Talleha was now wondering if she'd have lived forever around the little village of Cedar Springs. What a shame it would have been! She had to confess that she was excited about the strange new worlds she was learning about.

It filled her with a wave of sadness to think that her

mother and Hunter and his wife, Salina, never saw any place but Cedar Springs. Already her mother's life was over, and Talleha had no doubt that Hunter and Salina would live out the rest of their lives right there in Cedar Springs. Their son, Boyce, would stay in the village to marry some girl living nearby, as she would have surely done, too.

Maurier noticed how entranced she'd become as he told her about the place he was taking her to, and he was delightfully pleased that she'd given him no fuss about his plans to take her to Captain Crawford's house on the coast of Brownsville.

His eyes were filled with love as he'd declared, "Ah, yes, I can already see you, my little sea nymph, running down the beach with your black hair blowing in the swift sea breeze."

"You have me eager to get to this place, Victor. You make it sound so wonderful. You seem to love it, so I know I will."

"I know you will too, Talleha. I think you will be a good little sailor, too," he told her.

"Sailor, Victor?"

"Sure—when I get you aboard the *Destiny*."

"Oh, will I get to do that, too?"

"Of course, you will, Talleha," he said eagerly. He could not know the wild elation she felt, for she could not have been happier. Her wild, reckless heart had assumed that he was sailing from the Texas shores with her with him. Nothing could have made her happier than this.

"And where will we go?" she anxiously asked him.

"I—I don't know," he stammered. "I can't tell you that right now, Talleha." He gazed upon her lovely face with its expectant expression and he wished he'd not gotten so carried away when he was talking about his ship. He had no right to promise her anything right

259

now, no right at all; his future was just too uncertain.

His mood had changed so quickly that she did not know what to think. The way he was acting now had her utterly confused; she became withdrawn and quiet.

After an endless silence, Maurier pressed her by inquiring, "Something wrong, Talleha?"

"Wrong? With me, Victor? No—no, there is nothing wrong." After she said that, she immediately put up her armor of reserve again, and he found it impossible to invade her private world the rest of the night.

The morning hours did not ease the mysterious tension consuming them. Maurier had not rested, trying to figure out Talleha's complex moods, and Talleha could not understand why he had spoken with such a lying tongue last night. It was obvious to her that he didn't want to commit himself with a direct answer to her question.

Why would he act that way after they'd talked so intimately about the wonderful times that lay ahead for the two of them? After all, it had been Victor who'd initiated the conversation, and she had then enthusiastically joined in with wild anticipation. She would have had to be a fool not to notice the sudden chilly mood that gripped him.

She did not lie in his arms as she'd been doing the other nights, and she did not kiss him good night. She gave him a quick, hasty good-night and turned her back to him.

That was not his Talleha, and it was such a startling shock that he lay there dumbfounded by her mercurial moods. The only thing to which he could attribute her troubles was that particular time of the month when a lady just wanted to be left alone.

Come morning, her waspish mood would be gone. Tomorrow, she would be his sweet-faced angel again, he consoled himself. When he'd managed to convince himself, sleep did overtake him.

Talleha heard his heavy breathing and resented that he was able to rest so well when she was so wide awake. It had not bothered him that they'd not enjoyed the midnight swim in the river a short distance away. Why should she let it trouble her either? But damn it, it did!

Her stubborn streak urged her to make a point, then, of rising before he did in the morning, so she could take a refreshing dip in the river. Knowing how vulnerable she was to his persuasive charm, she'd not be caught in the river naked. No, she would make a point of getting up well in advance of him, having her bath in the river, and getting dressed before he got up.

So strong and determined was her will that she managed to do just that. It was laborious effort when she'd managed to have only a few hours of sleep. But the cold river water was delightfully refreshing and she felt invigorated as she strolled back to their campsite.

This was the glowing, radiant woman Maurier saw when he first opened his eyes, and her gleaming wet black hair told him what she'd been up to. Ringlets curled around her face and her head was held high with that pert little nose stuck up in the air. She gave off the air of an invincible maiden, and it made him wonder how she was going to respond to him this morning.

He rose up from the bedroll, mumbling to himself, "Well, guess I might as well find out." He bent down to roll up the blankets on the ground before taking time to pull on his boots.

With his back turned to her, he heard her lilting voice humming a tune: it would seem that her spirits were high and lively. He grinned, chiding himself that he was more experienced than she: he should be able to deal with this young lady and her moods.

It was ridiculous that she'd disturbed his sleep as she

261

had. After all, he was almost a decade older than she. He was a man who'd been on his own and traveled all over the world, and she was a simple little girl raised in the backwoods. She could not be as smart and clever as he was, he tried to assure himself. Having convinced himself of this, he lifted up the bedroll so he could sit on it to pull on his black leather boots. It was an arrogant, self-assured expression Talleha saw on his face as she approached him.

"Well, you look like you're full of vigor. Had a swim, did you?" he casually remarked as she walked temptingly close to him. She'd not taken the time to make her usual long braids, so her hair hung loose, falling freely over her tiny shoulders. The dampness lingering there made it look like glossy black satin. His observant eyes noticed that she'd changed her blouse and now was wearing a loose-fitting tunic of pale yellow.

While the tunic itself was simple, exquisite embroidery lined the neck and the long, flowing sleeves, and around her tiny waist the blouse was cinched by a silver-tooled belt. She made quite a striking image as she stood there before him.

"I've never seen that before, Talleha—your blouse and belt. They're nice," he told her.

"Yes, I like them. They were gifts."

"Gifts?" He wore a quizzical look. Who had given her such nice gifts, he wondered?

"Wasn't he sweet and generous?" She fingered the lovely silver belt, lightly stroking the links.

"I guess a lady would think so." There was an embarrassed look on his face, for he'd never given her any token gift to express his love for her. Actually, when he thought about it, he had not been the most gallant of men in his courting of Talleha. He'd really not been as generous with her as he had with some of the courtesans he'd visited when he was in ports along the English and French coasts. His face reflected his thoughts at that moment and he felt remorse.

While Talleha did not know what he was thinking, there was something about his face which made her wish to end whatever the anguish was, so she flippantly quipped, "Ah, but then who am I to tell you what a generous man Señor Cortez is."

"Señor Cortez—Emilo gave them to you?"

"But of course—who else?" She turned sharply around so that she was not facing him as she added, "You're so smart I figured you knew that without my telling you."

He opened his mouth to speak and decided against it. He tightened his lips, feeling impatient with himself. The little imp! She'd played him and she knew it.

He'd even the score with her, he vowed!

Chapter 32

There was a stiff, guarded air about Victor and Talleha as they started out on their day's journey, and that tension had not eased up by midday. It seemed to Talleha that the landscape never changed in the Texas countryside. It was flat and the farmlands seemed to stretch endlessly with their late summer and early autumn crops of vegetables and orchards of fruit trees.

There were no grazing herds of cattle in the grasslands as there had been back in the rolling hills near the Casa del Lago. For the first time in her life, Talleha saw shrubs and trees she'd never seen before. She forgot about being aloof and reserved when her inquisitive nature got the best of her, forcing her to ask Victor what they were.

Politely, he informed her she was seeing mesquite trees, which the farmers used for fodder because of their sweet pods. The sagebrush had also caught her interest. If he'd been impatient and irritated by her puzzling behavior, he now found himself becoming more forgiving. He couldn't help himself! She was adorable, with a childlike quality of eager curiosity.

What a handful she was at times, he thought. Yet she brought out something in him he'd never experienced with any other woman. He wanted to protect her. The thought of anything happening to her or of some other man taking his place upset him immensely. A voice deep within him seemed to be laughing and telling him, "Well, fellow, you've only one choice left, and that is to marry the girl. Simple as that!"

Now, it wasn't that Victor Maurier had not expected someday to claim himself a wife and have heirs; it was the conventional way of doing things. But he'd always pictured himself doing this a good ten years from now, when his roaming and wanderlust had calmed somewhat. For a few more years he wanted to sail the seas aboard *Destiny*. There were still some places he yearned to see. A wife just was not practical in the current scheme of things.

So in private, this thought argued with the voice of conscience, but in an unrelenting firmness, his heart told him he could not have it both ways. He'd have to marry her or leave her behind. He was so caught up in his whimsy that he almost yelled out an angry protest.

"Did you say something, Victor?" Talleha inquired.

"No, I didn't say anything," he curtly replied.

"Guess I was imagining it, then," she said, shrugging her shoulders and turning her attention back to the countryside.

However, she knew she was not imagining the distinct sound of galloping hooves in the distance a few minutes later, and she spurred Amapola up to cover the distance separating her from Victor and his stallion, Sultana. "Did you hear what I heard, Victor?"

He'd been preoccupied with his own thoughts and had not heard the riders in the distance less than a mile away. "Hear what, Talleha?"

"Riders—behind us!" she told him. He halted his mount, making the highstrung Sultana jump back and forth nervously, as if he resented Maurier reining him so tight. She was right, he realized. It had to be the Indian blood flowing in her veins that had made her perception so keen.

The land lay flat, and the miniscule image against the horizon appeared to be of three individuals. Maurier cursed the fact that the damned land was so flat—there were no hills and valleys to conceal oneself. A degree of panic seized him, not for himself but for Talleha. Instinct told him that she was the one in jeopardy. His blue eyes quickly searched the countryside for a hiding place. Perhaps the riders were just drifters on their way south—perhaps to the border, on their way into Mexico.

The flourishing rows of vegetables gave no cover for them and their horses, he realized; neither did the neat rows of fruit trees. Where could they go, he wondered?

Talleha saw the concern on his tense face. He did not have to speak for her to know what he was thinking. Her black eyes scanned the horizon and she saw a hiding place which obviously Maurier had not noticed.

"Victor, look! Over there to the west."

He heeded her call and saw where her finger was pointing. "All right—go!" He wondered with amazement how her eyes had spotted the shed beyond the thick grove of fruit rees. It might just work, he tried to assure himself. He followed behind Talleha's little mare, now weaving and bobbing in and among the green-branched trees. They made it to the shed.

It was very tight quarters with Talleha's little mare and the huge stallion inside the three remaining walls of what was once a shed. Now, all they could do was wait to see if the riders galloped on by or not.

Maurier hoped his fears were unwarranted. Never did he doubt that he could protect Talleha against one man or maybe even two. But he was only human and three man could prove too much for him.

His eyes strained through the weathered strips of wood as he heard the trio come down the trail. His heart was pounding erratically as they halted their horses near the edge of the orchard. What he wouldn't have given to hear their conversation as they lingered there before spurring their horses back into action.

That was enough to tell him that they were up to no good, he decided. It created an abrupt change in his plans which he didn't exactly relish, but at least it would be safer, he figured. It would mean a longer day of riding for them tomorrow, but that didn't matter if it proved to be safer for Talleha.

By the time Maurier felt it was safe to leave the ramshackle shed, dusk was falling over the countryside and they'd enjoyed the tasty fruit from some farmer's harvest. If Talleha was willing, he planned to go longer this evening.

He changed his plans after he'd taken a glance at the map that Emilo had marked for him as the best route for their journey. But Maurier's firm instinct was to veer sharply to the east and not follow the trail due south they'd been on. They mounted up and prepared to ride.

Because she gave him no hint of being tired, he pushed on long after darkness was all around them. It meant they were that much closer to Brownsville. Talleha seemed to understand his feeling, for she voiced no protest.

Maurier was thinking she would surely be tired of their long ride when his seaman's nose detected the smell of a salt breeze. He knew this was impossible; the only way he could explain it to himself was that he was exhausted and should camp for the night and rest.

He pulled up the reins, causing Sultana to stop and allow Talleha to join him with her little mare. "I'm ready for some food and rest, Talleha. Does that sound good to you?"

"Sounds wonderful," she confessed. Her thighs, hips, and back throbbed with an aching pain. They had surely ridden an extra two hours today, and the extra time spent at the shed must have added a good five hours to this long day's journey.

He reined Sultana toward a nearby grove of trees. "Let's see about over here. Should provide a cozy little nest for us tonight."

She gave him a nod and reined in Amapola. Her keen senses were sharper than Maurier's and she pointed out to him the rushing stream to the south. "What stream is that, Victor—straight ahead?"

It took him a moment—it was too dark to see the map in his pocket—but then he recalled something Emilo told him. This was all new, strange country to Victor. "It has to be the Colorado River, I think. I can tell you for sure once we get a fire built and I can look at Emilo's map."

After they dismounted neither of them confessed just how sore they were as they worked to put together a hastily prepared meal and take from their saddle bags the gear they'd need.

This was one night Talleha did not intend to indulge herself in a midnight swim. The dirt and grime from the trail could remain until morning, when she'd had a good night's rest; Victor could do as he pleased. It would be heaven to lay her tired body down.

While she could not know it, her sentiments were his tonight, too. By the time they'd finished their meager fare, he was questioning just how wise his decision had been to ride on so long after the delay in the orchard.

He still had a sense that they were close to the shoreline of Texas, and yet he knew this to be impossible. They could not be that far south so soon.

However, he was not imagining it; in fact, they were

less than thirty miles away from Matagorda Bay and the Gulf of Mexico. Just a few miles to the east was a little port town called Port Lavaca. Had they been traveling in daylight, Maurier's keen eyes might have seen signs of the nearby bay.

Once the two of them had satisfied their hunger, Talleha was the first to admit that she was ready to enjoy the comfort of the bedroll. Maurier nodded that he understood. "I'll be joining you shortly. I'm tired too." He gave her rump an affectionate pat as she rose up from the ground and it brought forth a complaining retort, "God, Victor! Why did you do that? I'm so sore I can hardly walk."

"Just couldn't resist, with you flaunting it, honey," he confessed, winking his eye.

She hobbled slowly away from him and gave out a disgruntled mumble, "Well, I can assure you it wasn't intentional. Goodnight, Victor." Wearily she walked over to the bedroll and sat down to remove her boots.

A warm, loving smile was on his face as he called out to her, "Goodnight, ma cherie." He spoke from the heart, for she was the dearest thing in the world to him.

Sitting there alone with the embers of the campfire burning lower and lower, he thought about the fact that once he'd met Captain Crawford and gone aboard his ship, he'd stopped speaking French. Only on very rare occasions had he sought to do so, and it was usually when very deep emotions were involved.

It was strange, really; it was the language he'd spoken throughout his boyhood.

He glanced in the direction of the bedroll where Talleha lay all curled up like a kitten. He didn't have to be by her side to know that she was already asleep. There was a strangeness in the air tonight, he thought to himself as he sat there alone. He felt his mother, Colette's presence there with him at that moment.

269

In a soft voice he declared, "You would like my Talleha, maman. I know you would."

He spent a few quiet moments alone before he rose up to join Talleha on the bedroll. He suddenly realized that with all his philandering, he'd never spoken the endearing words of love to any woman as he had to Talleha. Never before had he pursued a woman with sweet persuasion by speaking his words of love in French.

Only Talleha had ignited that desire.

Chapter 33

As reluctant as he was to awaken her, Maurier knew he must, for dawn was breaking and it looked like a good day for them to travel. At least they'd been lucky after that first morning to be spared from rain and storms. How miserable it would have been if the rains had remained with them, he thought.

"Come on, sleepyhead! That's all the beauty sleep you need for one night," he murmured softly as he bent over her still body. He grinned, thinking to himself that it looked as if she'd not moved all night long.

Still dazed by her heavy sleep, she flopped over to lie on her back, and in doing so, she flung out her arm, causing Maurier to quickly lean backward in order to keep from getting slammed. "Hey, you little savage," he chuckled.

"Victor—oh, Victor, is it you?" she drawled.

"And just who else would it be?" He teased her with his finger, tracing a line over her cheek to her forehead and back down the other side of her face.

Her long lashes fluttered open and closed again as she continued to lie there, making no effort to greet the new day. A little smile came to her face and she stretched her body like a cat.

271

"Come on, Talleha, or I'll ride off without you," he threatened.

Her eyes opened and life was springing in them now. "You'd not do that, Victor Maurier. I know you wouldn't," she declared, the hint of a pout on her lips.

"I might be tempted if you keep trying my patience as you're doing by lying there when we need to get started." He moved away to prepare for their departure. He glanced back at her to see her cradling her chin in the palms of her hands. She had been bone-tired, he realized, and the tiredness was still with her.

They surely had to be within a day or two of Brownsville, to judge by his map. He hoped so, for her sake!

"Come on, honey! We still don't know about those riders we spotted yesterday."

That had an impact on her, and as she raised her face up to look at Maurier, she realized that her fears about them had faded, though Victor was still concerned.

She tarried no longer, but immediately started rolling up the blankets. When they were tightly rolled, she tied each end with leather straps.

Now that he'd got her moving, he marveled how speedily she applied herself to the task of doing as he'd requested. Much sooner than he'd expected, they were mounted and ready to go.

As they spurred their mounts, he called her attention to the fact that she'd not braided her long, thick hair.

She gave forth a lighthearted giggle, "Didn't have time." But her burst of gaiety quickly changed to a more serious air as she insisted on knowing from Maurier, "You—you must think those men were posing a threat to us. Tell me honestly—did you?"

"I don't know, but it was enough to make me want to be bloody cautious. Perhaps it was just coincidence that they stopped by the orchard, but I had to assume it was because they'd lost sight of us and were trying to figure which way we were going. I can't afford to chance anything—not with three hombres against me."

In a somber, serious tone, she firmly declared, "But I'm with you, Victor, so it's three against two." The look on her face told him she wasn't trying to be flippant, but rather spoke in earnest. He never loved her more, and he knew that if the occasion arose, he would probably find her to be as brave as she was beautiful. That was amazingly rare with fragile-looking beauties.

He gave her a wink and replied, "I can't think of anyone I'd rather have fighting by my side than you, ma cherie."

"I appreciate those kind words, sir," she smiled prettily. She thought how dashing and handsome he looked this morning, so bronzed he seemed almost as dark as the halfbreed, Hunter.

A feeling of love rushed over her like a tide, and thoughts that had disturbed her the day before were swept away. Doubts and fears no longer existed for Talleha. All she knew was that she loved the man at her side. What tomorrow held for her did not matter, for all she cared about was being with Victor.

Many miles separated Maurier and Talleha from Harrison County, but Emilo had greeted the glorious golden dawn enthusiastically. He was impatient for Estaban to return to the Casa del Lago, as he'd promised to do after he'd informed his mother of his plans to stay with Emilo during the roundup season to acquaint himself with the ranch's operations.

Like Emilo, Marjorie had greeted the new day with determined plans. She could not recall how long it had been since she'd gone out alone in her little gig to pay a call on one of her neighbors, as she'd regularly done when Frank was alive.

Last night, she'd decided to pay a call on Emilo Cortez, and it was long overdue. Marjorie realized that it was not her dear friends and neighbors who'd failed her; she had failed herself. It was time to do something about it. Such a wonderful morning seemed to confirm her decision.

When Lucita had helped her dress, Marjorie announced her plans for the morning. "Alone, señora?" the Mexican girl asked, expressing her surprise.

"But of course. Has it truly been so long, Lucita? I guess it has, but if you'll recall, I used to do it all the time."

"Si, I do remember, señora," Lucita confessed.

"Now, why don't you look in on Ralph while I'm away as I've been doing every morning?"

"Si, señora—I'll check on him while you're away," Lucita assured her mistress.

"I would appreciate that, Lucita. I'll return by early afternoon. I'm going to pay a visit to my dear friend, Emilo Cortez. It has been far too long since I've seen him."

"Ah, Señor Cortez—he is a very nice man. Yes, it is good that you go to see him, señora."

"I don't wish Eliot to know, if he should inquire as to where I've gone, Lucita."

"Oh, no—no, señora, I will tell him nothing," Lucita quickly replied.

"Very good." She gave the young girl an affectionate pat on the shoulders. "I can always count on you, can't I, Lucita?"

"Si, señora—always!" She watched her mistress go out the door, and it was like the good old times to see her so alive and pulsing with vigor. Lucita smiled slyly,

274

thinking to herself that Eliot Penwick had not accomplished what he so fervently desired. He had not conquered and subdued this woman, and he'd never rule the Greenfield ranch. She was sure of it now!

Lucita was glad that her little escapade with him had lasted but one brief night. Eliot was not that exciting a man in bed anyway, she recalled. She'd take her hot-blooded Castillo in their little hayloft over him anytime. Brad Castillo truly knew the art of making love to a woman and sought to please her. Eliot was so concerned with himself that Lucita was left wanting, but he could not have cared.

There was no time to waste on those thoughts now, for she was going to see about Señor Ralph, as the señora had requested.

As the feisty little servant went down the hall to Ralph's room, she had to admit she enjoyed spending time with him. He was always so grateful for her time, and he was kind and gentle. Perhaps he was a bit ugly, but she found he possessed a most magnificent body; she sensed he was not aware of it. She found him to be a shy gentleman, most unsure of himself.

During his recuperation, the earthy little Lucita had given him his baths, and those dark eyes of hers had missed nothing. He was more of a man than he realized. She appreciated the gentle touch of his hand and the tenderness in his voice when he thanked her for the smallest favor she bestowed upon him. He was quite a contrast to the rugged Brad Castillo, who could be overbearing at times.

For a year she'd been Castillo's woman and he'd been her lover, but he had offered her nothing for the future. Being around the mistress so much and absorbing some of her knowledge, Lucita was shrewder than most of the servants in the household.

Her señora did not know that Lucita was very

275

ambitious. She did not wish to live all her life as a servant, as her mother had. She had more glorious visions for herself. A few days ago she'd had a brilliant idea about her future and how she could change her station in life. Marjorie's suggestion that she look in on Ralph fit into her plan perfectly. Ralph could be exactly the "savior" she needed to escape a dull fate.

She took a moment to smooth down her hair before she gave a soft rap on the door and called out, "Señor Ralph, it is Lucita."

When she heard his strange English-accented voice bidding her to enter, she went through the door, sensuously swaying up to his bedside with a provocative glint in her black eyes. "Good morning, señor. I came to see if there is anything I could do to make you comfortable."

The very sight of her was like a tonic to Ralph. She was beautiful and he swore he could have spanned her tiny waist with his two hands. Those doelike eyes of hers were the most tantalizing eyes he'd ever seen. He recalled a pair of exquisite onyx earrings his aunt wore; Lucita's eyes reminded him of them.

He tried to keep his voice from cracking when he replied, for her effect on him was overwhelming. He didn't want her to think ill of him. "I'm—I'm fine, Lucita." He propped himself up straighter in the bed and pushed the pillows up behind his back. Conversation did not come easily to Ralph, but he made a feeble attempt at it by remarking on the beautiful morning.

She sighed as she pushed back the sheers at his windows, "Ah, si—it is a beautiful day, and a shame you have to be confined in this room, señor."

Ralph gave her one of his big, friendly grins and declared with a new boldness which amazed even him, "But you brighten up the room, Lucita."

His comment surprised Lucita, but it also pleased

her. "Gracias, señor. That was a nice thing for you to say." She turned away from the windows and gave him her most attractive smile.

"It is true. I always enjoy your visits and it always adds pleasure to my day. You and the señora have been so kind to me since I was injured."

She fluttered around the room, straightening various objects here and there, but actually it was an attempt to linger near him. She moved closer to his bed and said, "You, señor, are easy to be kind to, because *you* are always kind. Your uncle could use some of your good nature, señor."

"No, I guess we don't have very much in common. I sure didn't inherit his good looks," Ralph remarked thoughtfully.

She leaned over closer to him in the bed, which gave Ralph a very exciting glimpse of her silken cleavage, her scooped neckline slightly gaping. "A handsome man is sometimes ugly; and an ugly man can be most handsome, through the eyes of a lady who might just happen to care for him—love him," she softly purred. Ralph's eyes brightened as he heard her revelation. Could what she said be true? She appeared to believe what she was saying.

She gave a cute little flip to her floral skirt and sat down on the bed beside him, which she knew was far too much liberty for a servant to take. But Lucita knew she had Ralph entranced; she wanted to play this moment for all it was worth.

Her black eyes danced over his face as she told him, "I knew an hombre once who was very ugly, but all the señoritas sought him out because he was so romantic. It is the truth, señor."

"Really, Lucita?" He straightened up even more on the bed, and their bodies were just a few inches apart now.

277

"Really, señor!" She let her fingertip lightly touch his cheek and then quickly drew her hand back to her lap to feign embarrassment. "I—I think you are very good looking."

Ralph felt like he'd been hit by a bolt of lightning; his body was afire with an overwhelming urge to kiss the gorgeous little Mexican girl. His male pride had never soared so high, and he gave way to the impulse to do just that.

Not only did he amaze himself, but Lucita was stunned by his powerful, stimulating kiss and she was filled with excitement.

When Ralph finally released her, he gasped breathlessly, "Dear God, Lucita—I—I think I've fallen helplessly in love with you."

She was breathless too as she sighed, "Oh, señor! I—I think I, too, am in love! But I know I've no right. . . ."

"The hell you haven't, Lucita!" Ralph fervently declared. "You can't imagine how happy you've made me; nothing could make me any happier—well, one thing might—and that is if you'd promise to marry me, Lucita. I guess I'm rushing you too much."

She looked at him lovingly and sighed, "Ah, señor, I am as impatient as you, I guess. I need only to get my mistress's blessing."

Lucita prayed she wasn't having one of her many romantic daydreams. Madre de Dios, she could not believe this! She'd planned to entice him, but she'd never expected to receive a proposal of marriage.

As she'd told Ralph when she'd first entered his room, it was a glorious day!

Chapter 34

Marjorie had not felt so exhilarated or so in charge of her life in many months. All she could ask herself was why in God's name she had not done this months ago. Why had she wasted so many precious months of her life?

She'd looked in her full-length mirror this morning as Lucita was tying the sash of her frock, and she was still a striking female, even though Eliot had long tried his best to debase her and destroy her confidence. She still had her trim figure and her breasts still stood high, with no sagging.

Once she'd stopped allowing Eliot to browbeat her and started defying him, her face had a better color and was no longer tense and drawn.

She liked the feel of her little gig and the power of the feisty little bay that pulled it. Ah, it was a grand day, of bright sunshine and blue sky, completely cloudless.

She anticipated seeing Emilo again, for she'd always admired him. He was a part of her life when times were good. She felt Frank's presence very much this morning, and she could almost see him nodding his head with approval. Frank used to say about days like this, golden with autumn's approach, that there was a certain magic in the air. It was there this morning, she felt it.

When she arrived at the Casa del Lago, Emilo opened the door, and the expression on his dear face was enough to assure her that she'd done the right thing in coming.

"What a delightful sight you make, my dear Marjorie. I can't imagine a nicer surprise than to see you here at my house. It's been far too long," Emilo said, patting her hand and giving her a light peck on the cheek.

"Entirely too long, Emilo. But it won't happen again, I promise."

He nodded and told her, "Good—I'm glad to hear you say that. Very glad." They strolled down the tiled hallway, with Emilo still holding her hand in his.

"What about some coffee on the east veranda, Marjorie? Would you enjoy that? And maybe some little spice cakes?" He smiled slyly, recalling how she loved his cook's nutmeg and cinnamon cakes.

"Oh, Emilo—you devil! You know I can't resist them." How wonderfully relaxed it was to be around him again; it was as if all these miserable months had never separated them.

An hour passed swiftly. The house servant served them the coffee and cake and they'd talked about everything. Marjorie suddenly realized that her dear friend, Emilo, was as lonely as she was to just have someone to talk to.

There was a compassionate look on her face as she asked him, "You miss her as much as I miss Frank, don't you, Emilo?"

His dark eyes clouded with the sadness he felt, and he confessed, "Every day of my life I miss my Carmalita. It grows no easier. It's like a pain in the body that you learn to live with and accept, I guess, Marjorie." He reached over to take her hand in his. "I have no need to ask you, Marjorie—do you feel the same about Frank?"

"I do, Emilo, and I don't have to tell you that Eliot Penwick was a horrible mistake."

"I know, Marjorie—I've known for a long time. I'm just glad you came to me and told me today. Now I feel free to offer to you what I've wanted so desperately to offer long ago. You know you have my help, my home, and me—anytime you need them."

Marjorie could not keep the tears from flowing. Emilo comforted her by enfolding her in his arms and consoling her, "Frank and Carmalita would want us looking out for one another—si?"

She looked up into his face with tears streaming down her cheek, managing a weak smile. "You know, Emilo—I truly think they would. Your dear wife and my Frank were two of the kindest people I ever knew."

"Then, Marjorie—it is settled, yes? We have a pact? I will look after you, as I know Frank would wish me to, and I know Carmalita would rest better knowing I have you looking after me."

Marjorie's smile made him realize that she understood exactly what he was telling her. It was nice to be with a lady like his beloved wife again.

"Oh, Emilo, the years go by so fast, don't they?" she said, feeling completely serene with the comfort of his arms around her.

"Si, Marjorie. But you know something I've just begun to realize? There are still some good days left for us, some very fulfilling days that the two of us can enjoy. I ask you—why should we not do it? We've shared so very much through the years and we share the love of this wonderful state and the land. Is it not so?"

"It is so, Emilo! I've hated Eliot when he's looked down his nose at my dear friends and what he called

281

this 'primitive' place."

"Ah, Marjorie—that only shows his ignorance. We know better. What other state boasts a prouder heritage than Texas?"

"None, Emilo, that I can think of. Oh, I admit that I am prejudiced."

He squeezed her tighter and chuckled, "And don't you ever apologize for that, Marjorie Greenfield! It is wonderful to know someone who has a passion for the land as you do. You see, I remember when you and Frank came to Harrison County, and I know how hard you both worked. I must confess that it was my greatest concern that you'd let it all slip through your fingers to a man like Penwick. The fear caused me great pain!"

"Don't worry about that, Emilo. It will never happen. I'm very much in control now, though I confess that I went through a period when it might have happened. I've thought about this very much lately, Emilo, and how life plays crazy tricks on you. I guess that it was the reason I felt so compelled to help Talleha get away from the ranch."

"I'm glad you did, Marjorie. We both know that she did not deserve that fate."

"Oh, it was more than that, Emilo. I know it sounds crazy, and I don't have to tell you that I went through many months of foolhardy insanity, but I reserved one room in which to keep all of Frank's momentos. Eliot resented this but he could never get me to do away with them. We had many fights about that."

"Good for you, Marjorie!"

"Do you recall a man Frank befriended by the name of Talbert, an artist?"

Emilo thought for a minute and confessed, "Only vaguely, Marjorie. Frank was always helping someone, as we both know. He was a man with a generous heart."

"Well, I knew there was something about this little

Talleha that was calling from my past, and I went to that room one day. It was one of Talbert's paintings he'd left there. It was a painting of a half-breed woman he'd lived with when he'd stayed up on Lake Tawakoni near Cedar Springs. Emilo, I have the strongest feeling that Talleha could be Talbert's daughter by the woman named Dawn. I have no proof except what I feel here," she said, "in the gut. Do you know what I mean?"

"Never sweep away a gut feeling, Marjorie! Never! It is possible, because Cedar Springs is where Talleha came from," Emilo told her.

"Well, if you could see Talbert's painting of the woman he became involved with there, you'd see the remarkable resemblance to Talleha. It is easy to see where the girl inherited her rare beauty. I tell you, Emilo, it is uncanny."

Emilo was extremely interested in what Marjorie was telling him about Talbert. "Why do you think this man—Frank's friend—would desert such a lovely woman and the child they shared?"

Marjorie confessed to Emilo that she was not as fond of Talbert as Frank seemed to be. "We spoke about him after he left every now and then, and Frank wondered why he'd never sent for his paintings. He left several with us when he left Harrison County. We finally came to the conclusion that he was dead after so much time passed without any word from him."

"It is a most interesting tale, Marjorie; and I'm sorry to say I can't recall the man right now."

"Well, I can only recall one meeting you had with him, Emilo, so that's understandable. You came over one afternoon, as I recall, to see Frank's new horse, and he, Richard, and you went out to the stables together. That was perhaps the only time you saw him during his stay at our ranch."

Emilo apologized, "I guess I am getting old,

Marjorie—but I just can't recall it."

"We're both getting old, Emilo." She gave forth a good-natured chuckle and patted his hand.

"Guess that's the reason we shouldn't waste our precious time."

"I have no intention of doing that anymore, Emilo. Not one minute! That's why I'm ridding myself of that worthless Eliot Penwick." She couldn't even bring herself to call him her husband anymore.

Emilo wondered how easy that would be, for he knew Eliot to be an obnoxious egoist who would never accept her ultimatum. He feared Eliot's violent, erratic temper—who knew what he might do to Marjorie?

"May I ask you, Marjorie—just when and how are you going to rid yourself of Eliot? Do you want me to help you?" A sober look etched Emilo's face.

"I can't answer you, Emilo, as to exactly when I will inform him. I can tell you it will be soon—less than a week. I appreciate your offer to stand by me, but you see, Emilo, I'm no longer afraid of Eliot. There was a time when he had me cowering, but no longer."

"But the man is capable of anything, I think. There is also a nephew of his under your roof, isn't there?"

"Oh, I have nothing to fear from Ralph. He is nothing like Eliot. The truth is, Eliot has been so horribly rude and inconsiderate to Ralph that I think his loyalty and devotion is to me. No, Ralph is a nice young man whom Eliot had not been able to influence with his evil ways."

Emilo was glad to hear that; it eased some of his concern. Marjorie gave him a warm, loving smile as she declared, "Oh, Emilo—my dear, dear friend, it is so good to have you caring about my welfare. It is most comforting, indeed. I only wish I'd come to you a long time ago." Next to her beloved Frank, Emilo Cortez was the most honorable, honest man she'd ever known, a rare breed.

"You came, Marjorie—that is all that matters now."

It was hard to leave the peaceful surroundings of the Casa del Lago, but Marjorie forced herself to say farewell. As Emilo went with her out to the hitching post, he, too, wished she could have remained there with him longer. How fast the time ahd gone by and how pleasant those two hours had been!

When Marjorie was seated on the seat of the gig with the reins in her hand, Emilo insisted that she get word to him so he'd know how things were going for her over at the ranch. "I'll get there as fast as Paco can bring me, Marjorie," he promised her.

"I will. I promise. Thank you for a wonderful afternoon," she told him, urging the bay to move out.

Emilo walked back toward his house with a thoughtful look on his face. Marjorie's sentiments were his, too. It had been a wonderful afternoon. He felt new life churning within him. In the same way that Talleha and Victor had brought a feeling of springtime to him, Marjorie had brought the sensation of a bright, sunny day of summer. He felt alive with feeling, and the feeling was good.

There was a touch of magic in the air, with the golden moonlight reflecting down onto the bay waters. Talleha loved the cool, damp sand teasing her bare feet as she and Maurier sat on the beach. She'd never seen such white sand as this on the beach of Corpus Christi Bay. Maurier had certainly been right when he described this place.

Everything had utterly fascinated her. The tall, majestic palm trees lining the shore were intriguing to her. But darkness had prevented her from picking up very many seashells.

They had been like two frolicsome children as they collected pieces of old driftwood to make their fire for the night. Victor had stopped a fisherman on his way home with his catch. He'd talked the man into parting with a pair of nice-sized fish and they'd made them into a very delectable meal.

As they sat there by the smoldering flames eating the last of the fish and potatoes they'd roasted in the coals, Talleha playfully teased him, "I didn't know you were such a horse trader, Victor. First, you haggle with the farmer with his wagon filled with vegetables and get potatoes for our meal and then you talk to the fisherman for our fish. You have talents I never suspected!"

"Lady, you've not seen anything yet," he laughed, tousling her hair playfully.

"You mean you have more surprises in store for me?"

"Hundreds!" His eyes danced over the beauty of her face in the flickering light of the fire. It never ceased to amaze him how gorgeous she was without the fancy frills and adornments most women used. Not Talleha —she didn't need them. In her simple cotton tunic and black divided skirt, she looked more alluring than any woman he'd seen in a fancy ball gown. She needed no jewels, for her black eyes were exquisite gems.

"Hundreds?" A provocative, challenging look reflected in those black eyes of hers as she daringly commented, "That could take a long time, Victor . . . a lifetime."

A slow grin creased his handsome face. The little minx! Was she doing what he suspected she was doing? Was she trying to wangle a proposal from him? Was this his sweet, innocent Talleha? It was at times like this he had to question just how naive she was.

He leaned over so close to her that his sensuous mouth was almost touching her lips. In a deep voice he declared, "That depends on how fast I work, honey."

A smug little smile came to her lips. Without any hesitation, she retorted, "And on how fast or slow I respond, my darling Victor!"

For a brief moment he was taken aback by her bold wit. But then, his strong, muscled arm lashed out like a whip, encircling her waist to draw her to him so swiftly that she didn't realize what had happened until she felt the flaming heat of his body searing her.

"Ah, ma petite—you'll respond, and very fast!"

Chapter 35

So ardent was his lovemaking that Talleha was left breathless as they lay there on the sandy shore. When his lips finally sought to release her after that first endless kiss, she stared up at him, startled.

"You see, my darling!" he told her, knowing that she was as impassioned as he was.

"Damn you, Victor Maurier! How come you are so devilishly smart?" she hissed, disgusted that she had so little control over herself. She had absolutely no will where he was concerned, and the scoundrel knew it!

He broke up in laughter and adored her all the more for her honesty. "Because I am honest, like you, and our love is too strong to deny, Talleha darling. It is as simple as that. You must know this, too, by now." But he gave her no opportunity to answer, for his hungry lips sought hers once again. It would not have mattered to Maurier what she said, for her soft, supple body was speaking to him already, answering eagerly as she arched toward him, her arms encircling his neck and her fingertips playing at the back of his head.

The slight rise of the sand dune provided a cozy bower, secluding them from the long strip of beach, and the gusting winds had calmed to a light, gentle breeze. There was only the golden glow of coals left from the fire.

Maurier raised her up to pull the tunic over her head, cursing at the delay it was causing. Talleha giggled at his impatience. She teased him as she wiggled out of the riding skirt and laid it next to her tunic, "I don't want to arrive in Brownsville half-clothed."

But he was too busy removing his own clothing to hear her. She merely smiled, pleased that he felt such a wild, surging passion to have her. It also told her something else which pleased her feminine vanity. He was just as helpless as she was in controlling his emotions and desires for her.

He looked up to see her staring down at him as he wiggled free of his pants, and he wondered what was behind her wicked, sly smile. She was thinking that he would have made a magnificent Indian warrior in a loincloth of hide like those worn by her mother's ancestors. He had a wonderful body with rippling muscles and broad shoulders. His arms and legs were strong and powerful. She felt no shame at staring and admiring his virile body, for it seemed the natural thing to do.

Maurier cajoled her, noticing her dancing, ogling eyes, "Come here, you little vixen."

"I don't know if I'm in the mood to," she impishly teased him. She turned slightly to kick her toe in the sand. Maurier's expert hand reacted with such speed tha she was once again taken by surprise. Victor admonished her once again, "I don't know what it's going to take, you little savage, to teach you that this isn't a time to tease me. I want you too much to play games right now."

When he had grabbed her foot and Talleha suddenly found herself beginning to fall backward, she let out a scream. But Victor had no intention of allowing her to fall, so his arm was there to support her back. "Now, are you ready to quit all this nonsense?" he grinned with such a twinkle in his eye that she smiled at him and nodded.

He sank down on the blanket beneath them. His two hands scooped a thick mane of hair away from her neck and placed it on the blanket so it wouldn't fan out on the sand. He gave her neck and throat featherlike kisses, working up to meet her luscious lips. Already, he heard her soft little moans and sighs and felt the throbbing tips of her breasts pressing against his chest. His hand moved to cup one in the palm of his hand and his finger teased the rosy tip. Talleha tingled at feeling the wonderful sensation, and she slithered her hips underneath him to urge him to fill her completely.

"Oh, Victor—I want you!" she pleaded anxiously. "I want you so much!"

He thrust himself into her, declaring, "Then you shall have me, ma cherie!" She arched closer to him and together they moved as the fury of their passion mounted higher and higher. It seemed to Talleha they were surely soaring to the heavens.

She felt the jarring quake of Victor's powerful body in the same moment that she gasped with her own sweet anguish. It was of a sensual splendor that she'd never imagined possible; never had their lovemaking soared to this lofty peak of sensuality.

Victor felt her heavy breathing as her petite, damp body lay stilled now against him and he, too, knew this was one of those rare nights of true sensual delight. She had loved it and that pleased him most of all.

Talleha was his, he told himself. No other man would ever touch her lovely body, but him!

When she finally spoke to him, it was as a woman completely fulfilled by the love of her man, and Maurier felt as if he owned the whole world. She sighed sweetly to him, "Oh, Victor—this was paradise—here on this beautiful beach tonight. If this moment never comes again for us, I will have no regrets."

He pressed her closer to him and could not hide the irritation in his voice as he questioned her, "Why in bloody hell would you talk like that—like it was the end, Talleha? Hell, it's just the beginning—not the end!"

"Oh, I hope you are right! I hope it goes on forever. But I know that nothing goes on forever. I—I just wanted you to know how I felt, Victor. It seemed important for me to tell you."

He was frustrated by this mood of hers; once again she was proving to have the ability to completely befuddle him. He tried not to show her how much she'd disturbed his pleasant mood, to mask the turmoil churning within him, keeping his voice calm as he replied, "I'm glad you told me your thoughts, Talleha. It was a very special night for me, too. But I guess I don't think as seriously as you do. I dream of many more nights like this."

She suddenly sat up. "Oh, God, Victor—I do too!" Her black eyes searched his face, knowing she'd given him the wrong impression of what she meant to say.

"The truth is, Talleha—I plan even more exciting interludes in paradise for us."

Wide-eyed and curious, she could not imagine a more rapturous, exciting night than this one. That unabashed, candid honesty of hers gave way as she sighed, "I—I don't know if I could stand it! I swear to you I don't know!"

"That is the point, ma petite amie! You don't know, and I'll be the man to show you. Trust me, Talleha— trust me completely, and I'll show you pleasures you never dreamed possible. We'll share a world of wonders few people ever know. I knew it the moment I first laid eyes on you. I know you felt the same mysterious way I felt that day down by the river."

"Well, I know I felt something I'd never felt before. But I must admit to you now that a part of me was frightened."

He gave a deep throaty laugh, "I would damned sure hope so! But you are certainly not frightened anymore, are you, Talleha?"

"Heavens, no!" She laughed.

This was what he adored about her—that truthfulness which left no shadow of a doubt!

He reached up to pull her to him as he lay on the blanket. "There's one thing about you, Talleha: you tell the truth. You don't waste time trying to flatter a man or play up to his pride."

"Why should I? More to the point, it would be foolish with a man like you: you would see through a simple person like me anyway."

Their eyes locked, piercing one another. Each was measuring the other. He wondered if she'd been born with an innate sense of womanly wiles to manipulate a man as she wished. She was the most intriguing, mysterious woman he'd ever encountered.

His blue eyes sought the depths of hers as he honestly confessed, "Talleha, ma cherie—I wouldn't swear to anything where you're concerned. I think sometimes you must possess magical powers. I've often wondered if you don't beguile me with your beauty and bewitch me with that tantalizing, tempting little body of yours. Do you suppose I'll ever really find out?"

She smiled and bent down to kiss his cheek. He could have sworn the expression on her lovely face was that of the most experienced courtesan as she murmured, "Now, you don't think I'll tell you all my secrets, do you? I'll just let you find out for yourself."

"You're wicked, Talleha!"

"And don't tell me you don't like my being just a little wicked?"

"As long as it is with me! As long as it is with me, you can be as wicked as you want." He noticed a dramatic change taking place on her face as soon as he spoke, and he was once again puzzled as to why she'd changed so abruptly.

"Victor, tell me the truth! Am I wicked to act as I do with you even though I am not your wife? I have often wished that I could seek my dear mother for advice. I gave you my love and my heart because I wanted to. Love was natural between me and my mother and given very freely. Perhaps you don't understand what I'm trying to tell you."

"More than you can possibly know, Talleha. To answer your question, you are exactly what I desire in a woman but never hoped to find. You are more woman than any lady I've ever known. Don't you ever change, ma petite!"

"Oh, Victor—you mean it, don't you?"

"Every word! Talleha, no marriage vows or piece of paper could bind me to you any more than I feel bound right now. Will you believe me, my darling?"

"I believe you, Victor. I must! If I didn't I would surely die!" she confessed with tears streaming down her face.

"Of course you must believe me, Talleha, for you know we could not have shared what we already have if there were not strong, deep feelings." His arms held her protectively as he wiped her tear-stained face. "You've no cause to cry, little one. God knows, you'll never die for lack of love."

He laid her back on the blanket with him, never taking his arms from her. She snuggled to fit herself into the curve of his body. "Hold me—hold me close!" she softly pleaded with him.

"I plan to, all night long. You, my pretty one, close your eyes and go to sleep, for we have a long ride tomorrow. In fact, we are going to be riding along this shore all the way to Brownsville."

That aroused her attention and she questioned, "On the sandy beach all the way?"

He gave her a lazy grin, "All the way, Talleha."

She gave a pleased little sigh of delight and curled back down beside him; she didn't have to tell him that this intrigued her. It also pleased him, for he told himself that his beautiful Talleha would love sailing on his schooner, letting the spray of the ocean wash over her face, the strong sea winds blowing her hair.

Shortly, he closed his eyes and wonderful, whimsical thoughts engulfed him.

It was his future he was thinking about—his and Talleha's.

Chapter 36

Talleha was the first to wake up the next morning, and the first thing to catch her eye was a strange thing crawling along the beach near their blanket. It fascinated her; she sat up quickly, wide-eyed and curious! What in the world was this mysterious little creature?

Maurier slowly opened his eyes to see her sitting there, utterly spellbound. She was so absorbed she didn't sense that he was now observing her.

"Odd-looking little critter, isn't he?" Victor finally spoke up. She turned toward him with an expression of astonishment. "What is it, Victor?"

"A sand crab," he told her, and she repeated the name, as though she wanted to be sure to remember it forever.

The episode of the sand crab was just the first of many inquiries Talleha was to make during the day as they started to travel down the long, endless beach of the Texas coastline.

Once they were dressed and their gear was packed back on their horses, Talleha found herself famished, and she recalled the wonderful tasting fish Maurier had bartered from the fisherman the evening before. "I'd love to have some more of that right now. I don't know about you, but I'm starved, Victor."

He soothed her to be patient, "There's a small fishing village up ahead, and we'll stop there to get something." This seemed to pacify her somewhat.

"I can't recall any of the fish we caught out of our lakes or rivers tasting like that. What did you call it, Victor?"

"They are redfish, caught out in Laguna Madre. And no, my little Talleha, you would not catch redfish in your lakes. I do agree with you that they are good." He added that if she was so hungry she should quit asking questions, so they could be on their way toward the village.

He didn't have to tell her twice; she frantically gathered up the last few articles and tied them up in her lightweight cape. She marched over to mount the little mare. Out of the corner of his eye, Maurier had been watching her, and it was one of those times she seemed like a wonderful child.

The calm breeze of the night before was gone, and in its place was a strong, galelike wind sweeping over the sandy dunes. As they rode along the shoreline, Talleha noticed the effect it seemed to have on the choppy waters of the bay beyond: the lazy, lapping water stroking at the beach was now an angry, rushing tide slapping at the shore.

She was also fascinated by the strange sight of what the wind did to the sandy dunes. They seemed to change before her eyes, as if a giant hand of a sculptor was applying his craft there on the sand.

Maurier rode by her side, listening to her constant chatter about all the things which were new to her. If he'd not formerly appreciated the fact that she was as smart as she was lovely, he certainly did now. Nothing escaped her. She absorbed everything around her, and her insatiable curiosity reflected a sharp, keen mind.

As the day went on, he was certain that she was a woman who would never be happy to live within the confining walls of a house . . . walls would be boring to Talleha. She needed bridges to cross and places to go. Perhaps her childhood on the Lake of the Pines had made her this way. Whatever it was, he was glad to be able to share his life with this kind of woman.

As they spent the day together, he saw a new side of her nature and was amazed by her awareness of the surroundings. She pointed out the magnificent, but grotesque sight of the old live-oak trees growing on the shoreline. He would have ridden right by them, taking no time to admire them as she had.

He thought that by the middle of the afternoon, her enthusiasm would have dimmed after many hours of riding. But he found out he was wrong. In fact, she was bubbling with excitement at the first shrimp boat she'd ever seen. Then, too, she'd yelled out to him with a wonderful childlike excitement, "Oh, Vic—look—look over there! What kind of a bird is that? How beautiful!"

He'd looked in the direction she was pointing toward and saw that it was nesting cranes. He had to agree with her that they were a most impressive sight. "They're cranes, Talleha."

It was then and there that Victor decided they would stay one more night on the beach, which seemed to be enchanting her so much. He was glad that he'd bought enough supplies for them to enjoy a hearty meal by another driftwood campfire, as they had last night.

The sight of a steamer plowing through the waters heading south made him anxious to see his own schooner again. The smell of the salt air so close by invigorated all his senses, and he knew just how much he'd missed it all during these many weeks on land.

But never would he have lingered so long on land

297

had it not been for her. But for Talleha, he would have stuck to his original plan when he'd first arrived at Casa del Lago, when he'd found out from Emilo that Eliot lived only a few short miles away.

When they reached a spot which could make an ideal place to camp and the sun was beginning to set very low on the horizon, he announced his plans to her. "One more night on the beach before we make Brownsville, Talleha. Hope you don't mind, knowing that tomorrow night you'll finally have a comfortable bed to sleep in."

"It sounds wonderful to me!" she exclaimed delightedly.

"Good! I'm glad you feel that way. I confess to you, I bought enough food back at the village so we could have a nice little feast if we didn't make Brownsville tonight."

"What a thoughtful man you are," she declared with a loving smile on her face. There had been times when she'd found him impossible and bossy, but there was about him a gentle tenderness that she loved with all her heart.

By the time she'd dismounted and untied the little bundle secured behind her saddle, Maurier was taking his gear from Sultana, the moon was rising, and its light shone on the waves a short distance away.

"Shall we search for some driftwood, ma petite?" he asked her, and she gave him an eager nod of her head. Like a doting puppy, she skipped along to catch up with him, and they held hands like all young lovers to stroll in the moonlight. Talleha, loving the feel of the sand on her bare feet, had already removed her boots, and the feeling was divine.

They didn't have to go too far before they came across a massive piece of driftwood, and Maurier took it along with them until they came across another huge piece of wood. "I think this should do it," he told her, turning around to go back to their campsite.

Happiness was hers tonight, Talleha thought as she strolled beside the handsome man she worshipped. Since they left Casa del Lago, their time together had been so special, and it almost frightened her. It was almost too good to be true.

She looked up toward the heavens and she saw diamond-like stars twinkling down on them. A silver moon seemed to light their way back to their campsite. it was a night made for lovers like her and Victor.

Maurier took notice of her quiet mood, but he had only to see the serene look on her face to know she was blissfully content. That was all that mattered to him. So he smiled and held her hand more tightly in his.

When their meal was cooked over the bed of coals and Maurier had put the coffee pot down into the coals to warm up the last of their coffee, he was thinking that this wouldn't be a bad place to settle down someday. To be near the sea and breathe the salt air appealed more to him than the ranch life of the Casa del Lago.

Captain Crawford had told him there was a most lucrative business to be made in salvaging up and down this coast with its many coves. Victor had not thought about it too seriously then, for his mind was on tracking down Eliot Penwick. Settling anywhere was the last thing on his mind, but tonight that idea was not so foreign as it had been then, Maurier realized.

When there was no more coffee to drink and their hunger was sated, they lay back on the blanket, pleasantly contented to gaze up at the stars. There was no need for conversation between them. They just lay there, holding hands affectionately. A peaceful languor washed over them.

Neither of them knew that two terrifying characters stood above them on the slope of the sand dune. The two nudged one another, giving forth an agreeing nod of their heads. In the lovers' favor, they'd not disrobed just yet, but the sight of Talleha's body fully-clothed was enough for the two who ogled her figure to be tempted.

The two drunken sailors were already late in returning to the steamer in port at Brownsville, but they were too drunk to concern themselves about that.

The sight of Talleha whetted their sexual appetite, and the man lying at her side did not appear to pose a problem to these two robust sailors. Once they took care of him so that he couldn't interfere with their anticipated pleasure, they could use her to satisfy their lusty desires as long as they wanted.

The two huge man were amazingly light on their feet as they moved slowly down the dune. Each was armed with an ugly, sharp-bladed knife which he could use effectively.

It was not the noise of their movements that alerted Maurier to the danger lurking nearby, but that particular odor so familiar among a particular breed of seamen. It was enough to make every muscle of his strong body tense with fear and concern for Talleha. He should have been more cautious, knowing they were here by the bay, he chided himself. His hand snaked backwards, praying he could reach his pistols a short distance away. He didn't want to alert Talleha if he could keep from it. The element of surprise would be to his advantage.

The touch of cold steel fitting into the palm of his hand was a welcome feeling to Victor, and he gripped the pistol firm and tight.

His blue eyes moved to search the darkness on his side for some menacing shadow sneaking down the sand dune, but he saw nothing. So it would be on Talleha's side the enemy would be approaching, he concluded. He was greatly relieved that Talleha lay so quiet and still by his side.

Suddenly, Maurier did not have to wonder who his enemy was as two massive figures towered over him and Talleha. "Look at this, Cutter—look what a pretty little thing she is," a deep husky voice laughed, bringing a shocked Talleha up from the pallet. Her black eyes darted over to see Victor still lying there, almost as if he expected them. How could he be so damned calm and cool, she wondered?

"Yeah, she's already primed by this bucko for us to take over, wouldn't you say?"

Rubbing his groin lustily, one of the seamen took a step forward, licking his lips as if he were about to devour a fine beefsteak. "Well, I'm about to find this out for myself."

"Get your fill of her, Cutter, 'cause I'm already hurting to have my fun," his friend chuckled.

Another voice made itself known. It was as cold and final as death. It was an edict, firm and resolute. "You'll not find out anything, bastard! You're about to die!" With those words, an explosion of Maurier's pistol hit the target and one of the intruders tumbled to the ground.

But suddenly another explosion came from up above the dune and found its mark, causing the one named Cutter to fall to the ground, moaning in anguish and grabbing ahold of his thigh.

Talleha and Victor were both startled as they gazed upward to see the imposing figure of another man standing there with a pistol still held in his hand.

There was a cocky air about the man as he announced, "Captain Dorsey Loper—at your service!" With that, he sauntered unhurriedly down the dune, and when he reached the felled man lying so close to Maurier and Talleha, he addressed the man moaning in

301

agony, "Cutter, maybe you'll behave yourself now for awhile."

He turned his attention to the puzzled pair there on the pallet and explained, "This obnoxious rascal is one of my crew, I'm sorry to say. I do apologize for his behavior; I only wish that I had been closer, so this wouldn't have happened."

By now Victor was standing, and he offered a hand to express his appreciation to Captain Loper. "I'm Victor Maurier, captain, and the young lady is—is to be my wife. This is Talleha, Captain Loper." He could not bring himself to call her just a friend.

"Nice to meet you both."

"Nice to have you come along when you did, Captain Loper," Talleha managed to say, for she was in a state of shock at the strange, unconventional way he'd chosen to propose to her. Her black eyes turned from the captain to go back to Maurier, who seemed somewhat frustrated and a little nervous.

"My pleasure, ma'am," the red-haired Loper replied. He saw that she was a ravishing beauty, and he was as guilty as the two members of his crew, for he was churning with wild desires himself. He forced his piercing, admiring eyes to turn back to the man at her side. "Where were you heading, Maurier?"

"To Brownsville," Maurier told him, adding that he, too, was a man of the sea; his schooner was moored there.

"Well, then you've arrived at your destination, in case you didn't know it. Right across the way over a couple more sand dunes, Maurier," Loper chuckled.

Maurier didn't realize it, for he'd traveled a different way when he'd left Brownsville many weeks ago to go to Harrison County. "By chance, Captain Loper, would you know an old sea dog named Crawford?"

"And who doesn't? Is that where you're headin'? If

302

so, you could have been in a comfortable bed this night!" Dorsey roared with laughter because he'd passed the captain's little cottage near the beach as he'd tracked his two wayward sailors to this spot.

"You mean we're that close to Crawford's house now?" a puzzled Maurier inquired.

"Mean just that. Get your stuff together and I'll escort you and your lady there myself," Dorsey offered.

"But what about him?" Talleha pointed to the distraught figure lying there on the sand still moaning with pain.

"Ah, I'll send two of my men back here for him after I direct you to Crawford's place. He deserves a little discomfort," the rugged looking steamer captain said, shrugging his hefty shoulders.

Victor detected that Talleha was about to make a remark, so he hastily urged her, "Get your things together, Talleha, so we can get going."

She noted the bossy air about him as if he were already her husband. She was right, for Victor wished to project this manner. He'd noted the way Dorsey Loper's eyes danced from the top of her head down to her bare feet. While he was grateful to Loper, there was a limit to that. That gave him no special privileges with Talleha!

Chapter 37

Dorsey Loper bade them farewell. Then he turned toward the docks to dispatch two of his seamen to the beach, to bring the two members of his crew back to the steamer. He wore an amused smile on his ruddy face. Whether Victor Maurier approved of Loper or not, he was beholden to him. Victor had shot and killed one of his seamen, and Loper had assured him as they'd walked the distance to Crawford's cottage that he'd handle that minor detail.

"Hell, Maurier—you know like I do how these idiots get themselves killed once they hit land. The best sailors on my steamer are fine as long as we're out at sea. Let them hit land and they go crazy. If it ain't the liquor, it's the ladies." He quickly turned in Talleha's direction and, embarrassed by his big mouth, apologized, "Pardon me, ma'am. Ain't got the best of manners sometimes, I guess."

"That's all right, Captain Loper," she said, trying to keep from smiling. She found it amusing that such big, husky men like Loper and Maurier could become as embarrassed and shy as a woman at times.

"Well, he was your man, so I'll go along with that. We both know he'd asked for what he got. I have no qualms. I'd do it again," Maurier admitted.

So this was the bargain struck between the two of them. The only other commitment made by Victor was the invitation to Loper to come aboard his schooner, *Destiny*. "She's a slick-lined lady I'm very proud of. Be glad to have you see her."

"Yeah, Maurier—I'd—I'd like that. I surely would," Loper accepted. He had to admit that this Frenchie had a talent for picking slick-lined ladies—be it a ship or a woman!

When they said their good-byes and Victor secured the horses to the hitching post just outside Crawford's cottage, he noticed that a lamp was burning brightly inside the house. That old night owl was still up, and he recalled the man's irregular hours of the past.

In a way it pleased Maurier, because it told him there was still a lot of life in the dear old man. Maybe his health had not deteriorated as much as Victor had feared during the time he'd been gone. He took Talleha's hand to guide her up the plank steps to the narrow little roofed porch.

Maurier knocked on the door and he heard Crawford's gruff voice call back, "Well, come on in and quit knocking!" Victor gave out a chuckle, recalling how the captain had told him he never locked his door. He took the lead, holding Talleha's hand.

A broad grin was on Victor's face as he announced, "I'm back, captain. I've a friend with me, too."

Glenn Crawford turned in the wooden rocking chair to see the face of the young man who he considered his son. Victor wore the expression of boyish enthusiasm Crawford remembered on many occasions over the years when the young man was triumphant over some feat he'd just accomplished.

A slow smile lit up Crawford's face, and as ill as he was, he'd not lost his sense of humor. "Well, tell you

305

what, sonny—you can go back, but just leave your pretty friend here with me."

A deep, throaty gusto of laughter broke in Maurier's throat, and he released Talleha's hand to rush over to embrace the old man he loved so dearly. It was hard to keep a tear from coming to his eyes, for he knew the old man was not feeling all that randy, but trying to put forth a brave front for him. But then he'd never known any man to have so much guts as that old sea dog.

"I wouldn't trust you alone five minutes with such a beautiful girl as Talleha. You taught me to be too clever for that, captain," Victor teased him. He motioned Talleha to come over so he could formally introduce her. Her black eyes sparked brightly, enjoying the warmth of the scene. She was reminded of that special bond she shared with her mother. She understood and appreciated it.

What a remarkable face this Captain Crawford had, she thought. The tanned, weathered look of his face and hands confirmed what Vic had already told her about Captain Glenn Crawford and his life as a seaman. The etched lines of his face told her he'd lived his life to the fullest. Her eyes had seen the genuine affection in his eyes as he looked at Victor and she knew the gentle heart of the man.

She especially liked his straightforward manner when he addressed her. "Talleha—an Indian name and a beautiful one. But then so are you, my dear. I welcome you to my humble home."

She could not resist the impulse taking hold of her and she did as her heart yearned to do. She bent down to kiss that weathered cheek of Crawford's and told him, "I think I like you, Captain Crawford. I think I like you very much."

He grinned, "So you form an opinion very fast, eh, Talleha? And may I ask, are you usually right about your first impressions?"

Now she knew she liked him. "Rarely am I wrong, sir!" she replied with a smile.

He gave out a chuckle and patted her hand. "Then we do have something in common, young lady. My first impression is usually right. We must talk one day soon about our first impressions. We might just discuss you, Victor." He gave Talleha a wink of his weak eye.

"Ah, now that could be most interesting, Captain Crawford." She gave forth a soft laugh.

"Now, come on, you two. This is not fair. I feel like you are ganging up on me," Victor protested.

"Oh, bucko—you can bet on that. We are going to make you walk the straight and narrow, Victor."

It was a lighthearted gaiety the three indulged in, and Crawford could not have had a better tonic than these two young people sharing his humble little cottage and his evening.

Talleha enjoyed her time with them, but she felt very strongly that they would appreciate a private time by themselves. She knew not quite how to manage to excuse herself. Finally, her straightforward honesty urged her to say, "May I be excused, gentlemen? I'm going to fall on my face if I don't lie down."

"For God's sake, Talleha—forgive an old man for not being more considerate of a little lady," Crawford said, noting the look of weariness on her pretty face. "Take her to the back bedroom, Victor. You can share my room."

These might not have been the sleeping arrangements Maurier would have wanted, but he said nothing as he motioned to her to follow him from Crawford's small parlor.

The little cottage was so compact that it took only a few steps for Victor to usher her through the doorway to the cubicle of a back bedroom, which was sparsely furnished with a small, narrow bed and a dressing table. One small nightstand nested beside the bed with a lamp on it and he lit that for Talleha before reluctantly bidding her good night.

"This is going to be changed by tomorrow night, ma petite. I'm not going to share a bed with Crawford when I've got you here," he grinned devilishly.

She could not resist taunting him, looking over at the very narrow bed against the wall. "I think with your huge body on that bed I'd have a devil of a time finding anywhere to sleep, Victor."

"Ah, ma cherie—never you fear. We'll manage!" He bent down to kiss the pert little nose. "See you in the morning."

"Good night," she replied, closing the door as he left.

What a hectic night it had been, she thought now that she was all alone! It had started out so well. But Victor had ended up killing a man tonight, and who knows what would have happened if Captain Loper had not come on the scene when he had. Yet now as she sat on the bed she had the distinct impression that Victor did not wholeheartedly approve of Dorsey Loper.

It was obvious to her that Maurier did approve and admire Captain Crawford, and she could see why. She recalled the circumstances of their meeting years ago. Now she knew why Victor's eyes glowed with such warmth when he talked about his captain. She already adored the elderly man.

As she began to undress, she took notice of the meager furnishings of the room. The narrow bed and little dressing table took up almost half the tiny cubicle. The nightstand beside the bed was the only other piece of furniture except for an old chest at the foot of the bed. There were no pictures on the painted walls, nor anything reflecting a lady's touch. Victor had told her that Crawford had never married. That would explain the plain, simple decor of his little cottage.

Smugly, she smiled to herself, thinking she would change all that with the beautiful shells she'd picked up along these wonderful beaches. But there was something within these walls that she valued far more than any lavish furnishings, and that was the great love and warmth of a gentle man. This was not to say that Talleha thought any the less of that dear Emilo Cortez for this was not the case. She adored him, too. But to her way of thinking, Glenn Crawford was as wealthy as Emilo in a different way. Her conception of wealth would have been considered by most strange and unconventional. Yet her values were far more enduring and long lasting than those of the masses.

What Talleha could not know at this glowing time of her life was that she was much wiser than most, and for this she could thank her mother, who was pure in heart and possessed a gentle soul. Talleha could not know now just how much she was like her.

Vic Maurier's arrival into her life had opened the door for her to discover the woman she was. Gradually, she was finding out about herself—things she'd never known before or given any thought to until now.

Realizing how she felt about Victor and knowing the depth of passion she felt when he made love to her, it stirred her curiosity to know more about the man her mother had obviously loved. But Dawn was the only one who could give her the answer to that, and she was dead.

However, it was not Talleha's nature to give in to defeat. Somehow, there had to be another way, she told herself.

Now, disrobed down to her undergarments, she slipped between the sheets, ready to lay her head on the soft pillow and sleep.

Her last thoughts were about Victor and his friend, Crawford. Were they talking about her? She realized Victor had to explain her presence with him.

The captain had certainly been cordial tonight, and she could only hope he would greet her as warmly in the morning.

The two men did talk for quite some time after Talleha went to bed. Dawn was breaking when weariness insisted that they retire, and Maurier admonished himself for keeping Crawford up far too long. But the cantankerous captain would have no part of retiring until he was told the whole story about Talleha and Victor's many weeks in Harrison County.

"My good friend, Emilo, is all that I said he was?" he'd asked with an assured smile on his face.

"That and plenty more, captain. I consider him my friend, too, now," Victor told him.

"Now, tell me, did you accomplish the feat you set out to do? Did you find this Eliot Penwick and avenge your dear mother's death?"

It was difficult for Victor to have to admit that he had not yet done so, and that he must return to Harrison County to finish things up before he could go on with his life.

A frown creased Crawford's brow and he insisted on knowing how it all went wrong. Victor spared none of the details as to why it had failed. "It is uncanny to think how simple it was to locate the bastard almost as soon as I arrived there and how complicated it became to do what I'd gone there to do in the first place."

A sly grin came to Crawford's solemn face, for he was a firm believer that every man had a destiny. Victor's had led him to a beautiful girl named Talleha, instead of punishing the killer of his mother. For whatever reason, that was the way it was meant to be.

"So you intend to go back, son? What about the girl?"

"I'd like for her to stay with you until I can return, sir, if that's all right."

"You know it is. This time you will not fail, Victor. This time will be the right time," the captain assured him.

As it had always been in the past, so it was now, for Maurier never doubted the wise words or advice of Glenn Crawford.

"No sir, I won't fail this time. When I return, Eliot Penwick will be dead!"

Chapter 38

During days and nights of golden splendor Talleha stayed in Captain Crawford's little cottage on the beachfront, sharing wonderful times with the man she loved and his friend, the dear old sea captain. She could not believe how swiftly time passed; she was completely happy and content.

She could not imagine anyone wishing for more than to dwell here by the sea and roam the endless beaches. The beauty of the surroundings kept her constantly enchanted.

It was certainly true, as Victor had told her, that there was nothing like the fresh sea breeze to make one's vitality surge. She was truly in her element as she rarely wore her slippers or boots, preferring to go barefoot around the cottage or the beach. She cared not that Victor constantly teased her, calling her an uninhibited little savage. She knew the captain approved of her informal air and was amused by the two of them. She also sensed that he rather admired her not yielding to Maurier's demanding nature at times.

When they were alone one afternoon, he confessed that he liked her spunk. "You're the kind of woman Victor needs, Talleha. I'd—I'd like to think you'll be around to keep that young rooster straight after I'm gone." It was the first time he'd mentioned his grave condition, and she found it hard to believe that he was going to die soon: he was too alive and his mind was too alert.

She refused to accept it. For almost a week she'd lived here now, and she'd observed him daily. He ate heartily and slept like a baby. The only thing which indicated that Glenn Crawford was an ailing man was the enormous amount of time he seemed to have to confine himself in that old rocking chair in the small parlor. But even those hours were not spent in idleness, for he enjoyed reading when he was not engaging her or Victor in conversation. Often she'd caught him gazing out the window to the horizon. She knew he was secretly wishing he was out there, sailing to some faraway shore.

She loved this remarkable man and all he stood for. He set no boundary on anything in life, and he thought nothing was impossible if a person wanted it badly enough. He'd told her about the simple rule he'd laid down to Victor when he was just a lad. "I told him, Talleha—I told him to have the guts to just try. He might even fail, but that was no disgrace. The disgrace is in not trying. The little monkey fell on his face many times, but by God, he came up stronger every time. I was do damned proud of him, even when he did fail."

She'd given him a warm, loving smile. "You remind me of my own mother, Captain Crawford. You and she would have been a great match."

He gave forth a goodhearted chuckle, "What a shame I never met a woman like your mother. If I had, I might not have ended up an old bachelor."

"Did you never fall in love, captain?" she dared to inquire of him.

He'd have resented that query from anyone else. He

answered her honestly, "Only once, my dear, and she was taken from me. She took quite ill even before I could ask for her hand in marriage. After that, I just never met any girl who could quite measure up to her, and I could not settle for anyone else. So I had a love affair with my ship, and you know what, Talleha? I discovered that women and ships are very much alike. They can be unpredictable and tax a man beyond his limits, but they can also give a man a satisfaction that words can't describe."

"Well, you've given me much to think about, captain," she replied with a sober, thoughtful look.

"Sorry, my dear—but I don't understand—how would that give you something to think about?"

"It's really quite simple, captain; I speak of Victor. He must surely feel the same way about his own ship. How can I possibly conquer such overwhelming competition as that?" The minute she'd bared her soul to the captain she was sorry she'd made such a confession.

Crawford's face mellowed with affection as he studied the girl's face. He appreciated her candid, straightforward manner in speaking so confidentially to him. "My darling Talleha, there is no ship on any sea that could compete with you! You missed one very important part of my statement, I guess. Victor is not faced with the sad situation I was faced with. The lady I loved happened to die. You, my dear, are very much alive!"

A slow, comforted expression came to her face, and it brought forth a glowing radiance that Crawford instantly noticed. "Oh, captain—I do love him . . . so much so that it frightens me sometimes." Once again her guilelessness took over as she admitted, "I never loved a man before I met Victor, and he can be a most forceful individual."

"And a most persuasive one, too," he added lightheartedly. "What I don't think you realize, my sweet girl, is the tremendous force you possess in your own way. You must have had a volcanic impact on Victor. Remember one thing: I raised this young man. I know him if anyone does. Victor never needed a lot of people around him to make him happy. I always thought it was because he and his mother lived a pretty secluded life on the wooded estate he told me about."

"He told me he was about eight or nine when you took him in."

"That's right, and I thought he was downright scrawny for a lad that age, remembering my sister's boys. But those next four or five years he shot up like a sapling. Filled out too—he did! Yes sir, the sea air and all his work around the ship made him eat hearty—put some meat on his bones. He took to it, I can tell you."

Talleha listened enraptured. The captain seemed to enjoy reminiscing about the past.

"Glad he got back from Harrison County when he did. I'm a selfish old man and I wish he didn't have to go back there," Crawford told her.

"But he hasn't mentioned anything in the last few days about it, captain. Maybe he's decided not to go, after all." This was Talleha's secret hope.

"No, child—no, he'll go back—he has to, and I can't fault him for that. You must not either, Talleha."

She gave him no reply but sat silently, looking down at her hands in her lap. She was bothered by the captain's words, for she'd enjoyed the last several days immensely and the thought of Harrison County had been the furthest thing from her mind. She should have known better than to pretend that these wonderful days would continue forever, that Victor would not end up doing exactly as he'd said he would.

Not even their paradise on the beach would distract

315

him from the ultimate goal for which he'd crossed a vast ocean.

Why did she continue to delude herself that to be by her side was the most important thing in Victor's life? The answer was crystal clear: she yearned for him to feel as strongly about her as she did about him. But perhaps he never could.

As the good captain had just explained, she could not fault Victor for wanting to avenge his mother's death, and she admired him so very much for it.

After her talk with Captain Crawford, Talleha knew she had a decision to make about herself and her feelings for Maurier. It was really a simple one though it bent her stubborn pride tremendously.

What was she willing to settle for? That was what she had to decide. Was she willing to go back to her village, marry someone like Hunter's son, and have a houseful of kids by a man she could never love?

She'd taken this time of rapture with Maurier, luxuriating in the pleasures he offered, though it was without the bonds of marriage. But why not, while she was young and ripe for experience, shouldn't she enjoy life to the fullest? There was nothing wicked about that!

The only thing that troubled her was the fearful possibility that she could have a baby, as her mother had. She did not want a baby—not even Maurier's baby, if he would not be around to act as father to the child.

These disturbing thoughts consumed Talleha when Victor next encountered her. Her sudden change of mood completely baffled him. He was in the company of Captain Loper, who'd accompanied him to Crawford's cottage after Maurier had taken him on a tour of the *Destiny* moored at the docks.

"One damned beautiful lady, your *Destiny*, Maurier! Don't see how you can stand to be away from

316

her so long," Loper told him as they approached the front step of Crawford's cottage.

"Can't deny it's been hard, and I've got a fierce itch to be sailing out of here," Victor confessed. He'd never felt such mixed feelings about a man before. He disliked Loper and he knew why. But he also liked the man he was. Everything about Dorsey reflected boldness and daring; he was a man who took no quarter from anyone and let nothing stand in his way. And this was exactly what ignited Maurier's dislike for Dorsey: Dorsey was attracted to Talleha.

But, hell, how could he fault him for that, Vic equivocated. He was a hot-blooded Irishman in the prime of his life. Why wouldn't a tantalizing creature like Talleha arouse him?

That old, annoying voice which had plagued him once before was back again. There *was* a way he could rightfully stake a proper claim to the woman he loved, and that was to marry her. He'd even told Loper that when Loper had come to their rescue, but in the eyes of a man like Dorsey Loper, the fact that Talleha was to be Victor's wife meant nothing until they actually tied the knot.

Maurier knew how a man like Loper thought, and he was damned reluctant to leave Brownsville with this lecher still on shore. He knew he was lingering here longer than he'd intended to; he'd seen that Talleha was comfortably settled in with Crawford days ago.

As they were about to part company, Dorsey pointed out to Maurier the sight of Talleha sitting on the beach, staring out across the water.

"Oh, look—the little lady's out there all by herself. Think I'll just go and pay my respects before I leave, Maurier—my old steamer may be pulling out any time now. I got myself one hell of a cargo—ten barrels of whiskey, twelve barrels of wine, and forty barrels of

317

bitters. Can't even tell you how many barrels of molasses we've got. Tell you, I'm going to make myself some money when I get all this cargo delivered. Kerosene oil, soap, and lard brings nice prices in certain places."

"Glad to hear that you're prospering so, Loper. Hope to be doing the same thing myself in a few weeks," a disgruntled Maurier told him, trying to hide his true feelings.

"Thanks, Maurier! Well, I'll say farewell to you and wish you smooth sailing. I'll just mosey on over and tell Miss Talleha good-bye. You don't mind, do you?" But he knew damned well that Victor resented it like the devil.

"No, of course not!" Victor told him, watching as the rugged figure sauntered down the sandy beach toward Talleha. The girl sat very still, her arms embracing her knees. She wore a gathered floral skirt and a sheer batiste peasant blouse. Her pert little chin was resting against her propped-up knees, and Loper wondered what was going through that pretty head of hers.

Maurier lingered a moment once he reached the porch to gaze once more in her direction. Her long mane of black hair was blowing wildly as a strong gale assaulted the shoreline, and compassion filled him as he stared at her. Maurier knew he had a decision to make: did he leave Brownsville or did he stay? Suddenly, he knew it was a matter of trust—a trust of Talleha's love for him.

He had no doubt about his love for her. He loved her beyond all reason, but he could not rest until he killed Eliot Penwick.

He had to have faith that Talleha would be waiting for him when he returned to Brownsville.

Chapter 39

Maurier confided to Crawford that he was going to leave for Harrison County. Crawford was sitting alone in the parlor, staring out the window in the direction of the beach. He saw Talleha sitting there on the sand, saying a fare well to Dorsey Loper.

"Have you told her yet?" Crawford wanted to know.

"Not yet—haven't had the chance. I just returned along with Loper. Showed him the *Destiny* this afternoon. He's about ready to leave Brownsville, and I'd promised him a tour of my schooner the night he helped us out."

"I see," Crawford commented. "Did you mention to *him* that you were leaving?"

A frown creased Maurier's face as he snapped, "Hell, no! Why would I have told him that?"

How quickly he'd bristled, the captain thought. He knew that Victor was a little leery of Dorsey's attitude toward Talleha. Victor's disgruntled mood was because Dorsey was down there on the beach alone with her. The captain didn't blame him.

He felt much better now about what he'd told Talleha this afternoon, for he would not have wanted to give the girl false hopes.

Now, he watched Victor pace the floor. Crawford knew his mood was getting blacker by the minute as Talleha lingered on the beach with Loper. They seemed to be enjoying each other's company.

Crawford prepared himself for a stormy evening with the two young people—their personalities were volatile. He decided that he might allow them time alone to iron out their differences. He yearned for Maurier to take his leave in good spirits, without any burden of worry about the woman he loved back here in Brownsville.

The foxy old captain decided that he'd start playing a little charade right now with Victor. "I think I'll go have myself a nap, son. Hope you don't mind if I leave you to yourself. Maybe if I rest now, I'll be able to join you and Talleha for dinner."

"Oh sure, captain—sure! A nap would do you good," Victor told him, assisting him from the rocking chair, and into his bedroom. He closed the door, having told him, "Have a good rest. We'll see you later."

Crawford was glad to see Victor close the door, for he wasn't the least bit sleepy. He sprawled across the bed with a book to read. He realized that there were times he was glad he'd been spared the agony of jealousy over a woman. Oh, he'd known the pain of loving and losing the woman he loved, but never had he experienced the stabbing hurt of jealousy.

But he could imagine how Victor must be pulled two ways right now, and how reluctant he was to leave Talleha. If he himself were a well man, Victor would not have to concern himself about the likes of Dorsey Loper, Crawford mused dejectedly. But he was not, and no one knew that better than he. Each day there was a little less strength to make it to nightfall.

No one else would ever know. But Crawford was

glad that Talleha would be here with him while Victor was gone. It was hard for someone with his independent nature to admit—but Crawford was also an honest man.

The little black-haired miss would be good for him—the last week had proven that. If he were a gambler he'd wager that Victor had nothing to worry about where Talleha was concerned.

As it happened, he read only two pages in his book. He was wearier than he'd realized, and his eyes grew so heavy he was forced to close them. Sleep took him; in fact, he slept so soundly that he knew nothing about Talleha slipping in to cover him with a light blanket.

She'd returned to the cottage. The house seemed quiet, and she saw no sign of the captain or Victor. She put down the basket of shells she'd picked up on the beach.

Victor had heard her soft footsteps, but he did not wish to face her right then. He was far too angry, and he did not want their last night together to be one of arguments.

He knew himself, and it was far better for everyone at times like this that he let his temper cool. He was smart enough to know that he might carelessly say something that could send her rushing right into the obliging Dorsey's arms. Damned if he'd play the fool!

If nothing else had convinced him just how much he cared for Talleha, this did! The damnable voice which seemed to enjoy plaguing him lately once again demanded to know just what he was going to do about it.

To the empty walls, he mumbled softly, "I'm going to marry the little vixen when I've carried out the vendetta for my mother. That's what I'm going to do!"

"See that you do, Victor Maurier," the voice admonished. Victor was startled that the voice ringing in his ear seemed to be familiar, one that he'd not heard for many years. It was a soft, but firm voice with a very distinct French accent; it was the voice of Colette Maurier.

Now this rugged twenty-five-year-old could have been a lad of eight or nine as he mumbled in a faltering voice, "I intend to. I love Talleha with all my heart and soul."

"Then happiness will be yours, my son, for she loves you, too," the voice assured him. Maurier felt better and he was better prepared to face Talleha later. His anger was now gone; he was once again in control of his emotions.

When he emerged from the room, he was a man with a plan: he was going to tell Talleha that he was leaving Brownsville to return to Harrison County. He had already planned how he was going to ask her to marry him when he returned: they would sail away on the *Destiny* to honeymoon on the high seas, going to any corner of the earth she wished to visit. He wasn't exactly a wealthy man, but he'd acquired enough to live more than comfortably. He was so sure that Talleha would love life aboard the *Destiny*.

He'd even decided that should she desire a home somewhere on land, he'd agree with that; such an idea was not so distasteful as it would have been to him a year ago. Slowly, he realized that this had been one of the effects of Talleha on his life.

He marched into the small parlor with his usual self-assured, cocky air and was greeted by the captain and Talleha. It was the same old Captain Crawford he encountered, but there was a mysterious quality about Talleha's demeanor. Never had she looked more beautiful. She wore a coral blouse and a skirt of brown and coral challis, and for the first time that massive mane of hair was piled atop her head; it made her look older and more sophisticated. Whatever had urged her to style it that way he did not know but it was very appealing.

It had been worth the effort when she'd made her appearance; Captain Crawford had generously praised her when she'd entered the parlor. She would have expected the same exuberance from Victor, but he just stared at her without saying a word.

Was he thinking that she looked more like a mere child trying to play grownup? He, of all people, should know better than that! Perhaps he was comparing her to the worldly women he'd once courted. Maybe she could never be anything to him but a simple maid he'd chanced to meet and had taken pity on. It never had dawned on her to ask him if he was already engaged to marry some other young woman.

Maurier's self-assured feeling quickly faded by the time they sat down to dinner. He could not understand Talleha's cool reserve. No one would suspect that they were lovers, the way she was acting tonight!

He went through the motions of eating, but he could not have said what he'd eaten. He carried on a conversation with the captain, but he did not know what he'd talked about. Why was Talleha doing this to him on their last night together? It could be weeks before he'd kiss those sweet lips and hold that satiny, sensuous body close to his.

The natural inclination was to blame her attitude on Dorsey Loper. Maybe old Dorsey had really made an impression on her on the beach this afternoon. Her expression gave him no hint as to what she was thinking, except that she wasn't concerned with him or his yearnings for her.

Glenn Crawford found himself in an impossible situation during the evening meal. Victor was directing his conversation to him, and so was Talleha. He knew

323

what the two young people were doing and he didn't like being used this way.

Well, he would outfox these two rascals, he decided, and as soon as he finished his dinner, he pushed back his chair, and taking hold of his walking cane, he announced, "Well, you young people finish your meal, because this old man is going to bed." He saw that Talleha's half-parted lips were about to say something and he suspected she wished to protest his leaving her.

Victor's blue eyes darted from him to Talleha and back to him again as he rose up. "Here, captain—let me help you to your room."

"Now look, you young pup, if I want your help I'll ask for it! Sit where you are. You've a beautiful young lady to entertain, and such a gorgeous woman as Talleha should not be neglected. I taught you better manners than that."

Maurier was not about to let Crawford know of the tension engulfing him and Talleha tonight, so he forced himself to reply flippantly, "You certainly taught me well, Captain Crawford!" He could not resist adding, "Sometimes I can't do justice to all your expert teaching, captain."

Crawford turned back to look at him. His rheumy eyes pierced Maurier as he parried, "I don't believe that for a minute, Victor." The captain saw that Talleha was battling utter confusion; this young woman was not one to play games.

There was nothing he could do; he left their problems to them.

An awesome quiet shrouded the small dining room after Crawford left. Neither Talleha or Victor spoke for a few moments.

Finally, Victor rose and went to the captain's cupboard to get a bottle of whiskey. He knew he had to tell Talleha he was leaving in the morning; he could no

324

longer delay it.

He prayed that she would rush into his arms, show some tears of regret that he was leaving, and declare that she would miss him. But he was also smart enough to prepare himself in case she didn't.

With a generous glass of whiskey in his hand, he returned to the table. Her black doe-like eyes slowly turned upward to lock with his, and her honey-sweet lips tempted him as he gazed down at her.

"I—I'm leaving in the morning, Talleha. I'm heading back for Harrison County. I've held up just as long as I can here in Brownsville." He could swear he could hear his own heart pounding wildly as he awaited her response.

As had happened so many times before, he was not prepared for her answer. She spoke with composure. "I've known all day long. I woke up this morning feeling this." As brazen as any wanton, she rose up from the chair and her hands went to the sides of his face as her eyes locked with his. Her lips invited him to kiss her as she murmured seductively, "I want to be with you tonight, Victor. I want to be with you all night long."

He heaved a husky sigh of delight, "Ah, ma cherie— you will be! All night long!"

Chapter 40

He had to satisfy his curiosity—how could she possibly know that he planned to leave in the morning? Her lovely eyes searched his face for a brief moment before she proceeded to answer him. "You must promise you will not laugh, Vic. Promise me!"

Trying to keep his deep voice lowered so they would not awaken the captain, he murmured softly in her ear, "I swear to you I will not laugh."

"I'll tell you when we get to my room," she whispered.

When they were in the room and he'd closed the door, he immediately insisted that she keep him in suspense no longer.

She sat down on the bed and the expression on her face told him she felt very deeply about whatever it was she was about to tell him. "I've never told anyone this, Victor, and I never got the chance to talk to my mother about it, even though it had happened a couple of times. I regret very much I didn't speak to her, for she would have given me a good answer, as she always did."

A frown creased Maurier's face, for she had him puzzled, to say the least. "*What* had happened, Talleha?"

"Please, don't be impatient with me, for I must tell it my way," she gently admonished him.

"I'm sorry, sweetheart. You tell me and I'll keep silent."

"Well, I know of no other way to say it, so I'll just blurt it out. I've—I've a gift, Victor," she told him in a faltering voice. "I sense things that are going to happen before they happen."

"You're telling me you have visions?"

"No . . . I have thoughts. I'll never forget the first time—I woke up thinking Hunter's son was going to have something happen to him before the day was over, and it did. He almost drowned in the lake. I was so frightened I was afraid to tell mother, and God, I wish now I had."

"When did it happen next, Talleha?" he asked her, sincerely interested now.

"A few weeks later when Hunter, who is a seasoned trapper, got his foot caught in a trap. It was exactly the same. I woke up in the morning thinking about Hunter. I was going to talk to mother that night, but she was so tired when she returned from their house, having helped Salina tend to the horrible injury to Hunter's foot, that I didn't have the heart to keep her up any longer. She was exhausted."

"Have you never had a good prophesy, Talleha?"

"Only one."

"You have another one, then, to tell me about, sweetheart?" he asked her, feeling compassion as he saw the melancholy look on her face.

"I should tell you about the worst one of all, on the day my mother was killed and I was taken from my village. If only I'd told her maybe she would not be dead now. But I didn't!" The mist in her eyes urged him to rush to her side and take her in his arms.

"You can't blame yourself for that—you know that, Talleha. But you told me you had one good prophesy.

327

Tell me about it."

A few tears lingered on her cheek and her long lashes fluttered as she looked up at him. "It was on the day I met you by the riverbank, when you slept and the fish got away."

"Tell me more," he prodded her.

"I woke up that morning feeling that something was going to happen that would change my life; I could never have guessed that it was to be a man. But I remember vividly that as I rushed away from the Penwick house to go down by the river, I was very eager to get there, though why, I didn't know."

His arms pressed her closer and he murmured softly in her ear, "And you found me lying there asleep against that old log, and a fish running away with my bait." He smiled, feeling quite pleased that she considered this one of her good visions.

"I'll never forget the sight of that." She gave out a soft little giggle.

"And I won't forget the sight of you when I opened my eyes and saw a breathtakingly beautiful maiden standing there staring at me with those big black eyes." His voice was husky with emotion. "I'd never seen anything so lovely in my life, Talleha!"

"Oh, Victor," she sighed, throwing her arms around his neck, her half-parted lips inviting him to kiss them. He needed no urging, for he was more than eager to kiss her honey lips.

It was a long, lingering kiss, and their wild desire grew with intensity as their bodies pressed together.

He was glad to find her blouse and skirt easy to remove. He was an impatient man tonight, and he did not apologize for that. He intended to give her all the love he could, enough to last them both until he could return from Harrison County. In the same way that old Emilo branded his cattle with a special brand to claim them as his own, Victor planned to do the same thing to Talleha with his lovemaking. After all, it was the last night they would share before he took his leave at dawn.

As his lips caressed her, so did his hands. As his strong arms encircled her, so did his muscled thighs. His fierce, powerful touch had its effect on her, for she'd never felt such a wild recklessness as he made her feel this night.

He stroked her with caresses of gentleness as he removed the wisps of curls from her face, and his lips whispered tender words of love in her ears.

Amid this sensual frenzy, she wondered how she could possibly stand it when he was not with her. How would she endure being alone? It made her arch against him desperately; she wanted his forceful maleness to fill her completely.

Her silken body drove him to a heightened passion he feared he could not control. It seemed she had the power to drive him insane, and he silently cursed, for he did not wish this paradise to fade so fast.

Suddenly, she felt the weight of his searing body leave her, and at the same moment, she felt herself being lifted just enough to fit with perfection atop him. He raised her up just enough so his lips could capture the tip of her breast. He allowed her undulating body to play against him as long as he could endure the sweet agony before thrusting into that velvety, satin flesh of hers.

He felt her breathless sigh of pleasure and he knew she was soaring to the same lofty heights of delight as he was. He knew, too, that he'd delayed the inevitable as long as possible. If wishing could have made it so, he would have wanted this moment to go on endlessly, but that could not be.

When that quaking moment shook both of them and

they clung together so very close as if nothing could ever divide them, Maurier made a wish. It was a wish he'd never made before, not even with his beautiful Talleha. He wanted to leave his seed within her. He wanted her to have his child.

He wanted this more than anything, he suddenly realized. No one was more shocked or surprised by this than Victor himself!

While Talleha could not know his thoughts at this moment, she knew that they'd shared a very special night—a very special love. She lay in the circle of his arms overwhelmed by very mixed emotions. It was going to be more heartbreaking than ever to tell him good-bye in the morning, but she had never been more sure of his love for her than she was this night.

Doubts and fears were swept away, for she could not believe that a man could share such all-consuming passion with a woman he did not truly love. This gave her an assured feeling she'd not known before with Victor, and the exaltation of that was beyond description. All that clouded this glorious feeling was how soon he would be leaving her now. But she remembered Captain Crawford's words to her this afternoon: this was something Victor had to do. He had to return to Harrison County. She knew she must not try to stop him, as much as she yearned to do just that.

After a long period of silence passed between them, Victor was the first to speak. "I am not going to wake you, Talleha, when it's time for me to leave. I want no farewells between us. I want just what we've had. Just know this, darling: I will return to you as soon as I do what must be done. You understand?"

"I understand, Victor. And I want you to be careful, for I'd just want to die if anything happened to you. We both know how evil and vicious Eliot can be."

"Oh, you can rest assured I plan to take every precaution, ma petite. I want no other man stepping in to console you. I'm selfish that way." He gave a husky laugh. "You've not known me long enough, Talleha, to know that I, too, can be vicious if I must. I don't consider myself evil, though. That makes a great deal of difference."

Her shapely body snuggled up closer to him and she teased him by saying, "Oh, I think I saw a little of that primitive, vicious man in you tonight."

"And I must say that I noticed that you seemed to enjoy it as much as I did, you wild little savage!" He kissed her so ardently he dared her to deny it.

She was not foolish enough to try that!

There were no farewells when he left her side as the sun was rising. But she felt the sudden chill after he'd left her bed. She also knew when he'd slipped through the door and lingered to look back at her. He was convinced that she was sleeping.

Only when the door was closed did she allow the tears to flow and dampen her pillow. She could already feel the tremendous void in her life with Victor not around. Now she realized how much her life had evolved around him ever since the day they'd left the Casa del Lago together. They'd been together constantly since then, and it was as if she was missing a part of herself to know that she'd not see his handsome face for days and maybe weeks.

Was it as painful for him as it was for her? Was that why he didn't awaken her to say a final goodbye? She was selfish enough to want to think so.

Tossing aside the quilt, she struggled to get her feet out and over the edge of the bed. She argued with herself as to why she was getting up, for the day offered no cause except to do a few things to help the captain. There was at least another good hour she could have enjoyed the leisure of sleep, but she knew she wouldn't sleep. She'd merely lie there, tossing and turning nervously, so why put herself through that torment?

She dressed and combed and brushed her hair until it had a glossy sheen, then made two neat, long braids. She heard the calling of the seagulls just outside her window and as she peered out she saw a massive flock of them flying over the beach below. She decided that once she fixed the captain a good breakfast, she'd take some crumbs of bread in her apron to feed them. That was a very pleasant pastime. She'd already spent many hours doing just that.

As she made her way toward the kitchen to start brewing a pot of coffee, she was sure that the captain was already up. She'd wager he'd made a point of having a last word with Victor before he galloped away.

But the house was ghostly quiet, she was surprised to see; there was no one in the small parlor. She went back into the kitchen to start the coffee.

She prepared the coffee and had it brewing. There were two stoneware cups on the table, handy to pour the coffee into as soon as it was ready. Now she planned to check on Crawford before she prepared anything else, for she was a light eater in the morning. Of course, on the trail with Victor she had always been ravenously hungry when she got out of that bedroll. Perhaps it was the country air that had enhanced her appetite.

When she was about to check on the captain, a man's deep voice stopped her as he remarked, "Something smells awfully good, missy."

She turned to see a ruddy-cheeked Captain Crawford standing there giving her a warm smile. She knew he'd been out walking on the beach and the wind had brought forth the rosy glow to his weathered cheeks. It amazed her that he'd found the strength when he'd looked so weak last night, excusing himself from the dinner table to go to his room.

Putting her hands on her hips with a bossy, demanding air about her, she insisted on knowing, "Now just what have you been up to, sir?"

A sheepish grin etched the old man's face; it was nice that this pretty lady was so curious about his whereabouts. She looked as cute as could be in her little white apron, her braids hanging down over her shoulders.

"Took myself a stroll on the beach, just hoping when I returned that you'd be a good girl and have me some strong black coffee made. Damned if you didn't! Now that's a girl after my own heart!"

She broke into laughter and went over to embrace him. "You're an ornery rascal, Glenn Crawford, but I love you."

"Ah, you do, do you? Well, to heck with Maurier! Let's you and me just get married, my sweet Talleha," he playfully jested. He didn't know whether it was that delightful, refreshing sea breeze or this enchanting little sea siren, but the captain felt like he'd had a healing balm. No woman had ever bossed him before, but somehow he didn't resent Talleha's bossing him.

Maybe it was just his age that had mellowed the cantankerous old man he knew himself to be!

Chapter 41

The Casa del Lago was a beehive of activity. The roundup was in full swing; Estaban had returned to the ranch; Emilo Cortez was still searching the countryside for some sight of Victor Maurier's return. Emilo had lost track of how many weeks it had been since Victor and Talleha had departed that miserable, rainy morning. He knew it had to be at least three weeks now, but then he reminded himself that it was a long trek down the coast of Texas to Brownsville.

But many things could have delayed or changed Victor's plans. His old friend, Crawford, could have died. There was the distinct possibility that Victor had found a very stubborn, determined little señorita to deal with once the two were on their way; Victor may have had to return her to her village instead of taking her to Brownsville.

The wise señor finally decided that he could speculate forever, but it was only when Victor did return that he would know for certain. Nevertheless, he could not occasionally stop his thoughts from returning to the two young people he thought so much of. He wished only the best for them, wherever they were.

As far as Emilo was concerned, he could not recall

having enjoyed a more wonderful season than this autumn in a long time. There was the camaraderie he shared with his nephew, Estaban, and he'd never have believed this possible. His faith in the young man was warranted, he was happy to say.

The last few weeks had been gloriously rewarding with Marjorie's visits to the ranch, too. He knew that she shared his feelings about this new development in their longstanding friendship. It surpassed any romantic affair, as far as Emilo was concerned. There was a time and a season for everything and he'd already had his season at being the romantic Latin lover. She understood this, for her life had taken a similar course.

Yet each of them felt a great passion for one another, and they enjoyed a serene rapture when they held hands or Emilo's arm encircled her waist as they strolled around his gardens. It was a good feeling and just the comfort both were now seeking.

Emilo's only complaint with Marjorie was why she allowed that English bastard to remain under her roof.

"If you don't know, Emilo, then I'll tell you something that has been going on for over a year between my maid and your foreman, Castillo. It seems my Lucita and Eliot's nephew, Ralph, find themselves madly in love. Call me the matchmaker if you will, but I've been biding my time for Ralph to be able to travel as they both wish to do, so they can leave Texas. They intend to marry and I've given Lucita my blessing to do so."

"But why does that have to stop you from tossing Eliot off the ranch?"

"Oh, Emilo—I can't explain the many complicated problems it could cause, but take my word for it, I hope to get Ralph and Lucita away first so they can be well on their way before I order him to leave. Trust me about that."

335

"I fear I must, Marjorie. I just hate that you have to continue to put up with such a despicable man even one minute longer."

"One more week, Emilo, and it should all be taken care of. It was only after Lucita came to me, confessing about her and Ralph, that I sought to delay my plans."

In a hesitating tone Emilo replied, "I—I guess that is not too long, my dear. I just caution you not to let your guard down."

"We might as well be strangers in that big house, Emilo. He rarely comes near me anymore, and he gets stranger by the day. He rides for hours or locks himself up in his study night after night. By way of the servants' gossip, I hear he spends a lot of his time at a cantina in town. I don't care what he does, as long as he leaves me alone. Now even his devoted English servant, Flossie, has no respect for him."

"All the more reason for you to be careful, Marjorie. A terrible rage might be festering there, ready to explode at a moment's notice," Emilo advised her.

"I know, Emilo. I'll tell you just how guarded I've become: I lock my bedroom door at night and I sleep with Frank's pistol close by."

"Dear God, Marjorie—that is dangerous!"

"But it is not for long, my dear friend. I promise nothing is going to happen to me. I decided that a long time ago. I'll kill Eliot if I must to save my life."

Emilo's dark eyes locked with hers. "See that you do, my dear Marjorie. He isn't worth your little finger."

"Oh, Emilo, I feel very honored that you hold me in such high esteem. I really don't think you know how much this means to me—how much the last weeks have meant to me," she told him, her eyes warm with affection.

Emilo was tempted to say something to Marjorie Greenfield that had been brewing within him for the

336

last week, but he restrained the impulse. His dignified reserve of his won out.

When she finally went to board her gig with Emilo helping her up onto the seat, he gently urged her, "Do what you must for the two young people under your roof. I admire what you are doing to help them. I've always known you to be a generous, kindhearted lady, so this doesn't surprise me, Marjorie. But I can't deny that I'm eager for you to be rid of Penwick."

She gave him a slow, sweet smile. "You know, Emilo, I've known you all this time, yet I feel I'm just beginning to really understand you. All those years I saw an Emilo Cortez who was aristocratic and gallant and never let anything make him fret or worry. Now I see that you worry just like the rest of us if you are concerned about something. Thank you for caring so much about me."

Emilo bent his head, and as he looked back into Marjorie's searching eyes, he admitted, "I'm not all that noble, Marjorie. The truth is, I'm a little greedy and selfish."

"You, Emilo—selfish?" She gave forth a girlishly soft laugh. "I find that hard to believe."

"My dear Marjorie, I'm going to disillusion you. I have my own selfish reasons for wanting Eliot Penwick out of your life, though that is really more than I intended to say at this time. You—you made me forget myself. You see, you've made me forget my usual logic. You've made me feel young again, Marjorie—young, and maybe a little reckless."

Did he mean what she thought he meant? she wondered. She prayed so! One thing was certain: Emilo was sincere in what he was saying. He was not the silken-tongued, smooth talker that Eliot Penwick was. It was Emilo she should have sought out for companionship after Frank had died, but she had been blind and stupid. If only she'd sought him out before, all the misery of the last year would never have happened.

She found herself feeling girlishly shy as she stammered a parting reply to him. "I—I feel young again, too, Emilo. I have you to thank for that!"

She swore she was blushing as she waved goodbye to Emilo, and she felt flushed and giddy as the bay broke into a fast trot to take her back to her ranch. It had been a long time since she'd allowed herself to dwell in the daydreaming she did this late afternoon.

When she got home and rushed immediately to her room, Lucita instantly noticed the radiance on her face. "I'll swear, señora—I'll swear you look more beautiful than I ever remember seeing you."

"Oh, Lucita—I'm a lady who can no longer even call myself middle-aged. I'm flirting with fifty." This didn't bother her this afternoon as it would have a few months ago.

"That was easy for me to believe some weeks ago—that you were a lady of almost fifty—but you don't look that way now. I tell the truth, señora."

As she helped the señora change out of her clothes, Lucita told Marjorie of the plans she and Ralph had discussed this afternoon. "He swears he is able to travel, señora, and wishes to leave immediately, if that is all right with you. He told me to tell you that he appreciated your generous offer, but he has quite enough to keep us comfortably until we get settled. He tells me he has a place in mind, señora. It is a place called Baton Rouge, Louisiana. He stayed there a few days on his way to Texas when he came to see his uncle, and he knows a man there who took a liking to him. My Ralph is a very smart man in his quiet way, señora, and he tells me he can keep a very fine set of books. This I do not understand, but if he says so, then I know it is true."

"So you are saying Ralph could be an accountant for this man in Baton Rouge—be his bookkeeper?" Marjorie wanted to know.

"Si—that is what he says. He says he will get a little house and live quite well. Is—is that all right with you, señora?"

"Go, Lucita—whenever you and Ralph wish—and know that you have my blessings," Marjorie told her, giving the little Mexican maid a warm, affectionate embrace. "But I won't be denied giving you a wedding gift."

As Emilo had remarked just that afternoon, Marjorie Greenfield was generous to people she liked. She'd become very fond of young Ralph Penwick, and Lucita had become very dear to her over the last years. The maid had always stood by her, devotedly loyal. Lucita had seen her in agony and despair, and Marjorie could remember times when she felt she was wandering in a maze between sanity and insanity, and the soft, encouraging words of Lucita had always helped her.

Her wedding gift to them was most generous. When the hour of their departure came, they had their own gig and a bay from Marjorie's stable to pull it. She'd casually announced to them, "Well, I have a new one, and I certainly can't ride in two at once, so you might as well have this one."

The fine roan mare was a superb animal which Ralph knew did not come cheap, and he was awestruck by the señora's lavish gift. He was not to know until much later, as they traveled through the Texas countryside after night had descended (Eliot was away from the ranch), that Lucita had been given a sizable dowry. He was stunned by the amount. It told him just how much Marjorie thought of Lucita, and it told him how truly remarkable Marjorie Greenfield Penwick was. He had been right about her all along. Everything his Uncle Eliot had told him about her had been a lie. Ralph was so glad he'd seen through it all. Now, as he traveled away from the ranch toward a new life with Lucita, he could feel almost sorry for Eliot. Like most people weaving their little webs of deception, Eliot had got caught up in his. Now he was strangling on his own rope. Ralph saw a man doomed, and it was a sad ending.

He was not greedy, nor did he desire a vast fortune. He just hoped to enjoy a happy life with the beautiful woman who'd promised to be his wife. He'd never expected someone as lovely as Lucita to fall in love with him, and to find out that she also had a dowry was more than he could have ever wished.

All he wanted was a cozy, comfortable cottage where he and Lucita could live and he could work to make a living to support her. If they were blessed with a family, he would be a man fulfilled.

He could not resist reaching out to take Lucita's hand. He gave it a little squeeze and smiled. "I'm the happiest man in the world tonight, Lucita. You can't know how much I love you. We're going to have a good life, I promise."

"I know, querida! We will work very hard to make it so—si?" she agreed, snuggling closer to him on the seat of the gig. "I've worked hard all my life, and I shall work twice as hard for us, querida."

He bent over to kiss her cheek and confessed, "I still can't figure out how an ugly bloke like me could have been so lucky to catch a beautiful girl like you. I know we are going into the unknown, Lucita, but I am not afraid with you by my side. It is so good to be away from all the evil I know is brewing back there. My only regret was leaving the señora there with that bastard uncle of mine."

"I know, Ralph. But I have a feeling that she will be all right." She made a gesture toward her heart as she added, "I have felt in here that she is going to be just fine. If I had not, I confess to you I could not have left."

"I hope you are right, Lucita! I truly do!" Ralph sighed.

"I tell you something, Ralph—the Greenfield ranch and cattle would never have come about but for a strong, determined lady like the señora. Oh, it is true that Frank Greenfield was a forceful man, but he could not have done it without the support and help of his woman. She stood by him all those years. When he died, she was devastated. That was the only reason she was gullible enough to be taken in by the likes of your uncle."

"Were you there when they married, Lucita?"

"Ah, si—I was. I saw a lovely spirited lady go to hell and back, and it frightened me. He did have a talent for bewitching a woman, I confess. I was swayed by his charm in the beginning, Ralph. I will not deny it, but it soon became obvious to me what a horrible, mean man he was. It took the señora a longer time to realize this, but once she did, she seemed to gather her strength again."

"Lucita, please don't hold it against me that he is my uncle. I can't help what he is. The only thing we share is the name of Penwick," Ralph pointed out to her.

"Ah, do you think I would? Do you think I would be sitting here beside you now if I did, querido?" she murmured softly and leaned over to kiss his cheek.

"No, Lucita—I guess I just wanted to hear you say it," he told her as they traveled onward into the night.

"Then I say it, Ralph. You are a mucho hombre and Eliot Penwick is a culebra!"

Ralph gave out a lighthearted laugh as he declared, "I'll swear, Lucita, you are going to have to teach me your language so I'll know whether to be happy or sad. You see, my darling, with a little spitfire like you, I could be in big trouble. You could be cussing me and I'd not know it."

She giggled and assured him, "Ah, you would know the difference, I promise you, Ralph. Just hope that I will never call you a culebra, for I would be calling you a snake. If I should do that, then I would be very angry with you."

"Oh, God forbid!" He turned to stare at her, cleverly concealing his amusement. He observed the sparking black of her eyes and the cute pout of her sensuous lips. She looked very young. Lucita was a mere child when he considered the years dividing them, and he'd not thought about it until now.

Somehow, he knew that she'd lived a life that would make his pale by comparison, and he did not wish to know about that. That was the past and all he cared about was the future.

Chapter 42

Eliot Penwick wore blinders, whether he was looking at himself in the mirror or trying to sort out the reasons everything had gone wrong for him. He stubbornly refused to admit that he was not as clever as he'd thought. He dared not face the fact that his excessive drinking was taking its toll on both his health and his looks.

His irregular hours and forgotten meals were already obvious to anyone who knew him. His once-fine physique was showing signs of weight loss and he no longer had an arrogant, self-assured air to his pace. He moved slowly and sluggishly, if he was not swaying and stumbling from his overindulgence.

The fine-chiseled features which once had made him seem so aristocratic were lined now from his dissipation.

There was no one at the ranch for him to turn to. He no longer had Flossie's sympathy; he'd sought to engage her in a few moments' conversation this evening when he'd returned from his ride in the woods, and she'd urged him to go off and get some rest.

For the last few weeks, he could not leave the house even for his ride in the woods without filling his silver flask.

By the time he'd turned his thoroughbred over to Romano and begun to stumble along the pathway toward the house, he was in a foul mood. He mumbled, "Damned Mexican—looking down his nose at me!" He'd sensed the distasteful look on the Mexican's face as he'd handed him the reins and left the barn.

His mood got even blacker as he'd walked through the front door to encounter Flossie. His prim and proper housekeeper had glared at him harshly. He sought to be playful and grabbed her around the waist, but her plump figure flinched with disgust when he slurred his words. "Come on, Flossie—what's the matter with my Flossie? You forgot about our plans— going back home to England, my dear. You still want to, don't you?"

She saw his glazed eyes and his tall body swaying back and forth. There was very little about this man that reminded her of the fine English gentleman she'd been so devoted to for so many years. Now she wondered if she'd been a fool all along to have admired him so much.

Dejectedly, she shook her head. "Oh, sir—what a shame it is that you ever left England and came here. What a bloody shame! Go to bed, Lord Penwick. Go to bed and rest. It's what you're needing, sir. Not drinking the night away." She turned and waddled away down the long dark hallway.

Eliot stared at her as she left him and his lips curled up with a smirk. "God damned old bossy bitch! Who does she think she is, anyway, talking to me like that— telling me what I should or shouldn't do?"

He was like a young boy defying a parent after he'd been told not to do something, for it was his study he made for as he walked on down the hall. He slammed the door and turned the lock.

He didn't trouble himself with getting a glass. Instead, he took down the bottle of brandy and uncapped it to guzzle greedily straight from the bottle.

As he did nightly, he cursed all the members of the household, especially Marjorie and Ralph. He got so caught up in his rage and hate that he sought to vent it on his nephew, Ralph. Like a rampaging bull, he stormed out of the study to race up the steps to Ralph's room. When he entered to find the room dark, he assumed his nephew was already asleep.

He stalked quietly toward the bed, but he was shocked to find the bed empty. "What the hell?" he exclaimed, as he frantically searched the room to find all of Ralph's belongings, including his one valise, missing. He was so stunned that he sank down on the bed. A feeling of giddiness engulfed him as he sat there staring into the empty space of the bedroom.

Had Ralph left to return to England? Eliot was of the opinion that he was not well enough to go on such a long journey yet. But maybe his nephew had made some improvements he'd not realized, now that he thought about it. He'd not taken the time to look in on him the last two or three days, Eliot reminded himself.

He loathed the idea of asking Marjorie where Ralph was, but he knew no one else could tell him. God, he detested having to seek her out! As he sat there on the bed, a new rage built within him, and it was directed toward Marjorie. That bitch had been a hellish torment, and it was the worst day of his life when he'd met her. The worst decision he'd made in his life was when he'd married her, thinking that she could provide the lavish way of life he desired. This miserable Texas countryside and this rancher's widow had driven him to a madness he was not sure he could conquer now. He hated her as he'd never hated another human being.

There was only one bright spot in all the many

months he'd spent in Harrison County—Talleha. But Marjorie had destroyed that for him. He knew she'd played a hand in helping Talleha leave the ranch. Maybe she'd even manipulated Talleha's abduction, his clouded mind reasoned.

There could be no other answer, Eliot told himself. It had to be that crazy wife of his who had forced Talleha to leave because she was jealous of a young lady so breathtakingly beautiful. God, such wonderful dreams he'd had for the two of them! Such marvelous plans! Talleha was the one woman who could have been everything he'd always imagined he wanted to have in a wife. Now, that had all been destroyed and ruined for him—he could thank Marjorie for that.

He rose up from the bed, a strange look on his face. He pulled out the silver flask and drank deeply from it. He walked unsteadily toward the door of Ralph's bedroom.

It was to Marjorie's boudoir he was going; he needed to find out where Ralph was, and he planned to tell her more than she'd have liked to hear. In fact, he was going to tell her exactly how he felt about this damned old ranch that she was so proud of. To hell with the land, he'd never cared for land. The money it could have brought if he'd sold it was all that ever interested him.

Marjorie Greenfield would never have caught his eye for a second back in England, for he found her very pale and dull compared to the fancy ladies he'd squired around London.

Talleha was the vision of feminine charm he'd romantically fantasized about. That was why the first night he'd seen her was like a dream become reality. He was utterly dazzled by her striking beauty. Those onyx eyes, that black, glossy hair reminded him of the woman in his dreams, and he knew Talleha was the woman he'd waited for all his life. She was the reason he'd never married but had remained the elusive bachelor back in England.

Only his strained finances had urged him to propose to Marjorie Greenfield, and he recalled how effortlessly he'd won her hand in marriage. Nothing was as easy as a lonely widow like Marjorie—a sophisticated man like Penwick could get just about anything he wanted.

Boredom on this miserable ranch had driven him crazy after they'd been married only a few short weeks, and he was so hungry to have one grand night of reveling back in good old London, he'd decided then and there that he had to get the most he could out of this marriage. Then he could walk away from it and her and get back to England, where he belonged.

When he discovered that he could easily browbeat Marjorie, even to the point of making her ill, he realized he'd found the weapon he needed to accomplish his goal. For weeks he'd applied this tactic, and the results had been remarkable. She shriveled and withered like a flower. He was amazingly pleased with himself as he anticipated what a mere few months of sacrifice on his part could yield. It was well worth it for the vast wealth he'd inherit as her husband.

What had been the turning point in his grandiose scheme? Looking back on it now, Eliot realized when everything seemed to be crumbling and falling apart. When one plan failed, he tried to set in motion a new one, but it had not worked either.

There was not point in lying to himself any longer, he had to admit tonight. As drunk as he was, he knew the night that was the beginning of the end was the night his emotions became involved, causing him to think with his heart, instead of his head. It was the night he'd found Talleha in the woods.

347

From that moment on, he was a man beguiled. She clouded his good judgment and clear thinking. And her arrival on the ranch seemed to have had a strange effect on Marjorie. He realized now that the once spineless, weak-willed Marjorie was insidiously growing stronger and more self-assured. He found he was unable to subdue her. The stronger she became, it seemed to him, the more futile it was for him to carry forth with his quest.

As he now stumbled down the darkened hallway, he told himself he could easily justify wringing the necks of both Marjorie and Talleha. If he had a full coffer, he could turn his back on the whole damned state of Texas and its loathesome people and go back home—home to England.

To hell with that disloyal Flossie, too! He'd not take her along when he did leave, he vowed.

Another neck he'd like to wring was that of the deceitful little Lucita. He smirked as he raised his hand to knock on Marjorie's door. He'd decided to delightfully tell Marjorie this very night how he'd made passionate love to her "devoted" servant less than a month after they were married.

Revenge consumed him as he prepared to rap on the door. He figured that Lucita was sequestered inside with Marjorie as she had been so often the last few weeks. Oh, they thought he didn't know, but he'd known all along that they consoled and comforted one another so the big, bad Eliot could not harm them.

As he stood there knocking on the door, he gave out a crazed howl of laughter, caring not that they heard him. Before the night was over, they were going to hear many things they might not want to hear!

Marjorie heard the disgusting, high-pitched voice of Eliot out in the hallway. All night she'd prepared herself for the scene she knew she was about to endure.

It was inevitable—one last trial before the fresh, clean air could once again flow through the rooms of her home and the vile evil of Eliot Penwick was swept away. She could not avoid it any longer.

To say she was not scared would have been a lie. She was terrified. It had been desolate and lonely this evening without the consoling company of Lucita; but she was happy that Ralph and Lucita were heading toward a happy life together, wherever they went. Lucita had promised to write her as soon as they were settled.

Marjorie had requested a carafe of coffee brought to her bedroom at a later hour than was her custom. She didn't want to drift off to sleep tonight too early. She'd placed Frank's two pistols so they were conveniently near to her, should the need for them arise. Her usual routine for changing into her gown and wrapper was not followed tonight. She had remained dressed in the afternoon frock she'd worn, but she had taken the two tight coils from her hair and let it flow down loose and free. That seemed to ease the tension in her throbbing head.

But there was comfort to be had in the room tonight, and Marjorie felt it most strongly. There was the voice of Frank, encouraging her to stand up to the bastard who was now outside her door.

"What do you want, Eliot? The hour is late and we have nothing to talk about that can't wait until morning," she finally responded to his ranting voice.

"No, it can't! I demand to know where my nephew is!"

"If that's all you want to know, I can answer you quickly. He has left the ranch! He is gone!"

"Gone where?"

"Maybe back to England. I'm not certain. Now go to bed, Eliot. I'm tired." She bent close to the door, straining to see if he'd started to leave. She heard nothing, and she heaved a deep sigh of relief, praying that he'd left. Her lock was secure. Slowly she moved away from the door and went over to sink into the overstuffed chair. Her hand was trembling so, she wondered if she could have used the pistol if she'd needed it!

She felt a wave of panic washing over her as she leaned her head back against the floral chintz chair and closed her eyes. Taking a deep breath, she gave out a moan, wishing the night was over and it was already morning. What was it about the night that made everything seem so eerie?

As she sat there trying to gain her composure, it seemed she heard Frank's voice calling out to her again. He cautioned her to not let her guard down. She swore she heard him call her by his pet name for her. "On guard, Margie! Open your eyes!" the voice warned.

When she did open her eyes, she became very alert, for there was a noise nearby. She could not figure where it was coming from or what it was. Her hand searched for the pistol and gripped it firmly.

Having been Frank Greenfield's wife for many years, she knew well how to use a rifle and pistol. As petrified as she was, she posed, ready to fire, her finger teasing the trigger. She listened attentively to see if she could hear what she thought she'd heard earlier.

Eliot's conniving, devious mind was not completely numbed by liquor. He knew there was no way she was going to admit him into her bedroom, but he remembered that the next room down the hallway was the adjoining sewing room. When he tried the door it was unlocked. He did not want to enter just then. Quietly, he sneaked down the hallway to his own room, and when he found the object he sought, he made his

350

way back down the hall.

Along the way he paused long enough to gulp all the liquor remaining in the silver flask, and when he found it empty he dropped it casually on the fine carpeted floor. His dizziness caused him to stumble, and he steadied himself by grabbing for the wall.

When he slipped through the doorway leading into the sewing room, he could see the dim lamplight from Marjorie's boudoir. He knew it came from the lamp sitting on the table next to the comfortable chintz chair. What he was not prepared for was finding no Lucita sleeping on the little daybed in the sewing room. The bed was empty! Eliot had intended to make one fatal swipe at her throat to enjoy his revenge on her, but it was not to be!

This added to his madness and frenzy. He was a man consumed with fury as he stalked toward the doorway to Marjorie's bedroom, his sharp, silver-bladed knife raised and ready to plunge into his prey.

Marjorie saw the ominous, shadowy figure moving in the dark adjoining room. She knew it was Eliot and cursed herself for being so careless as to forget to check the sewing room before coming to bed. How could she have been so stupid! But it was too late to worry about that now. She had to act and act fast. Now she was faced with a wild beast raging toward her with a knife; there was no doubt where this demented madman intended to place it.

An amazing calm settled over her as she took aim and pulled the trigger. She heard the explosion and she smelled the acrid odor of smoke. At the same moment, she heard Eliot's agonizing scream as he fell to the floor.

She collapsed in the chair with the pistol still in her hand. Her dark eyes were glazed as she stared at the stilled figure. In a stammering voice she murmured,

"We did it, Frank! It's finally over!"

That wild scream and the explosion in the still of the night spurred into action the rider on the black stallion who'd been stationed in the pine trees a short distance from Marjorie's house for the last hour.

Emilo Cortez spurred his stallion, Mirlo, into action, praying that the scream he'd heard was not Marjorie, but Eliot Penwick. He was glad he'd listened to instinct and come here.

He'd never prayed so hard in his life as he galloped toward her house.

Chapter 43

It was a panic-stricken, ashen-faced Emilo Cortez who quickly dismounted from his stallion and rushed up the flagstone walk to the entrance of the Greenfield house. He was more than concerned when he found the heavy oak door ajar. This should not be, he told himself. He could not know that Eliot Penwick had been the last one to enter and had carelessly failed to close it properly.

It would not have happened if Lucita had been there, because every evening after she'd left her mistress's bedroom to go to her quarters, she always checked the front door. Emilo moved cautiously down the tiled hallway, knowing not what he was about to encounter.

There was a pervasive quiet that made him tense with apprehension. All the time he prayed that the scream he'd heard was not Marjorie, for it would plague him the rest of his life that he hadn't taken a firmer hand with her the other day. He knew the chances she was taking, but she was so determined that she had it all planned out. He should not have dismissed it so lightly. He should have demanded that she let him take charge of the situation, he chided himself.

Moving slowly with his six-shooter ready, he moved

along the hallway. The entire downstairs seemed to be deserted; there were no lamps burning. The scream he'd heard seemed not to have brought any of the servants scurrying. This disturbed him greatly. He could only conclude that poor Marjorie had been here all alone this evening with that despicable English villain.

Suddenly, he heard a soft, feminine voice calling to him from above; it was tremulous and stammering. To Emilo, there could have been no sound more wonderful. He turned to see Marjorie standing there at the railing. Her face was pale and she looked like a helpless child.

He turned and rushed to her; he mounted the steps with agility. When he got to her side, he embraced her, holding her close. "Ah, querida—thank God! Thank God, it was not your scream I heard. I was so worried!" he confessed to her.

He held her. Amid the sobs, she confessed to him that she, too, had never been so scared. "I killed him, Emilo! I killed him and I am glad!"

"And so am I, querida! Oh, so am I, and I do not apologize for such a horrible confession."

Suddenly, she pushed away from Emilo just far enough to look into his dark eyes. "I laughed, Emilo! Can you believe that as I pulled the trigger and killed the man who was my husband—I laughed! I find it hard to admit even to myself! But I swear to you, Emilo, that Frank was there in the room guiding me tonight all the way. I swear it!"

Emilo patted her shoulders and assured her that he could believe that. Often, he'd sworn that he'd heard his dear wife talking to him. Most people might think you were crazy if you told them that, but Emilo knew it was true.

"I heard Frank say to me, 'Remember everything I

taught you, Margie. Remember, for your life depends on it.' Dear Lord, it did! He came after me with a knife."

Emilo pressed her closer to him and praised her, "Oh, Marjorie—you're so brave! You can be very proud of yourself. Frank would be proud of you, too. I know I am!"

In the comforting circle of his arms she could not see the mist of tears in Emilo's eyes. He knew now that he would delay no longer the proposal he'd been thinking about for the last week. He would ask Marjorie to be his wife. But first he had things to do.

"Marjorie, my love—do you think you could brew your old friend a cup of coffee? The house seems to be without any servants tonight," he told her, feeling her body beginning to calm. There were things he must see about, and it was far better that she remain downstairs as he went about the unpleasant task upstairs.

Marjorie had always known that Emilo Cortez was a man of finesse and tact, and she knew exactly why he'd suggested that she occupy herself with brewing them some coffee. She knew she was going to need to rely on the sage wisdom of Emilo before this whole horrible mess was over and done with.

She was not so overcome with grief that she had not heard the terms of endearment Emilo had used. It was crazy to have happened at a time like this, but Marjorie was in the highest of spirits. Why shouldn't she be? She was rid of Eliot Penwick once and for all! She had her ranch and he'd not succeeded in his evil plan to rob her of it and destroy her as she knew he surely planned to do. Now she knew that Emilo cared very much for her! What more could any woman want?

To have had one wonderful man like Frank Greenfield was a blessing, but to be blessed this way twice was more than any mortal could ask or expect.

"I'll have us some coffee made by the time you get downstairs, Emilo," she told him as she broke away from his arms.

Only when she had descended and Emilo had seen her reach the base of the stairway did he turn to go to where he'd seen the lamplight burning.

The scene was far more gruesome than he'd expected. He saw the fierce, long-bladed knife that Eliot Penwick had obviously threatened his wife with. He bent down on the expensive carpet and performed the grisly task of closing the staring, lifeless eyes of Eliot Penwick. A crazy thought flashed through his mind—he'd never realized how brilliantly blue they were until now.

Lying there on the floor as he was now, Eliot seemed so gaunt and decaying that he looked pathetic in death. That once aristocratic face now looked twenty years older. What a very sad end the man had to come to!

Emilo roamed Marjorie's bedroom and the adjoining sewing room. His shrewd, clever mind had reconstructed the last moments of Eliot Penwick's life and the horror of the moments Marjorie had lived through. What nightmares she was going to have in the nights to come! He was going to be there to hold and comfort her if she'd allow it, he vowed silently.

As he finally moved along the dark hallway to go downstairs, he realized Marjorie had managed to get Ralph and Lucita away from the ranch. As soon as they had a steaming cup of hot coffee, Emilo was going to suggest that the two of them leave, too. He was determined to take her back to the Casa del Lago with him, and he would send one of his men for the sheriff once they got there.

There was no question in Señor Cortez's mind that the killing of Eliot Penwick would be considered an act of self-defense on Marjorie's part. It could not be

356

otherwise, he told himself. The devil was coming at her with a knife and was going to plunge it into her flesh. Luckily, Frank had taught her so well!

He went into the kitchen. She turned around to face him and give him a friendly smile. "It is ready, Emilo. Here, let me pour it for you." As the two of them sat alone at the little oak table, Marjorie sipped her coffee and thought about the request she was about to ask of Emilo.

She couldn't bear to stay in this house alone the rest of the night. She wanted to go to the Casa del Lago, but would it be too brazen of her to ask this of him? As close as they'd become the last few weeks, she would never want Emilo to think her presumptuous.

She swore he had to be reading her innermost thoughts as he said, "Marjorie, I want you to go with me to the Casa del Lago. I'll send a man to town to tell the sheriff what has happened out here tonight. You do not need to be alone, querida. You need to be with me."

Though startled, she didn't try to deny it. She softly replied, "I do, Emilo. I admit I do."

He gave her a warm smile and his hand reached out across the small table to take hers. There was a very solemn tone to his voice when he next spoke. "I think, Marjorie, that I should take charge, as you say. I think we both know—have known for a few weeks—that it's time we start taking care of one another. We can both have a wonderful life together and enjoy whatever time we have left." He gave forth a lighthearted chuckle, "I know it is a most untimely moment to bring up such a subject, but circumstances make it so."

She gave him an approving nod of her head and remarked, "Dear God, Emilo—have you wondered as I have lately about how we both could have been so stupid? About the marvelous times we wasted? I was a widow over a year before Eliot Penwick came into my life, and here you were so near."

"Perhaps, Marjorie, that was the reason why. I was close and Penwick came into your life and it was new, different, and exciting. As for myself, I can only say that when my wife died, I closed and locked doors that I never intended anyone to open again. I can be a very strong-willed person, Marjorie. I might as well alert you to that right now."

She gave him a sly little grin, "Really, Emilo? I'd have never guessed that! You and Frank Greenfield have a lot in common, you know?"

He could only give her an affectionate smile, for he knew of no man more strong-willed than his old friend, Frank Greenfield. He sat there holding this lady's hand and wondered how he could have been so blind all those years—and they were lonely years.

He was not an unfeeling man and he knew this was a night that had been horrible for Marjorie, but as they sat there together now, he knew she was not feeling any remorse. Neither was he.

Already, he was thinking to himself that as soon as she finished her coffee and could pack an overnight bag, he was going to suggest that they ride to the Casa del Lago. Dawn was fast approaching. Another day was beginning and Emilo was eager to greet it with Marjorie by his side.

When they arrived at the Casa del Lago, Emilo immediately took charge, insisting that Marjorie get settled into one of his guest bedrooms. "You've had enough for one night, little lady. You need to get some rest."

She did not seek to argue with him, for it was true. She suddenly felt she could fall from the exhaustion and trauma she'd experienced this long, long night.

When he'd left her in the capable hands of one of his Mexican servants, he summoned one of his men from the bunkhouse to ride into town to inform the sheriff of what had happened at the Greenfield ranch earlier tonight.

It was one of those times Emilo needed the quiet solitude of his study and a talk with his beloved wife, and that was where he went. The moment he closed the heavy oak door and stared up at the portrait with the serenely smiling face looking down on him, he relaxed.

This spot was always his haven, and nothing would ever change that, Emilo knew. If he did ask Marjorie to be his wife, there were certain things she'd have to understand. Somehow, he felt she was probably the only woman who would.

He poured a glass of the amber Madeira wine which was his wife's favorite and he looked deeply into the crystal glass, thinking about how flattering the lovely amber color was to his wife's tawny skin.

He looked up at the portrait and vowed to Carmelita that Marjorie could never take that special place she would forever hold in his heart. "No woman was ever as breathtakingly beautiful as you, mi vida, and no woman ever will be."

The room was ghostly quiet, but Emilo had his answer, and it was the one he was sure he would get. Carmelita was always a kindhearted, loving woman, and he felt she was urging him to help their friend, Marjorie. He swore he could hear her saying to him, "I can't be there with you and Marjorie to comfort you as I would like to do. You two comfort one another, Emilo. You need one another."

"Si, querida—it is true," he murmured softly. He sat thoughtfully for a few minutes longer and sipped the Madeira. "So it will be, beloved, until I join you—si?" Never did he love his wife more than he did in that special moment. Theirs had been a rare love; he'd always known that. Their hearts and souls were joined in all-consuming, endless depths of passion and love.

When he emerged from the study, he was a man revitalized for the numerous tasks facing him. He immediately summoned the Cerventes family along with their daughter, Miranda, to go to the Greenfield ranch, to stay and see that certain things were not disturbed by any of the Greenfield servants until the sheriff could check the dead body of Penwick. Emilo wanted the scene to remain as it was for the sheriff's eyes to observe. The fierce knife Eliot had held in his hand was evidence that Marjorie's life had been threatened. He wanted to establish beyond any doubt that it was a case of self-defense.

It was not until two hours later that Emilo finally allowed himself a brief period of sleep and rest. But he was pleased that he'd accomplished all the tasks he felt necessary before he sought to retire.

There was a strange feeling of gratification churning within him. There was still a lot of stamina in this old man, he told himself. He was not ready for a rocking chair just yet, and this was enough to make him rejoice!

Emilo had some more living to do and he planned to do just that.

Chapter 44

The news of Eliot Penwick's death stirred no great wave of grief in Harrison County. He'd never endeared himself to anyone during the two years he'd lived there. The small crowd who attended the funeral did so out of respect for his widow, Marjorie.

Some still harbored deep resentment toward Marjorie for marrying Penwick. Marjorie saw this as she stood by the graveside observing the crowd through her black-veiled bonnet. She was glad that the veil covered her face and concealed that she was not overcome with grief. She shed no tears during the ceremony, for she felt no loss, and she had never been a woman to lie about her feelings.

Emilo stayed by her side as he had since the fateful night it had all happened. However, she had returned to her ranch the next day. She was more than grateful that there had been no questions about the circumstances of Eliot's death after the sheriff had investigated the scene up in her bedroom. She had to wonder whether he'd have been so eager to accept her story about what transpired that night if he'd liked Eliot. But he, like most of the people of the surrounding countryside, detested her husband. He'd made that perfectly clear to her when he'd come to the ranch once, having been summoned about Talleha's disappearance.

Marjorie said a fervent prayer, hoping just to get through this funeral so she could once and for all put the episode of Eliot Penwick behind her. Until she heard from Ralph and Lucita, she could not inform him about his uncle's death. But she was eager to throw herself into the workings of her ranch and was ready to put her life back together.

As she'd told Emilo the other night, they could enjoy one another's companionship until a proper amount of time had passed. If they felt the same way when springtime came, then she'd discuss marriage with him.

There was no hint of weakness in Marjorie, but she had to be sure that Emilo's feelings for her were not out of pity. And she did not want any offer of marriage out of Emilo's loyalty to Frank or any feeling of obligation, for she knew Emilo was one of the true gentlemen left in this world. She wanted to marry him only if his feelings were for her and her alone.

When she confessed this to Emilo, his esteem and admiration was only heightened. Now he understood Frank's devoted love for his wife. He understood many things now, too. It was Marjorie who had played a tremendous role in making Frank the outstanding man he was.

Of course, he would agree to her terms; he knew she was wise. They were not two reckless youths who felt they had to rush into marriage. They were mature individuals who'd experienced life. It was a bond of understanding.

He told her it would be as she wished it, and he sincerely meant it.

Two days after Eliot's funeral, the usual routine of the ranches was resumed. There was one exception which Marjorie had gratefully accepted from Emilo, and that was that the young Mexican girl, Miranda, became her maid, since Lucita was gone.

Only after Marjorie had insisted upon having a talk with Emilo's housekeeper, Miranda's mother, did she agree to such an arrangement. Emilo was not completely truthful about his reasons for sending Miranda over to her ranch. He could not be completely sure of Estaban and his behavior. So until he was, he thought that it might be the perfect maneuver to ensure Miranda's best interests.

He was delighted when Marjorie agreed to have Miranda under her roof. He assured her, "She is a good girl, Marjorie, and very trustworthy. She comes from good stock. Her family have been with me for years. I have great respect for all of them."

"She is a beautiful little thing."

"Si, she is." He had not intended to say what he said next, but Marjorie seemed to have a way about her which made him unguarded and relaxed. "My Estaban found her most tempting."

Marjorie broke into laughter, "So, you sly old devil—you're trying to protect little Miranda from that hot-blooded nephew of yours who's staying for the roundup?"

A sheepish grin came over Emilo's face. "You are too clever, my dear, far too clever for me to fool. It is true that I would not want Estaban trifling with such an innocent girl as Miranda, and it could happen so easily."

"Then, querido—we've hit on the perfect solution to keep that from happening." She bent over to kiss Emilo on the cheek.

Emilo left the Greenfield ranch feeling happy. He had not felt so lighthearted in years. Life was wonderful. A man was not whole without a woman.

363

This blissful state lasted for the next twenty-four hours. But when Emilo happened to be looking out his study window the next late afternoon and saw Marjorie riding frantically up his long drive, his heart started pounding. Something was wrong and he knew it instinctively. What had gone so wrong in one day's time, he wondered? He rushed out of the study to meet her at the door.

He watched her dismount and thought to himself as he was hurrying toward her that she could have been the woman he'd known some thirty years ago. Hair was flying back from her face, cascading freely down her back, over her flat-crown felt hat. She wore a faded blue tunic with a pair of tight-fitting dark-blue pants. He'd known about Marjorie's habit of wearing men's pants for riding, instead of the traditional lady's divided skirt.

She looked marvelous to Emilo, but right then he was concerned with the look on her lovely face. A million thoughts ran through his mind as they approached one another.

"You'll never believe what I'm about to tell you, Emilo," she gasped breathlessly. She took the kerchief which had been tied around her neck and dabbed her forehead and down her cheek.

"And I probably never will if you don't calm down. Come, Marjorie—let us go to the veranda and sit calmly so you can gather enough breath to tell me—si?" He took her arm and guided her.

When he had her seated comfortably and had summoned one of the servant girls to bring them something refreshing to drink, he insisted that she tell him what had her in such a frenzy of excitement.

"A man came to the ranch today, Emilo, an agent working out of a firm back east. It—it seems he has been searching the area for months, Emilo. He represents a law firm that was handling the affairs of Richard Talbert. Remember I told you about him? Remember I told you about the portrait I found among the ones he'd left at our house?"

"Ah, yes—the half-breed lady, Dawn—the one you thought looked so much like Talleha. Yes, I do remember—wasn't Richard Talbert Frank's friend who stayed with you awhile after he'd been up in the Lake of the Pines country?"

"That's right, Emilo!" she exclaimed, excitement still churning within her. Emilo was aware of this as he looked at her flushed face. "Was the agent sent by this man, Talbert?"

"Oh, no, not Talbert. He is dead, and that is why this Mr. Hemphill was here. Richard Talbert is dead; he died a year ago, but it seemed that even after all these years he never forgot the woman who carried his child, and it is the child they are searching for now. She has inherited a fortune. Hemphill recognized the portraits I showed him in my storage room as Talbert's work. There was no doubt in his mind. He is returning in a week, Emilo."

"Wait a minute, Marjorie—I fear I'm lost. Why is he returning in a week?" Emilo asked.

"My God—don't you see, Emilo? We've got to get word to Talleha and Victor. Did he take her back to her village? You were the only one to have the answers to that. Don't you know what I've been telling you? There is no doubt that Talleha was Dawn's and Richard Talbert's daughter."

"Please, my dear Marjorie—you are going too fast for me. How can you be so sure it is Talleha who is Talbert's daughter?"

"Hemphill said Talbert's journal was turned over to his attorneys. The daughter who he called Nicole was given an Indian name by her mother—one of love and

365

endearment. The name 'Nicole' was the name of Richard Talbert's mother, and Talbert adored her. It seems, according to Hemphill, that Talbert returned to the village a few months ago to find Dawn and his daughter when he knew he was dying. He could not linger there long, for he was too ill, but he did learn that Dawn was murdered and his daughter was taken away. Talbert returned to the east, but since he knew he was a dying man, he turned over his journals to his attorneys."

"What could the journals tell his lawyers about his daughter, Marjorie?" It was Emilo's understanding that the man had left this half-breed Indian woman and a child he could know little about.

"Ah, Emilo—more than you might think. He wrote of their mutual friends in the little village where he once lived with the woman, Dawn. Mr. Hemphill had spoken with their friends, Hunter and Salina. They confirmed that the daughter of Dawn had a birthmark on her right shoulder, and they gave definite details as to the size and shape of it."

"I see," Emilo replied slowly. Victor Maurier would surely be an authority on that, Emilo considered.

"Oh, Emilo—it is really a bittersweet love story, and I was so very wrong about Richard Talbert. He was a man capable of great love, and his leaving Dawn was not to desert her—just to tie up the loose ends of his life so he could return to her and his daughter. He did not try to explain the complicated circumstances to Dawn, for he knew this sweet, simple Indian woman would not have understood."

"So he was not a scoundrel and a drifter just using this poor innocent maiden for his own selfish pleasures?"

"Of course not. He'd come to America, all the time painting canvases of the various landscapes and people he'd met along the way. Richard was the kind of man who had obviously never cared about worldly goods like his wealthy family back in France. He'd never stayed long in any one place until he came to the Lake of the Pines and met Dawn."

Marjorie added that he had no way of knowing while he was in that isolated area of Texas that his many paintings, which he'd been sending back to a friend in the east, were selling. His friend had had no way to contact Talbert.

"Talbert did not realize his success until he'd left Dawn. He'd traveled back east to go to France to see his family and tell them he intended to return to America and stay. But when he arrived in France, he found the mother he adored was dying, and so he remained much longer than he'd planned. Almost three years would pass before he was able to sail back to the States."

"Pardon me, Marjorie, but what delayed the man for another decade or more from getting back to a woman and a child he loved so much?" Emilo asked.

"Fate, Emilo. A crazy turn of events. He arrived back in Boston a very sick man from a malady he contracted on the crossing. He was befriended by a most generous widow returning on the same ship. After months of residing in her palatial home in Boston, he married her out of gratitude. Richard was a very handsome man. He obviously forgot about the woman and daughter. His obsession was with his painting during that time, and he made quite a name for himself."

"So it was when he found himself to be a dying man he decided to try to find his daughter again?"

"According to Mr. Hemphill, he began that quest about three years ago." Marjorie noted something about Emilo's expression and manner that urged her to

367

inquire of him, "What is it, Emilo? I sense that you don't approve of this man too much."

"The truth is I don't, Marjorie. I don't approve of him at all."

"Neither do I, Emilo—but I'm not asking for approval. I'm merely telling you what Hemphill told me. But what is really important about this is that our little Talleha as we knew her is actually an heiress—a very wealthy heiress! We must try to locate her, and I want your help."

"But Marjorie, my dear, my hands are tied until Victor Maurier returns. He swore he would. We can only wait."

"Then let's pray that he returns within the next two weeks. Hemphill is going to contact me again then, and I promised to see what I could find out for him."

Ever the wise philosopher, Emilo pointed out to her, "It is in the hands of fate, querida. We both know that."

"Si, Emilo—I know that!" Marjorie told him as she snuggled closer to him, glad that fate had brought the two of them together.

Chapter 45

Maurier found his days and nights to be lonely without the company of Talleha. He left Brownsville and rode across the countryside northward toward Harrison County. There was no lighthearted laughter to share during the endless days and he found his bedroll the loneliest without her sweet, warm body there beside him at night. It was all the incentive he needed to spur Sultana to a faster pace to get to his destination so he could have this miserable task over and done with. Only then could he ride back to Brownsville as fast as Sultana could take him to return to the woman he loved.

He hoped she would enjoy the nice little surprise he'd managed to work out before he'd left Brownsville. He'd sought out a seamstress in the town and ordered some very fancy lingerie, a promise he'd made her when her chemise was lost in the currents of the river back on the trail. He'd insisted on black lace and scarlet satin.

When the seamstress and owner of the shop, Madame Charbeau, found out that Maurier was French, she was most obliging. Victor was suddenly stricken by the fact that of all the ladies he'd squired and courted, he'd done nothing to really let Talleha know he adored her. What better time than this, he told himself. She had brought precious little with her when she'd hastily left the Penwick ranch that night.

He'd admired the fact that when she'd left the Casa del Lago with him that morning, she'd left behind the fancy articles of clothing which had once belonged to Señor Cortez's wife. There was no way anyone could call Talleha a greedy female.

So this last-minute act before he left Brownsville had given him much pleasure, and he was generous when he'd placed the order. Madame Charbeau was a happy lady and very impressed with the handsome young Frenchman. He was obviously enamored of the young mademoiselle about to receive such a magnificent bounty of gifts.

He had paid her in advance and given her very specific directions as to where they were to be delivered.

"You will not be disappointed, Monsieur Maurier. It is exciting to me to prepare such an order. I haven't had an order such as this since I left New Orleans. You must know that Brownsville is not the flamboyant city that New Orleans is. The people of Brownsville are more practical," she told him.

Maurier gave her a broad, knowledgeable grin, "Ah, there are few cities to compare with New Orleans, Madame Charbeau. Would you not agree with me?"

"Oui, Monsieur Maurier, I would agree. The closest I've ever found to my beloved France was New Orleans." She was enjoying herself; she wouldn't have cared if he'd purchased nothing in her salon. Such a man as Maurier was refreshing compared to some of the gentlemen who came into her shop with their ladies or their wives. Her curiosity was fired to see the young mademoiselle for whom he had selected such fine gifts.

She was even more impressed when she presented

370

him the final tally: he did not flinch. He paid her and gave her a most alluring grin as he prepared to leave her shop. "It's been a pleasure, Madame Charbeau, and I hope to do business with you again in the future. I know my lady will be pleased when you deliver the articles to her."

"Oh, oui, Monsieur Maurier—I know she will be pleased. She is a very lucky lady to have such a man as you. I must admit that I can't wait to meet her."

Victor smiled, "When you see her you will realize that I am the lucky one. Bonjour, Madame Charbeau." He turned to go through the doorway, for he still had things to attend to before the afternoon had slipped away.

"Bonjour, Monsieur Maurier," the middle-aged seamstress called out to him as she watched his tall, muscular body move out the front door and mount his horse. It had been the most stimulating interlude she'd had here in Brownsville in a long time. Such encounters did not happen often for Madame Emily Charbeau, and certainly not in Brownsville.

It was times like this that she wished she'd never left New Orleans. She'd caught a packet ship to sail across the gulf to Brownsville to escape an unhappy love affair. Ah, she had escaped, but she'd doomed herself to a very weary, routine existence which had swiftly consumed almost twenty years of her life. Time had gone by too quickly, Emily had to admit. Now she was too old to dare to be reckless or adventuresome. Brownsville would be where she'd live the rest of her days, and Brownsville would be where she'd die. She accepted that.

Victor Maurier could not have known the glorious pleasure he'd provided for the little French seamstress that afternoon. However, as he rode through the Texas countryside all alone, he thought about his visit in Madame Charbeau's salon and he wished he had been able to give Talleha the fancy lacy chemises and other lavish gifts he'd purchased. He'd give anything to see those sparkling black eyes of hers when she opened the boxes of silks and satins!

He envisioned that lovely face of hers lighting up; he could imagine her soft, lilting laughter ringing out with glee, and he could hear her gasps of delight as she pulled the lovely garments out of the boxes or her lazy sigh as she smelled the sweet fragrance of the toilet water.

Was he wrong to have left, he wondered? Was his quest foolhardy after all these years? Maybe his loyalty was misplaced and he should have remained to help care for the dying Captain Crawford, who needed him more now than his dead mother.

Now that he thought about it all, he wondered if he was really a stupid fool to have left the vulnerable Talleha back in Brownsville with that lusty, ogling Dorsey still in port. He realized it was one hell of a time to start questioning all this, now that he was closer to Casa del Lago than he was to Brownsville. He cursed himself.

Victor questioned just how shrewd he'd been under the circumstances. It wasn't easy for him to confess that he wasn't as clever as he'd always credited himself with being. He wondered now if this was what Crawford was trying to tell him that last night before he'd left. He was a man with many doubts as he crawled into his bedroll.

He hated to think that he'd ever disappoint Crawford after all the faith and confidence the captain had bestowed upon him. He owed that old man so much that he could never repay him, Victor realized.

372

He loved Talleha with all his heart, but he could not rid himself of the guilt: to question the wisdom of his decision to leave her back there in Brownsville with an ailing old sea captain barely able to protect himself, let alone her.

These troublesome thoughts made sleep impossible for Victor and he stared up at the starlit sky. The stars were like diamonds, reminding him of the black brilliant sparkle of Talleha's eyes, and the midnight blackness engulfing him was as dark as her lovely hair. Suddenly, passion and desire overwhelmed him.

But all he could do was just think about her, for she was many miles away. Already the few days he'd been gone seemed like months. He swore one thing as he lay there under the vast Texas sky, and that was that he was not going to let anything delay him this time. The execution of Eliot Penwick would be carried out immediately once he arrived at the Casa del Lago.

Nothing was going to distract him this time!

Lovers like Victor and Talleha could never really be separated by distance when their hearts were so consumed by their love for one another. Talleha was just as lonely and empty without him by her side as he was alone in the bedroll. She lay in her bed, staring out the small window of Crawford's cottage by the sea, and she looked at the same stars in the dark sky. She saw the brilliant blue fire of her beloved Victor's eyes and the black of his hair. The bright full moon in the heavens brought back vivid memories of those moonlit nights of ecstasy they'd shared as they'd traveled to Brownsville. The rapture she'd found in the circle of his strong, powerful arms was wonderful, and she felt flushed just recalling the heat of their passion and the sensuous bliss of his lips. These thoughts made her restless.

She could not believe he'd only been gone a few days, for it seemed so much longer. Although she'd tried to keep herself busy in Captain Crawford's small cottage, it was not enough to fill the endless hours of day and night.

Crawford had complimented her that afternoon; he'd never had his home so spic and span, with everything in its proper place. She tried especially hard to fix meals to whet his appetite, for he seemed to grow thinner every day. After their evening meal, she'd washed the dishes and read to him before he retired. Some evenings she took brief walks along the beach close to the cottage, never roaming too far away.

It did no good to lecture herself that Victor would be away many days yet, for he'd not had time to arrive at the Casa del Lago. It was a long trail ride from the southern tip of Texas to the Casa del Lago. Now that so many miles separated them, she was at the point of wishing she'd had him take her back to her village. At least then she would not have been so very far away from him!

Quickly she reminded herself that had she not come to Brownsville, she'd never had met this remarkable captain.

Getting to know Crawford had been a rewarding experience to Talleha and one she would not have wanted to miss.

Many hours had been spent with the two of them talking the evenings away after dinner. She knew that by now there was nothing left for her to tell Captain Crawford about herself. They'd laughed together about her tales of childhood pranks back at her village. He'd chuckled, "I find it awfully hard to believe such a pretty little thing like you could be so full of mischief, Talleha." She'd sheepishly confessed that everything she'd told him was true.

She realized that he was enjoying their conversations, and it was a source of entertainment to this old man who was surely dying. This was another concern to Talleha; she prayed Victor would be back before that happened.

She saw death in the old man's eyes, and she remembered that her mother had told her once that you could see it in a person's eyes when it was approaching. Dawn was a reflective thinker with the primitive perception of her Indian heritage. Often Talleha remembered how people of their village sought out her mother for her advice. When Talleha questioned her about it, Dawn had replied, "It is the legacy which came from my ancestors. It is a precious gift, Talleha. It is something I cherish and guard carefully."

Talleha did not pursue the subject then, but later, she'd thought about her mother's comments, and it was only after her mother's death that she had wondered if she, too, had been given the gift of her mother's ancestors. By then it was too late; her mother could not answer her.

Dawn had been a remarkable woman with a loving, gentle nature. Talleha recalled that their life was ruled by the land, the sky, and the waters of the rivers and lakes. There was always a planting of their garden in the spring and the autumn, but the moon had to be just right so that their plants would grow and thrive. Dawn could always tell when a storm was coming in by the winds and the reaction of the creatures in the woods surrounding their house.

"Open your eyes to all that is around you, Talleha, and you will learn. Take the time, my darling, and many things will be told to you," Dawn had advised her.

So many times it had dazzled Talleha that Dawn

would foretell a snowfall on a chilly winter's evening. Sure enough, Talleha would awaken the next morning to find a snow dusting the grounds around their cottage.

Only now could she begin to understand the many things her mother spoke about a couple of years ago. If only they could talk together now, Talleha mused.

When she looked into Captain Crawford's weak eyes this morning, she saw a man in his last month of life. Not only did it sadden her, it frightened her.

"Hurry back to me, Victor," she silently prayed. She knew that the poor captain was ill and helpless, but as long as he was alive she felt the force and the strength of him there with her. If he died, she wasn't sure she could carry on without Victor by her side.

But a voice she knew so well admonished her severely by saying, "Oh, yes you can, my darling! Oh yes, you can!"

She knew it to be Dawn speaking to her.

Part IV

The Fury of Heaven and Hell

Chapter 46

Captain Dorsey Loper had always considered himself a lucky son-of-a-gun and never more so than this afternoon, when he'd chanced to be in the right place at the right time. That was at the elegant dress shop of Madame Charbeau. He was privy to the conversation going on between the owner and one of her assistants by the name of Mignon.

The poor Mignon was getting a harsh reprimand for being so slow in finishing sewing a garment. Madame Charbeau was obviously irate, Dorsey Loper realized as he listened to her yelling at the pretty young girl. "I promised Monsieur Maurier I would be delivering these things to the mademoiselle by tomorrow. At the rate you are going, I will not keep my word, and he will be back in Brownsville by the time you are finished, Mignon!"

Dorsey smiled as he clutched the scarlet nightgown he'd just purchased for a woman who'd been sharing his bed the last few nights. The news he'd just heard about Victor Maurier being away meant that the gorgeous Talleha was here without her overprotective suitor, and it fired Loper with excitement.

It immediately ignited the idea that Dorsey should

pay a visit on the beautiful Talleha. He'd rather liked the captain of the *Destiny*, but where a good-looking woman was concerned, Dorsey was after his own interests first. That black-haired miss had tantalized him the first minute his eyes saw her on the sand dune with Maurier. He had envied that good-looking devil lying so close to her sensuously curved body. She presented a tempting sight.

Oh, he'd take Mimi the scarlet nightgown he'd promised her last night, but then he planned to wander down the beach to Captain Crawford's cottage. If he was lucky enough to find the sweet Talleha alone on the beach, he intended to use that old Loper charm, which usually proved successful where the ladies were concerned.

It was not a nightgown he would take to Talleha. For her, he'd bring a lovely autumn bouquet.

Fortunately, he came across a flower vendor as he walked back toward the docks, and he purchased a beautiful bouquet of chrysanthemums in yellow and white.

When he got to his cabin and placed the flowers in an empty jar, filling it with water, he went to his desk to scribble a brief note. Placing the note inside the package containing the gown, he called out for his cabin boy.

A barefooted, frizzy-haired black youth came rushing through the cabin door to respond to Dorsey's call. "Yes, sir—you call me, sir?"

"Yes, Billy—I've an errand for you to run for me. It goes to the Sea Siren. This package is to be given to Miss Mimi Moran. You tell them that Captain Dorsey Loper wants to make damned sure that it gets to her. You understand me, boy?"

His frizzy head nodded up and down. "Yes, sir—I—I understand you. I'm to tell them Captain Loper says so. Miss Mimi Moran—right, captain?"

"That's right, Billy. Now be off with you." Dorsey quickly dismissed the boy, for he had other things on his mind. He intended to shave and get out a clean white linen shirt. Once he was shaved and he'd taken a brush to that thick, unruly red hair of his, he was going to put on his white shirt and his best pair of fine-tailored pants, which he rarely wore except for special occasions.

With the bouquet in hand, he would go to the beach to court the beautiful maiden who'd stolen his heart the first time he'd seen her. The cocky, conceited Dorsey figured to woo and win her.

It was on rare occasion that Dorsey Loper slicked himself up like he did this evening. He felt awkward in his fine-tailored pants and frosty white shirt, instead of his usual seafaring garb. But as he scrutinized himself carefully in the mirror after he'd brushed his hair neatly in place, he decided he looked as good as any other man he'd seen along the streets of Brownsville.

More important to Dorsey was what the tantalizing little Talleha would think when she saw him like this instead of in his seaman's clothes.

He gathered up the bouquet, wrapped the damp stems in an old newspaper, and proceeded to go out of his cabin. The deck of his ship seemed to be deserted except for a few sailors gathered at the far end. He was just as glad that they weren't within speaking distance as he walked across the deck with a bouquet of flowers in his hand. It would have been an amusing sight to most of his crew, and he was well aware of that. The rugged Loper was not known to them as a gallent gentleman. He would not have enjoyed seeing them smirk at him, amused and curious.

By the time he walked down the gangplank to step onto the wharf, he gave out a deep sigh of relief and

381

began to relax. But a familiar voice called out to him, and he turned to see his cabin boy, Billy. The shocked look on young Billy's face told Dorsey just how different he looked this evening.

"Didn't know you for a minute, sir!" he exclaimed to the robust seaman. "I—I carried out your orders, sir. Is there anything else you wish me to do tonight, sir?"

"Don't think so, Billy. I'll be out late, I imagine," Dorsey informed him.

"Yes, sir," Billy drawled, trying to convince himself that this was the Captain Loper he knew. He looked so different from the hardnosed, demanding commander of the steamer, yelling his orders and cussing the crew when they were not carrying out their duties as they should.

Must be some lady who could bring out this miracle of behavior in Dorsey Loper, Billy concluded as he slowly walked up the gangplank. He walked aimlessly across the deck, realizing his services were not going to be needed the rest of the evening.

Dorsey had noted the look in the black boy's eyes as he bade him goodnight and sauntered on up the darkened wharf. There was no activity on the wharves now, for the dockhands had put in their day and the port of Brownsville was idle and quiet tonight.

As he left the wharf to take the dirt road which would lead him along the beach, he glanced over at the small cove where that good-looking trim-lined schooner of Maurier's was moored. Damn, if he wouldn't give an arm and a leg for such a fine ship! He'd have found it hard to leave that magnificent ship to attend to business as long as Victor Maurier had obviously done. But then Dorsey also questioned why anyone would leave such a lovely girl as Talleha here in Brownsville alone.

Dorsey was a man with an inquisitive nature; he

wondered just what kind of business Maurier was about. To leave two such lovely ladies as Talleha and *Destiny* boggled his Irish mind. If he'd sized Victor Maurier up right, he figured that it had to be a most pressing matter.

His happy-go-lucky nature could not be troubled about that, not on a glorious night like this. It was always wonderful to Dorsey to walk along a beach in the moonlight. It mattered not what part of the world it was. Dorsey had visited many shores and faraway places, but he could not have lived away from the smell of the salty air and the echoes of the pounding surf on the shore. If he wasn't riding the waves and feeling the sea breeze on his face, he swore he would surely wither away and die.

Lamplight appeared in the darkness now as he got closer to the little cottages which lined the beach, and one of those little clapboard cottages belonged to Captain Crawford. All were similar in structure, with their little shutters at the windows and white picket fences enclosing the front yards. Crawford's window shutters were green, Dorsey recalled.

However, as he came closer, he could not have possibly been confused about the cottages. Sitting there on the steps of the cottage a breathtaking, etheral vision caught his eyes. She was a heavenly sight to behold with the moonlight shining down on her!

As she turned to see him standing there, Dorsey forgot that he planned to use his smooth, silver tongue charm on her. He spoke from the depth of his heart as he declared to her, "You make an enchanting sight sitting there in the moonlight, Talleha. I can't remember a more beautiful sight in my life, I swear it!"

Somehow, Talleha knew he spoke the truth, even though in her heart she could not have trusted this man who'd rescued her and Maurier that night on the beach.

Yet she felt he meant what he said. She gave him a smile and replied, "Well, I thank you, Dorsey Loper." She saw the lovely flowers he carried, and she knew they were meant for her. It was a sweet, thoughtful gesture and tonight she needed such thoughtfulness. It had been a lonely night up to now, and the sight of Dorsey was a welcome one.

Dorsey swelled with delight at the sight of her welcoming, warm smile. He could not believe his good luck this evening. A surreptitious individual, Dorsey set great store by his hunches and instincts. He just knew this was going to be a wonderful night.

As he walked jauntily through the little gate of the picket fence, he wore a broad happy grin on his face. His spirits were soaring.

"You are obviously enjoying this wonderful night, Talleha?" He glanced up at the sky and then back at her. "I—I hope you'll enjoy these, too," he said as he handed her the flowers, feeling somewhat awkward and ill-at-ease.

She accepted them graciously and thanked him. "Oh, they're beautiful, Dorsey. It's so thoughtful of you to bring them to me. I—I love flowers."

Slowly he sank down on the step beside her. "I'm glad they please you. I figured you did like flowers."

"Now, how did you know that, Dorsey?" she said, turning to look at his face.

"Don't know! I just did," he told her, feeling suddenly shy around this lovely young girl. It made no sense at all to the experienced Dorsey, who'd had many women and who'd spent much time this last week with the promiscuous Mimi, a lady of pleasure down at the Sea Siren.

"Well, you were right. I really miss the woods and the wildflowers to pick for myself. Here, I pick up shells instead of flowers." She gave out a soft little giggle.

"Well, we'll just have to take care of that for you, Talleha. You just have to know where to go to find them, and I will take you there. There are wildflowers growing here in Brownsville, too, you know."

"I—I don't go very far from the house, Dorsey. The captain is too weak—I'd dare not leave him too long, in case he needs me," she told him.

"So the old man's doing poorly?" Dorsey asked her.

"He had a very bad day today. Once he scared me, Dorsey, and I don't scare easily. I've been around ill people before," she told him.

The expression on her face reflected her concern for Captain Crawford. "You're really worried about him, aren't you? Do you know when Maurier will be returning?" The minute the words were out he cursed himself for bringing up the subject. Damned if he wanted her thinking about Maurier right now!

"I don't have any idea when Vic will be returning," she replied.

"Talleha, everyone needs a friend to call on from time to time, and I'm ready to come to you anytime you might need me. Remember that, will you?" His eyes searched her face as she stared up at him for a moment without saying anything.

"You've come to me once already in a time of need, Dorsey. I shall always be beholden to you for that. Those men were up to no good the night Victor and I were camping on the beach. Now, you offer me help again if I need it. You are a good man, Dorsey. I like you very much." She smiled at him sincerely.

Dorsey would have been the first to admit that he yearned for more than that, but he was willing to settle for that for the time being. "There are a lot of people who would not agree with you about being a good man, Talleha, but if you think so, then that is all that matters to me." He gave her a broad grin and one of his infectious laughs.

Her small hand reached out to pat his, but it was merely a friendly gesture for Talleha. "Then those people don't know the Dorsey Loper I know."

Dorsey's other hand covered hers. "Tell you something, Talleha—if I wasn't a good man you'd inspire me to try to be one. A woman like you is worth more than all the gold in the world."

"Dorsey, you say such nice things. I fear I'm blushing. Thank goodness, it's dark; my embarrassment won't show."

"I only say what is in my heart, Talleha."

Funny that he should say that, Talleha mused. That was a statement she had heard her mother make many times. "When spoken from the heart, it is the truth, Dorsey. So I appreciate all the more your kind, generous remarks." There was a comforting warmth to the feel of Dorsey's huge hand on hers, and there were confusing thoughts rushing through her mind at the same time.

There was an urgency churning within her that she didn't understand with the good-looking, red-headed sea captain sitting so close to her. Whatever the effect was he had on her, she didn't know how to deal with it. The only thing Talleha could think of doing was to escape into the cottage.

"I—I must go in, Dorsey. I really need to look in on Captain Crawford," she told him.

Dorsey reluctantly released her hand and told her he understood. He was not a greedy man, and to have sat in the moonlight and held her hand for a brief moment was enough to make him happy tonight. There were always ladies like Mimi to satisfy his sexual appetite, but a woman like Talleha meant more to him than a brief moment of physical pleasure.

He bade her goodnight and watched as she clutched

his bouquet close to her breasts. He savored the sight of her graceful body moving across the porch and through the door.

It was enough for Dorsey Loper as he walked away from the cottage and down the beach to swell with the hope that he might have a chance of winning Talleha's favor.

He knew one thing for sure: he was going to try his best to woo and win her.

Chapter 47

Glenn Crawford was well aware of Talleha tiptoeing to the side of his bed to see if he was asleep. Oh, he pretended to be, but he'd not been in his bed a full minute. He'd been holding a vigil at the cottage window until he saw Dorsey Loper go through his gate and down the dirt road away from his house.

He had been asleep when Talleha had been there on the step alone, but the sound of a strange male voice had invaded the quietness of his room. His sleep was a restless one anyway, so Glenn had sat up on his bed to listen as he heard Talleha's soft voice conversing with someone there on his front steps.

For a moment, he thought the deep, husky voice was Victor's, and he was heaving a sigh of relief that he'd changed his mind about the foolhardy quest of vengeance for his mother. That had all happened so many, many years ago, and Glenn figured the young man he'd raised would have been wiser to get along with his own life and forget the past. It was dead and gone forever. There was the present and that was far more important.

To Crawford's way of thinking, a smart man didn't leave a beautiful lady like Talleha behind as Victor had decided to do. He had not told him this, even though he wanted to. Victor should have been smart enough to figure that out for himself at the age of twenty-five.

After he peered out the narrow window of his cottage to see Captain Loper sitting there on his step close to Talleha's side, he knew what poor judgment Victor had used in deciding to travel all the way back to Harrison County without her. The rugged steamer captain was a fine specimen of a man, Crawford considered. He'd heard that he had quite a way with the women, and he could see why.

Crawford figured Loper to be a few years older than Victor, but he was not so old that a pretty young thing like Talleha could not be attracted to him. The captain knew that she was lonely here without Victor, and that alone made her vulnerable to another man's attention. Crawford knew that he was unable to pose much of a threat to a virile, robust bloke like Loper.

Oh, there had been a day when he could have been a formidable foe to the likes of Dorsey, and he would have done it without blinking an eye. That was now history for Crawford and he'd accepted it reluctantly. It was all he could do, and it took great effort to just sit at the window and spy on the couple.

There was another thing that puzzled Glenn about Victor making his departure. Didn't he realize that Talleha had no protector in him? What was the young rascal thinking, Glenn wondered?

When he saw Talleha bid Dorsey goodnight, he exhaustedly staggered to his bed and slipped between the sheets, pulling the quilt up over him. He expected that she would look in on him, which she had.

It took him awhile to calm his disturbed thoughts, even though he was weary with exhaustion. During that time he came up with an idea which he considered the best he could do under the circumstances to protect

Maurier's interest and Talleha's welfare.

It did not please him to consider sending such a tempting female as Talleha down to the harbor, but Crawford knew Davy Carron, Victor's first mate, and he'd seen the giant of a man, Bruno, aboard the *Destiny*. He was going to write a message to Carron, but he wished to hell he had someone else to carry that message instead of Talleha.

Carron could carry the burden of responsibility which was far too heavy for his weak shoulders. With this in mind Crawford went to sleep, for he planned to get up early in the morning.

At the first light of dawn, Crawford woke as he'd planned, and this rather pleased him, for he knew that his strong, determined will was still there. Oh, his body urged him to stay in bed, but he did not listen to it. Laboriously, he moved from his bed and to his desk to write his note to Carron. By the time he was signing the missive, he heard the padding footsteps of Talleha moving around his kitchen. He had to admit he was more than ready for a steaming hot cup of black coffee.

Reaching for his walking cane to steady himself, he secured the plaid woolen robe around his thin frame and tied the belt. He walked over to the low chest to get his hairbrush and make a few hurried strokes through his thick mane of gray hair. Looking at himself in the mirror, he decided it was time that he got Talleha to shear some of his hair off. It hung over the collar of his robe.

Before he alerted her to his presence, he watched her scurrying around his kitchen. She was still in her gown and robe, her long black hair flowing back and forth over her shoulders as she moved to attend to the task of preparing breakfast. He'd been pleasantly amazed by her skill at cooking and cleaning his cottage. There was not a lazy bone in this lovely girl. She'd not been coddled or pampered, that was for sure. He admired this and credited it to the way she'd been raised by that half-breed mother of hers.

To Crawford's way of thinking, it made her a far better woman than the wealthy ranchers' daughters who'd had a household of servants to wait on them or the offspring of the southern plantation landowners, who were lavishly spoiled and lazy.

He just hoped Victor knew what a rare jewel he had in this little minx with her sparkling black eyes. He had found himself stunned more than once when she'd spoken to him with a primitive wisdom and very sound logic for one so young.

When she turned to see him and gave him that radiant smile of hers, Crawford swore he'd never seen a young lady more gorgeous than Talleha. He could see why any man would lose his head and his heart over her! There was a certain mysterious charm about this young lady that Crawford could not pinpoint. In his experienced, worldly adventuring, he had encountered women from every corner of the globe, but he'd met few like Talleha. Very few!

She was not one woman but an exciting mixture of many women. This was the intriguing quality about her. If Maurier allowed this rare gem to slip through his fingers, he was the worst kind of fool, Crawford considered.

While they enjoyed a pleasant meal together, Crawford was a little perplexed that she made no mention of Dorsey Loper coming to the cottage last night. If only she'd casually mentioned it, Crawford would not have been half as disturbed as he was when she avoided the subject completely.

By the time he'd finished eating, he was satisfied that he'd made the right decision last night to write a message to Davy Carron. Now he was preparing to ask

Talleha to take this message to the *Destiny* and see that Carron got it.

Perhaps Victor would not have approved of this move, but Crawford figured that he should not have left him with such a tremendous responsibility—one which required him to send the note in the first place.

It took Talleha by surprise when he requested that she go to the harbor and deliver something to Davy Carron onboard Maurier's schooner.

"This morning, captain?" she asked.

"Most assuredly. As soon as you can get ready." His voice reflected a certain insistence which troubled Talleha. He certainly didn't seem to be worse this morning, nor had he picked at his food. Actually, he'd eaten a hearty breakfast.

"All right, captain. I'll get dressed right now and be on my way. The dishes can wait until I return." It was hard for Talleha to mask her feelings, and Crawford saw that she was perplexed as she rose from the table slowly.

A half hour later, he watched her go through the gate to do his bidding. He continued to watch her youthful swaying body all the way down the dirt road. There was a graceful movement to her curvy figure which was free and natural, and he noticed how she held that black head of hers high and proud. Ah, there was a spirit in that girl he had to admire, he thought.

Now, Glenn Crawford could only hope he'd made the right move, and as he well knew, time would prove him right or wrong. He knew one thing about Davy Carron, and that was that his loyalty to Victor was genuine and unquestionable.

When the captain had just got himself comfortable in his favorite rocking chair and pulled the woolen shawl over his legs, he was disturbed by an annoying knock on the door. The next few minutes left him agasp and speechless as an entourage from Madame Charbeau's salon paraded into his small parlor, their arms laden with boxes. Bringing up the rear of this strange parade invading the parlor was Madame Charbeau herself. She was greeted by a disgruntled, utterly confused old man who did not hesitate for one minute to express his feelings. "What the bloody hell is all this, madam?"

Madame Charbeau sought to turn on that particular charm and finesse she used upon the patrons of her salon. But Crawford was not impressed. It was only when she mentioned Victor Maurier's name that it began to register what this whole fiasco was about.

"Victor, you say? Well, he could have give me some warning about this," Glenn grumbled with irritation.

"Monsieur obviously forgot. He told me he was pressed for time," Madame Charbeau purred sweetly. "The lovely mademoiselle—is she here?"

"The lovely mademoiselle is not here, ma'am. It would seem that Maurier also forgot to tell her. You're telling me he purchased all this stuff for her before he left?"

"Oui, monsieur—he did, and now I've delivered it as I assured him I would," she told him. This man was a most intimidating old rascal, and she realized none of her charm would work on the cantankerous fool. It was best she did not try.

"Well, at least you are a woman of your word, then. More than I can say for most, Madame Charbeau. But as I've already told you, Talleha is not here. She is on an errand for me."

Madame Charbeau was obviously crestfallen. Crawford admired the fact that she did not try to deny her disappointment when she told him, "I've got to confess that I was eager to meet the young lady for whom the handsome monsieur was buying such lavish gifts."

Observing the mountain of packages the madame's helpers had piled in the center of his parlor, Crawford remarked, "I can see why you would be most curious, Madame Charbeau. Did that young rascal buy out your whole shop?"

She could not resist laughing as she told him, "Not at all. But he was most generous, shall we say. He is a man most devoted to this young lady, Monsieur Crawford."

"Yes, I think one could surmise that."

By this time Madame Charbeau had dismissed her employees back to the carriage. She was about to bid the captain goodbye, feeling sadly disappointed that she would not be meeting the object of Monsieur Maurier's affections. But there was something about the wizened face of the old sea captain which fascinated her. She found him most entertaining.

Perhaps her face reflected these feelings, for Glenn Crawford offered her a cup of coffee before she took her leave. With a wicked twinkle in his eyes, he enticed her, adding, "Maybe we should lace it with a little brandy, madame?"

She gave forth a lilting little laugh, "Ah, Monsieur Crawford, that sounds wonderful."

Together, they shared a pleasant moment, sipping on their coffee laced with fine Napoleon brandy. By the time Madame Charbeau left Crawford's humble cottage there on the beach, she felt she had formed a bond of friendship she would cherish for a long time to come. As she rode back to her salon in silence, she realized that the brief minutes she'd spent with Crawford were more wonderful than hours she'd wasted on others.

A simple cup of coffee laced with brandy and a lighthearted conversation had given her more pleasure and enjoyment than she'd known in a long time.

By the time she'd taken her leave, she felt free to be

bold, so she asked if she might call on him again. There was no doubt in her mind that he was unable to call on her. She would never know how much her request would do to raise the spirits of Glenn Crawford. In fact, he was completely overwhelmed by it. Christ, why did he not meet such a woman like her when he was enjoying good health?

How could he possibly refuse her? He extended the invitation to her to come as often as her schedule allowed.

She'd smiled sweetly as she'd replied, "Oh, Captain Crawford, I'll look forward to our next visit. I truly will. I have to tell you I work very long hours all week long, but my first free moment I'd like to come again to see you."

"Please do, Madame Charbeau. I shall be anticipating that more than you know," he told her.

"And I shall, too," she replied. The two of them looked deeply into each other's eyes. There was no need for any more words to be spoken. They had an understanding.

Each of them was thinking the same thought: what a shame it was that they'd not met much sooner, at another time and place.

Chapter 48

Emily Charbeau had to admit feeling somewhat letdown; she had not gotten to meet the young lady who was being gifted with the lavish array of garments that she and her seamstress had tediously worked on all week. Never would she have wanted any of her handiwork not to fit or please a patron. In this case, though, she thought there might be cause for a slight adjustment, and she hoped so. That way, she could meet the young lady, and more than that, it would give her an excuse to call on Captain Crawford.

Some might find it strange that she found the ailing old sea captain so attractive, but she could imagine how he was before ill health had ravaged his body. Perhaps his body was frail, but there was nothing frail about his mind.

Emily enjoyed their brief, pleasant hour together, and she hoped they would have the opportunity to share more time. When Madame Charbeau returned to her dress shop, she had time to reflect on this unusual week in her life. She had not only met one fascinating gentleman, but two. When the handsome Victor Maurier had come into her shop, Emily had gazed up into his handsome face and yearned to be a young woman again. Few men take your breath away as he did.

Now, today, she'd met Glenn Crawford, and she was enchanted in a different way, but it was just as impressive. Had they met only a few years ago, the attraction could have led to an affair, for she knew his weak eyes sparked with admiration as he looked at her. A woman can always tell when she's being admired.

Emily Charbeau was not the only one to enjoy a very pleasant day by an encounter with a man. Talleha had met three men who'd intrigued her. Those three had been just as intrigued by the time she'd departed the deck of the *Destiny*. She'd delivered her message as the captain had instructed her to Vic's first mate, Davy Carron.

As loyal and devoted as he was to Captain Maurier, young Carron could not stop his eyes from devouring the beauty of this young black-haired lady. Not for one moment did he allow himself to forget that she was the captain's woman, but he damned well couldn't stop the pounding, wild desire surging in his muscled seaman's body.

The big, burly Bruno took one look at her and vowed instantly to become her devoted slave, if she wished him to be.

The *Destiny*'s cook, old Snapper, considered her about the cutest little trick he'd ever laid eyes on. Nobody had to tell the skinny, toothless little man he was ugly, but Talleha had not made him feel that way when they'd been introduced by Carron.

When Carron offered to take her on a tour of the schooner, the giant, Bruno, and the scrawny Snapper trailed along behind them. Talleha was naturally impressed by their generous attention. She was like any other female who enjoyed being admired by the opposite sex.

The day had been a glorious one by the time she returned to the cottage, and she'd lost all measure of time. The sight of her entering the front door was one of great relief to Glenn. He was becoming concerned when she'd been gone much longer than he'd expected.

But upon entering, she found the clutter of packages in the middle of the parlor, and Glenn's explanation as to what they were completely dazzled her.

"For me? All of this? Glory be, what was Victor thinking of?" she stammered, for she'd never owned this many clothes in all her life. She could only smile as she sank down on the floor to start opening the first of the many boxes stacked there.

Crawford thought for a minute before he answered her, "I think Victor wanted to express just how much he thinks of you, Talleha. Perhaps especially since he had to be away." The sly old man had Dorsey Loper on his mind and was worried about him coming around to seek out Talleha, knowing Victor was away.

In a soft, subdued voice she remarked to the captain, "Victor doesn't know me very well if he felt the need to impress me with gifts. I never ask him for anything. All I ever wanted was his love, Captain Crawford. I—I certainly don't need all these fancy gowns to remind me that he is away and how much I miss him."

There was a cracking of emotion in his voice when Glenn spoke. "Victor Maurier is a most lucky young man, I think. Maybe you will be teaching that young man a thing or two as time goes by." He gave her an affectionate smile.

There was a flippant air about her as she told Crawford, "I think I shall, just as soon as he gets back here, and he just better not keep me waiting too long, I can tell you, captain."

Glenn did not know just what she meant by mentioning that he'd better not be away too long, and he didn't care to know at this time. He did decide that he'd excuse himself so she could enjoy some privacy to open the packages piled there on the floor. With this in mind, he left the room.

Her curious nature urged her to see what the boxes contained, so she eagerly explored their contents. Each box brought forth a glorious new delight for her eyes to behold. There were lacy undergarments, sheer stockings, and darling little satin slippers. There was a pair of soft leather boots in shining black leather. Soon she was to discover why he'd purchased the black boots when she opened a box to find a wonderful, fine-tailored riding ensemble in a rich berry color trimmed in black braid at the hem and collar.

She could not help giggling when she opened the box containing a lacy camisole to replace the one he'd so eagerly yanked from her and let get swept away in the current of the river. It was so diaphanous and daring, she knew what his devious mind must have been thinking when he made the purchase. She was glad now that she hadn't been here when these things were delivered by Madame Charbeau. She was also grateful that the captain had left the room. There was a thing or two she planned to tell Victor when he got back here. Until he did the honorable thing and asked her to be his wife, he could at least not flaunt the fact that she was a woman who came to his bed when he desired her.

To pretend it was anything else would have been false, she thought to herself sitting there on the floor. She was a wanton woman and would be until he sought to marry her. Yet it was impossible for her to believe that the love she felt for Victor was wrong or wicked.

Maybe it was a way to justify what she wanted, for God knew, she wanted Maurier. She had no doubt that he wanted her, too. The difference between their yearnings was that she wanted to be Victor's wife, while

399

he had not yet expressed the desire to be her husband.

By the time she'd opened all the packages, flung the lovely frocks across the chairs, and piled the undergarments on the seat of the divan, she heaved a perplexed sigh of amazement about Victor's lavish buying spree. She'd never known this side of him and for him to spend so much he had to be a wealthier man than she'd realized. She really knew so little about him.

A few hours later, when she'd found places for all her expensive new clothes and changed into one of the simple new muslin frocks Victor had ordered from Madame Charbeau, she sat at the little dressing table to take the braids out of her hair. Captain Crawford could give her some of the answers she sought; and she intended to ask him for some of those answers tonight.

She liked the simplicity of this gown he'd bought. The deep purple matrial sprinkled with little white flowers pleased her. The lace edging around the squared neckline and long sleeves gave a soft, feminine effect.

A young lady like Talleha, who had come from such a humble background, was thrilled beyond words to find an exquisite pearl necklace and earrings in the velvet pouch. She saw no reason to wait for some particular occasion to wear them, so she put them on to prepare dinner for the captain and herself.

In her attractive new frock, with the pearls around her throat and the earrings on her dainty ears, she marched into the captain's kitchen and tied the crisp white apron around her to prepare their meal.

A tempting aroma that met the captain's nose as he slowly ambled down the narrow hallway was enough to whet his appetite. He loved the skillet bread she made, and he smelled the fish she was frying. The crew of the *Destiny* had given her one of their catch of the day, which had been a fine-sized red snapper. His sensitive nose smelled onions steaming in the kettle of beans at the back of the stove. She was a frugal miss, he concluded, and she wasted nothing. He recalled the beans had been left over from last night's meal. Crawford approved of that kind of economy.

When he stood at the doorway observing her hasty dashing around his kitchen, he could not suppress a smile. She was a wonder! One would have thought they were having company tonight, with her all decked out in those pearls and that pretty deep purple muslin gown. Here she was only cooking for an old, sick man like him. It made him love her all the more.

He was moved with such depths of emotion that he shuffled back a few steps so that he might wipe the mist from his eyes. He could not endure the thought of her seeing him cry. He still had some pride left in that shrinking body of his.

Talleha would never have imagined that the man who entered her kitchen was the same man standing with tears in his eyes only a couple of minutes before. There was a jaunty air about him as he declared to her, "This calls for a fine bottle of white wine, missy, to go with that good-smelling red snapper."

She smiled sweetly and agreed with him. He acted spry and seemed in such fine spirits. This gladdened her heart, for she adored the old captain. She was glad she'd worn her finery for him.

"Well, when I find such a beauty as you are tonight, I insist that I toast her with wine. I'd consider myself an oaf if I didn't. You look so beautiful, Talleha. A part of your new wardrobe?" He pointed at the gown.

"Yes, it is. Do you like it, captain?" she asked, turning slowly around so he could see the entire effect of the lovely frock.

"I got to say, that rascal has good taste. The dress is quite pretty and the pearls very, very nice. 'Course, you enhance it with your loveliness, my dear." Crawford was having private thoughts of his own, realizing as Talleha had earlier that Maurier was quite wealthy. Although Victor had said he'd done well selling his cargo, it was obvious to Crawford that he'd been far more prosperous than he'd figured.

He was certainly no connoisseur of ladies' fashions or their cost, but he knew Madame Charbeau's bill must have been a tidy sum. Glenn was convinced now that Talleha meant a great deal to Victor, but he was still displeased with the rascal for leaving her here.

"I—I didn't realize Victor was such a wealthy man, captain. In all the time we've been together, we never talked about such things. Oh, he spoke about his schooner, and about going to all those faraway places—but I knew nothing about his wealth," she confessed.

"Well, honey, I guess I didn't realize myself how well Victor had done since we said farewell in England. The *Destiny* was my gift to Victor, for as you know, I look upon him as the son I never had."

"Now, that is one thing I do know about Victor. I know he thinks the sun rises and sets in you, and he could not possibly love a father anymore than he does you, captain," she declared.

He gave her a warm smile as he told her, "Well, Victor was a blessing in my life, and whatever force brought us together, it was the most wonderful thing that ever happened to me. I've never regretted the decision to take that young tadpole along on my ship that foggy night back in Dover. Never have!"

"How many years ago was that now, captain?"

"Oh, lordy, missy, as best as I can remember, it had to be about sixteen or seventeen years ago, I guess."

Talleha thoroughly enjoyed the captain's marvelous tales about their times together aboard his ship. She listened intently. The evening meal was pleasant and conversation was entertaining. She couldn't believe that the clock was chiming nine.

"Mercy, captain—I've got to get these dishes done or it's going to be midnight," she laughed, rising up from her chair. She began gathering up the plates. Crawford laughed, giving a nod of his head as he rose from the table to get his pipe for a smoke before he retired.

The rapping on the door surprised him and he told Talleha he would see who it was so she could attend to her dishes. Besides, Crawford suspected who that late-night caller might be.

If it was who he suspected, Crawford was going to turn him away from his door. He was still the master of this cottage and he could still speak his peace.

Dorsey Loper was not welcome here tonight!

Chapter 49

That cunning old fox, Crawford, had been right about the caller darkening his door, and Loper got a blunt, firm dismissal from the gruff, surly captain. Dorsey knew better than to insist that he speak to Talleha. He didn't seek to do anything which would make Talleha displeased with him. There would be another time to see her, Dorsey soothed himself.

He gave the old man a cordial goodnight and gallantly apologized for disturbing him. It was certainly not to his advantage to promote more ill-will with Crawford, he realized.

When Talleha inquired about who was at the door, Crawford shrugged his shoulders and gave her an offhanded reply, "Oh, just someone walking the beach who'd lost his direction." Talleha had turned back to the chore of doing the dishes and accepted his words without any doubt that he was telling her the truth. Crawford wasn't too happy about so brazenly lying to the girl. He would have preferred not to have resorted to this, but Dorsey was a forceful man with a great deal of charm, and Crawford had heard gossip of the harbor about his prowess with the ladies. He could not take any chances where Talleha was concerned.

He knew what he was gambling if she found out that he had lied, but he had to chance that and pray she'd never find out. If she did, though, and she was displeased with him, it was still worth it to have saved her from the likes of Dorsey Loper. Crawford justified his actions by telling himself that it might be the last favor he could do for Victor.

When he excused himself to retire, he only hoped his face didn't show an expression of guilt, but his concern was needless.

After she had put the kitchen in order, she went directly to her bedroom. When she removed the lovely pearls from her throat and ears, she fingered them lovingly, for they were the most beautiful gift anyone had ever given her. She would treasure them forever. Carefully, she placed them back in the velvet pouch as if she feared that she would break them.

Removing her dress, she gave it a shake and hung it up. Once she had slipped into her gown and wrapper, she could not resist examining the rest of her finery. Although she was tempted to try on the lacy, sheer chemise, she stopped herself. She decided that she wanted Victor's eyes to be the first to behold her in that particular garment. Perhaps she *was* a wicked little vixen, as he was always calling her, to have had such a devious thought. But she could not lie to herself. Where Victor was concerned, she could not control those wild, wicked, but wonderful feelings. She loved him and wanted him to love her. When his strong arms held her, she could not resist surrendering to his overwhelming charm.

He made her abandon any cares or concerns except that he fill her with his love. Until he'd come into her life, she'd never known or imagined such a savage, primitive passion was concealed within her. It had been Maurier and his sensuous magic that had breathed this

405

new rapture into her.

Was he as hungry for her lips tonight as she was for his? Did his body ache with longing for the feel of her flesh pressed against him? She yearned to feel the heat of his muscled body resting next to hers! She could imagine the stimulating feel of his firm thighs encircling hers with his searing maleness invading and conquering her. Ah, that sweet surrender which always left her breathless and carried her to the lofty heights of Heaven and back was more than she'd ever imagined in her girlish dreams of romance!

Feeling as strong and assured about her love as she did, why did she have certain disturbing doubts about Victor's love for her? Today, when she returned to Crawford's cottage to find all the lavish gifts he'd secretly bought for her, should have swept all that away.

What was this elusive air about Vic Maurier that left her with such questioning doubts? Would he ever ask her to be his wife? Talleha was determined that she would not be an unwed mother as her own mother had been. She could not explain to herself why this was such an obsession with her. It had never entered her mind to fault Dawn; never had she felt anything but the greatest admiration and respect for her mother. She was just determined that she would marry the man she loved. The son or daughter she bore this man would have a legal name—a last name.

Sitting there in the small bedroom, she suddenly sat up in the bed, rigid and stiff. There was a startled look on her lovely tawny face and her long black lashes fluttered nervously. Like the thick fog she'd watched rise off the rivers near her village, she had the answer to her obsession. All her life she'd always been known as just Talleha, with no last name.

As a child, she recalled she felt cheated, as though something was missing, because all the other children

406

had last names. Why didn't she? In their village, her mother was known only as Dawn. When she'd questioned her mother about this, Dawn's reply was always a question. "Do I not give you a happy, good life, my little Talleha?"

Talleha would truthfully reply, "Of course you do, Mother." Dawn would always lovingly enclose her in her arms and hold her close to her bosom and declare, "Then that is all that is important, my little darling."

At times like that, it was really all that *was* important to Talleha, for she felt so much love from her mother that nothing else really mattered. It was only that last year they'd spent together that the obsession had gnawed constantly at her. Reflecting on that now, Talleha wondered if Dawn sensed the torment that had plagued her at times. Perhaps she did!

As much as she loved Maurier, she would not be willing to sacrifice as her mother had. Maybe she was her mother's daughter, but there was a part of her that belonged to her father. At this time in her life, she yearned desperately to know about the father she'd never known.

Yet she felt helpless, for she knew not where to turn to find out about this man, who her mother had obviously loved so dearly that she gave herself to him and demanded no commitment.

This was why she had to reserve a part of herself from Maurier. She could not allow him to completely possess her; she would be completely consumed. She knew she wanted more than her mother had asked for. Victor Maurier had to be willing to give her more than her father had given to Dawn.

Late autumn was painting a glorious vista on the countryside of east Texas as Victor rode Sultana toward the archway of the Casa del Lago. He had to confess this was beautiful country. He liked Texas; of all the states he'd been in since he'd left England, he'd never found any place as interesting. It offered everything with its plains, pine forests, blacklands, and seacoasts. He knew of no other state which provided such contrasting landscapes.

How dramatically different this region was from Brownsville, with its sandy beaches, majestic palm trees, and tropical breezes.

Thinking about Brownsville made him think about Talleha. He wondered if she'd received his order from Madame Charbeau's shop and if she was pleased with his selections. He hoped she was.

His welcome at the Casa del Lago was warm and friendly, as he would have expected from Señor Emilo Cortez. What totally devastated him as they sat sipping the señor's favorite brandy was that his mission to kill Eliot Penwick had already been accomplished by Marjorie Greenfield.

"It was how it should have been, amigo; this was Marjorie's revenge. She was faced with protecting her life, Victor. He was drunk and threatening her with a knife, and she shot him. Frank had taught her well. She is a skilled marksman with a pistol. Thank God, her aim was deadly!"

While he listened to Emilo relating the details of this, Victor thought about the long, weary ride he'd endured to just get back here. He felt cheated. It didn't matter that the deed was done. He had been denied the satisfaction of doing it himself.

But this was not the only shocking surprise in store for him. Emilo told him about Mr. Hemphill's visit to the Greenfield ranch and the possibility that Talleha was Nicole Talbert. If so, she was heiress to a vast fortune.

"You can probably enlighten Hemphill about a particular birthmark that will be a determining factor in this, or so Marjorie was hoping. She came to me, but I didn't know when you would return to the Casa del Lago," Emilo told him.

"I found it very hard to leave Brownsville, sir. Captain Crawford is a dying man, and I hated to leave Talleha with that responsibility."

His masculine pride refused to admit to Emilo that what was causing him the most torment was knowing Dorsey Loper was till in the Brownsville harbor. His practical mind told him that nothing was going to prevent Crawford from dying when the time came. He had no control over that, and his presence there in Brownsville was not going to delay it.

He never doubted for a minute that Talleha could handle it if she had to. After all this time, he knew she'd faced a fair share of precarious situations for one so young. He had to say she'd fared all right. He never worried for a minute that she'd lack the guts and spunk to take charge.

But as a man who'd knocked around and traveled the seas, he knew how scoundrels like Dorsey Loper thought and how they tricked beautiful, tempting females like Talleha. That was what had already given him a few nightmares as he'd put so many miles between him and the woman he loved.

Now that he'd arrived back at Casa del Lago to find out that his journey was for naught, he was utterly dispirited. Emilo had only to look at his tense face to know this, but it was understandable.

He expressed these thoughts to Maurier. "Marjorie did not know she was cheating you of your justified revenge, amigo. It was a matter of life or death for her, and she did what any of us would have done under the same circumstances. I know you realize that."

Victor's blue eyes darted up to look at Emilo. "Oh, of course I do, Emilo. I'm—I'm just glad her aim was good and hit the target. I thank God Eliot Penwick can do no more harm to nice women like Marjorie Greenfield or my mother. I am just damned glad he never got to accomplish his vile plans for Talleha."

"I'm glad to hear you speak like that, Victor. That, after all, is really all that matters. Of course, she was cleared of any crime, so all is well and good. I might add that during the time you've been away, Marjorie and I have become very close. We—we understand one another, and it's been wonderful for me to share this time with her."

A slow, devious grin appeared on Victor's face. His black brow arched upward as he quizzed, "Are you telling me what I think you're telling me, Señor Cortez?"

Emilo sheepishly grinned, "If you're thinking that I've become very fond of Marjorie and I've asked her to share the rest of my life, then I must tell you I have. She's promised me an answer in the springtime."

"Ah, the springtime—a time for new beginnings and new life—si?"

"Si, amigo! But I must confess to you, that I feel like a new man already. It is wonderful to be given a second chance to enjoy the bliss that I'd never expected to experience again in life. Si, amigo—I'm a most happy man!"

Victor gave him a comradely pat on the shoulder as he declared, "I am most happy for you, Emilo, and for Marjorie, too. You both deserve all the happiness in the world. I think you will have it."

"If there is a wedding in the spring, could I expect to have you and Talleha back here at Casa del Lago? That would be my fondest wish. It truly would!"

"If the *Destiny* is not too far away, then I vow to you that we will be here. It would be my wish to be here, señor, and I know it would be for Talleha, too. Speaking of Talleha, sir—you didn't tell me where this telltale birthmark was."

410

"Ah, si—I got too busy talking about myself, I fear. The birthmark is on the right shoulder. Hunter and his wife, Salina, told Señor Hemphill, and Marjorie told me."

He needed to say no more. Victor sat for a minute with a thoughtful look on his face and a slow smile finally emerged. Never could he have conceived of his little savage, Talleha, as a wealthy heiress. Selfishly, he was torn by thoughts that if vast wealth should change her, he'd rather she wallowed in ignorance the rest of her life. But he knew he could not deny her the right to live her life as she wished. Greedily, he wanted her to share his life, but she had to want that too, he realized.

Looking at Victor's face, Emilo did not have to ask. He affirmed, "It is there—si?"

"It is there, señor. Our little Talleha is an heiress, it would seem," Victor replied.

The reflective, perceptive wisdom in Emilo Cortez voiced itself. "Well, Talleha already possesses great wealth that few people have. I found that out the first night I met her and I'd wager you did, too. No ordinary young lady, that one! No, she has that special charm to arouse and hold one's interest. It is a rare gift given to only a few in this world."

Maurier gave him an agreeing nod, saying nothing. At that moment, his thoughts were private ones he did not choose to voice even to his good friend. Right now, he yearned more than ever to be back in Brownsville by Talleha's side. Emilo had expressed with perfection the description of his beloved.

Never before and never again would any woman captivate his interest as Talleha had. What a fool he had been if he'd gambled too much on her love for him!

Now, he had to hope that his absence would only make her heart grow fonder. He knew one thing, though, and that was that he would not linger here in Harrison County.

Chapter 50

A brisk, invigorating breeze blew across the Texas countryside as Señor Cortez and Maurier rode their high-stepping stallions toward the Greenfield ranch. The pungent aroma of the pines was exhilarating as they rode through the thick, dense forest dividing the Greenfield ranch and the Casa del Lago. The two riders made a most impressive sight with Maurier astride the spirited Sultana and Emilo on his fiery thoroughbred.

While they ate breakfast, Emilo suggested that they ride over to speak with Marjorie the first thing this morning. "Mr. Hemphill is to contact Marjorie soon and she needs to have the information about Talleha. I know, amigo, that you are going to be eager to return to Brownsville. I could see that on your face last night."

"You're too smart, Emilo," Victor laughed good-naturedly.

"You, amigo, are a man in love. That makes you very vulnerable," he cajoled his young friend.

Victor threw his hands up in a gesture of surrender. "What can I say, Emilo? You are right!" The two of them exploded into a duet of laughter.

Now, as they rode through the countryside, Emilo remarked that there were already indications of winter approaching, and it was the season he liked least. "But there is always the spring to anticipate. Do you have a favorite season, amigo?"

"Never really thought about it, to be quite honest. Guess I'll have to give that some thought." Maurier quickly added that he was going to look forward to this particular spring: "Who knows, Emilo, there might be two weddings instead of one," he jested.

Emilo shook his head. "No, amigo—no, you will not wait for spring, I think. Youth is impatient. Madre de Dios, I have to admit that I envy you."

There was no time for Victor to reply because they were already entering the large double gateway entrance of the Greenfield ranch. The young Romano gave them an enthusiastic wave of his hand and Emilo returned his greeting. Emilo had been a regular visitor here for the last few weeks.

He turned to Maurier to comment, "A nice young man, Romano, and a hard worker for Marjorie."

There was a warm, friendly greeting from the young Mexican as Victor and Emilo galloped up to the corral. The atmosphere at the Greenfield ranch had completely changed, now that the despicable Penwick's insufferable arrogance no longer permeated all activity. Like Romano, some of the hired help had resented Penwick deeply; they'd often mocked him behind his back. They'd laughed at the clothing he wore, which made him remind them of some prissy peacock.

Señor Cortez was greatly admired by Romano; it was always nice to see him coming to the ranch, and it was obvious to all the ranch hands that their beloved señora was a much happier lady now that Penwick was dead.

Now it was more like it had been when Frank Greenfield was alive: Marjorie was more active. It gladdened the hearts of those who had worked at the ranch for so many years.

By now it was known that Lucita and Ralph had left to seek their fortunes together. The señora's new maid, Miranda, had been accepted by the other household servants and was well liked. Romano's dark eyes found her a tempting sight to behold. He was already making secret plans to attract her attention when the right opportunity arose.

After a moment of casual conversation, Emilo and Victor made their way to the house. One of the servants ushered them into the parlor while she summoned the señora.

A short time later, as Marjorie Greenfield moved through the archway to greet them, Maurier saw the miraculous transition which had taken place in her. As he gazed upon her serene face, it suddenly did not matter to him that she'd accomplished what he'd yearned to do. The only thing that mattered to him now was that Eliot Penwick was dead and could no longer bring pain and hurt to such nice, decent women as Marjorie and his mother.

He watched Marjorie walk over to stand at Emilo's side, her eyes gleaming in adoration, and he swelled with happiness for the two of them. It made him even more impatient to get back to the side of the woman he loved.

After the three of them had talked for over an hour, Marjorie turned her attention to Victor to say, "I have something to show you. Something I would like you to take back to Talleha."

She took Emilo's hand and guided the two of them to the locked room where Frank's belongings were kept. When they entered the room she went directly to Talbert's portrait of the tawny-skinned half-breed Indian woman. Marjorie knew this had to be Talleha's

414

mother, Dawn. When she held it up for Victor to see, she heard him gasp in recognition of the resemblance and she smiled.

His deep voice was filled with emotion. "Dear God! Dear God, she is lovely! The eyes—the eyes are Talleha's."

Marjorie knew he was right. Dawn's features were not as delicate, for Talleha had inherited Talbert's French ancestry, but there was no denying those black doelike eyes, nor the marvelous structure of the cheekbones.

"Take it to Talleha, Victor. She should have it."

"Thank you, señora. I shall be delighted to give her this. She will cherish it. I thank you from the bottom of my heart." He reached over to plant a kiss on her cheek.

"You do that again, Victor Maurier, and I'll forget all about Emilo," she teased; but as she said it, she gave Emilo a wink.

The three of them encircled one another with their arms in a binding embrace of friendship.

Before Emilo and Victor left the ranch, Marjorie insisted they enjoy a light lunch with her, and the topic of their conversation was naturally the beautiful Talleha.

Maurier confessed that he was still slightly dazed by the revelation that she was an heiress. "My little black-eyed Talleha," he sighed.

Emilo and Marjorie exchanged smiles. It was Marjorie Greenfield who pointed out to both of them, "Yet, you had only to look at her to know there was something unusual about her. You may not remember, Emilo, but Richard Talbert was a striking man. It is no wonder that Talleha is such a rare beauty."

Once again Victor expressed how grateful he was for her generous gift of the portrait.

Before they bade a fond farewell, Maurier could not

415

resist playfully jesting with the señora. "I have no wish to steal any of your and Emilo's thunder, but Talleha and I just might beat you two to the preacher!"

Emilo beamed with delight, for he had a marvelous idea. "I give you my Casa del Lago to have your wedding, amigo. Just go to Brownsville as fast as Sultana can carry you, then bring your bride-to-be back here and we will have the grandest fiesta Harrison County has ever seen!"

Ever the more practical, Marjorie pointed out, "It would be a wise move in Talleha's best interest, Victor. I will certainly convey your information to Mr. Hemphill." She could not help giving away to a more frivolous, capricious mood. "Besides, Victor, if you stay around us long enough you'll learn that Texans love nothing better than big shindigs. We do nothing in a small way, eh, Emilo?" she laughed gaily, giving Emilo a playful nudge, and he responded with an affectionate hug.

"She is exactly right, Victor!"

Maurier grinned. How could he possibly refuse such a gracious offer? And what Marjorie Greenfield pointed out to him made very good sense: it was imperative that he got Talleha back here to meet with Hemphill. How simple it would have been if he'd just brought her along with him on this trip, but he'd hardly anticipated this development. It seemed to Maurier that there'd always been some hitch in his plans ever since he'd docked in Texas. These things never happened at sea. He had to believe that the sea should be his home. It made him itch to get back to the *Destiny* and sail to some faraway port, but there was a difference now: he wanted Talleha by his side when he sailed.

It struck him suddenly that neither he or Talleha had any family. Emilo's suggestion that they marry at the

Casa del Lago seemed right and proper. Victor was honored by the señor's generous offer.

"I accept your offer most humbly, sir, and I think you are both right. I will go as fast as my horse can carry me back to Brownsville. But I plan to bring Talleha back aboard my schooner, for I am getting very weary of these long jaunts. I confess to you both that I'm a seafaring man," he laughed.

"For a man who rides the waves, you've become a very good horseman, amigo," Emilo remarked.

"But I'm ready, Emilo—ready to return to the life I love. I just hope Talleha can share that love with me," he told the señor, as if he had apprehensions about the possibility.

"Talleha won't mind where she is as long as she's with you," Marjorie declared, knowing that when a woman is truly in love with a man, that it is all that matters.

Victor was glad when Emilo suggested that they leave, for he was impatient. There was nothing holding him here now. Eliot Penwick was dead, and he'd now given Marjorie Greenfield all the vital information she needed for Mr. Hemphill.

Emilo glanced at his young friend as they rode toward the Casa del Lago in almost utter silence. He could see the firing eagerness on Maurier's face and knew his mind was busy plotting his departure. He understood and sought not to disturb his friend's reveries.

When Victor left the Casa del Lago, it was not astride the thoroughbred, Sultana. Emilo appreciated the value Victor put on such a fine animal; he'd explained his plans to sell the mount to board passage on a packet as soon as he hit the first port on the coast.

417

Reluctantly, Emilo sold Maurier one of his little roan mares, which would not bring a high price. Emilo realized that Victor had been quite serious about sailing *Destiny* up the Texas coastline when he brought Talleha back to Harrison County. When he confronted him about this, before he took his leave, Maurier confessed truthfully, "Yes, Emilo—I'm damned tired of riding horseback. I cannot lie to you."

They shared a comradely laugh before Victor mounted the little mare. He had to also confess that he already missed the spirited stallion; he'd become very fond of Sultana. He said nothing to Emilo at the moment, but he knew he'd face another dilemma when he got to Brownsville.

He'd have the devil's own time getting Talleha to part with Amapola. He could only pray that Providence would show him a way to convince that stubborn, headstrong little savage that she had to leave Amapola in Brownsville.

If Victor could have seen into his future, he'd have realized Amapola would be the least of his worries.

But the bold, dashing captain of the *Destiny* had no inkling of the trials he would meet once he got to Brownsville. In east Texas there was no hint in those late autumn days of what was about to happen down the coast.

Not even the old-timers along the coast saw any sign of the fierce, destroying fury soon to invade their shores.

As a seaman, Victor respected the ominous winds blowing in from the sea, and he knew the devastation they could bring to any port. What he did not know as he booked his passage on a packet traveling the southern route of the Texas coast was that a fierce hurricane was now heading in the direction of Brownsville.

Chapter 51

An indefinable restlessness engulfed Talleha from the moment she woke up and prepared to dress. It did not leave her as she went about her chores in Crawford's cottage. She thought to herself as she prepared the old captain's breakfast that she had certainly fallen into a routine. She'd lost track of how many days and nights it had been now since Victor had left. That first long week had been terrible, and by the tenth day she was miserable and lonely. By now, she could not tell herself whether it was two or three weeks. It seemed like forever, though.

She thought she was disguising her strange mood from the captain, for she tried to have a lighthearted chat with him, but the old man was not fooled. He noticed how she kept swiping her forehead with her apron as she moved around the kitchen. Perhaps she was suffering from the unusual heat. One would have thought it was midsummer instead of late autumn. The little kitchen seemed hot and stuffy, but even in the dining room with the windows open, the air was still sticky and oppressive. Glenn didn't like the feel of it. He knew all too well the dangers which could be brewing in the gulf beyond.

"You, miss—you are to get out of the house today and away from this old sick man. It is not right that you should be cooped up here so much just because Victor is away. Take Amapola and go for a nice ride along the beach. That little mare needs a good run as much as you do, I'd wager."

She could not deny that it sounded like a marvelous idea; she'd thought about doing just that. But she hated the fact that she'd be gone when he might need her, and she told him so.

"Nonsense, girl! What if you had not, by chance, come here with Victor? I would be here alone. I have a few friends who live along the beach. They'd have dropped in to see about me if you had not been here. No, I'll not have it, Talleha. I want you to go out for a while."

She adored him for his selflessness and reached down to plant a kiss on his cheek. "I shall go for a ride if you'll promise not to get into mischief while I'm gone," she teased him playfully.

"I'll be into mischief only if you don't mind me. Now scat, missy!"

She started to rush out of the room when she stopped suddenly to whirl around. Her black eyes sparked deviously as she accused him, "I know why you want me gone, captain—I bet you have a rendezvous with that Madame Charbeau you've been talking so much about." She gave out a girlish giggle to turn and leave before he could answer her.

Crawford smiled, thinking what an adorable little imp she was when she was in one of her teasing moods. He was glad he'd insisted that she leave the confining cottage and him. A young lady so spirited and full of life had to be utterly miserable in these surroundings. At the moment, he cursed Victor for being gone so damned long and leaving her with such a burden on her small shoulders. It was terribly unfair of him, Glenn thought. Maybe he'd not taught the young rascal as well as he'd thought, after all.

Talleha rather shared the captain's sentiments about that lately. Perhaps it would serve Victor right if she accepted Dorsey's invitation to go on a picnic down by Pirate's Cove or for a sail around Laguna Madre.

As she undressed to put on her new black riding ensemble for the first time, along with the brand new boots, she decided that the next time she might just take Dorsey up on an invitation. In the mirror she saw a young woman of great beauty that should not be wasted just waiting endlessly for some man to return. As much as she adored the captain, she asked herself how long she was expected to live like a recluse here in a tiny cottage.

As she yanked on the black skirt, a wave of guilt washed over her, but she quickly swept it aside. Why should she feel guilty for being young and wanting to enjoy the excitement of her youth while she had it? It was Maurier who should feel guilty—for leaving her here alone for so long with a responsibility that was his. After all, Crawford had not raised her or given her a magnificent schooner.

Finally dressed, she admired the attractive garments. Madame Charbeau was an expert seamstress, and Victor had a flair for ladies' fashions. Perhaps he had bought other ladies a handsome wardrobe like this one many times before. Perhaps she was just another mistress he had pursued and conquered, and that was all he'd meant her to be.

She'd managed quite successfully to style her hair in two smooth coils at the back of her head. She slipped the black vest over the long, white full-sleeved blouse, and she was pleased with the image reflected in the mirror. There was a touch of elegance about her today that she'd never seen before.

By the time she emerged from her small bedroom,

she was feeling not only restless, but reckless. She did not try to explain it to herself; she knew she could not.

When she jauntily bounced into the parlor, Glenn Crawford admiringly stared at her for a moment without speaking. She was utterly stunning, and he saw a new, sophisticated air about her. "Now, that's my girl. Give that Amapola a good workout."

"I intend to." She smiled and hurried toward the door as she waved good-bye to him.

The little shed and small fenced area at the back of the cottage had been very confining, and Amapola seemed to sense that Talleha was going to take her out. She kicked her heels up as she pranced and paced nervously while the saddle was being secured.

"All right, Amapola, I understand your eagerness," Talleha soothed the mare, taking the reins to lead her out of the gate.

As she was about to mount the mare, she heard a feminine voice beckoning to her, "Mademoiselle Talleha! Are you Mademoiselle Talleha?" and turned to see a middle-aged woman who had to be Madame Charbeau. The graceful plume on her fancy bonnet blew across one side of her face. A short cape draped across her shoulders was furled by the strong, gusting seabreeze now blowing in from the bay.

Talleha saw small wisps of dark auburn hair escaping from the frame of the bonnet, but what really impressed her was the lady's gardenia-white skin and her brilliant blue eyes. In some ways Talleha was reminded of Flossie, with her plump figure and friendly, smiling face.

"I am Talleha," she said slowly as she walked up to the woman, guiding Amapola along beside her.

Offering Talleha her gloved hand, Madame Charbeau introduced herself. "I see your riding ensemble fits perfectly. Ah, I am glad—but of course, you would make any garment look wonderful. It was such a pleasure to make up the things Monsieur Maurier ordered. I knew you had to be most beautiful, and you certainly are."

"Thank you, Madame Charbeau. I loved all the beautiful things you brought. Victor was most generous," she declared, feeling a sudden flush of embarrassment as she wondered what the woman's impression of her must be.

"Monsieur Maurier is obviously a man in love who wants to give his woman the sun, moon, and stars. That is all, cherie." She gave out a little laugh and winked her eye, giving Talleha the impression she might be an authority on men. Talleha liked her outgoing manner and friendly nature.

Any disconcerting feelings Talleha might have had were quickly forgotten and she felt relaxed and at ease now in the presence of Madame Charbeau. She would have had to be blind not to see that the older woman stared at her with true admiration.

Emily Charbeau suddenly noticed Talleha responding to her stare and she apologized, "Forgive me, mademoiselle, but beautiful ladies and their clothing are my life. I've rarely looked upon one so lovely as you, but then I'm sure you are used to such adoration and flattery."

A gleam lit Talleha's eyes and she answered the seamstress quite candidly, "I must tell you I have not." She turned to admonish Amapola, who kept jerking impatiently on the reins.

Madame Charbeau flippantly remarked, "How is that possible, ma petite? Someone as pretty as you would have to be stranded in some barren desert or back in the woods where there were no people around in order not to be noticed."

Talleha confessed, "You are right, madame. I did live in such a place—an isolated village in the woods."

"Oh, forgive me! I did not mean to make light of

your past." She threw up her hands in a helpless gesture as she sighed, "That is my way. It gets me in more trouble—my mouth!" She gave Talleha an embarrassed smile.

"You're in no trouble with me, I assure you. I could hardly feel that way when you've praised me so. I love flattery and compliments, I admit," Talleha told her.

Emily found her expression most interesting, for in a brief moment she'd changed from a sweet young lady to a frivolous little flirt.

"Ah, Talleha—I think I like you very much. I have to tell you I was most disappointed when I delivered your clothes the other day and did not get to meet you."

"Now that we have met, I am sorry, too. But after all the captain told me about you, I, too, was most curious to meet you, Madame Charbeau."

Emily Charbeau could not conceal her delight that Captain Crawford had spoken about her. She tried to sound casual as she inquired, "Oh, he spoke of me?"

"Constantly. He found you most interesting, madame. I think it was awfully sweet of you to visit with him, and I know he enjoyed it."

"Do you really think so, Talleha?"

"Oh, I certainly do—I know so." Talleha noticed a serious look on her face as though this was very important to the French seamstress.

A serene smile came to Emily's face. Talleha could not know what she'd done by telling her that. She'd had some misgivings about coming to see Glenn Crawford, for she did not want him to think her presumptuous.

However, when she'd gone to her shop early that morning, she found herself in a restless mood. There was a strangeness in the air which seemed to consume her. This troubled the well-organized Emily Charbeau, for she did not often give way to reckless impulse as she had today.

Without any explanation to Mignon, she'd left the shop. Mignon stood there, staring after her with a puzzled look on her face, for this was unlike Emily Charbeau.

She drove her little buggy along the streets of Brownsville, and a compelling force guided her out of the town along the street lined with tall, majestic palms towering high into the bright blue sky. A stiff breeze almost lifted her bonnet from her head, and the plume had blown across her face, almost blinding her view.

Emily knew she was right to obey her reckless impulse, and she was glad she'd come to see Glenn Crawford. In doing so, she'd been able to meet Talleha, and that had been worth the ride alone.

"You go for your ride now, as you were about to do when I stopped you. Take your time, ma petite, because I plan to keep your captain entertained. We can have a nice, long chat," Emily assured her, giving her an affectionate pat on the shoulder. "It will be my pleasure to share a pleasant morning with him. I find him a very interesting man, too."

Talleha responded with an understanding wink of her eye as she told Emily Charbeau, "I might just take a very long ride, then."

"Whatever would please you, my dear," Emily told her, turning to go through the gate. Abruptly, she stopped to call out, "Talleha, I'm glad we got to meet."

By now, the breeze was blowing Talleha's hair with such a fury that the coils broke free to fan wildly across her face. But she swept it away to call back, "So am I! I'll see you later, madame."

Emily watched her gallop off down the sandy beach and she thought to herself that it was no wonder Monsieur Maurier was helplessly in love with her.

What man would not lose his heart over such a woman!

Chapter 52

Glenn Crawford had watched the two women engaged in conversation. What magnificent women, he mused! As strange as it might seem, they had a lot in common.

He found himself swelling with delight at the surprising sight of Emily Charbeau riding up in her fancy buggy; he'd not expected this pleasure today. He let his imagination take him back to a time when she was Talleha's age; she must have been a seductive, red-haired siren who'd have caught his eye instantly.

But he found her damned attractive right now. He just wished to hell he was the man he'd been a year ago.

After watching them he realized that they were two very spirited women. One would have thought they were old friends instead of new acquaintances. Both were women of very intense emotions. He realized he was quite fond of both of them.

Talleha would surely have teased him if she'd seen him brushing his unruly thick mane of hair to make himself more presentable for Madame Charbeau. The little imp! He was glad she wasn't underfoot to see him, Glenn thought to himself as he quickly concealed the hairbrush. Emily was knocking at the door.

His deep voice replied, "Come in. It's open."

As she entered, it was like a ray of sunshine invading his doorway. Her eyes were a brighter blue than he'd remembered and her silken fair skin was far lovelier, too. Her deep-blue velvet bonnet was an attractive frame for her smiling face.

He loved the softly accented voice that greeted him. "Good morning, captain. You are looking chipper!"

"Good morning, madame. May I say you look stunning! I see you got to meet Talleha as you hoped. I'm glad!"

"Oh, la, la—so am I. She is even more beautiful than I imagined. Magnificent! And she is beautiful in spirit as well."

"I noticed that the two of you seemed to be getting along fabulously as you talked."

She shook her finger at him, playfully chiding, "So you spied on us—oui?"

"That I did! I will not deny it, nor do I apologize for it."

"Captain Crawford, you're a sly one! I see I'll have to be on my guard around you! You are too smart for me." She laughed as she removed her bonnet. There was no doubt in Emily's mind that she was going to stay for awhile. Everything about Glenn's manner told her he wanted her to.

"Granted, I'm a pretty sly old fox, Emily. Just living this long makes one smart. Would you not agree?"

It was the first time he'd addressed her so informally, and this pleased her. She took the chair next to his.

"Nothing makes one as smart as living. I've come to the conclusion that we've both done our fair share of it. I don't agree that one time around is enough."

Glenn gave out a laugh, "Nor do I, my dear. I'd damned well like to live it all over again. I'd just hope that I met someone like you a hell of a lot sooner than I did."

A demonstrative, liberated woman, Emily gave way to the impulse to reach out to take Glenn's weathered hand. Her eyes glazed with the depths of emotion she was feeling, for she knew that she'd not have such wonderful bliss forever. It mattered not to her. Her voice was soft as she murmured quietly, "What's important, Glenn, is that we did meet. Sometimes a moment in life can mean more than a whole lifetime."

Glenn knew what she was trying to say. He was so completely consumed by love for her, and it was a love such as he'd never known.

He could only stare at her, and he was struck numb, for the words to express his feelings did not come. He let himself drown in the serene blue pools of her eyes for one brief, splendid moment before he spoke.

"Holy Christ, Emily! What did I ever do to deserve such an angel as you? An old scoundrel like me doesn't deserve such a vivacious, lovely woman," he told her. A tear dotted the corner of his eye, for he was overcome with a wave of emotion. He was in a state of ecstasy.

Emily bent over to kiss his cheek; it felt very flushed. "You did nothing other than be who you are and have always been, Glenn Crawford. You are a most remarkable man, the most intriguing man I've ever known!"

"Dear God, madame—I can die a happy man after such praise from you," he laughed. The look on his face was not that of a dying man. There was a devious twinkle in his eye and a forceful strength in his hand as it held Emily's.

She admonished him in a playful manner, "Damn you, Glenn—I won't let you die yet. You hear me? I won't let you!"

"Then, by God, I won't. I swear I won't, Emily," he promised, and he sincerely meant it.

With an affirmative air, Emily said, "I'm going to

hold you to that promise, captain. I don't intend to let you slip away from me now that we've finally met."

Crawford laughed, "I'm an absent-minded old sea dog, so it will mean that you'll have to come around often to remind me of that promise."

They could have been two young lovers. Neither had enjoyed a morning so gay in a very long time.

Both knew that there were no boundaries on discovering love. The feeling was wonderful!

It had been a long time since Dorsey Loper had allowed himself to get as drunk as he had last night. When he'd opened his eyes to greet the morning sun shining down on him, he saw he was lying in a cove not too far from Glenn Crawford's beachside cottage, and he knew what had spurred his need to drown himself in liquor.

He and an old buddy had spent the evening at a local brothel. After they'd left the establishment, they'd staggered aimlessly down the road to the beach, taking turns swigging from the bottle of whiskey his friend had with him.

Vaguely, Dorsey remembered his friend trying to rouse him, but Dorsey had shrugged his suggestion aside. His friend had gone on his way when Dorsey had mumbled that he wanted to sleep longer. Loper was not a man to argue with, for he was known to have a volatile temper.

He had certainly slept later—a good six hours longer. The sun was high in the sky by the time he finally opened his eyes and forced himself to sit up straight and stare out over the bay.

He wondered if it was just the effects of all the liquor or a storm brewing out beyond the bay that made the air feel so heavy; it was hard to breathe. He had been a seaman long enough to know that the air was laden with moisture.

He laboriously staggered around the small secluded cove where he found the concealing privacy he sought. Stripping off his clothes, he took a dip in the water to cool his warm flesh.

When he had finally splashed around as long as he wished, he felt invigorated and refreshed. His energy restored, Dorsey felt ravenously hungry and he started to walk down by an old fishing pier extending almost a half-mile out into the bay. If he was lucky, he knew he would find the old Mexican vendor standing there with his cart, selling tamales. He felt like he could eat a dozen of them right now!

He was lucky; old Poco was there. He bought exactly a dozen, leaving Poco with a smile on his face from making such a large sale. He sank down on the beach and rested his back on a huge piece of driftwood.

He sat there munching on the tamales one by one, tossing aside the corn husks they were wrapped in, and he recalled the last time he'd been so drunk. That was when he and his first mate had indulged too much in his cabin aboard the steamer and ended up crawling the deck because they could not walk.

But he also recalled one night a long time ago when he was not yet a steamer captain. That was when he was a cocky young rooster knocking around the country-side with a friend named Murray Sharpe. As crazy as Murray was, Dorsey figured, he'd surely got himself killed by now. There was no man as wild as Sharpe and that half-breed friend of his, Lucus Bean. How he'd tied up with such a pair, Dorsey never knew. It could only be explained, he figured, by the fact that he'd been fired from a packet he was piloting when he'd made port in Galveston.

He was mad at the world and everyone in it. A pair

like Sharpe and Bean just happened along at that moment in his life, and what a spree they had for several weeks after that meeting! Later, Dorsey recalled that they'd done a few things he wasn't too proud of during those carousing times.

Sharpe was a man who had never gotten his life back together after the war. Like so many disillusioned southerners, he had nothing to go back to after the war, so he became a drifter. How he'd ever lined himself up with the young half-breed, Lucus, Dorsey never found out.

It was one of the craziest times of his whole reckless life.

But all thoughts of Murray and Lucus were quickly swept aside by the glorious sight he saw galloping along the beach. Wild as the wind, her hair flowing loose and free like the mane of her horse, was Talleha.

A sudden rush of desire swept over him to possess every inch of that silken flesh, and it mattered not to Dorsey if he had to force her to surrender to his demands.

The truth was that Dorsey liked to force his women to surrender and bend them to his will. It heightened his frenzied passion to a violent peak.

He'd never seen her look more sensuous, with her lovely legs straddling the horse, sitting so straight in the saddle, her lovely breasts jutting out to press against her blouse. Dorsey swelled with overwhelming desire! He had to possess her completely and he vowed to do it.

Amapola held her head high and swished her tail, giving vent to her exhilaration. The confining space of Crawford's yard was hardly to be compared to the large corrals of the Casa del Lago that she was accustomed to.

Talleha shared Amapola's mood. Long ago, Dawn had taught her about the creatures of the woods and

431

how they sensed instinctively when someone was kind and gentle. She loved the little mare, and Amapola sensed it.

She gave Amapola a loving pat on the mane. Her thoughts were of Victor, and she was flooded with a mixture of emotions. A part of her ached miserably for the sight of him and the rapture of his lips intimately caressing hers. Another part of her was furious that he could have deserted her for so many days and nights now, leaving her wanting him so badly. If he loved her as she did him, she could not understand how he could stand to be away so long.

Perhaps she did not understand the thinking of men. Perhaps they did not feel the same about these things as women did.

When she heard a deep voice calling out to her, she turned, hoping to see the black-haired, blue-eyed Maurier standing in the distance. Maybe wishes did come true!

But it was not Victor standing there in the little cove, waving wildly to get her attention; it was Dorsey Loper. She tried not to show her disappointment and forced herself to give forth a smile.

All the time her heart cried out. Why it could not have been Victor standing there instead of Dorsey!

Chapter 53

She'd turned in Dorsey's direction hoping to see Victor, but Dorsey could not know this. All he knew was that she was the most beautiful woman his lusty eyes had ever seen, and he tried not to wobble as he started toward her. But the truth was, he was still feeling woozy after having filled his stomach with all those tamales.

With each step he took, Dorsey found a stronger desire to bend this little minx's will. Why couldn't she have spurred the horse to move to meet him at least halfway? No, she sat there looking arrogant, as though she was challenging him. Dorsey didn't like this.

A conceited little lady, she was. He'd already sensed that she was independent and headstrong. In a way, it enhanced his desire for her all the more.

Talleha would have never suspected Dorsey's private musings as he came up, a broad, friendly grin on his face. "What a pleasant surprise to see you, Talleha," he greeted her.

"I was surprised to see you, too, Dorsey," she stammered. It was still hard to shake off the strong feeling consuming her that it should have been Victor's voice calling out to her.

"Well, let us enjoy it. Come, sit with me over there," he insisted, as he pointed at the little secluded cove where he'd been enjoying the tamales. It provided the privacy young lovers often sought here on their trysts.

Something told Talleha that she should say no. But his happy-go-lucky manner made it hard to refuse. Dorsey had never done anything to make her feel displeased with him. Actually, she had every reason to be grateful to him for coming to their rescue that first night on the beach. She was not so naïve that she did not realize what those drunken ruffians had intended for her that night.

So what could be the harm in sitting for a while with Dorsey before she returned to Crawford's cottage, she asked herself? The captain and Madame Charbeau were probably enjoying their private time alone.

Finally she consented, and Dorsey took the reins to lead Amapola toward the cove, then Dorsey helped her dismount from the mare. She allowed him to guide her to a particular spot he chose for them on the sandy beach. But casual conversation was not what Dorsey wanted, and he was cunning enough to know that this was not the time of day nor the setting for the seduction he craved. There was no cover of darkness to conceal what he was aching to do with this ravishing beauty.

Talleha was the image of an untouchable maiden, Dorsey considered. It was not that he doubted his prowess with women, but Talleha was not just any woman. He was not stupid enough to try to wrestle a screaming young woman on a beach in broad daylight.

Damn, he had to think of something to hold her with him longer. His mind was whirling crazily as to what he could do.

In the meanwhile, he played the perfect gentleman, inquiring about the captain. She told him about the delightful Madame Charbeau keeping him occupied while she was taking some time off to go riding on the beach.

"So, you see, Talleha—you might as well keep me company. Am I to assume that the captain and Madame Charbeau are attracted to one another?" Dorsey inquired.

An impish smile crossed her face as she declared, "As strange as it might seem, I think they *do* like one another. I think it's wonderful! They are both such nice people."

"I would have expected you to say something like that, Talleha."

"Why, Dorsey?"

"Because you are a romantic. Am I right?"

She gave him only a sly smile for a minute before admitting that she supposed she was. By now, Dorsey had been struck by a perfect solution to his dilemma.

"Then I have a place to show you that you will never forget. It is a most picturesque setting for watching the sun set over the bay, and Mama Rose is the best damned cook in these parts. There's nothing like a sunset across Laguna Madre."

He made it sound like a wondrous experience. She raised a skeptical brow to inquire, "Mama Rose?"

"Yes, she owns and runs a little inn. We'll eat and watch the sunset, and then I'll walk you and Amapola back to see you safely to the captain's cottage. We'll get there long before dark."

"Oh, Dorsey—I—I don't know."

"For goodness sakes, Talleha—what's an hour going to hurt? You'd still be home in time to fix the captain's supper."

There was no doubt about it—Dorsey had a talent for sweet persuasion when he really put his mind to it. There was no doubt he wanted Talleha any way he could get her. Once he got her to Mama Rose's, it

435

mattered not if she kicked or screamed, because no one would pay any attention to that.

He did not dare tell her about the small rooms at the back of the inn. They provided privacy to seamen constantly coming to Mama Rose's seeking a woman for an hour or a night. A port city, Brownsville had an overflowing crop of men making with nothing on their minds after many weeks at sea but a woman and some liquor.

Mama Rose had a most lucrative business in her little rundown inn, and the port authorities never gave her any trouble. Dorsey had met Mama Rose a few years ago and she liked him, so he knew she would accommodate him.

"Come on, Talleha. You deserve a little time to enjoy yourself. You can't just bury yourself in that house with a sick old man. Maurier left you high and dry with one hell of a load, if I must say so. He should not have left Brownsville when he knew the man was surely dying."

His words made an impact on her. She could hardly fault Dorsey when she'd had those same thoughts herself.

She had to question why Victor could take his leave so easily when he had seemed to adore her so much. How could he stand to be away from her so long? She'd given him her heart and all she had to give to any man, and now she was wondering if she'd sold herself too short. All the fancy clothes from Madame Charbeau's meant nothing to her. She felt like the cheap ladies of the brothels who were paid for their services.

Could this have been Maurier's way of telling her that he had paid her for the nights of love they'd shared? The thought was abhorrent. But how could she dismiss the possibility?

"All right, Dorsey, I'll go with you, but I must get back to the captain before dark," she firmly declared.

But that was all Dorsey asked, for he knew this night would grant him wildest desire.

"I'll see to it, Talleha," he told her. His heart pounded erratically. He would have told her any number of lies to have his way.

As they moved along the sandy beach, he realized she'd taken such a hold on him that he could not let go. She'd tormented him. Dorsey had a keen, sharp mind and a quick Irish wit. He considered himself knowledgeable about women's ways, but Talleha fit no pattern.

Touched by her enchanting magic, he found himself unable to break the spell. He knew it was crazy. He knew he should have left Brownsville with his crew and steamer five days ago, but he hadn't. She was the reason he'd delayed his departure and lied to his crew.

This obsession Dorsey had allowed to take hold of him was a tormenting madness. He had a sharp memory. It seemed there was no way this lovely girl could have crossed his path before, but something prodded at him that she had.

Talleha was first to spot the long pier built out over the bay. A few boats were docked there already, and Talleha could see the small frame building which she assumed was the inn Dorsey had spoken about. It could not service many patrons, Talleha concluded as they drew closer.

Dorsey had glanced back to see the scrutinizing look on Talleha's face. "I told you it wasn't a grand place, but wait until you taste Mama Rose's food!" He gave out one of his infectious gales of laughter.

"You have me very curious, Dorsey, about this delicious food, as well as Mama Rose," she confessed.

"Well, that curiosity will be satisfied before too long, honey," he replied, failing to add that he himself expected to be sated from the hungry ache in his groin

437

which had pained him for a long time. A wild anticipation swelled in him as he thought about how he was going to take his fill of the sweet nectar she'd tempted him with. He planned to kiss those honey-sweet lips until they were bruised. He planned to feast on that luscious body of hers until he was exhausted.

His friendly, grinning face gave no sign of the sadistic man seething within him. If it had, Talleha would have spurred Amapola into a fast, furious gallop to get away.

They reached the pier, where Dorsey instructed her to leave Amapola, and he tied the reins to a post after he assisted her in dismounting.

After they'd walked down the pier a short distance, Dorsey opened the room of Mama Rose's inn. Talleha walked through the entrance to find the place deserted. She saw not one soul. That seemed strange to her, for she'd seen the boats tied up in the bay.

When she was about to inquire of Dorsey if the place was even open, a statuesque, willowy woman with brassy blond hair came in from a back door.

"Good afternoon, Mama Rose," Dorsey greeted her. This was hardly the image Talleha had expected. She'd pictured a matronly, older woman with graying hair coiled at the back of her head, someone on the chubby side, like the motherly Flossie.

"'Afternoon, Dorsey. What's your pleasure?" the woman drawled casually. Her emerald-green eyes danced curiously over Talleha before they darted back to him.

Dorsey was far enough behind Talleha that she could not see the devious wink in his eye as he answered, "Promised this pretty lady some of your fine food, Mama Rose."

Talleha wondered how she'd come by the name of "Mama Rose," for she was hardly that old. Her voluptuous figure was clad in a bright-green frock almost the same color as her eyes, but Talleha was shocked by the low-cut neckline, which barely concealed the nipples of her breasts.

"Want some of Mama's food, eh, Dorsey?" Rose inquired, a sly smile creasing her face. Talleha observed the suggestive sway of her body, the flirtatious gleam in her eye, and the glib tone in her voice. Something about this Mama Rose did not impress Talleha favorably.

"Thought maybe we'd have some of your chowder or some of those good fried fish filets. Got some today?"

"Sure, Dorsey. Take me about an hour, if that's all right. Like one of the private dining rooms while I'm preparing it? How 'bout a bottle of wine?" Rose didn't know exactly what kind of game Dorsey was playing with this one, but she was willing to play along with him for her usual fee. Ordinarily, he brought a woman in and asked right out for one of the little cubicles so he could have his privacy and his pleasure.

"Yes, that sounds good, doesn't it, Talleha?" He impatiently urged her on before she could began to protest. However, he noticed she winced as he took hold of her arm.

Rose led them through another door at the back of the inn. From the pocket of her frock, she took a key to unlock the door, and as she invited them to enter, Talleha turned to Dorsey to remind him she had to get back to see about Captain Crawford before nightfall.

"That's no problem, is it, Mama Rose? Our meal will be done before then and we can be on our way," he flippantly remarked with a shrug of his shoulders. But the look on Rose's face was like a thunderhead, even though her voice was cool and calm. "Honey, you just make yourself at home while I get Dorsey to pick out the filets he wants me to fry up. Now, come with me a minute, Dorsey!"

Once again before Talleha could object, she found herself denied a response as Mama Rose and Dorsey left her.

Had she not been distracted by a noise in the next room, she would have heard the key turning to lock her in as Dorsey and Mama Rose prepared to walk away.

There was an evil foulness about this place; Talleha sensed it instinctively. Wishing not to face either Dorsey or Mama Rose, she did not dare try leaving by the door. However, she would try the window. If it did not open right onto the bay, she was going to crawl out and get to Amapola as quick as her legs would carry her. Without any hesitation, she rushed to the window.

Had she not been so petite, she would not have had a chance. She slipped cautiously along the narrow ledge just outside the window. There was no railing for her to hang onto. But her small body pressed against the side of the building as she slowly crept along the ledge, and her hands clutched the overlapped planks of the side of the building.

When she finally reached the end of the building, she stepped onto the pier and broke into a mad dash to reach the end of it and Amapola.

Her heart was pounding wildly as she fumbled to untie the reins. Wild as the winds now blowing in over the bay, she rode Amapola in a gallop down the sandy beach, her thick, black hair blowing across her face, nearly blinding her view.

Nothing mattered to her except getting away from that place!

Chapter 54

Rose marched down the dark, narrow hallway with Dorsey tailing behind her, and he didn't have to be told that she was mad as hell. About what, he couldn't figure out, but he had no doubt that as soon as they were out of earshot of Talleha, Rose was going to let him know what was riling her so.

Suddenly, the brassy-haired woman took Dorsey's muscled arm and yanked on it as she led him into a small room. Rose slammed the door shut, giving vent to the furious rage engulfing her. "You sonofabitch! I should have known that this girl was not the sort to be brought here. Damn you! I don't need that kind of trouble."

Her eyes were like green fire as she hissed angrily. For the life of him, he couldn't figure out why Rose was acting so saintly about Talleha.

He displayed his Irish charm as he sought to soothe her ruffled feathers. "Now, Rose, honey—I got to know what you're talking about before I can explain anything. What did I do to cause you any kind of trouble? We both know this isn't the first time I've brought a woman here, and I've paid you some damned good money, too."

"Not one like this one, Dorsey Loper. Never one like her," she told him, shaking her blond head with a dramatic gesture of disapproval.

"Come on, Rose—Talleha might not be what you think she is. Oh, I'll be the first to admit, she has the face of an angel, but what would you say if I told you she was certainly no virgin? What if I told you I know for a fact that she's traveled clear across the state of Texas with a man—been his woman?"

"All the more reason I don't want no trouble from some dude busting my place up, Dorsey." She took out one of the little cigars she purchased across the border and lit it.

"But that's no problem, honey. He's away from Brownsville for awhile. You got riled for nothing."

"I don't give a damn about that dude or whether she's a virgin or not, Dorsey. What matters to me is a dear old man I owe my life to. Glenn Crawford is my friend, and that's enough for me, if this girl's caring for him. It's enough to save her from the likes of you. I'm a whore, Dorsey, and I don't deny it. But I do have a little bit of decency left. Maybe, just maybe, there's a part of me that wants to keep a pretty little thing like her from being soiled from the likes of a bastard like you."

There was no point to try to fight a losing battle, Dorsey realized.

Rose gave out a laugh, observing Dorsey's dejection. "Cheer up, Dorsey. I'm sure you can always find a woman, if you're willing to pay the price. I'll tell you something which might surprise you. I was just as sweet and innocent as that one until I met a man like you." She took a deep puff on the little cigar and slowly moved to stand right in front of him.

Her green eyes locked into his as she spoke in a cold, calm voice. "Now, I'll tell you what you do, Loper. You get your butt out of here, and don't you ever show up

442

here again. In fact, you just follow me and I'll escort you to the front door."

"But what about Talleha?" he stammered.

"I'll see that she gets back safely to Crawford," she replied, pushing him toward the door. The two of them walked in silence through the inn.

When they got to the door and Rose took great pleasure in opening it to let Dorsey leave, she broke into a gusto of laughter. At the end of the pier, Talleha was mounting her horse. Rose knew the only exit the girl could have used was the small window.

She admired the lovely young lady, who was obviously as smart as she was pretty. She had instinctively sensed the danger she'd been in and had sought to escape. Rose applauded her and wished she'd been as clever. If she had, maybe she wouldn't have ended up in this dump.

"Look, Dorsey, my boy—your little pigeon is flying the coop. She's on her way home, so now we don't have to concern ourselves." She laughed again as she closed the door on Dorsey, who stood there watching Talleha ride her mare like the devil himself was after her.

God, she was a beautiful sight. But Loper was not stupid. The goddess of his dreams was utterly unattainable; he'd never have her.

Dorsey was not a good loser, and he started marching down the pier in a stormy rage. He knew exactly where he was going and who he was going to seek out. Mimi was always eager to have his money. There was a violence churning within him very much like the one rampaging in the waters of the bay.

Victor Maurier was a happy man as he swaggered down the long wharf which extended a good half-mile into the water. The harbor ran along Matagorda Bay and serviced many ship lines coming in and out to unload their goods from Texas, Mexico, and California.

Maurier had been lucky in securing passage on one of the packets making a run southward to pick up an assigned cargo of silver from Mexico. It had amazed him that he'd just happened to find this packet, the *Condesa*, which would follow the Texas coastline all the way to Brownsville and beyond.

There was no problem in selling the horse he'd insisted on purchasing from Emilo. He'd even had time after he'd booked his passage aboard the *Condesa* to buy a few things for Talleha.

He was a man on his way to claim his bride, and it was only seemly he should have a ring for the beautiful lady. He found exactly what he wanted in the first shop he entered. The exquisite diamond twinkled as brilliantly as her eyes, and the rich, deep-red rubies seemed perfect for her tawny complexion and jet-black hair.

He sought not to quibble with the jeweler over the extravagant price. On the contrary, he inquired about a pair of earrings to match. The jeweler delightedly pulled out a magnificent pair of teardrop rubies encircled with diamonds. They were exactly what Victor wanted to present to Talleha. He did not hesitate about telling the jeweler he would take those, too.

An hour later, he boarded the *Condesa* with his purchases and his valise. Under his arm in a leather pouch was the portrait painted by Richard Talbert. He was a man happily in love going to the woman he adored, bearing gifts to please her.

It was not until the next day, as he spoke with the captain of the packet traveling toward Mexico, that he found his lighthearted gaiety marred. The captain remarked that they could be heading toward foul weather.

The fifty-year-old Alex Haver spoke with the wisdom of his many years at sea, and Maurier immediately knew that. It was the hurricane season in the Gulf of Mexico, and Haver remarked that he didn't like the smell or the feel of the air.

"Now that you've pointed it out to me, I don't like it either, sir. Makes me know that I've been on land far too long, or I would have been more alert to it," Maurier told him.

"Eager to get back to it, aren't you? It's a fever, that's for sure. Once that salt air gets into your system, it's awfully hard to get rid of it." Haver gave forth a knowing laugh.

"Never intended to be away this long when I left the *Destiny*."

"Well, at least you've had a chance to see this part of the country. It's a damned nice one, don't you agree?"

"Oh, yes, sir. I have to say I like Texas the best of all the states."

"Now, that's what I like to hear. I was born and raised here. Wouldn't trade places with anyone I know. My parents were both immigrants. They took up their residence in a little German community not far from San Antonio, and raised a family of eight kids. Had themselves a darn good life, I guess."

Maurier grinned, "Raising eight children sounds like a handful."

"Yes, I guess you could say there's a lot of us Havers all over the state of Texas. Sisters all married and had a houseful of youngsters. Seems I was the black sheep of the family. Always liked the water better than the land. All my brothers are ranchers, except one who got himself killed by a band of renegade Comanches."

"Sounds like I might have missed something by

445

being an only child, Captain Haver."

"Nope, I wouldn't say that. Once you grow up and everyone goes his own way, your paths don't cross too often. Everyone is too busy working and raising their families."

"You married, Captain Haver?" Maurier asked.

"Oh, lord, been married three times! Lost my first wife to yellow fever when we lived in New Orleans. Lost my second one when she ran off with a gambler up the river in Natchez. That's when I decided to come back to Texas. Found myself a beautiful Mexican woman, and she gave me four of the most beautiful black-eyed children you'd ever want to see. It was the fifth child that took her from me. She died giving birth to him, and for the first few years of his life I couldn't stand to look at the boy, knowing he'd taken my wife from me."

There was anguish on Captain Haver's face as he spoke. Victor could put himself in the captain's place. If Talleha died bearing his son, he felt he could despise his own child. Right or wrong, that was how he would feel.

"And how do you feel about your son now, Captain Haver?"

Alex laughed, "Why, would you believe he now works by my side here on the *Condesa,* and we're closer than I am with any of my other children. You'll meet him, Captain Maurier. My Alfred is a fine man. The years bring a wisdom."

Soon Captain Haver had to attend to his duties. Victor lingered there by the railing as the packet plowed through the waters of the bay. He churned with an eager longing to get to Talleha.

He could only wish for fair days and swift sailing as the packet traveled the southern route hugging the Texas coastline. There were two ports they would stop at before they reached Brownsville, the captain had told him: Freeport, Corpus Christi, and then Brownsville.

Maurier prayed that that devil of a storm brewing out there in the Gulf of Mexico would give him time to reach Talleha, so he could take her and Crawford to some safe place where they'd be spared the ravaging destruction of those fierce winds.

He wondered how far out the storm was as he looked across the distant horizon. The most significant effect on his senses was the air he was breathing: he didn't like it. He'd been in these ominous winds before, and he recalled Captain Crawford's ship riding out a fury of such a storm. Maurier considered no one a better captain than Crawford, but this was a time when all his skill might not be able to overpower such fury.

All in all, a lot of one's success in such a storm was Lady Luck riding on your shoulder.

By twilight, Victor was a man consumed with tension and concern. Heavy rains pelted the deck of the *Condesa* and the winds blew strong and constant now. It was not fear for himself that bothered Victor, but gnawing concern for what might be happening many miles to the south.

It was only when they made the port of Corpus Christi that he'd be privy to information as to how the storm was affecting Brownsville.

He knew that one coastal town could be devastated while another was left untouched by such fury. He prayed that Brownsville would be spared.

He could not lose Talleha, now that he'd found the one woman he'd love all the days of his life. Maybe he was a rare man, but he would never settle for a second choice.

Now he knew why all his plans and his whole scheme in life had changed once he encountered Talleha. She was the woman he'd been seeking but had never found until now. He could not imagine the future without her.

447

Chapter 55

As Maurier thought about Talleha, she was consumed by thoughts of him. More than ever she desired the comfort of his strong arms, holding and protecting her as she rode away from the long pier and Mama Rose's. God knows what fate would have awaited her had she not made her escape from there when she had! She knew one thing, and that was that Dorsey Loper had nothing but dishonorable intentions. The look in Mama Rose's eyes told her that.

She faulted herself for her own stupidity to have accompanied him there in the first place. She could not justify her actions just because she was disappointed in Victor for the moment.

All she could think about was the safe, secure feeling of arriving at Crawford's cottage and how glad she would be to get there. The gusting winds tossed sheets of water against the shoreline as she rode along. The tall palm trees with their massive spreading branches bent to the wind's fury. She knew her little mare labored to gallop along the beach.

A fisherman cautioned her as they passed him, "Better get home, lady. We got ourselves a big blow coming in fast."

She'd happened to look across the bay the next

minute after she'd passed the fisherman to see a tremendous bolt of lightning. All she could think about was the wonderful, welcoming sight of that little white cottage. It seemed she would get there soon, yet nothing near these dunes looked familiar.

To have a better look at the surroundings, she reined Amapola up along one of the slight inclines of the dunes, instead of following the edge of the water. At least she'd be spared the damp spray off the waves. She surely had to look a sight! The captain was going to take one glance at her and ask alot of questions, she figured. Thank God, Madame Charbeau was there with him, at least.

Getting to a higher rise of ground did not give Talleha the clue she had hoped for. Now, she was frustrated by her dilemma. Where was she? She was not sure she knew.

Her lovely riding clothes were being spotted by the pelting rain, and she realized it was becoming harder every second to see clearly. If only she'd just politely bidden Dorsey Loper goodbye and ridden back to the cottage, she wouldn't be in this trouble.

By now, the pelting rain was becoming a torrent, accompanied by roaring bursts of thunder, loud as the explosion of a cannon. Amapola was frenzied to the point that Talleha had to exert herself to control her. Now there were streaks of flashing lightning and fierce, powerful gales of wind.

"Oh, God, Amapola! I'm sorry I got us in this mess," she cried out guiltily. She knew the little mare was in a panic. She was scared, too. She patted Amapola's damp mane and encouraged her, "We'll make it home!" The truth was that she wasn't too sure that they would.

For one brief second, her words seemed to calm the skittish little mare. But in the next moment, a mighty blast of thunder and lightning seemed to explode right on top of them, and Amapola gave way to terror, rearing up on her hind legs. One of the majestic palms bent to break and crash to the ground.

Talleha felt herself falling helplessly as her hand still tried to cling to the reins. She felt a sharp, excruciating pain in her leg and hit her head hard as she slammed to the ground, giving out an agonizing scream.

Then she was swept into oblivion.

Madame Charbeau had watched Crawford pace the floor and knew no words to comfort him. He stared out the window for some sight of Talleha. "Where the hell is that girl? I feel like wringing her neck."

Emily knew she'd got caught and was sitting out the storm somewhere. But that would not pacify him. He raged, "Here is where she should be, Emily. This is no spring shower we're having. I'm worried about her."

"I know, Glenn, and I feel so helpless. But I'm glad at least I'm here with you." She walked over to where he stood, staring out the window at the desolate beach. She gave him a warm embrace, which made him turn around to face her. "God, I'm glad you're here too!"

She gave him the best smile she could muster under the circumstances. Emily knew the hurricane out there would wreak havoc along the long strip of beach and the town of Brownsville. She'd been in Galveston when a similar storm had struck a few years ago.

Never would she forget that day. It was the cause of the foreboding she'd had this morning at her shop. That was why she could not concentrate on her business and decided to go see Glenn Crawford. Here with him was where she wanted to be.

"Oh, I think I know, Glenn. I feel the same way. Remember the hurricane that hit Galveston some years back? Well, I'd just come across the gulf from New Orleans. I got a speedy initiation to these devil storms

450

and what they can do."

Glenn moved with her back over to the little settee. He was feeling tremendously weak; the worry about Talleha had exhausted him. He knew he was unable to search for her as he would have only a year ago. He could only hope the girl was safe, wherever she was.

His wrinkled hand held Emily's as the two of them took a seat and Glenn suddenly realized why she'd come to him today. It gladdened his heart. There was still enough desire in him to want to clasp her face with his hands and kiss her ardently on the lips. "I love you, Emily Charbeau, and we'll ride this out together."

Her blue eyes twinkled and her face took on the radiance of a woman completely happy. In that soft accented voice of hers, she agreed, "We'll ride it all the way together, Glenn. This is what I want. This is why I'm here." He hugged her closer to him.

Neither of them took notice that the winds had become more fierce or that the rains were beating more heavily against the windowpanes. As the thunder resounded outside the little cottage, they clung closer to one another.

Surging waves assaulted the beach a couple hundred feet from the cottage, and each new round of waves came higher and higher.

Glenn heard the howling winds outside his cottage and knew instinctively that they had to be exceeding seventy miles an hour at least. He'd ridden out many a storm at sea and could gauge with fair accuracy the wind's velocity.

He found himself amazed at Emily's calmness. She had to be aware of the certain danger they were facing any moment, but she seemed not to be afraid of it. Crawford had no doubt that very little along the long beach would be spared destruction, and probably not his little frame cottage. In fact, he figured that most of his neighbors had already moved out to a safer shelter.

His closest neighbor, Elbert Ferguson, had stopped by late in the afternoon to offer to get him away from the cottage and over to his brother's house. But Glenn refused his offer, since Talleha had still not returned at that hour. He did not want to have her return and find him and Emily not there.

Perhaps, Crawford concluded, this was the way it was meant to end for him, for the sea to take him into its bosom. What better way could he go?

Actually, it was an answer to his prayers, for Glenn did not wish to linger, to deteriorate in his illness to a state of absolute helplessness.

Only one thing troubled him as the winds became more fierce and he felt the walls of his little cottage vibrating against the powerful gales. He wondered where Talleha was. He cursed Victor yet again. Damn his stupid revenge!

But Crawford could never have cursed him half as harshly as Victor Maurier cursed himself. He sat in the docks at Corpus Christi and listened to the speculation of the many sailors on the wharf. Right now that was all they could do, for the storm had hit Brownsville. There were no lines of communication to alert them of the devastation already taking place there.

But all the warning signs were there to see. These men of the sea respected the dangers of a hurricane.

Maurier feared that Captain Alex Haver, a man in his fifties, would not be daring or reckless enough to pull out of the harbor to make his schedule into Mexico by way of Brownsville. He would not want to risk what they would be heading into by sailing southward. God, Maurier wished he had his schooner. Nothing would have stopped him from trying to sail on.

But he was wrong. It was music to his ears when Haver came down the wharf and boldly inquired if he was ready to be on his way. "I'll gamble on my luck," Haver cockily declared as he looked at Victor with a challenge in his eyes.

"And so will I, sir!" Victor felt a new admiration for this middle-aged captain.

"Well, let us delay no longer. The harbormaster has told me about the possibilities of bad weather. I'm the captain, and the decision is mine to make."

Haver did not have to be told that Maurier was elated. The two of them had shared one another's company after Alex had discovered that Maurier was the captain of his own ship. As the *Condesa* had plowed through the waters from Freeport to Corpus Christi, Alex had heard about Talleha. He knew Victor was eager to return to Brownsville.

He'd watched Victor's fine-chiseled features cloud up as he'd heard rumors from the sailors roaming the docks. He sensed Victor's deep concern about his lady miles away to the south, possibly in the path of what they were now calling a killer hurricane.

Corpus Christi was still enjoying fairly clement weather and blue skies. But the air was heavy with moisture. The gusting breeze hinted at the danger beyond.

As long as Victor could see blue sky on the horizon, he dared to hope that the rumors had been exaggerated. Not all storms brewing built to a fierce intensity.

But all these optimistic hopes were dashed some seven hours later when the *Condesa* headed into dark, heavy clouds. A few moments later, a torrent of rain flooded the decks of the packet.

Maurier was in agony. Never had he felt such torment and pain, nor such fear.

He would give anything to know that his beloved Talleha was safe, for nothing in the world mattered as much.

Chapter 56

As the hurricane moved inland, its fury diminished quickly. The first mate of the *Destiny*, Davy Carron, would never figure out how the trim-lined schooner had been miraculously spared. Its moorings had broken loose and the winds had carried the ship into a secluded little protected cove.

He knew that freakish things like this happened at sea. Now he had witnessed one. He could not believe how lucky he and his mates, Snapper and Bruno, had been. They'd gone out to investigate the nearby beaches and coves along the shoreline and seen the ravages of the storm. It was an awesome sight.

Feeling a certain degree of responsibility to his captain, who was away, his first thoughts were for the captain's lady and his old friend, Captain Glenn Crawford. Knowing the cottage, Davy had no doubt it had been washed into the bay, but he could hope that the pretty lady and the old captain had sought refuge somewhere else.

Without further delay, he told his mates where they were going and what they had to investigate. Snapper was the first to point out to the others, "That old sea dog, Crawford, had to smell this thing coming inland.

Bet they hit for high ground."

"I hope to hell you're right, Snapper, but, from what I've been told, the captain was a very sick man. Talleha may not have managed to get him out of there. She's rather fragile," Carron reminded him.

Bruno's deep voice interrupted Carron, "Not fragile, Davy. Little, maybe, but not necessarily easy to break. No, that one is strong of heart and will."

"You're right, Bruno. She is brave. But I still don't know if she could have handled such an overwhelming ordeal as she'd have been faced with last night. I think we should go immediately to see about them."

The three wasted no time and started in the direction of Crawford's beachside cottage. The closer they came, the surer each of them was of what they'd find. It would no doubt be as devasted as everything else along the beach. Broken and shattered debris covered the sand, and giant palms had been blown over like they were saplings.

The deadly scent of doom surrounded them. They passed dazed, disoriented people walking about aimlessly, still in a state of horrible shock. Some wore kerchiefs stained with blood; others limped from the injuries suffered in the storm.

Boats washed loose from their moorings had crashed on the shore. Hungry seagulls soared overhead, looking for the fishing vessels coming in with their catch, but they were to be disappointed this morning. Carron, Snapper, and Bruno watched them dive down to search the desolate beach before they soared back up to the sky.

When the three happened upon the site where Captain Crawford's cottage should have been, there were no signs of the little white frame house. However, nearby, entangled in a huge length of wire fencing, was Emily Charbeau's buggy: on the side of it her name was lettered in gilt. A limp, feathery plume rested in the front seat.

Carefully, the three of them searched the area, each going in a different direction; but there was no sign of the captain or Talleha.

About ten yards away, Davy saw smoke rising to the sky, and when he went to investigate, he found the small cottage had been burnt to the ground, possibly from a blown-over kerosene lantern. He turned to go back to where the Crawford cottage had once stood. As he roamed the grounds, he espied the captain's old walking cane and his pipe. He gathered them up to give to Victor when he returned. It was all there was left, Davy realized. There was nothing of Talleha's to give to Maurier, he thought sadly as he stood there waiting for Snapper and Bruno to return.

Snapper was the first to come back. He'd found no clues to the missing captain or the girl. In silence the two of them sat on the sand to wait for Bruno. It seemed to take forever, but when they finally saw him, he was walking down one of the dunes with a tiny bundle flung over his huge shoulders. They broke into broad smiles: no one had to tell them it had to be Talleha that Bruno was carrying like a ragdoll. But the thought struck them both at the same moment that she could be dead, and their broad smiles changed to frowns of concern.

As the black giant of a man came nearer, they could see the pleased smile on Bruno's face. Davy and Snapper began to calm and their hearts swelled with overwhelming joy. Talleha was alive and that was all that mattered to them.

There was nothing more for the trio here, but they were all eager to do what they could for the little lady Bruno carried so protectively in his strong, muscled arms. They walked swiftly to the haven of the little cove where they and their ship had been mercifully spared.

Talleha could not have known the tender loving care lavished on her so generously as she lay in the captain's quarters aboard the *Destiny*. Snapper worked diligently to prepare her his nourishing beef stew. The task of undressing her and getting her into warm, dry clothing fell to Davy Carron, and he prayed his captain would understand the situation.

Davy was all man; he could not deny that he was aroused by the lovely, sensuous nakedness his eyes beheld. Christ, Maurier had to be the luckiest sonofabitch he knew! He wondered what miracle had spared her.

Her clothing and hair were completely wet. Davy had worked carefully to wrap her long mane in a towel to dry it. He'd dressed her in one of Victor's long-sleeved shirts and tucked warm woolen blankets under her thighs before putting a thick, quilted coverlet over her. He felt a little inadequate in his role as a nurse, but he did the best he could. He was happy to see that she had quit trembling from the chill.

When he finally emerged from the cabin to be greeted by his two pals, he calmed their concerns by telling them she was resting.

Brushing a straying wisp of his dark, wavy hair away from his forehead, Carron declared with a broad grin on his face, "Didn't realize what a darn good nurse I was. The truth is, I bet she'll wake up hungry as a bear. Snapper, be ready with some of that good soup of yours." He turned to Bruno to ask him about Talleha's clothing, for he knew there was nothing to salvage back at the site of the cottage.

"Got them all washed good and clean for the little miss and hung up to dry," Bruno answered proudly, for it had taken a lot of scrubbing to remove the dark sand of the beach. Bruno knew she'd been wet to the skin.

"Good, 'cause that's all she's going to have for a while. All her things are out to sea or awash in the bay. Those waters swallowed up everything, along with the captain and this woman, Charbeau." Davy knew this sad news was going to hit Victor hard, and he dreaded having to tell him.

But old Snapper eased the heavy burden somewhat as he thoughtfully remarked, "Got a feeling, Davy, that maybe the captain, being the dying man that he was, might have welcomed the sea coming to take him on."

A wan smile came to Davy's face and he gave the old cook a pat on the shoulders as he told him, "You might be right, Snapper. You just might be!"

The three were an amusing sight as the day wore on, playing the roles of a mother hen. Periodically, each took his turn checking the captain's cabin and the sleeping black-haired girl lying there with her hair fanned out on the pillow. The cozy warmth of the cabin had quickly began to dry it out, and she slept peacefully from sheer exhaustion. When each had observed that she was enjoying a good nap, they'd tiptoe quietly out the door.

With a gentle touch, Bruno touched her cheek to assure himself she was not running any fever.

When she did rouse from her long nap, her thick lashes fluttered to see old Snapper standing there. She gave him a lazy mumble, "Ah, Snapper. It feels so good and warm here. Never felt so cold and wet in all my life." Slowly, her hands and eyes examined the garb she had on, and she wondered if it had been Snapper who had changed her clothing. Reluctant to ask him, she merely thanked him for caring for her.

"Oh, I can't take all the credit, miss. Davy and Bruno did their fair share. We're just happy you're all right. Captain would have had our hides if something had happened to you. Captain Maurier has a fierce temper when he gets riled. Got you some hot stew ready to eat whenever you're ready."

"Oh, lord—I'm famished. That sounds wonderful to me," she sighed. Snapper gave her a nod of his almost bald head, assuring her that he would go fetch it right away.

After he'd left, she propped herself up on the pillows and for want of a comb, ran her slender fingers through the tangled mess of her hair. As if answering her secret desires for a comb, Davy Carron came through the door. Having heard the good news from Snapper, he'd come to the cabin to see her. Recalling his own younger sister and her pride in her looks, he brought a few articles he felt she might enjoy using, like a comb and a hairbrush. He wished he'd had something more to present this lovely girl, like a bar of perfumed soap, but no such articles were there on the schooner.

Tomorrow, he'd go into the town to see what else had been destroyed. Davy was also dreading having to tell her about Captain Crawford; he hoped to delay it at least until tomorrow.

Snapper reappeared. Sweetly, she'd thanked them, "You are all being so nice to me. I thank you so much."

In a way, Davy was glad Snapper arrived when he did with a tray filled with stew and his fresh baked bread. If she ate all of that and drank Snapper's steaming black coffee, Davy figured she would be feeling a lot perkier. Maybe he would not be pressed to reveal the sad end of the old captain just yet. Perhaps tomorrow she'd feel stronger and be able to tell them why she was almost a half-mile from the cottage so late at night when the hurricane hit the shore.

His other wish was that Victor Maurier would get back to take over the duties of his ship and his woman. Davy already knew Talleha was too tempting for him to resist. As much a friend as he was to Victor, it would take one brief moment for him to forget that.

Davy knew he would be powerless to stop himself!

Chapter 57

Davy Carron did not like the way he was feeling about Talleha. He considered himself Victor's closest friend, as well as his first mate aboard the *Destiny*. His good looks could rival Maurier's rugged handsomeness, and neither found himself hurting for the ladies' company when they were in port. Like Maurier, Davy had an assured, arrogant air about him and a jauntiness to his walk. This drew a certain respect from the other seamen. It also caught the wandering eyes of the ladies when they walked into any establishment.

Like Maurier, Carron had enjoyed the favors of many women, so he found himself as puzzled as Victor had been about Talleha's spellbinding effect on him. His head whirled with desire when he was around her, as if someone had hit him between the eyes with a big club. Her effect on him was hypnotic.

He had figured it exactly right when he mused that a good night of rest and a hearty meal prepared by Snapper would restore her vigor. By the time he checked in on her the next morning, she was sitting up in the bunk, eating ravenously from the breakfast tray Snapper had already brought her.

Her face glowed radiantly and those black eyes

twinkled. He could see why Victor had fallen so head-over-heels in love with her. All his grand ideas about being the elusive bachelor with no intention to settle down with a wife until he was in his late thirties must have been quickly swept away, Carron knew.

All Davy had to do was listen to him talk about Talleha to know his old pal, Victor, was smitten.

It was a glorious day of bright sunshine and clear blue skies. That was enough to brighten anyone's spirits after the dark, dismal storm. The waters of the bay lapping at the beach seemed calm and serene now, all their fury spent.

Davy bade her good morning and told her how pleased he was to see her looking so fine. She rewarded him with soft laughter. "Snapper's good food is the healing tonic. He is a fantastic cook!"

A devious look was in Davy's eyes as he asked, "And did you tell him that?"

"I certainly did," Talleha assured him.

"Oh, Lord Almighty! He'll be a pain to deal with now," Davy teased her lightheartedly.

"Not Snapper! I can't believe that of that nice little man. I think I adore him," she declared.

She was a darling! There was something of a childlike quality about her which enchanted him, yet he knew this was no child. After all, he had undressed her. Oh, no, she was all woman!

He tried to keep his voice casual as he taunted her, "Now, Bruno and I are going to be jealous. That old Snapper is beating us out."

That sweet honesty of hers came pouring forth without any hesitation, "But I adore all of you. I owe all of you so much, Davy. I've no doubt that I owe you my life." Such warmth and emotion gleamed in her black eyes that Davy ached to rush to her and take her in his arms to declare how glad he was that they'd found her in time.

Instead, he played the role of the happy-go-lucky fellow to cover up his more serious self. "Well, now I feel better, I admit."

"Davy, now that I'm thinking clearly again I must tell you I'm deeply concerned about Captain Crawford. I left him in the company of Madame Charbeau while I went for a ride, and I just pray that she stayed with him."

Davy had known it was inevitable that he would have to tell her that Captain Crawford and Madame Charbeau were dead. Talleha's honest manner demanded that he be just as straightforward with her, so he was. He told her how they'd searched the whole area around the little beachfront cottage. "There was nothing left, Talleha—absolutely nothing! I guess we could assume that the sea he loved so dearly took him."

He watched her lovely face and expected to see a flood of tears. But he saw only a misty glaze forming in her eyes. She sat there for a moment as though she were absorbing his words. What better way for the dying old sea dog to go, she silently thought. There was no reason to be sad.

"You all right, Talleha?" Davy asked, as she had remained silent so long. But she quickly assured him that she was fine, but added that Victor would be devastated by the news.

"Captain Crawford was the closest thing to a father Victor ever had, so he told me. I'm just sorry that he had to be gone."

"So am I, Talleha. So am I," Davy mumbled. Secretly, he knew Victor was going to be sorry about many things if he stayed away too damned long. The way he was feeling, Davy considered it a wise time to excuse himself from the cabin.

After Talleha was left alone, she allowed herself to

cry until there were no more tears left. She cried for the dear captain she'd come to love dearly. She cried for Madame Charbeau, who she'd instantly liked and hoped to share more time with. Most of all, she cried for Victor Maurier; but at the same time, she cursed him for not being by her side when she'd needed him most desperately.

She rejoiced in having such devoted new friends as Snapper, Bruno, and Davy there by her side. What would she have done without them, she asked herself.

With her strength restored, she was now wondering what she was to do without any clothing. This oversized shirt was not enough to cover her decently. She wanted to go up on deck to absorb some of that warming sunshine. She had no intention of being a prisoner all day in the cabin.

Bruno had told her this was Victor's cabin, and now that she'd had a chance to survey it, she found it to be very nicely furnished. From what he'd told her, this was the only home he had. For the next hour, she browsed around the cabin slowly, absorbing all she could about the man she loved.

She looked over the clutter of his desk, which engulfed one corner of the cabin. Behind it he had many shelves filled with books. She found herself fascinated by the multitude of objects from all over the world, and it whetted her interest of going to all the exotic places Victor had gone.

The longer she examined Maurier's cabin, acquainting herself with the many sides of the man who'd stolen her heart, the more she realized how far apart their worlds truly were. Perhaps that was why he had been in no hurry to return to her. A man so worldly as Victor must surely find a simple girl like her very boring.

She slammed the door of the low chest she'd just finished exploring because anger suddenly ignited within her. He certainly never gave her that impression when they were in the heat of passion, nor when she knew he was in a fever to make love to her. But maybe this was the way with men when they merely wanted to pleasure themselves with a woman's body, as if it were their plaything. She reminded herself what had happened with the smooth-talking Dorsey Loper.

He'd brought her flowers, and sweet were the honey-eyed words he spoke through his lying lips to get what he wanted. It pained her to think that if she'd not accompanied him to Mama Rose's, she might have helped save Captain Crawford and that nice Emily Charbeau.

But a soothing voice came to her like the soft, warming voice of her mother. It urged her not to dwell on such foolish whimsy as that. The truth was that she, too, could have been killed with the captain and Madame Charbeau. Dorsey Loper was a no-good scoundrel, but his urging her to go with him could have saved her life.

Dawn would have told her it was not her time to go, and Talleha felt this had to be the reason she'd been spared. She was yet to fulfill her destiny. This was what she wanted to believe deep in her heart. Whether it was selfish or not, she wanted to share more days and nights of rapture with the man she loved.

Emily Charbeau's words came back to haunt her as she roamed aimlessly about the cabin. The woman seemed so sure when they'd spoken briefly before Talleha had left to go for her ride on Amapola. She'd said Maurier worshipped her. How could Emily be so sure of that when Talleha wasn't? Madame Charbeau seemed like an experienced woman. Oh, if only they could have had more time together, Talleha lamented!

Talleha needed an older woman like Madame Charbeau or her mother to confide in now about something tormenting her. Once she'd been moved to be daring and to confide in Captain Crawford, but she'd dismissed the whole idea. She found it just too embarrassing to admit even to a kind, elderly gentleman like Crawford that she suspected herself to be pregnant, for it was a confession as to just how naive she was.

The thought of having a child of Maurier's thrilled and frightened her at the same time. She did not wish to follow in Dawn's footsteps . . . it frightened her. If only Victor loved her, then she would be the happiest woman in the world. It all depended on him.

By the time the steamer, *Condesa,* reached the port of Laguna Vista, a small fishing village, the reports of the devastation around Brownsville were well known. Luckily for the tiny fishing village, they'd only born the brunt of the outer edges of the storm. The hurricane's path had veered to the north and west.

The news was bad, and it was enough to send Victor Maurier into a frenzy. His strong resolve to prepare for the worst was failing him miserably, Alex Haver realized. He felt sorry for his young friend but was helpless to know how to ease his pain. His devoted old captain and woman he loved might surely be dead, from what they were told about the damage to the coastline.

In a feeble attempt to soothe Victor's frayed nerves, he'd assured him, "This lady, my *Condesa,* is pushing herself to the limits, Captain Maurier."

"I know, Captain Haver, and I appreciate all you're doing." Maurier was a man devoured by overwhelming guilt, and it was tearing him apart. Never would he forgive himself if something had happened to her now! When he thought about the sweet, unselfish love she'd

465

given him so willingly and how he'd so sadly repaid it, he hated himself.

If only he found her, he silently vowed, he'd never fail her again. Never!

It was now hard for Victor to envision the ominous skies that had shrouded the coast of Texas less than two days ago. It was lovely now: the sky was azure blue and the sea gulls soared. In the west the sun was beginning to sink, and Maurier figured that long before dark they'd be arriving in the harbor of Brownsville. Then he'd know what Fate had in store for him.

The sea breeze was calm, with no hint of the fierce, killing winds of the hurricane. Other ships and vessels came and went as if there could not possibly be any disaster ahead for the *Condesa*.

However, a short time later Maurier's eyes noticed the first telltale signs of disaster, which instantly made him tense and alert. It looked as if a giant monster had invaded the beach. Tall palms were flattened to the sand, and he saw small boats turned upside down on the beach where the winds had obviously tossed them.

Alex Haver had seen it all and gone to seek out Maurier as he stood by the railing. He was not a man to mince words as he confronted Victor, "Looks bad, son. Looks damned bad!"

Victor answered in a voice barely above a whisper, "Afraid so, sir." His eyes stared straight ahead.

Maurier looked to the west as the *Condesa* moved south. Only a few miles away and back only a short distance from the coastline was the little cottage belonging to Glenn Crawford. There was where he'd left Talleha.

Alex Haver could almost see the tension in his firm, muscled shoulders as Victor strained to see the shoreline. His black hair blew wildly across his face and he brushed it back so he could see clearly. He'd said nothing to Haver, nor did he know whether Haver had noticed what he'd seen, but he recognized a familiar spot. Once a cottage had been there; it had been Crawford's closest neighbor. Now it was no more!

Alex Haver had lived a long life and he'd experienced much, but he was hardly prepared for the wailing now coming from the young man standing there at his side.

He turned in horror to see Victor covering his face and shaking with sobs as he moaned, "Oh God! Oh, God—no!"

"What, Victor? What is it?" Alex asked, taking hold of his trembling shoulders.

"It's gone! Captain Crawford's house is gone! Oh, God, Talleha!"

Alex Haver felt an ache in his gut as if he were sharing the pain.

Chapter 58

Captain Alex Haver had never felt like a sentimental man, but he could not bring himself to just leave Victor Maurier alone in the harbor at Brownsville and sail on to Mexico. It was in his own best interests to move on, for he had no cargo to load or unload on the wharf.

He knew Victor was a bold, daring young man from the conversations they'd had the last few days. Now he saw a man crazed by the grief he faced. Haver wanted to be by his side to help in whatever way he could.

Leaving his first mate in charge of the crew of the *Condesa,* he accompanied Victor down the gangplank onto the wharf. Numerous seamen roamed the wharf aimlessly. Haver figured they were the crews of ships that had been caught out in the bay. Their ships were now in dock, being repaired or rebuilt.

The next hour was one Alex Haver would never forget. He walked down the beach road with Maurier to the cottage where Crawford and the lady Victor loved, Talleha, should have been, but they were not there, nor was the house.

Haver stood by helplessly as Maurier searched the grounds madly. Alex knew he would find nothing. When he could stand it no longer, Alex suggested to

Victor, "I think we'd be wise to start inquiring about your friends. Don't you think that would be the thing to do, my friend?"

Dejectedly, Maurier shook his head and threw his hands up as he mumbled, "I suppose, sir. I see nothing left here—nothing at all. God!"

Alex prodded him gently on the shoulder and urged, "Maybe we should go to your schooner. Maybe they are with your friends there. What do you say, son?"

Maurier would not argue with that, for he knew he wasn't thinking clearly at all right now. Never had he felt so completely out of control as he was now. He decided to listen to Alex, who was a very level-headed fellow. He'd come to respect him very much in the brief span of their friendship.

However, a half-hour later, when they arrived to find Maurier's schooner no longer moored where it was supposed to be, he was beginning to get as perplexed as Victor. He had no answers for the young man he sought to help.

Alex dared not voice to Victor his innermost thoughts: he could have lost his fine schooner as well as Talleha and his dear friend. It was one hell of a blow for any man to have to swallow all at once.

All Alex could think of to ease the pain for the moment was a good, stiff drink at a tavern they'd just passed.

"Come on, Maurier. Let's go have ourself a drink and put our heads together. We'll think of something. We'll question everyone left if we must. That's why I stayed, my friend. I won't leave for Mexico until I help you find your friends."

"You're a good friend, Alex," Maurier told him. He had never lived through such a harrowing experience as this. For once in his life his independent nature had failed him; he did need someone to lean on. Captain

Alex Haver was proving to be a pillar of support.

Once the two of them found a table in the dimly-lit, foul-smelling little tavern, it was obvious the main topic of conversation among the patrons there was the devil storm they'd all survived.

Just listening to all the talk about the disaster was enough for Victor and Alex to realize what a terrifying, ghastly experience the storm must have been.

"Excuse me, Alex, I must question some of these men. Maybe one of them might have some information for me," Victor said as he rose up from the wooden chair.

"Good luck, Victor." Alex took a hearty sip of the whiskey. He truthfully didn't expect the young man to hear any encouraging news as he watched him saunter to one table and move on to the next. By the time Maurier had questioned men at four tables, Alex figured he'd be coming back to their table feeling even more miserable.

But he was due for a surprise as Maurier returned, literally lifting him out of the chair, causing him to spill his drink down into the lap of his pants.

"The *Destiny*, Alex—it wasn't destroyed! A sailor told me it is now moored over in a little cove—a different spot from where she was moored before. Come on!"

Alex had never seen such a sudden change of mood. Victor's brilliant blue eyes sparked with renewed hope. There was spirit and vigor in his body once again as the two of them moved hastily out of the tavern into the street. Twilight was descending now on the Texas coast, and there was a glorious sunset. Alex hoped it was a good omen that this day might end with the reunion of two young people in love.

He found it an ordeal to keep up with the fast-paced Victor Maurier. Only once did he slow up, to look back and remark to Alex, "Don't see how in hell the *Destiny* could have gotten over to this side of the bay."

"Crazy freakish things happen in a storm like this," Alex called to him.

They'd walked up one sand dune and down another when finally the waters snaked into a small, secluded cove off the bay. Alex and Victor both spotted the schooner. It was a fine ship, trim and slick.

It was so good to see her! The *Destiny* was Victor's home. Just the glorious sight of his ship restored his faith that somewhere, he'd also find Talleha.

He realized that he felt a degree of passion for the ship that was all-consuming and rapturous! Words could not describe it.

But Captain Alex Haver understood. He'd felt that way about the *Condesa*. It was his haven and his home. He stood quietly a short distance away and said nothing.

Haver was as amazed as Maurier that the schooner had suffered no damage from the storm, yet it obviously had been swept from its moorings to drift here. It was a magnificent schooner.

He called out to tell him this, and Victor gave out a deep throaty laugh, "Told you she was a beauty."

It was then that Haver and Victor noticed the massive man on the deck of the *Destiny*. Victor instantly recognized Bruno. Haver was naturally curious.

"Who is that, Victor?" he asked.

"He is called Bruno, and a damned good man to have along, for his strength is amazing, Alex. Been with me for four years now and I couldn't ask for a better crewman."

By this time Alex had managed to catch up with Maurier. Together they walked up the dune and down the incline to the edge of the cove. Bruno had spotted

471

the familiar tall figure of his captain and gave out a howl.

His huge body moved with remarkable agility to greet Victor. There was a boyish eagerness on the black man's face, and Alex Haver did not need more evidence of the high esteem in which Maurier's crew held him.

Victor called out to the black man, "Bruno!"

"Ah, Captain Maurier, good to have you back."

Alex Haver watched as the two men greeted with a warm embrace. It was always nice to behold such a bond of friendship.

"Bruno, I'd like you to meet the captain of the *Condesa*, Alex Haver," Victor declared, as he patted Bruno's broad shoulder.

"A great honor to know you, Captain Haver." Bruno bowed respectfully as he spoke.

Victor wasted no time in expressing his gratitude and delight to find the *Destiny* not scarred by the storm. Bruno confessed that he was the first to admit he could not explain it. "It was almost eerie when we saw what had happened, sir. We seemed to have had a guardian angel riding along."

By this time they'd reached the deck of the ship. Maurier's next question was one Bruno had feared: he asked about the old captain.

"Yes, sir—the storm hit hard there, and the captain was caught in his cottage. Nothing was spared along that beach. Everything was destroyed." As Bruno spoke he saw the brutal effect his words had on his captain and he hated to be the one to give him such awful news. But Davy Carron had told him how much Victor cared about Captain Crawford. He could understand it, now that they'd stayed in the harbor of Brownsville all these weeks and heard talk about the man among the various seamen drifting around the docks. Captain Glenn Crawford was an admired seafaring man.

When Victor tried to bring himself to ask Bruno his next question, he found his voice cracking with dread and apprehension.

Instinctively Alex Haver knew what horrifying thoughts troubled his younger friend. He only wished he could have been as sensitive and perceptive with his own son. From the first moment they'd encountered one another there had been a camaraderie between them.

Haver noted the cracking in Victor's voice as he said, "Tell me, Bruno—is there any news of my lady, Talleha?" Alex watched as Maurier awaited the answer and he found himself feeling concern for what that answer might be.

But Bruno eagerly replied, "Ah, that one—she is fine, sir! She is just fine! In fact, she is out trying to catch herself a fish this afternoon. She told Davy she was not about to stay in that cabin all day. A bossy one, she is!" Maurier did not have to be told that his Talleha had won herself a friend in Bruno. He was her slave if she wanted him to be. She lived and Maurier could breathe again.

"Fishing, you say, Bruno?" Victor prodded.

"Yes, sir. I—I found her on the beach the next morning after the storm. We brought her with us and she's been with us ever since," he proudly informed Maurier. It was important to Bruno to let his captain know that he was the one who'd found Talleha. To Bruno, it was his way of paying the captain back for rescuing him a few years ago. The captain had been his savior, and now he felt he'd repaid his debt.

"I'm beholden to you, Bruno, and I thank you from the bottom of my heart."

How wonderful life was, he thought to himself! Talleha lived and that was all that mattered! How lucky could he be? His fine ship was there in the cove, and the woman he loved beyond all reason was safe. Somehow, it made the loss of Crawford easier to bear, and as old Snapper had said, Maurier knew that the old captain was happy out there, somewhere in the waters of the gulf.

Slowly, he turned to face Alex Haver. Haver's face told him he understood his feelings. It was Alex Haver who finally broke the silence as he urged Victor, "Go to your beautiful lady, son. I shall go on my way now, for I am not needed anymore. I'm so very glad you found her again and I've only one thing to say to you. Now that you've found her, never let her go, son. Never! I loved a woman once like that, and I made the biggest mistake of my life by letting her go. I lived to regret it the rest of my life, Victor. Don't you do that!" He turned and went.

As he moved over the sandy dune, Alex heard Victor's voice calling out, "Will I see you again, sir?"

Alex did not dare turn around, for he might have weakened and he did not wish to do that now. It was not the time nor the place. But his brilliant blue eyes sparkled brightly, and never had he been so happy or proud.

"If fate deems it so, then we shall meet again. God bless you, son. Be happy and know that I'll be thinking about you and your fine lady."

A mist gathered in Alex Haver's eyes as he moved along the beach, and he knew the answers to everything which had troubled him for weeks. Each time the two of them had talked, he'd learned a little more about Victor Maurier, and today the last piece of the puzzle had fallen into place. When he'd casually mentioned his mother's name, Alex had recoiled with a flood of memories coming back to him. He was carried back to a time some twenty-five or -six years ago. He and his

474

good friend, Edward Penwick, were in the south of France. His Englishman friend was a most serious young man and he was a dashing young seaman. They were an unlikely pair, but they had formed a binding friendship. It was a wild spree they'd enjoyed that summer in France until Alex had sailed away, leaving Edward there alone.

Alex knew that when he'd left France, he'd left the lovely French beauty, Colette, with his child, and the gallant, kindhearted Edward had taken on the responsibility which should have been his. Dear Edward, he was always the gentleman!

Perhaps it was better this way—that Victor should never know the truth that Alex was the father he'd never known. Maybe it was better that he thought Edward Penwick was his father.

Time would give him the answer to that, Alex Haver decided. For the time being, he had to make a run to Mexico and, Victor had a gorgeous woman to be reunited with. Who could say what the future held for any of them?

Pridefully, he knew by watching his son's blue eyes as he caught sight of his ship that he loved the sea as Alex did.

There was no doubt that Victor was his son. No doubt at all!

Chapter 59

As Victor watched the tall, long-legged sea captain walk down the beach, he hoped they would have an opportunity to meet again. He'd felt an instant rapport with Alex akin to what he'd always felt for Captain Glenn Crawford. Each was like a father, he thought to himself.

Somehow, in his boyish memories of the quiet, gentle-mannered Edward Penwick, he'd never seen any of his own traits. The secret locked within the heart of Alex Haver would have greatly pleased Maurier. Other than the news that Talleha lived, nothing could have made him happier. It would have explained so many things to Victor to know that his father loved the sea and ships with the same passion as he did.

But now that the image of Haver had faded, he turned to Bruno to ask, "Where is she, Bruno—where is she doing this fishing you spoke about?"

Bruno saw an amused grin on his face as his captain inquired about his lady, and he knew he was going to seek her out even before he went to his ship. The *Destiny* had been replaced by a lady named Talleha. No longer was the *Destiny* his first love.

"Oh, Davy would not allow her to wander too far,

sir. I must tell you that she was highly indignant that he put a boundary on just how far she could go," Bruno chuckled.

"Am I to surmise that Davy has had a taste of her headstrong nature?" Maurier inquired of the black man.

Reluctantly, he admitted, "Just a little, sir."

"Good, I'm glad to hear it. I'll thank Davy for that later. By the way you can inform him that I'll be escorting her back to the *Destiny* myself."

"Yes, sir. I'll tell him. Over there, sir—around the bend is where you'll find her," Bruno said, pointing to the east edge of the cove.

The two parted company and Maurier eagerly ran in wild anticipation of the sight of her beautiful face once again. It seemed like forever since he'd last seen her! Each week had been like a year, and far too many had gone by, but never again would he punish himself so painfully.

When he reached the top of the sand dune, he saw no sign of her anywhere, and his heart began to pound erratically. Now where was she? Had she defied Davy's order as she had with him in the past?

There was nothing there below except a huge old piece of driftwood and someone's old bucket cast away. He searched as far as he could down the length of the cove. But as old Bruno had told him, it was a fairly safe place to allow her to enjoy herself for the afternoon.

Suddenly, his blue eyes noticed something there on the driftwood which didn't blend in. He abruptly realized that it was a lank of her glossy black hair. She was there just below him. He wasted no time as he rushed down the slight incline.

But as he reached the spot to find her with her lovely head resting back against the driftwood, sound asleep, he had to suppress the laugh yearning to erupt within him. Her crude fishing pole lay on the beach, and her line was giving forth a tug. Her catch was taking the bait and getting away. But it was the amusing sight of her garb that made him want to roar with laughter. He immediately recognized the faded blue pants as his, though the legs had been cut off. His shirt swallowed her up, extending far below her hips, and the sleeves were rolled up at least three times.

Nevertheless, she presented an enchanting vision. Those long, thick black lashes caressed her cheek and her lovely rosebud lips parted just slightly. Already, he anticipated the sweet honey he'd taste when he kissed them. While the oversized shirt she wore swallowed her, the soft round mounds of her firm breasts pressed against the material.

Slowly, he knelt down to sink onto the sand beside her. Amazingly, she still slept soundly. His head moved so his lips could take hers in a kiss. In a foggy daze, she mumbled, "Davy?" She stretched her body lazily.

"Davy—hell!" Victor growled angrily.

By now, she was wide-eyed, looking up into his irate face, and she could go on no longer with her charade. She broke into uncontrollable giggles. She'd known he was standing there before he'd sunk down to kiss her, and it was all she could do to restrain herself from leaping up to rush into his arms. But the imp in her decided to have a little fun with the handsome devil who'd stayed away far too long to suit her.

When she continued to laugh until tears were flowing down her cheeks, Victor finally realized the wicked trickery she'd played on him. A slow grin came to his handsome face as he muttered, "You—you little savage! I'll make you pay for that, you know!"

He fell to the ground beside her and took her impatiently in his strong arms. Pressing her soft, supple body hungrily, he captured her lips with his to let his

478

firing passion sear her. Talleha gave forth a breathless moan of pleasure.

His kiss was a lingering one, for it had been a long time and he'd ached so for her sweet lips. The way she surrendered told him that she, too, had longed for him. That was all he needed to know.

"Ah, my darling, darling Talleha—I've missed you so very much," he sighed, letting his hand play along her face, removing the strands of long hair from it.

"And I missed you, too. I—I thought maybe you were never coming back," she murmured breathlessly as he held her so close to his broad chest that she felt she could hardly breathe. Yet she wanted to be held that close, for it felt marvelous to be enclosed by his strong, muscled arms once again.

As she'd told him, there were times when she wondered if those arms would ever hold her or those sensuous lips would ever brand her with their kisses again.

The very thought of never experiencing that wonderful rapture was enough to devastate her. But now he was here with her, holding her close to him, and nothing else mattered to Talleha.

All that existed at this moment for her was his forceful, overpowering presence, and she surrendered herself to it. He felt the wild sensation of her undulating body moving beneath him and knew her impatient desire matched his. This pleased him.

His fingers began to fumble to unfasten the buttons of the oversized shirt she wore. Damned if he remembered having this kind of trouble unbuttoning this old shirt of his when he wore it! But when the task was finally done, what joy it was to feel the warm flesh of her, and he let his hands caress it as he'd yearned so desperately to do.

He loved to hear the sweet moans of her delight as he

touched and explored the spots which seemed to thrill her the most. It was wonderful to discover all the mystery of her all over again.

"Oh, Victor—God! Victor!" she cried out.

"Yes, my sweet Talleha! It has been far too long, hasn't it?" he huskily replied.

Eagerly, he removed the old shirt and his cutoff pants so his eyes could behold her golden, silken skin. It was just as tantalizing as he'd remembered.

He wasted no time ridding himself of his clothing so that nothing separated them. As he flung his leg free of his pants, Talleha raised up from the beach to kiss his lips. His lips murmured softly as they met hers, "Ah, ma cherie—ma cherie. I missed you more than I could have possibly known. Never again, I promise."

His forceful male body sank down to bury itself between her satiny thighs and she felt the firmness of his sinewy legs press against her legs. His head bent so that his mouth could take her pulsing, jutting breast, letting his tongue caress the rosy tip. Her petite body arched for him to fill it with his powerful manliness. Greedily, she wanted him to consume her as only he could.

Never had she known such ecstasy as he claimed her completely. Such an all-consuming passion made her feel as giddy as if she were drunk. She gave forth a gasp of sweet anguish, digging her fingers into Victor's back as if she was holding on to him for fear he would leave her.

His deep voice whispered sweet words of endearment, and he smothered her face with his heated kisses as his masterful body performed its magic, swaying to and fro with hers.

Talleha followed as he led her. Once again, she was convinced that no other man could make her feel this way. What made this so? What made her so shameless

480

and abandoned with him, while she could only be indignant when someone like Dorsey Loper wanted to lie with her?

Just the touch of his heated body made her wild with desire. The touch of his hands on her body made her flame with a mounting passion. She could not resist the reckless ecstasy Victor ignited within her. From the beginning it had been this way.

Maurier was soaring to heights of rare passion as her exquisite softness encircled him. Never had he expected to find a real love goddess in this world. A woman like Talleha only existed in a man's wildest fantasy. He'd dreamed about such a woman, but he'd never expected to find one—much less one to love him back as Talleha did.

Paradise was theirs in this special moment on the sandy beach as their hearts and souls united one with the other. Their vows were spoken silently, but they were just as binding and just as sincere.

Never could they have loved anyone as much as they loved one another.

For the longest time, Victor lay with her enclosed in his arms. So anxiously had he desired her that he'd not troubled himself to remove his shirt. So massive was his body that he concealed her nakedness from a pair of eyes observing them at a short distance.

The two lovers lay in sweet repose, knowing not that they were being observed by a pair of eyes envying them desperately.

Davy Carron had received the news from Bruno that his captain had returned and gone in search of Talleha. Naturally, he was delighted, and he'd given them the private time he considered they'd need when they were reunited. Then Davy went over to the cove to seek them out.

The truth was that Davy was finding the time hard to

bear as he awaited their return to the *Destiny*. The ultimate truth was that it drove Davy crazy with jealousy and curiosity as to what they were doing so long.

Damned if he could help the way he felt about her now! There was a certain possessive feeling he could not sweep away, though he knew he must, now that Maurier was back. If he couldn't, he could no longer remain on the *Destiny*.

Looking down on them now, Carron wasn't so sure he was that strong. He saw Maurier's body covering her and he hated him! His emotions were tearing him apart and he was smart enough to know it. He was just having trouble convincing himself what he was going to do about it.

Until now, Davy had not realized how much fever was in his blood over Talleha. He had no claim to her, but his reckless heart refused to listen.

Slowly, he turned his back on the two lovers. Unhurriedly, he walked back to where the *Destiny* was moored in the next cove.

As Davy had observed the two lovers, he, too, was being watched with grave apprehension. The man watching Carron was now convinced that he'd been right in his suspicions.

Davy Carron was attracted to Talleha. Bruno knew that could mean big trouble! It disturbed the big, black giant of a man, for he cared for everyone involved.

Young Davy, as Bruno called him, had to accept that Talleha was the captain's woman. If he didn't, there would be bloodshed, and the blood would be Davy's.

Chapter 60

It was amazing how fast and how quietly the huge black man could move. The last thing in the world he'd want was for Davy Carron to know was that Bruno was spying on him even as he was spying on the captain and his lady down there on the beach. Because he was swift on his feet, he reached the schooner and was sitting on the deck, pretending to be occupied with whittling a whistle when Davy flung his leg over the railing.

"'Afternoon, Davy." Bruno never missed a beat to look up into Davy's face. Davy's reply was a sort of mumble as he walked by. But as Davy went below deck, Bruno rose up to seek out Snapper, for he figured the old cook was going to be putting on a feast tonight, with the captain back.

He thought he'd find Snapper busy cooking, and he was right. The aroma was enough to drive Bruno wild.

"Son-of-a-gun, Snapper—don't know if I can wait two or three more hours. I'm starved to death," Bruno declared, for he had a rapacious appetite.

"You'll get the blade of my butcher knife if you dare to bother any of my pots. You hear me, you big swine?" Snapper teased him as only his good friend could have. Had anyone else called Bruno a swine his massive hands would have choked the life out of them. "You understand? You gotta wait like everyone else."

But Old Snapper was too kindhearted and generous to deny him one of his flaky biscuits, and he tossed it for Bruno to catch. Stirring one of the large black iron pots Snapper said, grinning broadly, "Gonna be a happy night on the old *Destiny,* I'm a'thinkin'."

Bruno gave him a grunt and ambled on out of the galley. As he walked slowly down the passageway, he saw Captain Maurier guiding his lady toward the door of his cabin. So they'd finally decided to leave their little haven in the cove and come to the schooner! Bruno figured Davy was in the seclusion of his own cabin, in no mood to face Maurier or Talleha for a while. Bruno figured he was attempting to gain some control over his emotions before locking eyes with his captain and friend, Maurier.

It had been Bruno's experience that nothing could break up a solid friendship between two guys like a woman.

Actually, Victor was in no mood right now for Davy's company, even though he considered no one a better friend. But there was so much he needed to say to Talleha. Besides, now that he had found her and she was safely by his side, he was impatient to leave Brownsville just as soon as possible.

Now that they had shared wild moments of ecstasy, he felt they'd never been closer, and he was slightly nervous about many of the things on his mind.

Once the door of the cabin was closed and they were all alone, he teased her by saying, "So you've been making my home your home, eh? How do you like it, Talleha? Does it please you?"

"It's all very nice. I—I found a lot of the mysteries about you explained. I guess I didn't realize what a man of the world you were until I stayed in your cabin."

He walked over to the low chest to pour himself a

484

glass of brandy as she sank down on his bunk. "Does this man you've learned about meet with your approval, my darling Talleha? I hope so."

He turned to see her observing him intently. The expression on her face gave him no hint as to what was going on inside that pretty head of hers.

Her soft voice finally spoke, and there was nothing lighthearted about her manner when she did. "I realize we come from two very different worlds. It's a wonder that we ever met."

"Ah, thank God we did! Maybe, Talleha, it was meant to be. Maybe it was written long ago."

Her black eyes gazed up at him as she asked, "Do you really think that is possible? My mother would have said it was, but I don't know. I'd like to think so."

"If that's what you'd like to think, then think it, Talleha." He gave her a light peck on her pretty nose, for had he kissed her lips, he would have not torn himself away, and he had to talk with Davy.

"I'm not the same girl you left here, Victor. Things happened while you were away. I feel different than I did then. That simple, carefree imp, as you called me, must have grown up."

A frown etched Victor's handsome face and he wondered what she was attempting to tell him. Fearful he was not going to like what she had to say, he tried to cajole her. "You look like the same adorable, capricious vixen I left behind. The truth is, Talleha, it was a long journey for nothing. Eliot Penwick was dead when I got back to Harrison County. His wife, Marjorie, killed him. It was in self-defense—he was trying to kill her."

"Dear God!" Talleha gasped, unable to say anything else. Finally, she added, "The poor señora—I always felt very sorry for her, even when I felt she didn't like me. But when she offered to help me get away from that horrible man, I knew she'd changed her opinion of me."

"Oh, she knew you were a good girl, Talleha. She knew all along that you were not at fault where Eliot's actions were involved. The truth is, she credits your presence at the ranch for giving her back the courage and strength that Eliot had so cunningly robbed from her. She is doing just fine now, I'm happy to tell you."

"Oh, I'm glad to hear that. How is that dear Señor Cortez?"

"I have something to tell you, ma petite, that I think will truly bring joy to that romantic heart of yours. The señora and our Emilo are to be married in the spring. It seems they've become very close during this ordeal."

A tear came to her eyes, for she was overcome with joy for those two nice people back in Harrison County. It was wonderful that fate had decreed she get to know them. If a horrible thing had not happened to her mother and she'd not been in that woods where Eliot Penwick had found her that night in early spring, she would not have gotten to know Emilo or the señora. Never would she have met Victor back in the small village where she and Dawn had lived.

"I think it is wonderful, Victor. I think they make a wonderful couple—so right for one another."

He had to bite his tongue to keep from blurting out that they would make no more wonderful a couple than he and she would make. They were right for one another, too. But in all fairness to her, Victor felt he must first tell her she was a very wealthy heiress. A simple sea captain might not be what she wanted to settle for when she knew what a rich young woman she now was, having inherited her father's vast fortune.

What was behind that look on his face, Talleha wondered? They'd shared an ecstatic love less than an hour ago, but all his words of endearment had not included marriage. He'd not asked her to be his wife now that they'd been reunited, and she'd prayed for that more than anything. In fact, she was wondering what she would do if he did not offer her marriage. Was she to return to her village and have his baby, raising it without a father, as Dawn had raised her?

She watched him place his glass of brandy on the nightstand and slowly walk over to pick up a long parcel that had been resting by the side of his desk.

"Marjorie Greenfield asked that I give you this, Talleha." He presented her the portrait of the woman he and Marjorie were certain had to be her mother.

He had only to stand back silently and watch the flood of emotion displayed on her face to know that they had been right. This lovely, tawny-skinned lady was Dawn! Talleha was, in fact, Richard Talbert's daughter by the half-breed Indian woman. Talleha was heiress to the Talbert fortune.

"How, Victor—how did the señora get this? I'm confused by this," she gasped, looking up at him, a childlike expression of helplessness on her face. Victor warmed with love and compassion. If it was possible, he felt more than ever she needed him for her own protection. But then, he'd felt this way about Talleha since the first afternoon they'd met.

Before Victor could answer her question, her attention had returned to the portrait. She sat there, staring at it in a trance. "Wasn't she lovely—my mother?"

"She was almost as lovely as you, Talleha," he told her gently. "Can't help if I'm a bit prejudiced, my darling. I'm in love with you."

She smiled sweetly and motioned for him to come to her. "Tell me—tell me how the señora got this. Who gave it to her? I must know."

"And so you shall, my darling." Victor pondered how he should begin this strange tale and decided it should be sweet and simple. So he came straight to the point. "The man who did this portrait of your mother was a friend of Frank and Marjorie Greenfield. He left it with them when he left Harrison County to go back east, Talleha. The painting had been stored for a long time in a storeroom, and only your appearance at the Greenfield ranch revived the memory. For awhile, Marjorie told me, she couldn't put the pieces all together, but one afternoon she went searching in the storeroom where she'd kept all of Frank's possessions. It was one thing she'd defied Eliot about, that storeroom. He'd resented it highly after their marriage."

Talleha held the painting lovingly to her as she declared, "Oh, thank God, she did! I wouldn't take anything for this!"

"This was why she wanted you to have it."

"Oh, Victor—she is a kindhearted woman!"

"Marjorie Greenfield is a most remarkable lady, and our friend, Emilo, suddenly realized it. Thank God for that, too," he told her, yearning to add that they'd offered the two of them a wedding there at the Casa del Lago. But he could not do this yet, for there was more he must tell her first.

"This Talbert you spoke of, Victor—he captured so much of my mother in this picture. Her spirit is there."

He grinned. "I see it, Talleha. I see a lady proud and brave, with her head held high. I see the spirit and fire in her black eyes and the softness of her lips, along with the warmth of her sweet smile. Talbert captured it on canvas because he knew Dawn so well. He was your father, Talleha. He was the man who loved your mother and who she loved beyond all reason." There—it was said. Ironically, it had been easy once he began to speak.

For a moment she was silent, and she sat there with her lips half-parted. Finally, in a faltering voice she managed to ask him. "Are you telling me that my father was this Richard Talbert who was the señora and her husband's friend?"

"Yes. He stayed awhile with the Greenfields after leaving your mother back at the village, where they'd shared many months of happiness. He'd obviously done numerous paintings while he lived with your mother. For whatever reason, he felt he must leave her to go back east. He went back to his native France, and various things kept him from returning to your village as he had planned." He told Talleha everything he knew about Richard Talbert.

Talleha sat stunned and astonished as she listened to him. It was wonderful to have the answers she'd searched for for so long.

But when she thought he was finished with this strange revelation, he really baffled her by adding, "Talleha, your father left you everything he owned when he died—all his holdings and his art. He was a very wealthy man, and now the wealth is yours. You also have a legal name. You are Nicole Talbert—not just Talleha."

God, he could hardly breathe as he sat there waiting for her reaction! He anticipated a scream of glee or a gusto of wild laughter, maybe she would dissolve into tears for the father she'd lost and never known.

She did none of these. But the sweet innocence of the child-woman was gone and a vital, spirited womanliness emerged as she rose up from the bunk. Her eyes were like smoldering black coals. The rosebud lips were provocative as she murmured softly, "I shall always be Talleha in my heart and in my soul. It was my mother's wish that I be called that. But since it was my father's desire to name me Nicole Talbert, I shall be Nicole Talbert when it suits me." He saw a new assurance in her he'd never seen before. But never had he desired her more.

There was no reason to delay his torment any longer, he decided. Either she wanted to marry him or she didn't, so he might as well find out where he stood.

His manly pride insisted he act flippant, even though he wasn't really feeling that way. "Now, tell me, ma cherie—how the devil am I to propose to you? Am I to ask Talleha or Nicole to marry me?" There was a handsome grin on his face, and Talleha looked down on him with adoration as her whole being swelled with bliss. He'd given her more than any fortune could ever provide. He'd asked her to be his wife. That's all she really wanted. It was not completely selfish on her part, for she was thinking about the child she knew she was carrying within her.

She had stubbornly decided that he'd never know about the child until he'd proposed to her. With the arrogant pride of her mother, she held her head high and with great dignity replied, "I am Talleha now and forever!"

He sat there, letting his eyes savor the sight of her. Not only did he adore her; he admired her tremendously. His deep voice was husky with emotion. "Will you be mine and only mine, Talleha? Will you be my wife—share my life—now and forever?"

Suddenly, that sweet innocence of hers returned and she rushed, flinging herslf on his lap. Her arms encircled his neck. Utterly shamelessly, she confessed to him before kissing his waiting lips, "Victor Maurier, I thought you'd never ask me! I was about to die! I couldn't stand to live without you!"

He roared with laughter as he flung her back on the bunk, telling himself there would never be another woman like this one.

His deep voice whispered in her ear, "Sweetheart, I won't let you die. We're going to live and live forever. You believe me?"

Those black doelike eyes looked up and he saw her trust and faith reflected there as she declared, "I believe you, Victor."

He knew he must never fail her.

Chapter 61

Another two hours passed before Maurier finally persuaded himself to leave his cabin to seek out his first mate, Davy. All Davy had to do was to look at his smug and satisfied face to know how he'd spent his time in the arms of the woman he loved.

Davy was a practical man, and it was enough for him to decide to forget any daydreaming he had allowed himself lately where Talleha was concerned. He would have been fighting a hopeless battle, and he was wise enough to know it. There would be another woman for him someday.

His infatuation with Talleha would forever remain a secret locked in his heart. He greeted Victor with a comradely pat on the shoulders and a broad smile. Maurier would never suspect that he passionately desired his lady.

It was like old times as they sat and talked together and shared a glass of whiskey. Maurier told him of his wish to leave Brownsville as soon as an extra crew could be hired. "Think a day or two will be enough, Davy? I've nothing to hold me here now. The captain is gone, and I owe you a debt I'll never be able to pay for saving Talleha and taking care of her until I got back."

He admitted to Davy that the trip had been a waste of his time and he regretted it. "I failed Captain Crawford and Talleha as well. I've a lot to make up for, Davy."

"There's no problem about a crew, Victor. Men are just waiting to work because their ships were lost in the hurricane. I can hire on a crew tomorrow. Supplies may prove to be another matter. What is our destination?"

"Our destination, my friend, is due north, up the Texas coast to Port Arthur."

"Port Arthur? What the hell are you talking about, Victor? I—I thought we were ready to get the hell out of this part of the world," Davy stammered, confused and dismayed. He'd had enough of this Texas coastline and was chomping at the bit to head for the high seas.

Maurier saw the frown on his irritated face and he understood completely. He tried to soothe his good friend by telling him, "I know how you feel, for I have the same itch—but my beautiful lady must have a proper wedding. She deserves that after all she's endured."

Davy mumbled, "I—I can't fault that. But why in the hell have we got to go all the way up to Port Arthur?"

"Our wedding is a special occasion to me, Davy, for I'll only go through it once in my life. With the captain gone now, I have no family, and neither does Talleha. My dear friend, Emilo Cortez, wishes us to hold our wedding at his ranch, the Casa del Lago, in Harrison County. I've just now talked to Talleha and we have agreed on it. I figure we will sail up the coast to Port Arthur and travel by stage to Harrison County. You, being my best friend, are to accompany us. I'd like you there by my side, my friend. Will you come with us?"

Davy was glad he'd already come to terms with himself before Maurier had spoken of his feelings. He was more than pleased that Victor considered him his best friend, and he decided then and there to live up to those expectations. "I'd—I'd be honored to stand up with you, Victor. I don't have to tell you that I think you are one lucky sonofabitch!" The two of them laughed and embraced.

It was a gala evening the five of them shared that night aboard the *Destiny*. Old Snapper outdid himself with a most delectable meal. His turtle soup was superb, and his crispy fried fish filet and small potatoes were devoured eagerly by Bruno, Davy, Victor, and Talleha. Talleha declared, "No one can fry fish like you, Snapper. I swear it!" She forever won him to her side. But he knew she spoke sincerely, and he valued her praise.

None of them knew where he'd managed to get fresh butter, but it was wonderful to spread on his crusty bread. Victor had brought up from the hold some prized white wines to complement the fish, and he'd insisted that Snapper quit his chores as cook and sit at the table with them to enjoy the fruits of his labor. "Besides, Snapper—you must share with us a special toast. Right, Talleha?"

She gave out a soft, lighthearted laugh. "My goodness, without Snapper, it would not be complete. He must share this moment for it to be special."

The look on that old man's face was something Victor would never forget. His old cook would love her the rest of his days. She'd spoken from the heart. Oh, he knew the folklore about a woman being aboard a ship and the bad luck it brought. But none of these men would ever look upon her as a bad omen. Not Talleha!

Together, the five raised their glasses in a toast for their captain and his lady. A second toast was given to the *Destiny*. It was a festive night.

Now as Davy Carron watched his good friend, Maurier, sitting there beside the lovely Talleha, their

493

eyes glowing with love for one another, he was happy for them. Whatever he had felt for her had now vanished.

Observing Davy as he had all night long, Bruno could now rest easy, for he knew instinctively that the first mate had come to terms with the torment plaguing his soul this afternoon. His ebony face gleamed with happiness. Never had Bruno felt such elation as he did when Talleha reached across the table to take his hand to declare to Victor, "Dear Bruno was the one who found me, Victor. My poor Amapola was gone, and I was there on the beach wet to the skin with damp sand on my face and hair. I don't think I'd be alive today if Bruno had not found me when he did. Remember, Bruno? Had you ever seen anyone shaking with chill like I was?" She could laugh about it now, but then it was not so pleasant.

To Bruno, it was a moment he would never forget. He'd never felt so proud. When her black eyes turned toward him with warmth and adoration, he worshipped her. He loved her in the most respected way and would have fought to the death to protect her from any harm.

It was an occasion everyone sitting around the table that night aboard the *Destiny* would remember.

Talleha had no inkling of all the activity that went on around a schooner when it was preparing to leave port. But she found it wildly exciting as she stood by the railing watching the deckhands working. She'd never seen so many fine, muscled men in all her life and she had to conclude that seamen were a healthy breed. But she admired none of them more than her handsome, virile Victor.

He moved among the others with authority. She

smiled to think of the son she was probably carrying within her now. He would be like his father, she knew. Dawn would have been proud of the man she'd chosen to give her heart to.

At daybreak Vic had left their bunk in his cabin and she'd watched him dress, even though he'd thought she was still asleep. She'd known when he'd cautiously opened the door to leave the cabin. But what really amazed her was when Bruno had informed her after she'd dressed and gone up on the deck that a crew had been hired and supplies were being loaded. They were leaving Brownsville this afternoon.

All morning and most of the afternoon, she watched the activity of the decks. She went to the galley to share a light lunch with Snapper and firmly insisted that she could attend to her own plate when she noticed the vast pots of food cooking. "You've got enough to do, Snapper, with that mob to feed."

She admired Snapper's ability to fix such tasty fare and told the old cook she hoped someday to learn how to cook as well as he did.

"I'll teach you, missy," he told her, assuring her it wasn't all that difficult.

As the day went on, Talleha found herself utterly fascinated by life on the schooner. It intrigued her; it did not bother her to be left on her own to explore. She had nothing to fear as a woman walking around the ship, for all the men treated her with the utmost respect—she was the captain's lady. The formidable Victor Maurier had made that perfectly clear. If his warnings had not been enough to instill awe in his men, the powerful presence of Bruno was enough to make an impact.

Talleha did not know that he was keeping a watchful eye on her throughout the day. She never sensed his presence, but he was always nearby.

Late in the afternoon, Talleha felt exhausted and returned to the cabin. She had not intended to take a nap, but when she lay across the bunk, sleep overtook her immediately. When she woke up a few hours later, she realized that the schooner was plowing through the waters of the bay. They were leaving Brownsville as twilight settled in. A more beautiful sunset she'd never seen as she gazed out the tiny window of the cabin.

A feeling of happy contentment engulfed her as she felt the light breeze caress her face. Life was wonderful. The man she loved had asked her to marry him, and now they were sailing toward a bright, wonderful future.

She looked over at the smiling portrait of her lovely mother. The spirit of her mother seemed to be there in the cabin with her. She stood for a moment whispering this new name she'd heard Vic call her. Nicole—Nicole—Nicole. She liked it very much. It was a beautiful name her father had picked for her. He had to be a man of sensitive feelings to have captured the essence of Dawn with such perfection. He must have truly loved her, Talleha told herself. It meant everything to Talleha to believe this.

She was so absorbed in her own thoughts and Victor had entered the cabin so quietly that she did not hear him. When she turned around to find him sitting in the chair looking weary and tired, she rushed to him. "Victor, you look exhausted!" she declared, planting a kiss on his tanned cheek. It was then she noticed the papers in his hand. He sat there in silence with a strange look on his face.

"Victor—what—what's the matter? Tell me!" She sank to the floor in front of him with her hands resting on his thighs.

He placed his hand on the top of her head and gave her a weak smile. His blue eyes danced over her lovely

496

face as he dwelled for a fleeting moment of the parallels of their lives. Just yesterday, he'd returned with the startling news that her father, who she'd never really known, was the famous artist, Richard Talbert, and informed her she was a wealthy young lady.

Late in the afternoon he'd been handed a startling piece of news when one of his deckhands had given him a letter. He found it overwhelming, but he also had to admit that it could be possible as he read the letter from Captain Alex Haver.

Instead of trying to tell Talleha about this, he decided to let her read the letter herslf.

"Here, Talleha—it's a letter from Captain Haver. It was his ship I booked passage on to come to Brownsville. Remember I told you he'd come along with me to search for you and Captain Crawford? We—we became very good friends on the trip down the coast from Galveston to Brownsville."

"Oh, yes, I remember. You thought very highly of him. Liked him very much—almost instantly you said." Her black eyes darted over his face anxiously, and she hoped it wasn't bad news he'd received about the man.

"Well, there could have been a very good reason for the two of us to become so close so fast, it seems."

Her curiosity was at a peak as she took the letter and began to read it.

It stated that the captain had questioned the strange, magnetic force he'd felt when he'd met Victor after he'd boarded his ship, the *Condesa,* and how he'd enjoyed those moments they'd shared in long talks as they traveled together.

Alex Haver wrote in his letter how he'd wished he could have shared with his own son the close feelings he'd so easily shared with Maurier.

"We both love our ships and the sea with a passion.

When I saw your fine ship, *Victor,* I felt envy," he'd stated in his letter. He'd added that his son had not inherited that trait.

The letter went on to say:

By the time you receive this, Victor, I will be sailing to Mexico. By the time you finish this letter you may very well hate me. I could not blame you. I was a reckless, young seafaring man very much like you were before you met the woman who tamed your heart.

I did not honestly make the connection until you happened to mention one name. Then, the past came rushing back like a roar of thunder. In the end the conclusion and the judgment are in your hands. All I shall do is tell you the story as it happened.

A young, wealthy Englishman became friends with me when I was sailing to ports in France and England. When I was going to be on land for a few days, the two of us would get together and have a jolly good time. We were a most unlikely pair, because Edward was a serious, quiet-natured fellow and I was an ornery rogue.

Once, after I landed in France Edward had found himself a lovely French mademoiselle, and he was completely smitten by her.

When I met her, I had never been so challenged in all my life. I determined I would have her before I left France and I did—only once. One wonderful night I possessed her, and then I left, heartless bastard that I was. It never dawned on me that I might have left her with my child. Perhaps I just didn't give a damn.

I learned later that Edward took her back to England with him, but could not marry her because he was already married to someone called Elaine. But he and I never saw each other after that. I never gave it any more thought until you spoke to me about your mother, Colette. Then it all came back to me. I knew it for certain when you mentioned the name, Penwick. It had to be my old friend, Edward Penwick. Maybe you are Edward Penwick's son, but there is the possibility you could be my son, Victor. I had to write this letter and tell you this, because I can't think of anything I'd be proud of than to know you are my son. What a magnificent blessing that would be to me! You're everything a man could possibly want a son to be. So I tell you honestly and selfishly, I hope I'm the one who sired you. I ask your forgiveness that I was so young and thoughtless at that time in my life.

I'll think of you often,
Alex Haver

Talleha's black eyes misted as she folded the letter and handed it back. Her soft voice cracked with emotion as she spoke, "I'd like to meet this man someday, Victor."

"I—I think we shall, Talleha," he said as he bent down to take her in his arms. Had she been looking at his face, she would have seen a mist of tears in his eyes. Already in his heart he'd accepted the fact that Alex Haver was his father, not Edward Penwick.

He held her close to him, for he had need of her sweet body and loving arms. They embraced one another in silence.

No words were needed—just the sweet comfort of being together.

Chapter 62

Instinctively, Talleha knew her strong, handsome Victor needed her tender caresses and her love. She could see his torment. Alex Haver's letter was disturbing to him, even though he had great admiration for the man. She, too, had experienced the strange shock of learning after many years who her father was.

Her dainty hands moved to unbutton his faded blue shirt and she said nothing as she prepared to remove it so she could massage his back. No one had to tell her how hard he'd worked all day, for she'd observed his firm, muscled body moving around the deck of the schooner. As her fingertips stroked his broad shoulders, she purred softly, "Does that feel good? You work as hard as any of your crew."

"Wonderful, cherie." Her touch was sheer magic and he felt himself begin to relax. He could smell the aroma of jasmine water she'd dabbed behind her ears. It was a refreshing scent after a long day of moving amid sweating bodies.

Vic could not explain why he was in such a hellish hurry to be away from Brownsville. Oh, he understood his impatience to get back to Harrison County so he could marry the woman he loved, but the driving force to leave Brownsville he didn't understand.

There wasn't enough time to buy his lady a proper wardrobe, and he knew the magnificent attire he'd ordered from Emily Charbeau was washed away to God knows where. But he planned to make a stop in Galveston before they traveled on to Harrison County. His lady would arrive at the Casa del Lago with a wardrobe befitting the occasion, he'd promised himself. He'd not mention this to Talleha.

He turned to gaze up at her as she stood behind him rubbing his back and she gave him a soft, sweet smile. She couldn't know his secret thoughts, but she saw him look lovingly at her, and that was all that mattered. She swore he did not look so weary and tired now and she was pleased that her efforts had helped.

"Come here, you beguiling little witch!" his voice huskily beckoned.

She gave out a soft giggle as she felt him urge her with his strong hands to sit on his lap. "So now I'm a witch, Victor?"

"Must be, sweetheart. My spirits were low and I was troubled. All it took was your magic touch. Guess I'll have to keep you around just so when I get in a black mood you can get me out of it."

She taunted him, "Is that the only reason you want me around?"

"Hardly, my pet." Already his body was alert, letting her know of the wild desire pulsing within him. He grinned sheepishly as he teased her. "Do I have to tell you the real reason I always want you, Talleha?"

She sought to tantalize him more as she leaned closer to allow her pulsing breasts to press against his bare chest. She purred softly in his ear, "You don't have to tell me anything." His hands moved from her waist to cup the flushed mound of her flesh, and when he did, she gave a soft moan of delight.

Now it was Victor who was unbuttoning the front of

her cotton blouse. When he'd freed her soft, satiny flesh, his lips captured one of the rosy tips of her breasts, letting his tongue gently caress it. Talleha felt the mounting flame of passion burning her like liquid fire.

In no time they were naked, and it made her pretty head whirl with amazement how skillful his hands were. Perhaps he was the one working the witchcraft. She told him so.

"Just as long as you are a willing subject, my darling, I'll damned sure continue to try." By now he'd led her from the chair to the bunk. Sitting down, he had pulled her up on top of him. "Now, I demand you make wild, wicked love to me," he playfully teased her.

He felt the velvet softness of her thighs as she sensuously undulated against him. It was more than he could endure, and he sought to have that velvet softness consuming him. He lifted her just enough to fuse himself to her.

She moaned with rapture as her heart beat faster. "Oh, God, Victor—it feels so wonderful! I—I never tire of you loving me!"

He laughed and gasped with his own heavy breathing, "Well, I hope not, ma petite, for I intend to do it the rest of my life."

She gave one of those particular little movements which drove him wild with desire, and he could not delay the spasm of ecstasy engulfing him.

Talleha shared that ecstasy with him, and neither of them were aware that the *Destiny* was plowing through the waters of the bay.

Victor had given orders to Davy Carron to get them underway when he'd left to go to his cabin, but he'd not intended to be gone for all the hours he'd been asleep with Talleha in his arms. But Davy figured out what was delaying the captain, and it was an embarrassed Maurier who faced his first mate some eight hours later.

Davy cajoled him goodnaturedly as he left the deck to get some sleep himself. Victor was lucky to have a pal like Davy, he reminded himself as he stood on the deck of his schooner, the stiff breeze playing havoc with his hair. In his hurry, he'd forgotten his cap. He took a deep breath—it was exhilarating! This was where he'd wanted to be for so long. He'd be damned if he'd tarry long at Casa del Lago. Already he was laying out his plans for the route he'd take around the Florida Keys on his way to the open seas.

Victor Maurier could not remember a time when his life was filled with so much bliss. He marveled at the ease with which Talleha had adapted to life aboard his schooner. She loved it, and nothing could have pleased him more. He swore she looked more radiant than ever. Bruno and Davy agreed with him. So did Snapper, but he wore a sly smile when he turned his back on them. He was privy to information that none of them had, not even Maurier. It was Talleha's and old Snapper's secret. She'd confessed to the old cook that she was certain she was pregnant. "You utter a word and I'll scalp you, Snapper."

"Nothin' there to scalp, miss, but I promise to be quiet as a mouse. Snapper will keep his mouth shut."

She knew he would. When she departed to go back to the cabin, she found herself pondering just when she would find the right time to tell Victor. All she'd ask was that he be as delighted about it as she was, now that he'd asked her to marry him. She, too, was in a blissful state, and nothing disturbed her too long.

It was smooth sailing and perfect weather as the *Destiny* steadily moved on its north, northeast course up the coast of Texas. She believed all the signs of the elements were foretelling of their happiness and that this was meant to be.

503

True to his vow to get her a presentable wardrobe, Victor sailed into the harbor of Galveston and the *Destiny* stayed in the harbor for two days while he and his bride-to-be went on a shopping spree. Such lavish extravagance Talleha had never imagined, but she dared not dampen his obvious enthusiasm. So she allowed him to buy all the magnificent clothing he wanted to purchase.

When they returned to the wharf, it took Bruno, Davy, and Maurier to carry all the packages aboard the *Destiny*. Once, she was tempted to tell him that before too many weeks had gone by, her waistline would be too big to get into those trim gowns. But he had looked at her, his blue eyes gleaming, to declare, "I'll have the best-dressed bride the state of Texas has ever seen."

She cared nothing about what anyone thought but Victor. However, she would wear as many of the lovely gowns as she could during the next few weeks. Some of the gowns had large seams, she'd noticed, so maybe she could even let them out when the time came.

Bruno's black face etched in a broad grin as he laughed, "Looks like I won't have to be washing that black skirt of yours almost daily, Miss Talleha. I'd say I can get by now for a week or two at a time."

They were a happy-go-lucky group as they marched up the gangplank that late afternoon. The same festive air remained during the evening. At the first light of dawn, the *Destiny* sailed out of the harbor of Galveston to go to Port Arthur.

Victor had told Davy about his plans to take the stagecoach to Harrison County. For the last two days, Davy had worried about how he was to get out of going along with Victor and his bride-to-be to Harrison County. Oh, he'd accepted that his daydreaming about Talleha was futile, but he was not prepared to stand by Maurier's side as he married her. When they returned from Casa del Lago, she would be his wife; maybe he

504

could finally accept it then. Right now he was having a devil of a time. The last few days had been sheer hell.

The only person who realized that was Bruno. The big man felt sorry for him. He knew how hard it had been for Carron to keep up this pretense.

After Talleha and Victor had left their midst that night to go for a moonlight stroll along the deck, Bruno decided to seek Davy out. Maybe he could do something for the young man who'd always been a good friend to him.

It didn't take long for old Bruno to spot him standing by the railing of the schooner, looking out over the dark waters of the bay. He moved in that direction. The first mate was dreading their landing tomorrow in Port Arthur, for it meant he was honor-bound to travel along with the captain and his lady.

His big hand reached out to touch Davy's slumped shoulder. "What can I do to help you, young Davy? I owe you so much for what you've done for me. Tell me how I can help you get out of doing what you don't want to do."

Slowly, Davy turned around. How did that big devil know what was troubling him, Davy questioned? He gave forth a weak smile and admitted candidly, "Well, I could hope Snapper's food would make me deathly sick, but that isn't likely, is it?"

"Not likely, sir. But there's other things that can prevent a man from traveling by stage."

His remark was enough to get Davy's attention and he took out his cheroots, handing one to Bruno. Remembering some of Bruno's tall tales about his life before he joined the crew of the *Destiny*, Davy quizzed, "Then you tell me just one good excuse I could use to get out of going to Harrison County."

"What's the most common accident on the deck of a ship? You know and so do I that a slip on the deck can happen most anytime. Now, suppose you done took yourself one hell of a fall tonight and messed up your foot? Who's to be the wiser? You remain here and the captain leaves tomorrow for a few days. By the time he and his lady return, you can be all recovered. Makes sense to me. What about you, young Davy?"

Davy was silent for a moment, taking a deep puff on the cheroot. Hell yes, it would work. It was so damned simple he wondered why he'd not thought of it. "You rascal—how come you are so smart?" The two of them laughed and puffed on their cheroots. Carron's spirits were instantly lifted, for he had his answer, thanks to old Bruno.

Their little conspiracy was carried out smoothly, with Maurier cautioning Davy to take it easy while he was gone.

"I can assure you, I won't be gone too long this time, Davy. I'm itching as much as you to get back to sea. But my lady deserves a proper wedding, and she must meet with this Hemphill about her inheritance."

Davy displayed the proper remorse that he would not be accompanying them and Maurier bade him farewell. His first mate assured him that he would still be able to see to the duties of overseeing the *Destiny* until he returned.

Miraculously, Davy's "injury" was healed after Maurier and Talleha departed from the *Destiny,* and he confessed to Bruno how amazingly easy it had been to fool Victor.

"Right now, he is a man blinded by love, young Davy. Never has he been so vulnerable," the black man laughed.

It was like a homecoming when Victor and Talleha arrived at the Casa del Lago. When Talleha alit from the buggy, she looked like the wealthy heiress she was, a vision of elegance in one of the exquisite ensembles

506

he'd purchased for her in Galveston. The rich gold velvet of her bonnet was tied saucily to the side of her face, and it made her eyes look blacker. Small wisps curled attractively at her temples, and the rest of her long hair cascaded down around her shoulders and back.

The gold velvet of her skirt swished as she walked. Seeing them arrive, Emilo stood for a moment to admire her. Always, he'd seen her as a fine, spirited thoroughbred. Now more than ever, he knew he'd been right about her. He admired the graceful carriage of her body and the high, proud way she tilted her head. It was not the gold velvet she wore that made Talleha so rare, Emilo knew. It was the woman she was. He saw the wonderful changes in her which had taken place in the last few months. She was more gorgeous than he'd remembered.

It was a wonderful reunion when the three of them embraced on the front veranda. As Emilo led them down the hallway toward his parlor, he confessed, "I tell you I'm overcome with joy, my dear young friends. You kept your word to me, amigo. You are going to be married in my home—si?"

Victor laughed lightheartedly, "Si—we are if the offer still holds, señor."

"Oh, you know it does. Marjorie will be overjoyed to see you've arrived. She's due here any minute now." Emilo's exultation was written on his face for them to see.

As anxious as Victor was to be back on the high seas, he found himself glad that they had traveled back to Casa del Lago for their wedding. Emilo Cortez's delight to have them was so genuine it warmed his heart, and he knew Talleha felt the same way.

Emilo summoned one of his servants to bring refreshments, declaring it a festive time, and demanded a toast with one of his finest wines.

As the three of them were raising their glasses, Marjorie Greenfield came through the archway of the parlor and Emilo rushed to greet her, planting a kiss on her cheek. Talleha was delightfully surprised to see the transformation which had taken place in her the last few months. She was stunning!

Emilo's love and devotion were responsible, Talleha was certain.

Those next few hours were special to the four in the parlor. They laughed and talked as they sipped wine and ate from the tray of little finger sandwiches the servant had brought.

While Victor and Emilo were engrossed in conversation, Talleha and Marjorie sat in a secluded corner of the parlor behind a huge palm and had their own confidential chat.

Both of them suddenly began to giggle, and they rose up to go over to the men. Marjorie Greenfield startled and delighted Emilo when she asked, "Emilo, how would you like to have a double wedding? I think Talleha has convinced me I'm a fool to wait. I might lose you."

Emilo did not reply. Instead he rose up to take her in his arms and kiss her firmly on the lips as Victor and Talleha looked on, exchanging grins.

Later, Emilo declared to Talleha, "I don't know what kind of magic you possess, señorita, but I bless it, for I've tried to convince her we should not wait. Life is too precious at our age to waste one minute. I bless you, Talleha, for convincing her."

"Oh, señor—I possess no magic. I just think it would mean so much to all of us in the years to come to have shared such a special occasion of our lives, would you not agree?"

Emilo nodded his gray hair. He was amazed at this most unusual young woman who'd impressed him favorably from the minute he'd first met her. Maurier was a lucky man, indeed!

Two days later, a lavish wedding took place at the Casa del Lago. It was probably the grandest one held in Harrison County in decades. A fabulous fiesta followed the ceremony.

Multitudes of ranchers and friends of Señor Cortez and Marjorie Greenfield came for miles around to attend the gala occasion. This marriage was wholeheartedly accepted by her friends. The taint of Eliot Penwick was swept away forever.

True to his plans, Victor and Talleha departed the next day, saying their farewells to Emilo and Marjorie. However, they promised to return in a year to the Casa del Lago.

Somehow, Talleha had never found the moment she wanted to tell Victor of the baby she was expecting. As they traveled toward Port Arthur to board the *Destiny,* she still found it impossible to bring up the subject, fearing she would spoil this glorious time. Once aboard the *Destiny,* she'd tell him.

After their journey from Harrison County, as they prepared to walk up the gangplank to board the *Destiny,* Victor was delighted as she turned to him with a sincere smile on her face to tell him, "We're home, Victor. And I'm so glad!"

"You truly mean it, don't you, Talleha?"

"Of course I mean it! Why would I say it if I didn't?"

They'd received a boisterous welcome from the crew of the *Destiny,* and Talleha had enjoyed it tremendously. But they'd finally managed to slip away to the haven of his cabin and this was what Victor really wanted.

"I finally have you all to myself, ma petite. I think I shall keep you here for days, now that you are finally my wife."

"But as the captain of your own ship, you could not stay with me," she pointed out to him.

"Enough, woman. You're too bossy and too smart," he jested as he moved her toward the bunk. As he laid her back on the bunk and her hair fanned back to cover the pillow, he noted how the silvery moonlight seemed to focus on the loveliness of her face. She was absolutely breathtaking.

"What is it about you, Talleha? Are you a goddess? You seem to weave such spells on me—on everyone. Emilo had just gotten through telling me he wanted to marry Marjorie months ago, but she adamantly refused to until springtime. Suddenly, after the two of you talk awhile, she comes and announces to Emilo that she's ready to marry him. What did you say to her that made such a difference? Tell me, you little vixen! I want to know!"

Her black eyes looked as innocent as they had that first time he'd taken her and made passionate love to her. Talleha knew she'd found the right time to tell him her secret. Without further ado, she confessed the truth in that straightforward manner of hers. "I merely told her that come springtime, we could not be at the Casa del Lago for their wedding. Come springtime, I will be having your son or daughter, Victor."

For a moment, he was dazed and could not speak. When his strong arms reached to encircle her, he felt like a man who possessed the whole world.

His deep voice cracked with emotion as he told her, "You're a wild, wicked little vixen, but you're the most wonderful miracle of my life!"

"You're happy about the baby, Victor?" she cooed in that soft voice of hers.

"Honey, if I was any happier I'd be dead and gone to heaven," he laughed. His lips sought hers to convince her of the rapture he was feeling at that glorious moment.

He convinced her!

FIERY ROMANCE
From Zebra Books

SATIN SECRET   (2166, $3.95)
by Emma Merritt
After young Marta Carolina had been attacked by pirates, ship-
wrecked, and beset by Indians, she was convinced the New World
brought nothing but tragedy . . . until William Dare rescued her.
The rugged American made her feel warm, protected, secure—
and hungry for a fulfillment she could not name!

CAPTIVE SURRENDER   (1986, $3.95)
by Michalann Perry
Gentle Fawn should have been celebrating her newfound joy as a
bride, but when both her husband and father were killed in battle, the young Indian maiden vowed revenge. She charged into the
fray—yet once she caught sight of the piercing blue gaze of her
enemy, she knew that she could never kill him. The handsome
white man stirred a longing deep within her soul . . . and a passion she'd never experienced before.

PASSION'S JOY   (2205, $3.95)
by Jennifer Horsman
Dressed as a young boy, stunning Joy Claret refused to think
what would happen were she to get caught at what she was really
doing: leading slaves to liberty on the Underground Railroad.
Then the roughly masculine Ram Barrington stood in her path
and the blue-eyed girl couldn't help but panic. Before she could
fight him, she was locked in an embrace that could end only with
her surrender to PASSION'S JOY.

TEXAS TRIUMPH   (2009, $3.95)
by Victoria Thompson
Nothing is more important to the determined Rachel McKinsey
than the Circle M—and if it meant marrying her foreman to scare
off rustlers, she would do it. Yet the gorgeous rancher felt a secret thrill that the towering Cole Elliot was to be her man—and
despite her plan that they be business partners, all she truly desired was a glorious consummation of their vows.

PASSION'S PARADISE   (1618, $3.75)
by Sonya T. Pelton
When she is kidnapped by the cruel, captivating Captain Ty, fair-
haired Angel Sherwood fears not for her life, but for her honor!
Yet she can't help but be warmed by his manly touch, and secretly
longs for PASSION'S PARADISE.

*Available wherever paperbacks are sold, or order direct from the
Publisher. Send cover price plus 50¢ per copy for mailing and
handling to Zebra Books, Dept. 2251, 475 Park Avenue South,
New York, N.Y. 10016. Residents of New York, New Jersey and
Pennsylvania must include sales tax. DO NOT SEND CASH.*

SURRENDER YOUR HEART
TO CONSTANCE O'BANYON!

MOONTIDE EMBRACE (2182, $3.95)

When Liberty Boudreaux's sister framed Judah Slaughter for murder, the notorious privateer swore revenge. But when he abducted the unsuspecting Liberty from a New Orleans masquerade ball, the brazen pirate had no idea he'd kidnapped the wrong Boudreaux — unaware who it really was writhing beneath him, first in protest, then in ecstasy.

GOLDEN PARADISE (2007, $3.95)

Beautiful Valentina Barrett knew she could never trust wealthy Marquis Vincente as a husband. But in the guise of "Jordanna", a veiled dancer at San Francisco's notorious Crystal Palace, Valentina couldn't resist making the handsome Marquis her lover!

SAVAGE SUMMER (1922, $3.95)

When Morgan Prescott saw Sky Dancer standing out on a balcony, his first thought was to climb up and carry the sultry vixen to his bed. But even as her violet eyes flashed defiance, repulsing his every advance, Morgan knew that nothing would stop him from branding the high-spirited beauty as his own!

SEPTEMBER MOON (1838;, $3.95)

Petite Cameron Madrid would never consent to allow arrogant Hunter Kingston to share her ranch's water supply. But the handsome landowner had decided to get his way through Cameron's weakness for romance — winning her with searing kisses and slow caresses, until she willingly gave in to anything Hunter wanted.

SAVAGE SPRING (1715, $3.95)

Being pursued for a murder she did not commit, Alexandria disguised herself as a boy, convincing handsome Taggert James to help her escape to Philadelphia. But even with danger dogging their every step, the young woman could not ignore the raging desire that her virile Indian protector ignited in her blood!

Available wherever paperbacks are sold, or order direct from the Publisher. Send cover price plus 50¢ per copy for mailing and handling to Zebra Books, Dept. 2251, 475 Park Avenue South, New York, N.Y. 10016. Residents of New York, New Jersey and Pennsylvania must include sales tax. DO NOT SEND CASH.